THE GHOST OF
DARWIN STEWART

BOOK ONE OF
THE ISSACHAR GATEKEEPER

L. G. Nixon

Fitting Words

The Ghost of Darwin Stewart

Copyright © 2021 by L. G. Nixon

Published by Fitting Words—www.fittingwords.net

Library of Congress Cataloging-in-Publication Data

ISBN: 978-1-7357748-2-4

Cover design provided by Moon Designs www.moondesigns.com

Table of Contents

rologue

"You shall touch it no more," commanded the High King, his arms outstretched in front of him. A brilliant flash of energy bolted from his fingertips, smashing into the old, gnarled tree that stood majestically in the middle of the meadow. The sound of cracking and splintering echoed as the tree came crashing to the ground. The force of the explosion shattered the place's serenity as two lone figures plunged into the shadowy woods at the edge of the meadow.

The High King shook with anger as an overwhelming sadness crushed his heart.

The Tree of All Knowledge lay split in two, the timber broken and scattered on the ground. Its bright-red fruit lay smoldering to ash. He knelt beside the splintered remains. "I am sorry, old friend." A tear slipped down the High King's cheek as he caressed a piece of its bark. "You were so beautiful, a magnificent thing to behold. I shall miss your laughter." He uttered a deep sigh as he heard a snigger from the angel standing behind him.

"Oh, come now, you knew this would happen, old man," sneered Darnathian. "You can't pretend you didn't know I would search for the

Life Tree." The angel stood watching the High King. Darnathian twisted his head, cracking his neck, an odd quirk he couldn't control when he was angry. "Only a few more minutes with those two spineless creatures of yours and I *would* have found the location of the Life Tree," he hissed, his hands clenched at his sides. His shining white wings quivered behind him.

"You will never eat its fruit, Darnathian." The High King's voice resonated with quiet authority. "The Life Tree is no longer here in the garden. Knowing this day would come, I have made sure of its protection. Fire and sword guard it. Only the Bachar who are true of heart will enter the New Garden and eat the fruit. To those who serve, I will write their names upon a living stone. They will be honored for all eternity in the courts and halls of Ascalon."

"Blah blah blah, the 'true of heart.' What does that mean? They're your little minions, dutifully doing whatever you tell them to do?" Darnathian folded his large white wings, and they disappeared beneath the folds of his tunic. The sun sparkled like diamond dust on his skin, emphasizing his dark hair and angular features.

"They have free will, just as you do. Yet this is how you choose to use your freedom and knowledge." The High King drew himself up to full height, tall and elegant, thick white hair and colorful robe glowing with an inner brilliance. "Don't you remember, Darnathian? You once were true of heart. Everyone throughout the kingdom knew of your wisdom, benevolence, and compassion. Your actions showed your love for your King."

The King turned from the ruins and surveyed the angel standing before him. Darnathian was assuredly the most handsome and beguiling of all the creatures who served in Ascalon. And one the King loved like a son. Just now, Darnathian's eyes glowed like liquid amber; his tall, lithe shape wrapped in white linen folds that fell to his knees. His breastplate, adorned with purple jewels signifying his rank, gleamed of polished gold. The leather straps of his sandals crisscrossed their way up to his muscular calves.

"You have always loved your little minions, yet see what they have done, old man? They disobey the first chance they get. And look what you have done," said Darnathian, gesturing to the shattered remains. "You broke your favorite tree. Now, isn't that sad?" A smirk dimpled his cheek.

"You have become the chief of liars, Darnathian. Your thirst for power and control has corrupted your very soul. It was your venom that poisoned their hearts against me." The High King raised his gaze to the sky, drawing deep breaths of crisp air. Raising his arms he said, "Because of the evil you have done here today, Darnathian, you shall no longer be called a son of the High King, prince of Ascalon. You are stripped forever of your rank, your privileges, and your mighty wings. If it is power and a kingdom you want, then you shall have it."

The air quivered as the High King brought his arms down quickly, pushing a sparkling white-and-gold energy ball at Darnathian. It hit Darnathian's golden breastplate with such force the breath was knocked from his lungs and sent him stumbling backward. His mighty wings exploded into a full spread, flapping to keep himself from falling.

The white-gold orb circled the angel, slicing his wings from his back. "No!" Darnathian howled as the remaining bony nubs melted like lava into his skin, and his beautiful wings lay lifeless on the ground. The orb blew up in a startling flash, encasing him.

Darnathian thrashed and kicked against the orb without success. His eyes, filled with hatred, burned like fire as he stood glaring at the High King.

"The earth shall be your kingdom," said the High King, his voice booming like thunder. "For a time, you shall walk on its ground and gather your followers. The Fallen from Ascalon shall do your bidding. The fallen Daemonimini shall forever be known as the Irredaemon. They held the highest order serving before the King in the courts of Ascalon and understood the cost of their wicked, traitorous actions. Ergo, the most wicked shall be known as Daemon.

"For the remainder of the Fallen," the High King continued, "those creatures who were deceived with your lies and had their innocence stripped from them, they shall have the opportunity to be redeemed. They will remain in bondage until such a time as they repent from their disrespectful ways." The High King raised his arms again, the sleeves of his robe billowing in the wind as it increased and swept around him. "The impenitent shall be doomed to Shinar where the spirit lives forever, and their memories shall crawl like worms in their heads."

Darnathian struggled against the orb holding him. "I *will* have your throne one day, old man! It won't be easy to get rid of me. I will find the Life Tree, and once I eat the fruit, I will be your equal," raged the angel, pounding against the orb. Blue, green, and white lights bounced erratically around inside the orb. "I will take your power and destroy everything you have made! I will be exalted far above you!"

The High King flattened his lips, brought his arms down, and clapped his hands. "Begone!" The orb with the angel imploded and disappeared.

The wind became a gentle breeze, tickling the flowers among the meadow grasses. The sun sat high in the blue sky, its warmth caressing the meadow where the birds chirped and insects buzzed. The day seemed like any other day, except for the remnants of the shattered tree. The High King retrieved a piece of the bark and lovingly caressed it.

"A life given cannot be undone, old friend. I have an important mission for you. Are you willing to take another form?" asked the High King. The bark quivered in his hand. "Good, I thought so too."

With his white hair and his colorful, flowing robe, the High King strode quickly along the path that led from the meadow down into the city of Ascalon, nestled between the Eastern Mountains and the Crystal Lake. As he entered the city gate, the chief blacksmith and the chief carpenter met him near the Amethyst Fountain, its waters bubbling gaily in the sparkling purple-hued basin.

"Gentlemen," said the High King quietly as he placed an arm around each of their shoulders. "I require your services. I need special tools and a trunk in which to place them."

Of Spooks and Weird Stuff

Lucy's hand shook. The magnifying glass she held to her eye tapped a staccato rhythm against her cheek. The black-robed spirit she saw through the lens of the magnifying glass mesmerized her. It was following a woman down the aisle of the flea market, coming up behind the woman and whispering in her ear, its sleeve caressing her shoulders. The woman shivered uncontrollably, then moved on.

Lucy watched the spirit floating along the ground, the hem of its robe swirling, a hood pulled low over its face. The afternoon summer sun seemed weak against its darkness.

The spirit halted, sniffing. Turning, it pointed a bony finger at Lucy. She felt a chill wash over her skin like a gazillion insects were crawling along her arms to swarm down her back and legs. The spirit spun into smoke and ash and flew at her.

"Argh!" screamed Lucy as she fell backward, bumping the vendor's table. She dropped the magnifying glass and threw her hands to her face. It fell with a thud in the dust at her feet as the black cloud engulfed her and then disappeared. She peeked open an eye, leaned against the vendor's table, and gripped the edge, her knuckles turning white. An acrid smell of sulfur hung on the humid air. She gagged.

"What were those things?" asked Lucy, her voice quivering. She inhaled ragged breaths of air.

"What things, young lady?" The elderly gentleman was tall and thin with a shock of thick, longish white hair brushing his collar. His white eyebrows floated on his forehead. "Did you see something in the glass?" His gaze took in the contours of Lucy's face, the nut-brown hair that just brushed her shoulders and the clear, gray eyes, which were wide with fright.

"I think I saw a ghost in the glass!" gasped Lucy. "It was horrible. The sleeves of its cloak were all ragged. Didn't you see it?" She stared at him as though he had two heads. He must have seen it.

He smiled and glanced down, his thick mustache wiggling like a fat white caterpillar on his upper lip. "Really? Do you often see ghosts, young lady?" A light breeze ruffled his hair.

"No!" Lucy snapped. "I've never seen a ghost before." She rubbed a shaky hand over her goose bumps.

"Well, it is an extraordinary scope," he said. "It is called a Spectrescope, and it only reveals its secret to the true of heart. If you can see ghosts, then it has chosen *you*."

Lucy studied him. His blue eyes twinkled with mischief as he nodded his head, smiling. He seemed oddly out of place wearing a brown tweed suit at a flea market in July. His white shirt was open at the neck.

"The ghost in the glass flew at me. Where did it go?" She glanced around the aisle. "I saw others in the glass too. Some were beautiful, glowing, like sunshine." A shiver crawled over her skin. She wrapped her arms around her. "Was it real? Were they ghosts?"

"What do you think, young lady?"

She looked at him. He reminded her of her best friend Schuyler's grandfather, who was always smiling, helping others, and making everyone laugh. Grandpa Williams could make you feel safe just by walking into the room. She had often wished he were her grandfather too.

She picked up the scope with the tarnished silver handle and strange symbols. She blew the dust from the lens and held it to her eye, peering through the lens. The ghosts were gone. She blew out a huge breath that puffed her cheeks.

Lucy straightened her shoulders and then tipped her head to one side. "I don't think I believe in ghosts," she said lightly, a thin, wavering smile appearing briefly on her lips. "It must be a trick." She turned the scope over in her hand, running shaky fingers over the symbols. They felt warm.

Lucy's head jerked up. *What did he say?* "Wait a minute. What did you mean 'it has chosen' me? You talk like it's alive. You're joking me, right?"

"It will take time, but you will understand," he said, then he guffawed. "After all, it is a scope for the imagination." Smile lines crinkled around his eyes as he laughed.

Lucy squinted her eyes and pursed her lips. Questions exploded like popcorn in her mind, but she couldn't decide what to ask. "Uh-huh, right," she said, examining the scope. "It does look ancient." She glanced sideways at him.

"Yes, it is very ancient. It's nearly as old as Time himself." Despite the sticky heat, he looked strangely relaxed and comfortable in his suit. He stroked his mustache. "The Spectrescope is an extraordinary tool that can only be wielded by the true of heart. If it has chosen to reveal itself to you, then the time has finally come. You cannot escape your destiny, Lucy."

"My destiny?" Lucy giggled and started to relax. "Okay, I'll play along. How do you make it replay the ghosts? It will be great for telling spooky stories around a campfire or babysitting the Gleason boys."

She turned the Spectrescope over several times. *Hmm, there's no switch.* She gently placed it back on the table. Strangely, it was the only item on the vendor's table. She glanced across the aisle where her mom was still arguing with the kitchen-gadget vendor.

Lucy pointed at the handle. "What do the symbols mean? Do they spell something or tell a story?"

"It's an ancient language once used for storytelling. The ancient peoples of earth told stories to pass their culture and history on to the next generation." The vendor touched his finger to the ring of symbols under the glass lens. "The symbols contain memories, and when the symbols are in motion, they tell the stories of important events—past, present, and future. It is like the stories grandparents tell of meaningful times in their lives, a way to share their special memories."

"I get it. It's sort of like the tribal American Indians who used pictographs on rocks to tell their stories. That is cool. How do you make them move?"

"Why don't you look through the trunk? Perhaps you will find a few more interesting objects," the vendor said. He sat down on a wooden chair made from some sort of tree root. The breeze ruffled the leaves in the gnarly old tree overhead, the sound like whispering voices. The old vendor chuckled.

"Uh, what trunk?" asked Lucy. "I don't see a trunk."

"The trunk that is under the table. You set your backpack in front of the trunk." A worn wooden box peeked out from under the table.

Weird, Lucy thought. *It wasn't here a minute ago. The vendor must have pushed it forward with his foot.* She brushed a few stray hairs from her face, tucking the hair behind her ears, knelt, and pulled the trunk from under the table. It had the same strange symbols as the Spectrescope.

She wiped her sweaty palms on her shorts, then ran her hands lightly over the trunk's rough, aged surface, careful not to get a splinter. Tarnished handles hung from either side. Attached at the front center edge of the lid was a round brass doorknob. "So cool!"

Lucy lifted the lid and peered inside. The interior looked more exten-sive than the trunk itself had looked from the outside—several items nes-tled among the folds of black velvet cloth. There were a hat and a knitted silver vest, a glass globe, and a mirror. The globe base and mirror appeared made of silver metal with intricate leaves and vines swirling around the base and frame. Etched among the plating were the symbols from the Spectrescope. A second brass doorknob was in the bottom of the trunk. Lucy gave it a yank, but it didn't move.

She picked up the glass globe. It was about the size of a baseball. The sphere began filling with a thick, colorful mist with complex swirling shapes that dissolved into other new forms. *How is it doing that?* she thought. *That's so awesome!* She watched it a moment longer before placing it back in the trunk. She saw a shadow pass over her as two sandaled feet with red-painted toenails stopped next to the chest. She looked up at her mom.

"Oh, this shade is lovely!" Mom said. She dropped several packages from the kitchen-gadget vendor on the table and fanned herself. "Whew! What a wonderful relief from the sun! I think this is the only shade tree in the entire market!" She looked at Lucy kneeling on the ground. "So, what did you find, honey? Did you find a gift for Schuyler?"

Lucy grimaced. *Oh, no, Schuyler's birthday is Tuesday. Maybe there's something in here I can buy. It can't be just any gift.* She rummaged through the trunk again, pulling out the hat and the knitted silver vest. *No, all wrong.* She put them back and grabbed the globe. *Yeah, maybe this could be it.*

"Sir, how much for the globe?" She held it up so the vendor could see it.

The smile disappeared from the vendor's face. "You cannot separate the tools. You must take the trunk and all the items in it." The breeze kicked up and swirled around them, ruffling Lucy's hair and shaking the leaves overhead.

"Hmm," Lucy said as she placed the globe back in the trunk and stood up. "I don't have enough money for all of this." She pushed the hair away from her face.

"Remember what we talked about?" Mom interjected, swatting at a lock of light-brown hair the wind had pushed in front of her face. "We're going to stash some of your babysitting money away to buy your school supplies in the fall. You're thirteen now and old enough to help out." Her lips were a tight, thin line as she tilted her head. Lucy knew the "don't even think about it" look. She had seen it often lately.

"How much money do you have, Lucy?" The vendor smiled winsomely at Lucy's mom.

"Not a lot," Lucy said, "and I'm not supposed to spend it all." Head down, she scuffed her feet in the dirt, sending up little puffs of dust.

"If you are willing to give all you have, then it is enough," the vendor said. Lucy's mom glowered at him and harrumphed.

Lucy stared longingly at the trunk. "I can do extra chores and babysitting jobs to earn money for school supplies." She turned an expectant face toward Mom. "I promise. It's still weeks before school starts."

"Well . . ." Mom hesitated. She looked at the trunk of tarnished peculiarities. "Fine, but you still need a gift for Schuyler." She crossed her arms.

"Wonderful!" said the vendor. "You have made a wise choice, Lucy. There is a bracelet in the trunk. I think your friend Schuyler would like it. It would suit her perfectly." The breeze settled down and wafted gently around them. "And since Schuyler is your best friend, it wouldn't be separating the tools, now would it?"

"I guess not." Lucy rummaged through the trunk till she found the bracelet. Like the Spectrescope, it was tarnished and dull, but Schuyler would like it. She pulled money from her backpack, paid the older man, and thanked him for the trunk. He winked at her. She grinned. "It was very nice meeting you, sir."

The Ghost of Darwin Stewart

"When you come again, Lucy, I will be here if you need me." A smile lifted the corners of his mustache.

"Well, no point in carrying all these packages since we now have a trunk to put them in," Mom grumped. She dropped her packages haphazardly into the trunk and slammed the lid. She and Lucy each grabbed a handle and carried the chest between them.

Halfway back to the car, Lucy stopped, dropping her end of the trunk. It hit with a loud thump on the hard-packed dirt. Her mouth fell open. The older man had called her by her name. *What? How did he know my name? And how did he know Schuyler was my best friend?* Lucy thought.

"Lucy Hornberger! For heaven's sake! What are you doing?" Mom barked, still holding her end of the trunk.

Lucy turned to wave at the vendor, but he had disappeared along with his table and chair. Even the shade tree was gone.

It was as if he had never been there at all.

2 The Master

Grehssil, the servant, took a deep breath, turned the handle, and opened the heavy wooden door. He shuffled into the room and bowed. "Master, we have news from the battlefield. The Spectrescope is active once again. It has passed to a girl named Lucy Hornberger." He shuddered, clasped his hands tightly, and then continued. "One of the Ormarrs witnessed it, Master."

The Ormarrs made Grehssil almost as nervous as the Master did. He didn't like the nasty things, all creepy in their ragged black cloaks, slinking around in dark corners. It caused him to shudder just thinking about them, and having to relay his Master's commands to an Ormarr left him nearly catatonic. He never felt entirely alone, constantly checking the corners of a room to make sure they weren't darker than usual. He didn't trust the Ormarrs. He couldn't see their faces under the hoods. He wasn't even sure they had faces.

"So, it begins," said a deep, lilting voice. "I have been waiting for too many millennia for this very time. Are you certain it has passed to a girl?" The voice dripped with disdain.

A large, dark wooden desk with ornate carving sat in the center of the room. It was covered with books, papers, drawings, and a blood-red feather in an inkwell sitting next to a blotter. A tall, tufted leather chair faced the expansive floor-to-ceiling mullioned glass windows behind the desk.

"Yes, Master, it is what the message said." Grehssil cast furtive glances toward the chair, and his head bowed, limbs quaking. "It was a high-level Ormarr who obtained the information."

"Do stop your sniveling, Grehssil. You know how much I dislike it," the Master snarled. "It's hard to believe you once served in the courts of the precious High King. Do you require further correction?"

"No, Master," said Grehssil as his hand moved slowly over his deformed leg, a reminder of his previous correction.

"A girl? Does he think a mere child can defeat me? How insulting. Does he not expect my wrath?" The chair slowly turned. The Master rose gracefully to stand before the bowing servant. He twisted his head, cricked his neck, and smiled, revealing a perfect set of pearly white teeth. His deeply set eyes, the color and hardness of fossilized amber and rimmed with dark lashes, penetrated those of the anxious servant.

"Heh! Doesn't he remember? I once ruled countless legions! I was Prince Darnathian, like a son of the High King." His jaw clenched, distorting his classic features. "A single word from my mouth carried as much authority as that of the King. I still command legions of followers while he sends a child to thwart my plans. He surely must be getting old."

Grehssil remained silent, and his eyes averted as he listened fearfully. His Master neither wanted nor expected his response except to serve without question.

"Insolence!" The Master slammed a hand down hard on the desk. Long, thin fingers with manicured nails swept across the surface, sending papers and drawings fluttering wildly to the floor. A faint blue-green light flickered, dancing across the paneled walls and library shelves filled with dusty, ancient tomes.

"I will crush the impertinent child and throw her mangled body at him!" His eyes burned bright like the glowing embers of a dying fire. His hands curled into fists.

The air in the room instantly became supercharged and heavy. The intensity of the blue-green light increased, flickering wildly now across the walls. Wood logs burned fiercely in the giant stone fireplace, the flames leaping and swirling, belching heat into the room. Grehssil continued to look at the floor. Sweat dripped from his long, pointed nose.

The Master stood tall and slowly inhaled a deep breath, his eyes closed. His arms swept slowly upward and backed down again as his hands unclenched, features relaxed. The blue-green light calmed to a gentle flicker, and the flames settled down to tickle the logs in the grate. "I have a better idea." He laughed. The sound was almost musical, enchanting, and thoroughly evil.

The servant shivered despite the heat.

"I will show her just how invaluable a friend I can be. Once she learns he's just a moldering old fool, she will turn away from him. She may wield the power of the Spectrescope, but she will use it for my purposes, all the while thinking it's her idea. Oh, yes, I like this plan." He clapped his hands excitedly. "It should be quite easy to turn her. Humans are so gullible. She might become my best instrument yet."

"We have her scent, Master," Grehssil said, withdrawing a small glass vial from his coat pocket and holding it out for the Master to see. His hand quivered.

"Excellent! I want to know everything about little Miss Hornberger. Send the Hayyothalan to keep on an eye on her. If he can retrieve the Spectrescope from her, all the better. Eventually, she will give me what I need." The Master glared at the servant. "Go!" he bellowed, with a dismissive wave of his hand. He ran his hands down each arm, smoothing the wrinkles from his impeccable white suit, then casually slipped them into the pocket slits of his trousers. The flickering blue-green light dissipated. His shoulders shook with mirth.

Grehssil hurried from the room, closing the door behind him as his Master laughed heartily. The sound chilled him to the bone as he quickened his pace. The castle corridor echoed with his scuffling footsteps.

He limped stiffly to the spiral stone staircase. Holding tight to the cold, serpentine metal railing, he lurched up the stairs. His leg had never healed properly from the Master's last correction. Shuffling down the next corridor, he came to a series of doors carved with images of ancient creatures long extinct in the human world.

He opened a door adorned with a giant crow and stepped inside. Torches burned in charred sconces hanging on the stone walls, sending a feeble light gyrating across the room's exquisite furnishings. The warm glow could not dispel the chill that enveloped the Hayyothalan's abode.

A man stood looking out the mullioned window across the room. Smooth, shiny black feathers covered his head. He had an ashen pallor and wore a long black cloak.

"The Master has a task for you, Malpar," Grehssil said. He shuffled farther into the room. The bird-man turned to look at him with expressionless black eyes. "It is a crucial task. He has waited millenna for this opportunity. The Spectrescope has resurfaced. It has passed to a human girl named Lucy Hornberger." The servant held the vial in his hand. "We have her scent. Take it. It will help you track her. We need to know everything you can learn about the girl. If you can steal the Spectrescope from her, do it, and do it quickly."

The Hayyothalan walked forward, grabbed the vial from the servant's hand, and disappeared.

# 3 The Mirror Awakens

"Mom! He's gone! He's gone! Even the tree he was sitting under isn't there!" Lucy threw her hands in the air. "Just look!" She gestured back toward the market.

"Lucy!" snapped Mom. "Don't be so irritating. That is utterly impossible and ridiculous. Now, don't say any more about it. We've walked quite a distance. I'm sure his table is just out of sight."

"How did he know my name? I didn't tell him my name," Lucy insisted, stomping her foot and crossing her arms.

"*Stop.* The vendor probably heard me say your name," barked Mom. "Now, let's go!"

"You called me honey, not Lucy."

"*Lucy. Hornberger!*"

Lucy harrumphed, picked up the handle on her end, and began walking toward the parking lot, dragging her mother in her wake.

A stony silence filled the car during the drive home. A thousand questions bumbled around in Lucy's head. If the Spectrescope and the ghost were real, then the older man's disappearance would make sense if he were a wizard or something. The objects with the strange symbols in the trunk could be magical. It was all connected, but how? She needed to talk to Schuyler, but Schuyler was visiting her grandparents for the weekend. And though Mom didn't say it, Lucy heard the implied assumption that she was making up stories again. No matter what she said, Mom wouldn't believe her. Mom pulled the SUV into the driveway too fast again, hitting the edge of the curb and tossing Lucy against her seat belt. "Geez, Mom!"

"Do not bring that trunk into the house unless it is thoroughly clean and debugged," Mom complained. She slammed the gearshift into the "park" position, stopping abruptly. "And do it before you forget and drift off into that fantasy world of yours."

"Aw, Mom," Lucy moaned. "Couldn't I—"

"Not one more word! As pleasant as the old man was, you can never tell where that trunk has been, so scrub it clean before you bring it into the house, for goodness' sake!" grumped Mom as they took it out of the back of the SUV. "Now that you've wasted your money on this piece of junk, you're going to need to earn more. You should call the Gleasons and offer to babysit for them. I hear Mr. Gleason got a promotion at work. Naturally, he will want to take his wife out to dinner to celebrate. Or you could do some tutoring to earn some money. How about that kid, Paul, from school?"

"It's Saturday, and if the Gleasons haven't called for babysitting by now, it's not going to happen, and I'm not tutoring anyone. It's summer!" declared Lucy, crossing her arms and glowering at her mother.

"Lucy Hornberger!" Mom snarled. "Just you remember; you promised to earn money to help buy your school supplies."

"I won't forget because you won't let me!"

"I can't do it all on my pittance of a salary. There's only one of me to feed everyone in this family, so go call the Gleasons." Mom's voice quivered slightly, whether from anger or anxiety, Lucy couldn't tell.

"Fine. I'll call when I finish scrubbing the trunk!" Lucy retorted. Grabbing the handle, she began the trek to the backyard patio, dragging the trunk through the long grass beside the path on her way.

Lucy spent the rest of the afternoon cleaning the trunk and its contents. The work helped her forget the heated exchange with Mom. She knew Mom was worried, being a single parent trying to keep ahead of the bills and still provide a normal-like existence for two active teenagers. With her older brother, Dale, Mom hoped he would qualify for a scholarship in his last year of high school. Lucy pushed the guilty feelings aside and scrubbed hard at the Spectrescope, polishing its long, wide handle with some silver cleaner she found in the basement. The symbols sparkled, and in the sunshine, it looked as though they were moving.

Next, Lucy polished the bracelet. *The gentleman was right*, she thought, putting it on her wrist. *Schuyler will love this*. The purple stone, nestled in the center of the braided metal with intricate leaf etchings, appeared clear at times, yet it wasn't. No matter how she turned it on her wrist, the bracelet always centered itself on the top of her arm, so the stone was facing up.

"This is awesome!" Lucy squealed. She wrapped it carefully in a cloth and placed it in the trunk with her backpack.

Satisfied that the trunk and the oddities contained in it were clean, she tugged and pulled it through the kitchen and up the back stairs to her room. She pushed it into place at the foot of her bed and then retrieved the backpack and flung it on the bed before running back down to the kitchen for a glass of milk and two chocolate cookies. Sitting in the upstairs foyer windowsill, she munched the cookies, careful not to waste a crumb, and updated her journal. She filled several pages.

"Lucy, dinner is ready!" Mom yelled up the stairs, interrupting her work.

Before heading down the back stairway to the kitchen, Lucy dropped her journal on the table near the window. The aroma of grilled pork chops and hot rolls filled the air, making her mouth water. Once back down in the kitchen, she slid into her seat.

"Did you bring your dishes down?" Mom placed a plate of chops in the center on the table. "Or did you forget them again?"

"Oops, sorry, I forgot," Lucy replied sheepishly. She shrugged her shoulders and smiled goofily at Mom. She reached for a hot roll.

"What a surprise," mumbled Mom. "Go get them now and put them in the sink. You can wash them with the dinner dishes."

Lucy sighed, her hand hovering over the rolls. Forgetting the roll, she ran back upstairs to the foyer. The plate and glass were on the table next to her journal. "Oh, bugger," she muttered. The half-empty tumbler of warm milk had formed a ring around the inside of the glass. *If Mom sees this*, Lucy thought, *she'll make me drink it like she did the last time. Yuck!* Without thinking, she grabbed the glass and pitched the warm milk out through the screen of the open window.

Ha! Mom will never know! She dabbed milk droplets from the screen with the hanky she kept in her pocket. She grabbed the plate and turned toward the stairs when voices drifted up from below the open window.

"Aw, dang it! I just washed that car this morning," said Bill McGoo, their next-door neighbor. "That must have been one big bird to drop a mess like that!"

Lucy's hand flew to her mouth. *The milk!* She dropped quickly to the floor and crawled to the window. She raised her head slowly, peeked out the window, and grimaced. The milk had splattered over the front of Bill's car, parked directly below the window in the narrow driveway between the two houses. The milk had dried immediately on the warm metal of the car sitting in the evening sunshine. Bill's head swiveled as he checked the sky above.

Lucy rolled her eyes. *Oh, my gosh! I sure hope Mom doesn't hear about this one*, she thought. *I'll be grounded till I'm twenty-three! And that's if I'm lucky!* She crept away from the window, her heart pounding. Clutching the tumbler and plate, she clomped down the back stairs two at a time.

She put the dishes in the kitchen sink. Her brother, Dale, sauntered in, plopped into his seat, and speared a pork chop. His shirt was untucked, as usual, and his jeans had a new hole in the knee.

"Lucy, what did you do?" said Mom, passing the hot rolls to her. "Why is your face so red?" Lucy's gray eyes popped open wide, punctuating the startled look on her face.

"Uh, because I was running up and down the stairs?" Lucy scuttled into her seat at the table, grabbing the plate from Mom. "I was trying to hurry. I know you don't like the food to get cold," Lucy blundered on, the words rushing out of her mouth. "Thanks for dinner, Mom. It all looks good. I love pork chops! Yum!"

"Uh-huh," Mom said as she spread honey on a roll. "Did you get the trunk all cleaned out?" She glanced at Dale's rumpled appearance, pursed her lips, and took a bite out of the roll.

"Yeah! It looks great," Lucy said. She relaxed, breathed a sigh, and stabbed a pork chop with her fork. "You should see all the cool stuff! Everything cleaned up well. They must be antiques or something." She grabbed the bowl of peas and scooped some onto her plate. "There's the bracelet the vendor mentioned and a cool ring. I didn't see it before. It rolled out of the black velvet fabric tucked inside. There's a globe, kind of like one of those snow globes with the fake snow inside, only this one has smoke in it, and a mirror and some other things. I'll give the bracelet to Schuyler for her birthday present, as the vendor said." She sliced the chop. "It's bizarre, though. The stone always comes back to center on top of your wrist, no matter where you place it."

"Ith pa ba bee a hi oh coop," Dale mumbled through a mouthful of food. Lucy rolled her eyes and flicked a pea at him. It missed.

Mom heaved a sigh. She clenched her jaw as she stared at Dale with the "how many times have I told you not to talk with your mouth full" look.

Dale gulped his food. "It's probably a gyroscope. That's what gyros do. They balance themselves, so you always know which way is up. You know, Uncle Bob showed us the artificial horizon on the instrument panel of his Cessna when he took us flying last summer. It indicates when the wings are level. You'll learn about gyros in science class."

"Cool!" Lucy said. "Schuyler will love it. She likes weird stuff!"

Lucy didn't talk much during the rest of dinner. Her thoughts kept wandering back to the vendor, the Spectrescope, and the trunk and its contents. Dale chattered amiably about his afternoon adventures while Mom pushed food around her plate.

After dinner, Lucy cleared the table, washed and dried the dishes, and then headed upstairs to finish the next chapter in the ghost story she was writing. *Today's events certainly qualify as a ghost story*, she thought. She crossed the upstairs foyer and reached to pick up her journal. Voices drifted up from the driveway. She peeked out the window at the neighbor next door.

"Look, Vivian, how big that bird dropping is!" said Bill, pointing at the car. "That must have been one big bird. I wonder what it was. Turkey vulture, maybe? I've seen some enormous blackbirds around behind the garage today. Especially a big, ugly one, but he might have been a raven, creepy thing."

Vivian, his wife, stepped out the kitchen door and looked at the big white splatter on the front of the car. She smiled wryly and placed her hands on her ample hips.

"For heaven's sake, we can't drive that mess to the church in the morning. Get the bucket, and while you rewash the car, I'll make the dessert for the Sunday social tomorrow. I'm going to need plenty of chocolate chip cookies for those youngsters," said Vivian, her portly figure disappearing back into the kitchen. The screen door banged shut.

Lucy's head dropped. Her shoulders drooped. Her face burned. *It was childish, not something a teen should do*, she thought. *How could I be so stupid? Won't I ever learn to think before I act? Grr.* She bopped herself on the forehead, took a deep breath, and then hurried down the back stairs, through the kitchen, and out into the yard. At the side gate leading to the neighbor's driveway, she waved at Bill. The big car seemed out of proportion next to Bill, who was on the thin side. Water and soap from the wash bucket had splashed his olive drab pants and T-shirt. His dark-brown hair was tousled and streaked with gray strands.

"Mr. Bill, can I talk to you a minute?" asked Lucy, giving him a feeble wave.

"Well, hey there, Miss Lucy, how are you?" Bill gave Lucy a big smile. He liked it when she called him Mr. Bill.

"Not so good," Lucy replied, lightly running a hand over the crossbar on the gate. "It wasn't a big bird that splattered your car today. It was me." Her face went scarlet as she grimaced, looking up at Bill.

"You, Lucy?" Bill said, plunging the sponge into the wash bucket and swirling it around. He dropped it on the car and then wiped his hand on his pant leg.

"Yeah, Mom has this rule. I can take milk and cookies upstairs to my room, but I have to drink all the milk and not waste it. I didn't drink all my milk," she said, twisting her hands. "It got warm, and I threw it out the window so Mom wouldn't find out and get mad at me. It was stupid and a childish thing to do. I'm sorry I messed up your car. I didn't mean to make extra work for you."

Bill was quiet. He looked at Lucy as he rubbed his chin. Lucy thought he was going to get really mad at her. She gripped the crossbar and waited.

"Well, the way I see, it took a good heart and a great deal of courage for you to tell me what you did. I'm willing to forget about it and not tell your mom, but in return, you have to help me wash the car," Bill replied, smiling slyly, the lines around his brown eyes crinkling.

A few minutes later, when Mom looked out the kitchen window, she saw Bill, Vivian, and Lucy laughing and sitting together on the driveway, eating chocolate chip cookies. The wash bucket sat on the ground in front of Bill's sparkling clean car. She shook her head and mumbled, "That girl."

*   *   *   *

Lucy crawled into bed and turned on the bedside lamp. From the back of her journal, she studied an old photo found one day in a tattered box of yellowed photographs when she was rummaging in the attic. She knew it must be of her dad because she looked just like him. He was grinning in the photo, revealing smile dimples in his cheeks just like hers, and his button nose and nut-brown hair was the same as hers too.

She wondered why she had never heard from him. No birthday cards or Christmas gifts. Where was he now? Did he ever think of her? Did he even remember he had a daughter? Sometimes she could almost imagine the sound of his voice. It would be soft and clear and comforting, like snuggling in blankets and listening to the sound of rain on the window.

Schuyler's relationship with her dad sometimes made Lucy feel a little lonely. Mr. Williams was always teasing Schuyler, helping with her homework, and cheering the loudest at her volleyball games. It would be great to have a dad. Perhaps Mom would tell her someday why he left when Lucy was so young. She had no memories of him at all. Even Dale wasn't sure if he remembered their dad.

"Lucy, bedtime!" Mom yelled from downstairs.

"Got it!" Sighing, she tucked the photo back into the journal and padded down the hall to the bathroom.

Lucy washed her face and put her pajamas on, then brushed her teeth as she bobbed her head, counting the brush strokes. Leaning into the mirror, she grinned and dropped the toothbrush into the holder as a loud creaking noise caused her to jump. For a moment, the air in the room seemed electrically charged, and her skin prickled along her arms. *It's just the old house grumbling again*, she thought. *It's always creaking and groaning. Get hold of yourself, for goodness' sake.* She turned off the light, closed the door, and went to her room. She stopped abruptly.

The trunk lid was open.

Hmm, I thought I closed it. I know I closed it. Maybe Mom was checking out the excellent cleaning job I did. She kicked the lid closed as she climbed into bed.

Lucy turned off the light, snuggled into the pillows, and gazed out the window at the twinkling stars. She lay wondering about the vendor. Was he a wizard or something? Her eyelids soon became heavy, and she quickly fell asleep. She dreamed someone was calling her, whispering her name as gently as a breeze. The voice stirred a longing in Lucy as though she had lost something precious. She desperately wanted to find the owner of the voice. Just when she thought she could almost see him, she jerked awake.

The curtains were fluttering. Lucy yawned widely and blinked her eyes. Leaning on an elbow, she looked around the darkened room. There was light reflecting on the walls and floor. She sat up. It wasn't coming from the window, and the bedroom door was closed.

It was coming from under the closet door.

The bright knifelike sliver of greenish light pierced the dark room. As Lucy sleepily considered the curious light, something interrupted it, sending shadows creeping eerily across the floor. Something or someone was pacing inside the closet.

The Ghost of Darwin Stewart

The shadow stopped. The doorknob began to rotate. She sucked in a deep breath and held it with a hand to her mouth. Her skin prickled with electricity all its own.

The latch clicked.

The door slowly squeaked open until the sliver of light meandered from the floor and slithered its way to the top of the old, warped door, and then it stopped. Lucy gulped and pulled the covers tight around her, her heart pounding loudly.

The thing in the closet paced methodically back and forth, the shadows crawling like snakes on the carpet and disappearing into the dark recesses under her bed. Again it stopped moving. The shadows stayed where they were under her bed.

Minutes passed. Nothing moved. Slowly, Lucy reached up and switched on the lamp, its light dispersing the shadows. Pushing back the covers, she crawled cautiously out of bed.

Lucy tiptoed to the closet door, reached out a shaky hand, and gripped the knob. *This is where freaking stupid people get their brains sucked out by drooling zombies*, Lucy thought. Taking a deep breath, she threw the closet door open and stepped back. A loud, snarling *hiss* erupted from the closet. Lucy squealed, jumping on the bed and grabbing a pillow to throw at whatever emerged from the closet.

Wide-eyed, back arched, and hackles raised, a small gray cat stood in the harsh light of the overhead fixture. With lips curled in a snarl, and eyes wide, the cat stared up at Lucy.

Metrocom!

Lucy sighed with relief as she sagged down into the covers, clutching the pillow. The tension slowly ebbed from her shoulders.

"What are *you* doing in my closet, you silly goose? Are you opening doors again?" crooned Lucy, picking up the cat and stroking its fur with a shaky hand. The cat meowed and pressed against her hand.

"You gave me quite a scare," she said, head-bumping Metrocom affectionately. She cuddled the cat, scratching his ears and chin till she stopped shaking. Opening the bedroom door, she set the cat on the floor. "You go downstairs now where you belong." The cat, named Metrocom after a character in one of Dale's favorite sci-fi books, ran down the stairs, his tail as straight as a car antenna with a slight crook at the end.

Lucy turned off the closet light, shut the door firmly, and listened for the click. The old, warped door was securely closed. She turned toward the bed. The trunk lid was open again, and the mirror inside was flickering with light.

"What the?" Lucy picked up the mirror. It was sparkling, reflecting its light onto the walls. Laying it on the floor, she sat and watched the surface shimmer and ripple like raindrops falling on a pool of water. Lucy hesitantly reached her hand out and then slipped it through the rippling surface up to her wrist. She wiggled her fingers in it. It was as cool as water and as light as air. She pulled her hand out. It was dry.

She set the mirror in a vertical position and then pushed her hand through the surface again. Peeking around the back of the mirror, she expected to see her hand poking out the other side. It wasn't. She shoved her arm in deeper, waving it around, grasping for anything that might be there. *Holy moly,* she thought. *Where's my arm?* She felt her hand and fingers wiggling, but where were they?

Lucy heard a deep rumble of what sounded like laughter. She pulled her arm out and whirled around, expecting to see Dale watching her from the doorway, but no one was there. She looked at the mirror. *If I stuck my head in there, what would I see?* Lucy wondered. *Could I breathe in there, or should I hold my breath?* As she leaned closer to the mirror, it winked out and became a solid surface reflecting Lucy's pensive face.

Lucy was perplexed. What was going on here? *Noises, dreams, lights, the mirror,* she thought. *Things are getting creepy.* Several minutes passed, but the mirror remained quiet. She dropped it in the trunk and closed the lid. She sat looking at the box and then picked up the backpack and placed it securely on the top. Crawling into bed, she turned off the lamp and pulled the cotton blankets over her.

Lucy lay awake for some time with her hands tucked behind her head, staring at the ceiling. Dozens of questions bumbled around in her head as she thought about the vendor. *Who is he? Does he know about the mirror?* Lucy pondered. *Where did he go when he disappeared? What opened the trunk? Where would I have gone if I had gone through the mirror?*

There has to be a way to find out. Schuyler will have an idea. I know she will. Snuggling down into the pillows, she soon fell into a dreamless sleep.

*　*　*　*

The Master stood watching Lucy through the sister mirror hanging on his paneled library wall. These were the only two mirrors of their kind on this side of Ascalon. The others were left behind when he was exiled from the kingdom. He hadn't time to retrieve them. Without them, he could no longer spy on the King, and he couldn't make any more mirrors since he did not have access to Crystal Lake.

Incantations safely guarded this mirror. Its sister mirror, the one Lucy Hornberger somehow had possession of, had mysteriously vanished long ago. But now that he knew where it was, things were about to become quite intriguing for thirteen-year-old Lucy Hornberger. *If little Miss Hornberger can animate the Spectrescope, does she know its secret?* he wondered.

A sinister smile creased his face as he watched her. The skin around his eyes crinkled with amusement as she placed her hand through the mirror's surface. The hand floated in front of his face, the fingers wiggling.

He studied the hand. The skin was smooth and youthful with just a tinge of brown from the sun. The fingers were narrow, and the nails neatly trimmed, though two fingers had hangnails bitten off. *Were you worried about something, little Miss Hornberger? You should be.*

He reached his hand up and wiggled his fingers like Lucy's, just millimeters from touching her. Oh, how he longed to grasp that hand and yank her into his world. The hand shoved further into the room. He leaned back out of reach, laughing heartily. The arm quickly disappeared back through the portal.

He studied the inquisitive face with the clear, expressive gray eyes and the room with its faded wallpaper and old-style dresser and nightstand. He committed every detail to memory and then sucked in a breath and growled as the portal became a mirror once again.

The Bracelet
Has a Secret

Lucy was up early Tuesday morning. She took the bracelet from the trunk, placed it in a small gift box, and wrapped it with brightly colored paper. Mom would be ready to go in a few minutes to drop her off at Schuyler's house.

She couldn't tell her mother about the mirror or the ghosts in the Spectrescope. Her mom would blame Lucy's overactive imagination again. Once, she told her younger cousin not to step on graves in a cemetery because a ghost would follow him home. He didn't sleep for days, and she had to wash windows because of it.

After a quick breakfast, Mom dropped her off at Schuyler's house, coming to a stop in front of the two-and-a-half story white clapboard home that welcomed guests with a wide brick front porch and light-colored curtains at the windows. Colorful summer flowers in terra cotta clay pots lined each side of the steps.

"I have a few errands to run before I pick up groceries, so it might be a little while before I come to get you," Mom said, rummaging through her purse for the errand list. She placed it on the seat beside her. A flock of noisy blackbirds landed on the telephone wires across the street. The din of their cawing and cackling sounded like a heated parent-teacher conference in session.

"Great! Schuyler and I have important things to discuss. See you!" Lucy jumped out of the SUV, grabbing the backpack and Schuyler's gift on the way. She slammed the door, and Mom squealed away from the curb, disappearing around the next corner. Lucy shook her head. "And she's off to the races!" Lucy ran up the pavestone path to the house.

An enormous black crow landed on a branch in the tree near the house. His black beady eyes watched as Lucy ran toward the house.

The front door flew open, and a girl with wavy dark-blonde hair, flushed cheeks, and bright, hazel-green eyes burst across the porch and down the steps. "Lucy!" cried Schuyler. She gave her friend a tight hug.

"Happy birthday!" Lucy held the gift out to Schuyler. "I hope you like it. Boy, have I got lots of stuff to tell you."

"Come see my room. Mom and Dad redecorated it for me while I was at my gram and gramp's. It's so shabby chic. We can tell each other about our weekends." Grabbing Lucy's hand, she pulled her into the house. "I hope you're hungry. Dad's going to grill his monster burgers, and there are cake and ice cream for later too. Mom made her famous chocolate triple-berry torte. It's going to be so yummy."

"Oh, my gosh! Your mom is such a good cook, but the chocolate triple-berry torte is my absolute fav. I feel like it's my birthday."

They ran upstairs, and Schuyler opened her bedroom door with a flourish. "Voila! So, what do you think?" She stood aside to let Lucy into the room.

"Whoa. It's awesome." Lucy stood gaping at the room. "It's so you!"

The pale-green walls reflected the light from the open windows. Sheer white curtains fluttered in the breeze. Pink-and-green striped bedding, pillows, and a new tufted headboard in a light-colored fabric completed the redo. The high-ceilinged walls had a pale-pink chevron border painted around the top. The entire effect was light and airy.

"They've been saving up all summer for this. Isn't it amazing?" Schuyler said, admiring the room. Her hazel-green eyes sparkled. "Dad even painted my old wicker desk and dresser, so they look new too." Schuyler plopped on the bed next to Lucy and opened the birthday card.

"It looks like it came right out of a magazine. Your mom and dad are so cool," Lucy said, leaning back on her elbows. "I'd love to redo my old room. I think the wallpaper in my room has been there since the Civil War." Her hands rapidly slapped the bedcovers in excited energy as she spoke.

Schuyler laughed. "You're exaggerating again." She read the birthday card and grinned. It featured a squirrel with its mouth chock-full of nuts, saying, "Birthdays are nature's way of saying, EAT MORE NUTS!"

"Not really, Grandma says the house was built in 1830, so it might be the same wallpaper. It even smells that old." Lucy gagged.

"I wonder if our house is that old. I bet my dad will know." Schuyler pulled at the wrapping paper. "I know all the houses around here are old, and there's some kind of historic neighborhood society. I'm not sure, but I think Dad has to get their approval before making any changes or repairs to the house."

"Why? It seems silly since it's your house," said Lucy, a confused look scrunching her face.

"I think it's to keep all the houses looking like they did in the 1800s when the city was still pretty new." Schuyler dropped the wrapping paper on the floor.

"Oh, how was your trip to your grandparents," Lucy asked, chewing her bottom lip. Patience wasn't one of her virtues, and she was just bursting to tell Schuyler about the vanishing vendor.

"It was fun! We went to the zoo, and we saw the botanical gardens. The flowers were awesome. Gram and Gramps live in the country, and all kinds of animals tromp through their property. Gram feeds the deer, and I got to help. A mama deer ate a carrot from my hand. It was cool. Gramps even took me for a ride on his motorcycle. How wowza is that?" exclaimed Schuyler, her hair bouncing as she moved her head. "They don't act their age, so you never know what they'll be doing next. I overheard Gram say she wants to take up skydiving!"

Schuyler glanced at Lucy's hands, which were still double slapping the bedcovers, and pinched her lips with a smirk. "How was your weekend, Luce? Did you find anything unique at the flea market? Any scope for the imagination?"

"Oh, yeah!" Lucy popped up from the bed and turned to face Schuyler. "It was cool and creepy at the same time."

"Really? Well, come on—spill it." invited Schuyler. The gift lay unopened in her lap.

Lucy told her about the trunk, the Spectrescope, the old man's disappearance, and the strange lights in the mirror. Schuyler was shaking her head dubiously by the end of the story.

"A magnifying glass that's called a Spectrescope for hunting ghosts and spirits, and a shaggy ghost. And an old man and a tree that disappears. It's just too fantastic, Lucy." Schuyler stared at Lucy, one eyebrow raised. "The mirror is what? A portal to another dimension? Mars? This is one of your stories, isn't it?"

Lucy grabbed the backpack and pulled out the Spectrescope. "This is the scope I saw the ghost through." She handed it to Schuyler. "What do you think?"

"Whoa, it's ancient." Schuyler turned the scope over in her hands. She hefted it up and down. "And heavy! Look at the weird symbols on the handle. They're beautiful." The symbols appeared to glow with an inner light.

Schuyler peered through the glass. "I don't see any ghosts." She studied the symbols on the handle and traced them with her finger. "You're still writing that ghost story, aren't you?" She handed the scope to Lucy.

Lucy pinched her lips and grumbled. "Yeah, so?"

"Uh-huh, I thought so."

"Oh, just open your gift," Lucy grumbled. "The old guy said I should give it to you, and he thought it would be the perfect gift." She watched Schuyler open the gift box. "Wait till you see what it does, then maybe you'll believe me," she mumbled.

"Wait. What did you say?"

"Nothing, just open it already!"

Schuyler's mouth dropped open as she reverently lifted the bracelet from the box. "Oh! I love it! I do love it! It's so different," exclaimed Schuyler, slipping the bracelet on her wrist. She gently turned it around her arm. "The stone looks like a purple star amethyst with flecks of gold. It's beautiful." She gave Lucy a perplexed look. "The old man said you should give this to me? Why? It looks valuable."

"Yeah, he did." Lucy paused, scrunching her face and wrinkling her nose. "Uh, your bracelet may have some rather unique qualities."

"What do you mean by 'unique qualities'?" Schuyler blinked wide-eyed at Lucy. "Is it safe to wear? It won't turn my skin green, will it?"

"No, I don't think it's going to turn you green, but it might do something else. Turn it over on your wrist, so the stone is on the bottom."

"Okay." Schuyler squinted at Lucy. She turned the bracelet over, placing the stone on the bottom under her wrist. The bracelet vibrated and then flipped itself so the stone was back on the top of her arm, startling her.

"Oh, my gosh! How did it do that?" Schuyler squealed, holding her arm away from her body as though the bracelet might turn into an alien. She twirled the bracelet several more times, putting the stone on the bottom of her wrist. It vibrated and flipped itself over each time. Deciding it was probably safe, she grinned. "This is pretty cool!"

"Great, isn't it? I am not sure how it works. It always comes back to the top. Dale thought it was a gyroscope of some kind, but *I* think it's *magic*. It must be, like the other things I found in the trunk." Lucy leaned back on her elbows.

"I like the stone. It's my favorite shade of purple, though I'm not sure yet about the gyroscope thing," Schuyler replied. She rubbed her finger over the stone's smooth surface. "The metal is shiny too. I love it. Thanks, Luce!" She leaned over and hugged Lucy. The bracelet began to glow on Schuyler's wrist.

A shadow, black as ink, slipped unnoticed through the open window screen and slithered up the wall. It crawled into a corner of the ceiling where it looked like a giant spider waiting to drop on a delectable victim. The Hayyothalan, Malpar, clung to the wall, hoping to gather information from their conversation about the Spectrescope. Being a shapeshifter, he could make himself as small or as large as needed and change his form from a manlike creature to a crow or an inky-black shadow.

The bracelet suddenly tightened around Schuyler's wrist, forming to her arm. Schuyler squealed and jumped from the bed. The stone erupted into a long silver shield, emblazoned on the front with a white fox that held a purple flag with a golden cross.

"Get it off! Get it off!" Schuyler shouted, running around the room while shaking her arm and pulling at the shield. "Lucy, help me get it off!" Her face was terror stricken.

Lucy scrambled to her feet and, grabbing the shield, tugged on it. It held firm and wouldn't budge. "Hold still!" She tried prying it off Schuyler's arm with her fingers, but it was no use. Realizing there wasn't any danger, she finally let go, laughing. She watched as Schuyler frantically circled the room tugging at the shield, her shoulder-length curls bouncing wildly.

"Stop! Just sit down," Lucy giggled, rolling on her back on the bed, her knees pulled to her stomach. "You're killing me!"

"Kill you is something I'll do later! How do I get it to turn back? I can't go around carrying this thing," Schuyler fumed. She plopped on the desk chair, still shaking her arm and glaring at the offending object.

"I don't know, it didn't do that for me." Lucy rolled onto her stomach, her feet waving in the air.

"*Oh, by the way, it has unique qualities, says she*," Schuyler grumbled. She tapped the shield in several places, but it remained. She slapped it.

The unexpected appearance of the shield startled the Hayyothalan. He slithered quickly from his hiding spot near the ceiling, down the wall, and back out through the open window.

"Now what? It won't come off!" huffed Schuyler. She held her arm in front of Lucy.

"Dunno," Lucy shrugged. She muffled a giggle. "Sorry! What were you doing when it changed?" She held her breath, trying to look serious. She hiccupped.

Schuyler glared at her. "I think I was rubbing the stone with my finger."

"Well, try that. Touch the stone to see what happens," Lucy replied, tossing a pillow on the floor. She sat cross-legged on it.

"Where is the stone? I can't find it." Schuyler searched the shield with her free hand, swirling her fingertips against the surface. She finally found the stone on the inside next to the handgrip. As she touched it, the shield vibrated and shrank back into the bracelet. "Phew! Good to know how that works." Schuyler sighed.

"That was so awesome! Now that we know how it works, think how great it can be in a snowball fight!" exclaimed Lucy, clapping her hands.

"Lucy!" Schuyler scolded. "Yeah, I'm sure that is its exact purpose. Come on, Luce, think about it." She took the bracelet off and studied it closely. The weird symbols etched the braided metal. Hidden between the vines and leaves was a single tree with a flame of fire at its core. "Someone designed it for a special purpose and gave it magical powers. It has tiny etchings all around the bezel of the stone. They're the same as on your Spectrescope." She looked up at Lucy. "What about your Spectrescope? Didn't the old man say it has chosen you?"

"Yeah, he did. I don't know what it's supposed to mean, though. I just thought he was teasing me. You know, trying to sound all mysterious and spooky-like," said Lucy, rolling her eyes and wiggling her fingers in the air. "He said the things in the trunk were tools that can't be separated and that I can't escape my destiny. I thought maybe it was a gimmick to get me to buy the trunk." She smiled wryly. "Now, I'm not sure what to think."

"Try the bracelet on." Schuyler handed it to Lucy. "See if you can get it to change for you. I bet you can't."

Lucy put it on and stroked the stone in a swirling motion, just as Schuyler had done. The bracelet remained unchanged. She tried it again, nothing.

"The old man told you to give the bracelet to me. It must have been meant only for me, just like the Spectrescope was meant only for you. Even so, how did the old man know you would be at the flea market?" mused Schuyler. "Your Spectrescope probably won't work for me. They're magical, but what are we supposed to do with them?"

"I don't know. The vendor was just a friendly old guy. I only stopped to look at the scope." She gave the bracelet back to Schuyler. "It was kind of weird looking and just lying on the table. There's no way he could've known about me or that I was going to be at the market on Saturday. I've never seen him before. At least, I don't think I've met him before, and yet, I feel as though I've always known him." Lucy paused, a pensive look clouding her face. "No, that just sounds strange."

"Duh!" Schuyler threw her hands up. "You mean like this stuff isn't strange? I am sure a bracelet like this is perfectly normal, somewhere in the universe!" she said sarcastically. She polished the bracelet on her shirt hem and then suddenly sucked in a breath. "Oh, my gosh! Lucy! Did you have this engraved?"

"What? I didn't have anything engraved."

"The bracelet has my name engraved among the leaves," Schuyler said, pointing at the spot. "It says, *Schuyler the Protector.*"

"Seriously? I swear! It wasn't there when I was polishing it." Lucy gaped at the bracelet. "I would have seen it."

"Check the Spectrescope! Is your name engraved on it somewhere?"

Lucy took the Spectrescope to the window and studied the handle in the strong sunlight. Tiny etchings of leaves and vines swirled around the handle with the tree with a flame at its core. The words *Lucy the Gatekeeper* were engraved.

"No way! That was not there before!" exclaimed Lucy, staring open-mouthed at Schuyler, the Spectrescope trembling in her hand.

"Then it's all true! These things truly are meant for just us," said Schuyler, her voice crackling with excitement. She cautiously slipped the bracelet back on her wrist. "But why?"

"You know, if all those things in the trunk *are* magical—the Spectrescope, the mirror, the bracelet—what are we doing with them? Do you think he's a wizard?" Lucy giggled, then hiccupped. "Maybe he's an alien from outer space!"

"Lucy!"

"Geez, you're as bad as my mom," Lucy moaned. "No sense of humor."

"Maybe the vendor doesn't know they're magical. What then?"

"He had to know. He was selling them. That stuff is ancient, and you have to admit they're unique. They must be valuable."

"Well, I guess there's only one way to find out. We'll go back to the flea market and find him if he's there. We can ask him what it's all about. Is your mom going to the flea market this weekend?"

"I think so. I overheard Mom telling Dale she would buy him some new jeans for his camping trip. Holy moly, did he make a fuss about her buying his stuff from a flea market!" Lucy smirked.

"I'll ask my mom if I can go with you on Saturday. Maybe we'll find some answers there," said Schuyler, shrugging her shoulders.

*   *   *   *

The day had quickly flown past, with every minute chock-full of activities for Schuyler's special day. There were games of beanbag toss, Frisbees, and water balloons, which Lucy thought felt fantastic due to the sunny day and temperatures hovering near ninety, and there was a picnic-style lunch out on the back patio.

They were all feeling stuffed by the time Lucy's mom telephoned, explaining that she needed to go to the office for a while. Mrs. Williams agreed to have Lucy spend the evening with them, and Mr. Williams surprised the girls with a trip to the mall and a movie and then treated them to ice cream afterward. Both girls were sleepy by the time Schuyler's dad dropped Lucy off at home in the evening.

Lucy let herself in the house, pocketing her key as she dropped her backpack by the door. "Mom! I'm home!" she yelled. The timers had turned the living room lights on, and the soft glow made the empty room look cozy. "Mom! Is anybody home?"

"She's not home yet, Squirt," Dale called from his bedroom upstairs. Lucy could hear the blasters and *rata-tat-tat* of the video game he was playing.

"Mom's still at work? This late?" asked Lucy, trudging sleepily up the front stairs, dragging the backpack along beside her.

"Yeah, she called to say the other lady had goofed up the presentation, so Mom had to start over from scratch. Said she would be home by midnight at the latest." Dale rolled his desk chair to the open bedroom door, poking his head into the hallway. "You have a good time at Schuyler's?"

"Yeah." Lucy yawned. "Mrs. Williams is an awesome cook. There were three different types of salad and the monster-sized hamburgers Schuyler's dad likes to grill. And the best part was Mrs. Williams's specialty, chocolate triple-berry torte with buttercream frosting. I could eat that every day, it's so good. Then we went to the mall and saw a movie too." Lucy yawned again. "Best day yet of summer vacation."

"You better head to bed. Your eyes are barely open," said Dale, reaching out to ruffle Lucy's hair. "Goodnight, Squirt."

"Night, D," Lucy mumbled through another yawn. She dropped the backpack on top of the trunk, pulled her pj's from the dresser drawer, and headed to the bathroom. Five minutes later, she crawled into bed.

Curled up under the covers, she gazed sleepily at the night sky outside the window. Her eyes were heavy with sleep, and her stomach was still too full. She fell into a fitful sleep almost immediately, tossing around in the tangle of covers and being disturbed by a very unusual dream.

* * * *

Darnathian twisted his head, cracking his neck and wishing he could rid himself of this odd quirk. He leaned closer. The girl sent to thwart his plans tossed fitfully about in the bed while he hovered just above her. He blew softly in her face, his breath tickling her cheeks and lifting a few brown hairs that stuck to her forehead. Her nose wrinkled, and she suddenly sneezed, her head popping up off the pillow and missing his nose by centimeters. He reached a hand toward her.

"You shall not touch Lucy Hornberger," said the High King. He slowly stepped from the corner of the room and approached the bed as Lucy snuffled, turning her face into the pillow. He had exchanged his colorful, flowing robe for a brown tweed suit and white shirt. "She is not to be harmed."

"Another of your precious minions, isn't she? I have no intention of harming little Miss Hornberger," replied the Master, standing tall. He casually slipped his hands into the pockets of his trousers to hide his clenching fists from the King.

"Why are you here, Darnathian?" The High King gazed thoughtfully at the former angel, noting every detail about the creature on the other side of the bed.

"What? Can't I even walk about without your interference? I was out for a stroll and thought I would stop by and visit Miss Hornberger. It's as simple as that, old man." A flicker of hatred flashed across Darnathian's face before he could control it. The tension in his shoulders caused the bony nubs where his magnificent wings used to be to ache painfully. He smirked at the High King, a dimple appearing in his cheek. Strips of blue-green lights danced along the walls.

"It is never simple with you, Darnathian. Even now, you are struggling for control." The King sighed, shaking his head wearily. "Why must you be so antithetical? It is because of your own choices you lack tranquility. Will you never rest from this opposition?"

"Speaking of choices, what choice does she have?" said Darnathian, waving his hand at Lucy. "Why don't you just build a protective fence around her and lead her around like a puppy dog? She has no choice about serving you. Does she even know who you are and what you're capable of?" he snarled. "Do you think she will still serve you when she learns you're responsible for her father's disappearance? I think not."

"Lucy is intelligent and honest, sometimes willful and impatient, but always loving," said the King, smiling down at Lucy thoroughly tangled in the bedcovers. He waved his hand over her form, and she settled into a restful slumber. "I do not doubt as to the conscience of her heart that when tested, she will still be the Lucy Hornberger who wants to do right, to love and be loved. She has free will and must glean the truth for herself about who I am. The struggle will make her stronger. And our bond insepara-ble." The King was gradually fading from view. "Goodnight, Lucy," he whispered. Then he disappeared.

Darnathian leaned over the bed, reaching his hands out and flexing his fingers, wanting desperately to throttle Lucy in her bed. "You're wrong, old man. She'll turn from you. I will turn her." He became a swirling mass of blue-and-green light and, forming himself into a large ominous serpent undulating beside the bed, he hissed loudly and vanished.

* * * *

Lucy woke with a start. She sleepily looked about her room, feeling as though something had just happened. Misty images from the dream drifted away from her. She yawned widely, rolled over, and vaguely remembered two men standing on either side of the bed in her dream, talking about *her*, their voices silenced. The older man looked like the flea-market vendor, while the other man was younger with dark hair and golden eyes. The older man faded away. The younger man, however, became an iridescent blue-green snake leaning over her before he vanished.

Lucy shook her head. "Wow," she murmured. "Maybe I shouldn't have eaten the last slice of Dale's meat-lovers pizza right before bed." She yawned and was just drifting off again when a scratching sound began.

Dismissing it as a squirrel in the tree next to the house, or perhaps one running along the small, shingled overhang under the window, she pulled the covers over her head and wished for it to go away.

Tap. Tap. Tap.

Tap. Tap. Tap.

Lucy sat up. Awake now, she pulled the covers to her chin, clutching them tightly in her hands. She glanced around the room to find the source of the tapping.

Tap. Tap. Tap.

Tap. Tap. Tap.

It was coming from outside her window. Fearing it might be a bat sitting on the window frame outside trying to scratch its way in, she cautiously pulled the curtain to the side and peeked out the window. A dark shadow flittered past the window. She flinched, dropping the curtain and listening for more sounds, but heard nothing.

Slowly pulling the curtain back again, she peeked out the window once more. Everything was as it should be for a quiet summer night with the streetlights casting small pools of soft light around their poles, tree toads croaking in the tree branches, and crickets chirping in the grass. The night air drifting through the screen smelled of moist earth and flowers. Lucy leaned closer to the window.

Two glassy red eyes were staring back at her from the other side of the screen.

"Argh!" she squealed, scampering backward across the bed.

A thick, dark shadow rose, covered the window entirely in darkness, and then flew upward toward the top of the house. The room filled with scratching sounds as something crawled along the roof. Lucy looked around the bedroom. The sounds were everywhere.

Mom burst through the bedroom door.

"What are you doing in here?" Mom demanded. "I need to get up early in the morning. I have a project to complete before the boss arrives in the office. Now, quiet down!" She pulled her cotton robe closed and tied the belt. She leaned over to switch on the desk lamp.

"Mom! It isn't me. There's something on the roof. I saw it!" Lucy pulled the curtain back and pointed to the window. "It was outside tapping on the window frame, and then it flew up to the roof."

"Lucy, I don't have the patience for any more of your stories. Just go to bed so I can get some sleep." She turned and bumped into Dale, who was yawning and rubbing his eyes.

"What's all the noise?" Dale mumbled and yawned again.

"Lucy is telling stories again. Claims she saw something flying around outside and landing on the roof," sighed Mom. "Will everyone just please go back to bed?"

"There is something on the roof. I heard it too," said Dale, stifling another yawn. "It's probably just a squirrel. I heard it scratching at the shingles like it's digging a hole or something."

"Or something," Lucy murmured.

"Lucy Hornberger! Have you been feeding the squirrels again? I've told you a thousand times not to put peanuts on that shingled ledge. Enticing those pests will only cause problems," Mom grumped.

"I didn't put peanuts on the ledge! Mr. Bill feeds the squirrels, and they sit there and eat the nuts!" retorted Lucy, folding her arms across her chest.

Thump!

"What in the world?" Mom exclaimed, looking at the ceiling as though she could see through it. "Dale, grab a flashlight, and let's go see what's making all the ruckus." Mom padded down the back stairs to the kitchen, her fuzzy slippers flapping against her heels.

Lucy grabbed her robe and was struggling into it when she saw the Spectrescope. It was lying on top of the trunk, the symbols glowing around the headpiece and morphing into various birds' shapes. She snatched it and ran down the stairs.

Lucy charged ahead of her mom to the gate by Mr. Bill's driveway, threw it open, and ran along the side of the house. Using the Spectrescope, she looked up at the roof and caught a quick glimpse of a darting black shadow surrounded by a faint purple mist in the glass.

Dale joined her in the neighbor's driveway and turned the flashlight beam on the roof. As he panned the light back and forth across the shingles, several peanuts whizzed past their heads. They all heard the scratching sounds as something hurled more peanuts at them. The noises then faded toward the opposite side of the house.

Dale followed the ruckus around to the front of the house, flashing the beam over the siding under Lucy's window. Suddenly the scratching noise stopped, only to be replaced by a fast-paced chirping.

"See, I told you it was squirrels," snickered Dale. He flashed the beam on Lucy as a peanut bounced off the top of her head. "From one squirrel to another." He turned the light off and disappeared around the back of the house. When he was gone, footsteps raced across the roof and down the tree. They faded into the night.

"C'mon, Luce." Mom sighed. "Let's go back to bed. Lock up, will you?" She padded back through the gate toward the back door, leaving Lucy alone and staring after her. The night seemed eerily quiet between the light pools from the streetlamps. Even the crickets were silent.

"Heh, heh, heh," laughed a raspy voice nearby.

Lucy froze. Goose bumps popped up across the length of her arms. Unsure of where to run, she raised the Spectrescope and slowly looked in the direction of the voice. There, in the tree limbs above her head, an enormous black crow-like bird sat surrounded by a pale purplish glow. Its eyes glowed an eerie red-gold, looking much like the glowing embers of a campfire. Chills crept down her spine. She stared at the strange bird, which was staring back at her. A burnt odor drifted on the air.

"You are not very brave, are you?" the bird said. It tilted its head sideways, the beak glistening in the lamplight. "Give us the Spectrescope."

Lucy turned and fled, charging through the gate and into the house. Slamming the back door, she quickly turned the deadbolt, pulled down the shade, and leaned against the doorjamb.

Only a nightlight illuminated the dim kitchen. Mom had already turned the lights off on her way back to bed. The faint glow of the nightlight made the shadows lurking in the room's corners even darker. Lucy

The Ghost of Darwin Stewart

crept toward the back stairs, her breathing shallow as she listened for any intruders. Finally reaching the stairs, she raced up the steps and into her bedroom. She collapsed on the bed and sat, pulling air into her lungs.

"Meow."

Lucy jumped from the bed, clutching her robe at the throat. Metrocom lay curled up on the pillows, nonchalantly licking his paws. Shaking, she stuffed the Spectrescope under her pillow before reaching over and slamming the window firmly shut.

"I don't care what the rules are about pets on the bed. Tonight you're sleeping with me," Lucy said, crawling under the blanket. Metrocom turned around twice and resettled himself in the crook of Lucy's arm, his tail lazily swishing back and forth in contentment.

5 Wizards, Ghosts, and Warnings

Lucy drummed her fingers on the armrest with one hand while the other gripped the backpack with the Spectrescope tucked securely inside. Saturday had been long in coming to begin with, and now Lucy's mom appeared to have changed from her NASCAR driving habits to that of a centenarian who couldn't remember how to use the accelerator. Sitting next to her, Schuyler spun the bracelet around on her wrist.

An overcrowded parking lot and rising temperatures greeted them as they arrived at the flea market. Mom had barely stopped at the entrance when the girls burst from the SUV.

"Meet me back here in an hour," yelled Mom as she sped off in a cloud of dust to find a place to park down the road. Waving away the dust, Lucy and Schuyler headed into the market, winding their way through the meandering crowd of shoppers.

"Look for a large, gnarly old tree. The vendor wore a brown suit, and he was sitting in the shade under the tree last time," Lucy said, her hand raised against the sun. "I should have brought my hat," she muttered, fanning her-self with her free hand.

"What hat? You don't wear hats."

"The one I found in the trunk. It's rather cool. It changes color to match whatever you're wearing," Lucy said, grinning. "Maybe it's in the backpack." She rummaged through the pockets.

"When did you become a fashionista?" Schuyler snickered.

Lucy poked her tongue out at her friend.

"I bet this used to be a cornfield," Schuyler said, looking around and squinting against the strong sunlight. "There's hardly a tree anywhere except around the perimeter, and the trees here are quite young. A big tree should be easy to find."

"Let's try the outer aisles first. The vendor should be down one of those." Lucy led the way past rows of sunglasses, T-shirts, velvet Elvis paintings, and cheap plastic toys.

They searched for nearly an hour, jostling their way through groups of shoppers. Tired and sweaty, they wandered toward the outer aisle where they had begun. Lucy pulled two bottles of partially frozen water from her backpack and handed one to Schuyler. Uncapping the top, she drank deeply before replacing the cap. The cool water was refreshing.

"Phew! That's much better," Lucy mumbled. She put the water bottle back in its pocket and pulled out the Spectrescope. "I wonder if I can see him with this." She scanned the aisle for any sign of the vendor. Perplexed, she searched the area again. "Weird."

She saw people buying fruits and vegetables, people looking at dusty old furniture and poking at holes in the cushions, and children who were shuffling along after their parents. She didn't see anything unusual for a flea market.

"What's weird? You didn't see the vendor?" Schuyler asked between sips of water.

"No, I don't see the old man, and I don't see any ghosts. When I found the Spectrescope, I picked it up and looked through it. I saw ghosts, gobs of them everywhere. The thing that flew at me was horrible. It was creepy and wearing a ratty hooded cloak. It pointed a bony finger at me."

"Ew! Are those things here?" Schuyler glanced about, her eyes moving like pinballs. "Where are they?" She stared at a shaggy-haired guy walking past and squinted her eyes at him. He raised a questioning eyebrow but kept walking.

"Well, that's just it. The ghosts are not here. They're not anywhere. No creepy hooded thing, and no happy pieces of sunshine either." Lucy paced in circles and looked up and down the aisle. She leaned sideways, looking around Schuyler at three lanky teenage boys dressed alike in gray T-shirts and black jeans. They were watching her. "What?" she said, raising her arms in the air. They walked on.

"What are 'happy pieces of sunshine' supposed to be? A different type of ghost?" asked Schuyler, her brows scrunching together. She felt a little calmer knowing there weren't any ghosts in the immediate area.

"Maybe, I guess, I dunno. I know there were ghosts here when I found the Spectrescope." Lucy looked through the scope, trying to see any hint of a ghost but secretly hoping she wouldn't. Her experience with the creatures so far was unsettling enough.

"Do you think the Spectrescope is broken or just not working for some reason?"

"I used it the other night. We heard something crawling on the roof, scratching and tapping at my window. Mom and Dale heard the noises. We all went outside, and that's when I saw a purple mist through the scope."

"Was it a ghost?" whispered Schuyler. "Did your mom and brother see it too?"

"No, it was only visible in the scope. Oh boy! If Mom had seen it, she would have blamed me for it. It seems like she blames me for everything lately. Only this time, I'm afraid she would be right."

"If there are no ghosts, what do you think it means?" Schuyler mopped her forehead with a hanky and pushed aside her hair, which was rapidly frizzing in the humid air. She tucked the water bottle into a mesh pocket of Lucy's backpack.

"I wish I knew. We have to find the vendor. He must be here somewhere. He said he would be here if I needed him." Lucy sighed. She put the scope in the backpack. "Where are you, Mister?"

"Lucy! Look!" Schuyler grabbed her friend's arm and pointed down the aisle they had just searched. "He's here. We must have walked right by him."

Lucy saw the old man. "No, we didn't. He wasn't there before, and neither was the tree. We would have noticed. C'mon!" She darted around a man and woman holding hands and walking casually along.

"What's he doing?" Schuyler followed Lucy down the aisle toward the vendor.

The old gentleman had left his table and wandered out into the field behind. He made his way through the tall meadow grasses to the middle, where four horses were standing. The horses, each a different color with long flowing manes, had strong muscular bodies. He approached a horse and caressed its dark-cinnamon mane as he spoke softly to it. The horse nodded and shook its head. When the vendor noticed Lucy and Schuyler approaching, he patted each horse's neck and quietly whispered to it. The horses waggled their heads up and down as if answering. They turned and trotted back through the grasses and disappeared across the field. The girls looked at each other as they waited near the vendor's table.

"Good morning, Lucy! Good morning, Schuyler! How kind of you to visit me," called the old man, smiling. He returned to his table under the shade tree. "I dare say you must have a few questions to ask me by now." His longish white hair curled over his collar, and he wore the same brown tweed suit and white shirt. He still looked like Schuyler's grandpa.

Schuyler's mouth dropped open. "How did you know my name?"

"You are wearing the bracelet Lucy bought for her best friend, Schuyler. Therefore, I assume you are Schuyler," he replied softly, his eyebrows lifting on his wrinkled forehead. "Are you not?"

"Well, yes, I am, I guess," she said, her brows furrowed as she studied him.

"Don't you know if you are Schuyler?" he teased, wiggling his mustache.

"Of course I know who I am!" retorted Schuyler. "You know what I mean."

"Yes, I do know. Can't an old man tease two charming young ladies who were so kind to come to see him? I get so few visitors these days. I was just trying to be witty," he said, shrugging his shoulders.

Lucy studied the vendor's face as he conversed with Schuyler. There were deep lines etched around his eyes as though he smiled often. His white hair, mustache, and eyebrows were a bright, glowing white, as though they had their own light source. Lucy still felt as though she had known him from somewhere before but just couldn't remember where. "Hello, sir. Can I ask you something?" she said.

"You just did," he said with a laugh. "Do you have another question you would like to ask?" His blue eyes twinkled.

"Where did you come from just now? We walked all over the market, trying to find you. You weren't here, and neither was this tree. It seems like you just popped in from nowhere. Did you pop in?" Lucy asked hesitantly. A gentle breeze caught a strand of hair, floating it across her face and tickling her. She tucked it behind her ear.

"I was here. I am always here, although it was not until you asked that you found me," the gentleman replied, leaning toward Lucy. He casually slipped his hands into his pants pockets.

"I don't understand," Lucy said, shaking her head. "You mean all these people can't see you unless they ask? Are you a wizard or something?"

"Oh, they see me. As my dear friend Matthew was so fond of saying, 'They see, but do not observe. They hear, but they do not listen.' No, no, I am afraid they pay me no heed at all," the vendor said with a sigh. He didn't answer her question about being a wizard.

"If they ignore you, why do you come here?"

"Come here? Dear Lucy, I have never left."

"I still don't understand, sir," Lucy said. "Do you live somewhere around here? Is that what you mean?"

"In time, dear Lucy, in time, you will understand many things," he replied softly. A group of shoppers walked by, laughing and chatting. They took no notice of the vendor or the girls.

Lucy glanced at the passing shoppers. The air had a strange, shimmering quality to it as though she were inside a bubble looking out. She blinked her eyes. The shimmer was still there.

"Okay, but in the meantime, what do we call you?" interjected Schuyler, her hands on her hips. "You do have a name, don't you?" By this time, her hair was looking like a thick thatch from a woolly sheep with its tangled curls, and it was getting bigger.

"I am Iam Reynard," the man replied, and with a flourish of his hand, he bowed.

"Iam Iam?" said Schuyler, confused. "That's a strange name. What kind of name is that? Is it British?" She loved anything about England and the British.

"You may call me just Iam," he said, twisting his mustache. He gazed at Schuyler, who was closely watching him and smiled. "Reynard is from an old French translation meaning 'fox,' and it appears in European folklore and literature about a rather adventurous and crafty fox. Interesting, isn't it? Who knew there is more to a name than just a label we call ourselves?"

"While that's interesting, how did you know her name?" persisted Schuyler, pointing toward Lucy. "Lucy says she didn't tell you her name."

"Why, I suppose I must have heard her mother use her name. That would be logical, wouldn't it?" asked Iam innocently, tilting his head.

"That's what my mom said," Lucy muttered. "Yet I don't remember her saying my name. Anyway, I want to know about the objects in the trunk. Who made all of those things? They must be worth way more than what I paid for them. What are we supposed to do with them?"

"Oh my, it would take a long time to explain," said Iam, putting his hands in his suit pant pockets and looking down at his dusty black shoes.

"They must be valuable. They're antiques," Lucy insisted as Iam tugged at the collar of his shirt. "Are you sure you don't want them? I'll understand if you want me to return them." She pulled the Spectrescope from the backpack and held it out to Iam.

There was a short silence while he looked thoughtfully at Lucy, then he continued. "Yes, I suppose many people would consider them priceless antiques. Each is unique. Though, there are things worth much more." He paused briefly before continuing. "The trunk and all its contents are . . . necessary. The trunk contains everything you will need. The Spectrescope has chosen you, Lucy, so you must be ready."

"Ready? Ready for what?" Lucy asked, confusion and a frown appearing on her face and brow. She looked at Schuyler, who was still watching Iam closely. She took a step back from the vendor's table, still holding the Spectrescope.

"A battle," he replied.

"You mean, like a fight?" asked Lucy, incredulous. "I don't know how to fight. Why would I be fighting?"

"A battle has been raging since before this world was born. The forces of the Fallen are aware the Spectrescope has chosen you. They know your name, Lucy, and they will try to stop you. The trunk will help you. It will give what is necessary when you need help. It knows your every need." Iam paused. He stepped from behind the table to stand before Lucy. He sat on the edge of the table and looked in her eyes, his hands clasped before him.

Bewildered, Lucy watched him earnestly.

"You see, Lucy," Iam continued, "the universe is not only made up of the things you can see, but there is also the unseen as well. Spirits, powers, principalities. They hold it, shape it, shift it, and bind it all together. Not all of these things are good or well intentioned. Your Spectrescope has shown you some of the unseen forces."

"Spirits? Powers?" Lucy asked, confused. She was feeling slightly ill and frightened by what she was hearing. She took another step back. "You mean, like the ghosts I saw in the Spectrescope?"

Iam nodded slowly. "Yes, these are a few of the unseen forces that exist," he replied quietly. "The good, as well as the bad."

Lucy swallowed hard. "By bad, you mean the Fallen?" asked Lucy. She glanced furtively at Schuyler, whose mouth had dropped open and whose hazel eyes were wide with disbelief. The humidity had now frizzled Schuyler's hair into a mass that looked like a horrible perm.

"These are but a few of the invisible forces in this world," Iam continued. "They prey on people who cannot defend themselves, the weak and misguided. These spirits are not good."

"Who are the Fallen? Where did they come from?" Lucy asked, shuddering. An ill feeling in her stomach threatened to upheave the breakfast burritos they'd had from the drive through on the way to the flea market.

Iam hesitated, then continued. "They are fallen Daemonimini, banished from the kingdom of Ascalon several millennia ago." A pained expression flashed briefly across his face before he looked again at Lucy.

"They are now called Irredaemon, the irredeemable. In your world, they are called angels."

"I'm sorry, sir. I don't understand any of this. Fallen angels from a kingdom I've never heard of, spirits, ghosts?" Lucy shook her head. "Why would they do any of this?"

"They are evil and take pleasure in haunting and tormenting people, preventing them from finding their way home. You, Lucy, have been chosen to help those who cannot help themselves."

"I don't understand. How can I help? I'm not smart or brave or anything. I'm just a kid," Lucy said, feeling a bit anxious and shrugging her shoulders. "I mean, how much help can I be? Besides, who would believe me?"

"You have a very giving and loving spirit, Lucy," Iam said gently. "It is why the Spectrescope chose you. To be 'true of heart' means you have a genuine concern and love for others, whether they deserve it or not. That is the greatest gift." He smiled kindly at her. "It does not matter that you are young, only that you are willing to do what you can, to do what is right. Therefore, you must be ready."

"Will they hurt us? The spirits, I mean, these Irredaemon. Why would they want to stop me from helping someone?" Lucy shivered slightly, then rubbed her hands over her arms. She felt goose bumps popping up.

"I am afraid it will take much too long to explain. You will, I think, begin to understand," Iam answered gently. He stood with his hands still folded in front of him, studying her expressions. "The Spectrescope, the tools in the trunk, and the trunk itself will help you and protect you. You need only to ask. They will teach you what you need to know."

"What if I don't want to do this?" asked Lucy, watching her foot scuffing nervously at the dirt.

"Would you refuse to help someone you love if they were in trouble?"

"No, but what if I can't help them? I would try, I really would, but maybe I just can't help them. What then?" She looked into his blue eyes and saw gentleness and understanding. It made her feel less anxious.

"I would not worry, Lucy," Iam replied confidently. He smiled as he said, "The Spectrescope has never been wrong in its choice when selecting the next ghost hunter."

"Ghost hunter!" gasped Lucy. "Is that what I am?" Her eyes were like saucers, and the Spectrescope wobbled in her hand. Her goose bumps were multiplying at warp speed.

"Yes, a ghost hunter. Does that surprise you?" Iam laughed as he leaned against the table. "And a powerful one too. Once you've gotten the knack of it, you will be unstoppable."

"Wow! I'm a ghost hunter!" gasped Lucy, looking excitedly at Iam. She was shaking all over and could hardly believe it, rubbing the bumps on her arms. "Oh no," she said, suddenly deflated like a popped birthday balloon and wishing she could be someone else, knowing she would probably have to tell her mom about being a ghost hunter. "Should I tell my mom? I don't think she will believe me or let me go ghost hunting."

"Well, it is not right to deceive someone, so you should tell her if she asks," he replied his white mustache wiggling.

"Okay, but I know she isn't going to believe me. She'll think I am making up stories again. I am always getting into trouble for telling my little cousin spooky stories."

"If she chooses not to believe, it is her choice to make. You will have told the truth, and that is what matters most," Iam said. "Always remember, Lucy, the truth will protect you."

"Okay, I think," said Lucy, still somewhat confused. "How do I do this ghost hunting thingy? Who do I need to help?" The breeze played with her hair. She tucked the errant lock behind her ear again.

"What tools have you found in the trunk so far?"

"I found a belt-shaped ring with blue-and-white stones of some kind, a hat, a knitted vest, and the bracelet I gave to Schuyler for her birthday. There was also a mirror and a smoke-filled globe."

"Excellent, Lucy! How exciting! You have everything you need to get started. Keep the Spectrescope with you always. It will reveal the hidden things you need to see."

"What do all of those things do?" Lucy asked Iam. "Are they all magical?"

"In time you will—"

"In time, you will understand many things," Lucy quipped. "Yeah, yeah, just like my mom when she doesn't want to tell me something." She sighed, placed the Spectrescope in the backpack, and set it on the table.

Iam laughed heartily. "Dear Lucy, you are a treasure," he said, slapping his thigh.

Lucy smiled wryly. She watched his shoulders quiver with laughter. "Why is there a doorknob on the lid? There is another one on the inside bottom of the trunk too."

"I suppose it makes the trunk easier to open, does it not?" replied Iam merrily, his shoulders still hunching up and down with amusement.

"Uh, I guess so. What does the doorknob on the inside do?"

"Perhaps it is a spare?" Iam answered, raising his eyebrows and tilting his head.

"Humph." Lucy pursed her lips. She gave Iam her "really?" look. "What if I need to ask you more questions or need help? How do I reach you? Do you have a cell phone so I can call you?" Lucy asked, rummaging through the backpack for a notepad and pencil. She had left her cell phone on the car seat.

"Oh, dear!" Iam laughed, dropping his head. His shoulders shook again with laughter. "No, Lucy, I don't have a cell phone. However, should you need me, you can reach me anytime just by calling out my name. I will find you. I have excellent hearing. Is that okay?" Iam replied, smiling as he bent slightly to look her in the face.

Lucy puckered her lips and gave him a look that said, *"Yeah, right. Like I believe that's going to work."* She dipped her head and gave a little snort.

"What about me?" Schuyler asked. "What should I do with the bracelet?" She held out her arm to Iam.

"Schuyler dear, I haven't forgotten you," said Iam, turning toward her. "You are very important indeed. Every good ghost hunter needs a trustworthy assistant for help and support. Why, without you, Lucy would have a difficult time indeed." Iam smiled encouragingly at her.

"Ooh!" exclaimed Schuyler. Ghost stories were her favorite, and to be a part of one sounded exciting. "Okay!"

"Be sure always to wear the bracelet. It will protect you." He leaned toward Schuyler in a conspiratorial way and whispered, "Have you discovered its secret yet?"

"It vibrates and turns into a shield! It is long and not nearly as heavy as I thought a shield would be. And there is an emblem of a white fox holding a purple flag with a gold cross. Whose emblem is it?" Schuyler nearly vibrated with excitement, waiting for Iam to continue.

"Indeed?" replied Iam, raising one eyebrow. It twitched. "Always keep the bracelet with you, Schuyler. It is your shield and your help, just as the Spectrescope is your helper, Lucy. A ghost hunter must never let her guard down," he said firmly, looking at Schuyler and then to Lucy. "And you must never be without your special tools. Do you both understand?"

"Uh, sure, I'll keep it with me always," Schuyler stammered. Lucy hesitated and then nodded vigorously.

Suddenly, Iam looked sharply at Lucy, concern clouding his face. "Lucy, is there anything you need to tell me? Has something happened? Have you encountered any more ghosts?" His blue eyes, usually bright and sparkling with amusement, suddenly turned dark and piercing as he looked at her.

"Uh, well, I did see a mist the other night," Lucy replied, slightly intimidated by his unusually grave expression. "It seemed to surround an enormous black bird sitting in the tree. He spoke to me."

"Tell me exactly what happened," said Iam. He watched Lucy closely as she retold the event. He stood up and walked back behind the table. "A Hayyothalan," he murmured under his breath. His hand pulled at his mustache as he thought about what Lucy had just said.

Lucy interrupted his thoughts. "Iam? What does the mirror do? When I woke up in the night, the trunk was open, and the mirror was sparkling, kind of like sunshine on water. It looked so cool and inviting that I put my hand in it. It felt almost silky, not wet. I pulled my hand out, but it was completely dry. Why did it do that?"

"Be very careful when gazing into the mirror, Lucy," Iam admonished. "It is a window, a portal of sorts to see what is happening in other places. Others can also see you from the other side. Use it wisely, and it can be a great asset." Iam went silent. When he spoke again, it was to caution.

"Lucy, keep the mirror covered. You don't want someone or something watching you or coming through the portal."

"Who would be watching me? A ghost, maybe? Like in the Spectrescope?"

"Keep the mirror covered," Iam replied in a tone suggesting no objections would be permitted. "You will learn when it is time to use it."

She pulled the Spectrescope from the backpack again. As she looked down at it, she remembered something. "Iam? When I looked in the Spectrescope a little while ago, I was looking for you, and I noticed something weird. There aren't any ghosts at the market today. The day the scope chose me, there were dozens of ghosts in the glass. Where are the ghosts?"

"Lucy, you should always be aware of your surroundings," Iam warned. "The Dark Prince Darnathian is powerful, and he is gathering his forces. The forces of good gather also, to prepare their defense against the

Irredaemon." Iam's brow furrowed as he spoke, deep creases changing the gentle lines of his face.

"The Dark Prince?" Lucy asked. "Who's he?"

"Lucy!" called a loud voice. The girls turned and saw Mrs. Hornberger, her arms laden with packages and jeans for Dale, bumping her way through the crowd toward them. They waved at her.

"Iam, when will I see you again?" Lucy asked, turning around, only to discover he had already disappeared.

"Wowza!" cried Schuyler. "Even the tree and table are gone! How does he do that? We still didn't find out if he was a wizard or something. He must be a wizard!" She threw her hands in the air with a look that said, *Well, that settles it. He's a wizard!*"

"Man!" Lucy exclaimed. "I wish I could do that. I wouldn't have to ride the school bus. I could just pop in and scare my teacher!"

As the girls joined Mrs. Hornberger, a large brilliant white fox trotted across the field behind the market and disappeared into the tall grasses.

* * * *

Sunday afternoon, Mrs. Williams called to invite Lucy to dinner with the family. Mrs. Williams, the best cook *ever* in Lucy's estimation, served steamed green beans accompanied by roast beef with potatoes and gravy, followed by strawberry shortcake for dessert. Lucy was in food heaven.

"Oh, Mrs. Williams! Everything looks so delicious! Thanks for inviting me." Sitting down, Lucy pulled her chair closer to the dining room table and reached for the green beans. "I wish my mom would cook like this. Hey, I'd be happy if *I* could cook even half as good as this." Lucy laughed and plopped some beans on her plate. "You should write a cookbook. I'd buy it!"

"Well," Mrs. Williams whispered, a conspiratorial look on her face. "I've been entering some of my recipes in an online contest. The winner will receive a lump sum of cash and have their recipes published in a magazine. Isn't that exciting?" She giggled and blushed red under her short dark natural curls. "Don't tell Mr. Williams. He doesn't know I'm doing it," she said, putting a finger to her lips. Mr. Williams was in the kitchen retrieving another plate of roast beef with mashed potatoes and gravy.

"If you win, what exciting thing will you do with the cash? Publish your own cookbook?" Lucy whispered expectantly.

"I've always wanted to own a bakery," said Mrs. Williams, keeping her voice low. "It would be wonderful, hard work and early hours, but so rewarding. And Mr. Williams wouldn't have to work such long hours at the office anymore," she said dreamily. "I could even sell my jam as a side for buttermilk biscuits."

"Awesome, Mrs. W!" Lucy gave Mrs. Williams two thumbs-up and a huge smile. Schuyler snorted, nearly choking on a mouthful of food as Mr. Williams came in carrying his plate piled high with beef and mashed potatoes. Everyone at the table busily shoveled food into their mouths, looking a little too innocent.

"What did I miss?" Mr. Williams asked, squinting his eyes at the girls. Receiving no answer but stifled giggles, he sat down to enjoy his second helpings.

Soon they finished the main course, and Mrs. Williams served Lucy's second favorite dessert, strawberry shortcake. Lucy shoveled a big helping of the dessert into her mouth and sighed with contentment, a goofy grin on her face. When Lucy and Schuyler could eat no more, they helped clear the table and then went upstairs to play video games.

Lucy plunked down on Schuyler's bed. "I am so full. I think I'm going to pass out in a food coma. Your mom sure knows how to plan a meal. I would be rather large if I got to eat like that every day."

"Weekday dinners are usually a bit lighter, though Mom likes to make big meals on Sunday. Is it cold in here?" Schuyler scooted her chair up to the computer at the desk and grabbed the mouse. Suddenly, she shivered. The laptop awakened with a *bing-bong* sound.

"It seems fine to me," said Lucy, pulling the Spectrescope from the backpack and laying down on the bed. After polishing the handle on her shirt, she placed the Spectrescope to her face, looked through the lens, and sucked in a deep breath. A nearly transparent purple mist outlined the image of an odd-looking man standing in the corner. He didn't look like the scary ghosts from the flea market. Instead, he was tall and lean and wore a cape over a suit and knee-high stovepipe boots. The small squinty eyes moved quickly and were unnerving.

"Uh, Schuyler," whispered Lucy, sitting up. Her mouth hung open, and her eyes felt as though they were going to pop from their sockets.

"What's the matter?" Schuyler asked, scrolling through the video games on the computer, her back to Lucy. "Got a food coma? Or a stomachache? Wowza, can you eat!"

"I think there's a ghost in your room," whispered Lucy, pointing toward the corner. "He's by the creepy closet." Schuyler's closet had two doors, one opened from her bedroom and the other was in the back wall, which opened to the sitting area at the top of the stairs. It was an oddity no one could explain.

"A ghost? In my room?" cried Schuyler. Her face paled as she swung around in the desk chair. "Where?"

"Shh! I don't think you want your parents to hear us, do you?" hissed Lucy, waving a hand at Schuyler. "How are you gonna explain a ghost?"

"What're we going to do? I don't want a ghost in my bedroom!" whimpered Schuyler as she scrambled from the chair and, grabbing Lucy's sleeve, nearly pulled her off the bed.

"Can you talk to us?" stuttered Lucy as she struggled up from the bed, Schuyler still grasping her sleeve. She hoped the ghost wouldn't notice the Spectrescope shaking in her hand.

"Yes," hissed the ghost, the word slowly leaking from his mouth like air from a punctured tire. He silently looked from Lucy to Schuyler, studying each one in turn. He wavered in and out of focus like a TV losing the broadcast signal, distorting his image.

"What's your name?" asked Lucy, watching the supernatural image in the lens.

"It's not important," said the ghost. With quick, jerky movements, he tilted his head to the side and looked at Lucy. "You are both shaking. You needn't be afraid of me yet. I am not one of the very evil ones."

"Ooh, that's scary! Where is it? I can hear what it's saying, but I can't see it," whimpered Schuyler. Her grasp on Lucy's sleeve grew tighter as she shook.

"Um, can you make yourself visible so we can both see you?"

"Perhaps," he replied. "If I choose to show myself to you, then you will have reason to be afraid." The temperature in the room steadily grew colder as the ghost spoke. Lucy's and Schuyler's breaths puffed in front of their faces. "Today," he drawled, "I chose not."

Schuyler tugged on Lucy's sleeve. "Is it still in the corner?" she asked.

Lucy nodded vigorously, intently watching the form through the Spectrescope lens. She held it up so Schuyler could see. The purply image of the ghost darkened slightly in the glass.

"Uh, okay, I've never talked to a ghost before," said Lucy. "What are you doing in Schuyler's bedroom?"

"I was curious about you," hissed the ghost.

"Curious?" Lucy winced as Schuyler tightened the grip on her arm even more. She poked Schuyler in the ribs. Schuyler glared at Lucy and mouthed, "Ow."

"Why would you be curious about us?"

"I was curious why the Spectrescope would choose a girl, so I came to see for myself," he hissed, "and for my Master." He floated slightly above the floor, his cape billowing softly.

"You know about the Spectrescope? Do many people, uh, I mean ghosts, know about it?" asked Lucy.

"I cannot tell you. The spirits have always known about the Spectrescope," the ghost answered evasively, looking sideways as he spoke. "It is sought after by many and never found, and then suddenly it reappears, and you command it. Why? You must be very special, Lucy."

"So why did you follow me here? Why didn't you show up at my house?"

"I chose here and today," said the ghost, his gaze slipping quickly about the room as though searching for something. "I have been watching you."

"Watching? What is it you want?" Lucy asked, studying the spectral image in the glass lens. She kept glancing at the empty corner expecting to see the ghost.

"I must tell you something," he said.

"Tells us what?" asked Lucy, casting a sideways glance at Schuyler, who had gone pale and maintained a death grip on her arm.

"You, I am telling you, human girl. The Master wants the Spectrescope, and he always sends his favorite Hayyothalan to do his deeds," he snarled. The girls looked at each other. They slowly moved closer together and farther away from the ghost.

"Okay, well, that can't be a good thing." Lucy swallowed. "Wait, someone sent a what?"

"The Master wants the Spectrescope. Give it to us." He reached a pale hand toward Lucy, and she recoiled. He then pointed his finger at her. "Be very careful, human. When you see me again, you will be afraid. You may have the artifact now, but soon it will be ours!" He flipped his cloak around himself and disappeared completely.

6 Gravestones and Crows Aplenty

"Okay, then," Lucy squeaked. "Good talk." Standing stock-still, she stared at the space where the ghost had stood. The corner was empty, and the spirit was gone.

"Where is it?" Schuyler asked, finally letting go of Lucy's arm. She looked around her room. "Do you think he's gone?" She cautiously waved her hand around in the corner where the ghost had been floating.

"I don't know. He just disappeared." The ancient relic wobbled in Lucy's hand. "The Spectrescope is clear, I think." She peered intently into the lens as she swept her gaze around the room.

"What did he mean? Who's this Master, I wonder." Schuyler sat down hard in the desk chair and placed a trembling hand to her cheek. The color was just beginning to come back to her face.

"Yeah, not sure what he meant. You know, for meeting our very first ghost, that didn't seem too frightening," squeaked Lucy, her voice betraying the confidence she was trying to show. She plunked down on the bed.

"Maybe, but it's still unnerving to learn there's a ghost in your bed-room," retorted Schuyler. Her shaky hand ruffled through her dark-blonde curls. "Not to mention, creepy."

"Yeah, I'm not sure I would like to know there's a ghost in my house, either," said Lucy. She rubbed the handle of the Spectrescope.

"While it was kind of hard to see him clearly through the lens," said Schuyler, "it looked like his clothes were ancient. Remember the depart-ment store exhibit we visited on the school trip to the historical museum?" she asked. "The volunteer said in the 1800s rich people could afford the fancy trims on their clothes, and things like expensive wool cloaks. He must have been someone important. His boots were knee-high too." The girls sat in quiet thought for a moment.

"Do you know the history of your house?" asked Lucy, breaking the silence. "Maybe he was someone who died on the property or built the house. Grandma is always telling me stories about a ghost who lives at our house. I've never seen her, but Grandma claims she has. Grandma even thinks she died in our house."

"Oh, great, thanks, Luce. I won't be able to sleep ever again when I'm at your house." She scowled at Lucy. "I suppose you think this ghost died in the house and now haunts my bedroom?"

"Sorry," said Lucy. "I hope not. It was just a thought."

"I don't remember any stories like your grandmother's. We could go to the library, though. They should be able to tell us about local history," Schuyler said. "They might have newspaper articles about the property, land deeds, or obituaries for previous owners. We can check to see if there is men-tion of the owners of our house. The librarian should be able to help us."

"Better yet, we could go to that little museum house down the street! We might be able to find the local area records. It is open on Sunday after-noons." Lucy put the scope in the backpack and threw the bag over her shoulder. "C'mon!"

They ran downstairs to tell Mrs. Williams they were going to the nearby museum. She offered to drive them, but the girls were already out the front door and running down the street toward the small museum. Two minutes later, the girls arrived at their destination, breathless. A bell tinkled overhead when they entered the house.

One of the museum volunteers, an older woman, greeted them cheerily. "Good afternoon, girls! Welcome to Hall House Museum. I am Mrs. Bronson. May I show you anything in particular, or do you have any questions I might answer?" Her hair was nearly as blue as the vest she wore with the Hall House Museum logo neatly embroidered on it. Lucy pinched her lips into a smile, suppressing a giggle.

"We were wondering," Schuyler began, glancing at Lucy, "if there is any way to find out who owned our property or who built our house." Schuyler smiled sweetly at Mrs. Bronson. "My mom is doing a family tree, and I want to help. We think it could be one of our ancestors, someone prominent in the area."

"Oh! How exciting! It's so nice to know some children are still interested in learning," the woman gushed. "I'll be happy to help. Let me show you where we keep the journals." She ambled toward the back of the house to a small, musty room lined with tall thin books.

"This room was used by Mr. Hall himself as his study. He was a banker, and he also served on the city council. It just seemed fitting to keep the journals in here," she said. "These are the actual journals and registries dating back to when the first settlers incorporated Grand River Valley. The journals are on temporary display from the District Library while it is under renovation."

A velvet rope sectioned off the room, preventing access to the shelves containing the journals. Several small Plexiglas boxes stationed around the room displayed artifacts, including a pair of woman's silk dress gloves, hat pins, and a man's pocket watch on a chain. Another display held a pair of leather stovepipe boots and an inscribed placard that read, "Dated from 1847 to 1900." Lucy pointed it out to Schuyler, who nodded.

"Can we look through the journals?" Schuyler asked. She leaned over the rope to get a closer look at the books.

"Oh, no dear, the books are much too fragile to handle. There are copies of one or two of the registries on display, though. You may look at those," said Mrs. Bronson. "There are also numerous photographs throughout the museum depicting early life in Grand River Valley. The captions are quite entertaining and very informative."

"Is that going to help me find what I need? I thought maybe we could read through the journals." Schuyler's face was crestfallen.

"I am sorry, dear. You will have to wait till the District Library reopens. Their microfiche files are being updated and converted to digital. They had copied most of the journals to microfiche years ago to preserve the records."

The bell tinkled, announcing another visitor.

"Feel free to look around. I'll be in the front room minding the gift shop," said Mrs. Bronson, waving them off and shuffling down the hall.

"Phooey, I guess that's it," mumbled Lucy. She peeked into a display box, trying to read the inscription on a pocket watch.

"Lucy, you stand guard," whispered Schuyler, ducking under the rope. "Let me know if Mrs. Bronson comes back while I check out the journals."

"What are you doing? You're going to get us in trouble!" hissed Lucy, quickly glancing around. She could hear Mrs. Bronson talking loudly with another woman in the front room.

Schuyler put a finger to her lips. "Shh!" She shooed Lucy toward the hall to watch. Lucy leaned against the doorframe, looking bored and chewing a fingernail. She gave a friendly wave to Mrs. Bronson when the lady peered down the hallway. Mrs. Bronson smiled and went back to chatting.

The books had dates on their spines. Schuyler quickly leafed through journals and register books until she found a handwritten registry listing the town's local inhabitants. Despite the yellowed pages and the somewhat faded ink, it was still readable.

"Look!" whispered Schuyler, poking Lucy in the arm. "The Stewart family owned the property where we live now." She pulled out her cell phone, pointed it at the list of names followed by brief descriptions, and started snapping pictures. "A Darwin and Helena Stewart lived in the area known now as Stewart Heights. They owned nine hundred acres of property, which they used for lumber, and a sawmill. They also operated a carriage stop." She carefully turned the page and snapped several more pictures.

"I wonder if those two streets are named after him, Darwin Street and Stewart Street," said Lucy quietly.

"It was common to name streets after influential people back then," came Schuyler's scholarly reply. "If they owned a carriage stop and that much property, it is possible."

Lucy rolled her eyes. Sometimes Schuyler could be a know-it-all. "I wonder if they lived in the big brick house on the corner. It's supposed to have several bedrooms. The house looks old and has huge barns outback. They could've kept the carriages and horses there," said Lucy. "The older lady who lives in the house now grows flowers in huge wooden boxes in front of the barns."

"Oh! You mean old Mrs. Walters. She's a nice lady. My mom used to clean house for her twice a week."

"She did? Why?" Lucy asked.

"Mom likes to have a little extra cash on hand. She says she's saving for a rainy day, but I think it's for the little bakery she wants to open someday. Plus, Mrs. Walters would share her baked goods recipes with Mom."

"Okay, now I get it. Your mom is too cute," snickered Lucy.

"Anyway, the journal shows the Stewarts living in the carriage house from 1849 to 1866. According to the records, Darwin Stewart died of consumption, whatever that is, in 1864 after he enlisted in the Michigan regiment of the Union army," reported Schuyler. She carefully turned the fragile pages of the journal and snapped more photos. "His wife, Helena, continued to operate the carriage stop until October 1866 when she died suddenly. It doesn't say how, just that she died."

"If the ghost *is* him, it may explain the way he's dressed," said Lucy. "But the ghost didn't look all that old—maybe late thirties? So, it couldn't be Darwin Stewart, could it?"

They heard footsteps shuffling down the hallway.

"Hurry!" hissed Lucy, pushing Schuyler toward the shelves.

Schuyler quickly put the journal back on the shelf and ducked under the rope as the volunteer appeared in the doorway. Mrs. Bronson stepped into the room and saw Schuyler kneeling to tie her sneaker. Lucy was casually flipping through the pages of a sample journal on display.

"How are you doing, girls? Anything else I can help with?"

"No, thanks. We're just looking. You have a lovely museum," Lucy said, grinning widely and looking a lot like a Cheshire cat.

"Oh! Thank you." Mrs. Bronson gave her a confused smile. She dusted a display box with the feather duster she had brought with her.

Schuyler gave Lucy a look that said, *"That's the best you could come up with?"* She rolled her eyes. Lucy shrugged her shoulders.

"So, now what?" whispered Schuyler. "You're the ghost hunter, so what do we do? How does this information help us?" She picked up a brochure on the information table.

Mrs. Bronson moved a little closer to them, keeping watch as she pretended to rearrange and dust a display of brochures. When she heard the word *ghost*, she raised one eyebrow and pursed her lips into a lopsided pucker. Her duster hung in midair.

"Well, now that we know that his name could be Stewart, we should try to find Darwin and Helena's graves in the cemetery."

"You want to go to a cemetery?" asked Schuyler, as her eyebrows flew up and nearly disappeared into her hairline. Shaking her head, she leaned over a display box, pretending to read the placard for a worn pair of pointy button-up shoes. "Why would we do that?"

"Grandma says when ghosts stay behind, it is because they left something undone," murmured Lucy. "If we find a family burial plot and learn the names of the family, we can show him we want to help. Maybe that's why he's here. If we find out what it is, maybe we can get him to crossover, or go into the light, or whatever it is that ghosts are supposed to do." She leaned toward Schuyler and whispered, "It would get the ghost out of your bedroom."

"Yeah, but he said they knew about the Spectrescope." Schuyler pinched her brows together. "He also said this Master, whoever that is, wants it. How does that fit in with crossing him over?"

"It kind of confirms what Iam said about the bad ghosts, doesn't it? They know about the Spectrescope, and Iam did say some Dark Prince was gathering his forces, so maybe that's the 'Master' the ghost was referring to."

"Well, there are several small cemeteries around, but it would have to be nearby. It was common to have a family cemetery plot somewhere on your property."

"Isn't there an old cemetery with creepy headstones behind the small white church on the Maple Street hill? It isn't far from the big brick house. Maybe the family plot is there," said Lucy. "The brick house could be the carriage stop, and then it would be on the property the Stewarts once owned, just like your house."

"The church may have been built later. It isn't used anymore except for weddings. It's very quaint, and the inside is lovely. It's all wood with original antique lights like the Gaslight Village at the museum."

"How do you know what the church looks like inside? Have you ever been in it?"

"Mom made a wedding cake for the daughter of a friend, and I helped her deliver it to the church. They had the wedding reception outside. After we set up the cake and covered it, we went inside to check out the wedding decorations," beamed Schuyler. "Mom and I took a sneak tour of the church while we were inside. There's no access to most of the rooms because the building is in bad need of repair. We peeked anyway. It looked like everything was original to the building." She wrinkled her nose. "It certainly smelled like it too."

"Wow! Your mom was sneaking around an old building like a burglar." Lucy laughed. "I love your mom!" Schuyler punched her in the arm.

"We need to go to my house before we go to the cemetery," Lucy continued. "I want to look in the trunk. Iam said everything we need is in there. I have the Spectrescope, but let's look just to be sure. You're wearing the bracelet, aren't you?"

"Of course I am. Let's go. This could be fun!" said Schuyler. "Spooky, to be sure, if nothing else."

* * * *

Malpar stood waiting in the Master's chambers, the fire roaring in the grate as usual and belching heat into the room. The intelligence he had gathered on Lucy Hornberger would help the Master, though he was sure it would cause an eruption of anger. The servant, Grehssil, had left him alone in the room to find the Master. He had been waiting for several minutes already.

The room held a gloomy air, the furnishings sparse but large and ornate. Walking to the bookcases, Malpar saw numerous historical documents and ancient Bibles, and books from different countries and cultures filled the shelves. The ensconced torches burned brightly but did little to disperse the heaviness in the room, as though weighted with generations of discouragement and despair. The room itself made him feel unworthy even to exist.

Turning, Malpar noticed an object hanging near the corner of the room. At first, he mistook the mirror for an empty frame, but something drew him to its unusual yet familiar shape. Its dark surface rippled like water without reflecting any light. He stepped closer, his hand caressing its frame. A sigh escaped his throat.

The heavy chamber door crashed open, and the Master strode purposefully into the room. Quickly lowering his hand, Malpar turned toward the Master who now stood behind the great desk.

"Tell me! What did you learn about the Hornberger girl?" Darnathian snapped the words and sat in the leather chair. With his elbows on the desk and hands clasped, he leaned forward. His eyes glowed like liquid amber as he stared at the Hayyothalan. "Does she have the actual Spectrescope? Does she know how to use its powers? Why didn't you bring it to me?"

"I am sorry, my Master," Malpar said quietly. "I did not find the Spectrescope. However, she has the trunk made from the Tree of All Knowledge. It has carvings of the ancient language, and it contains oddities, like a hat and a vest and an empty globe. You know the ancient language. Why not use the trunk instead to finish your quest?"

The fire crackled and roared in the grate, the flames licking eagerly at the stone mantle. As it continued to vomit heat, Malpar noticed a change in the room; a breath of fresh air drifted around him. His bird senses detected two young individuals, humans, eavesdropping on the conversation. *The portal must be open behind him*, Malpar thought, but the Master couldn't see it because he stood directly in front of the mirror.

"The trunk is no longer of any use to me. Spells and ancient magic will protect it. I need the Spectrescope!" Darnathian twisted his head to one side and slowly rose from the chair to stand at his full height.

Malpar didn't move, only dipped his head. "I am sorry, my Master, I just thought perhaps you could use the magic from the trunk . . ." he began but fell silent when he saw the Master snarling and clenching his hands.

The Master erupted, flailing his arms and hands toward the Hayyothalan. "I have told you, Malpar, how important your task is to the success of my plan. Failure is unacceptable. You do understand the consequences if you fail again, don't you? Shall I show you what the consequences will be?" He raised his hand, palm up, in front of him. An object in his hand shimmered with flashing colors of blues and greens, the colors wrapping and swirling around his arm like a colorful snake.

"Yes, Master, I understand. You needn't show me," hissed Malpar through gritted teeth. "I will not fail you again. The girl must have taken it with her. I will find it. You need not be concerned." He casually slipped one hand behind his back, palm flat, waving it back and forth as though shooing away a pesky fly.

"Excellent! I am glad we understand each other." The Master smiled. He lowered his hand, and the shimmering lights disappeared. "You may use any means necessary to obtain the Spectrescope, but obtain it you will. Take one of the low-level daemons with you to scare little Miss Hornberger. It should be controllable enough for you to command. Just don't let it scare her to death. I may need her to reveal the secrets of the Spectrescope."

* * * *

The girls thanked Mrs. Bronson as they left Hall House Museum and hurried back to Lucy's house. They charged up the back stairs to her bedroom. Lucy opened her bedroom door and abruptly stopped.

"What're you doing?" Schuyler protested when she bumped awkwardly into Lucy. "Oh," she said, leaning sideways to survey the damage.

The trunk was lying open on its side, the contents strewn around the room. The hat and the vest were crumpled up and tossed into a corner along with the mirror. Someone had searched the dresser drawers; pajamas and socks hung carelessly over the edges. The bedcovers lay tossed.

"What happened to my room? I bet Dale was in here. Some prank," Lucy grumbled. She stomped around the room, picking up clothes off the floor.

"I don't think it was your brother, Lucy. What would he want from the trunk or your room? Is anything missing?"

"I don't think so, just messed up." Lucy sighed. "Yeah, you're right. Dale didn't do this. His fun idea is to hang fake spiders from my ceiling or drop them over the railing on my head to make me scream. Who would be looking in the trunk? What would they want?"

"They were looking for the Spectrescope. Iam did say to always keep it with you," said Schuyler, straightening the bedcovers and fluffing the pillows.

"Yeah," said Lucy. She took the Spectrescope from the backpack and looked at it with a curious expression on her face. "Schuyler! The symbols are glowing!" She held it in front of Schuyler. They watched the symbols shift and flow, like mercury, into different shapes. New symbols replaced the old ones.

Turning the Spectrescope slowly to view all the new images, Lucy studied them carefully, tracing each of the symbols with her finger. Then something new happened. The images displayed themselves across the floor, flickering and moving like an old film running through a projector. Both girls gasped at the same time. "Holy moly! How's it doing that?" whispered Lucy.

"Lucy, quick! Flash it up on the wall so we can see it better," exclaimed Schuyler.

"Oh, my gosh! They were looking for the Spectrescope!" The movie playing out across the wall showed someone dressed in a black cape and boots entering Lucy's bedroom door and opening the trunk, searching the contents. Then in anger, the person tossed the box aside and began rummaging through her dresser drawers. Lucy gave Schuyler a skeptical look. "It looks like a man. Wait, is that a bird on his head, or is his head a bird?"

The movie stopped playing when the creature morphed into a swirling mass and flowed out the open window.

"I'm not sure, but I think we need to be careful," said Schuyler. "If they can get into your house and search it without anyone seeing or hearing them, they must be very clever. They might even be dangerous."

"Mom was home all day, so she would have heard anyone messing around. How did they make this mess without anyone hearing it? The guy came in through the door. I bet he searched the rest of the house too."

"Maybe it wasn't a someone, but a something," replied Schuyler, pointing at the strange bird-man symbol. "Maybe that's a Hayyothalan like the ghost said."

"I guess it's possible. Iam did say there were unseen forces we don't know about," said Lucy, looking at the Spectrescope. "Though there is one thing Iam forgot to say. He forgot to tell us just how creepy some of these unseen forces were going to be. Yikes!"

"It's something to consider. Are we still going to the cemetery?" Schuyler's head swiveled from side to side. She had an anxious feeling about the cemetery.

"Right after we pick up this mess. If Mom sees it, she'll think I did it," huffed Lucy, laying the Spectrescope on the bed. They cleaned up the room, putting the clothes back in the drawers. The mirror was lying upside down under the hat and vest. It was shimmering when she turned it over.

"The mirror is doing it again!" Lucy quickly propped it up on the dresser. The girls watched the mirrored surface shimmer and ripple like water before it became as still and clear as glass. Drawing close, the girls found they were looking into another room as two people engaged in conversation.

An extremely handsome, dark-haired man in a light-colored suit was standing behind an enormous and ornate desk, his hands vigorously expressing his emotions toward the other person. The second man was also tall but narrow in build, with sleek raven-black hair. He was dressed entirely in black with a cloak over his shoulders, and he was wearing stove-pipe boots. His stance was stiff, and his hands were clenched at his sides. His back was to them.

"Who are they?" whispered Schuyler. She leaned closer to the mirror, trying to see farther into the room. Looking closer at the man in the cloak, she clapped a hand over her mouth.

"I haven't a clue. Whatever those two are talking about, the guy in the black cloak doesn't seem too happy about it," Lucy whispered. She was beginning to think nothing would surprise her.

"Listen. Can you hear what they are saying?" asked Schuyler.

Lucy leaned in closer. The tall man in the suit was speaking vehemently.

"I wish we could hear them," whispered Lucy. The images in the mirror flickered briefly. When it cleared, they could easily hear the men talking.

The tall man in the suit was speaking. "I have told you, Malpar, how important your task is to the success of my plan. Failure is unacceptable. You do understand the consequences if you fail again, don't you? Shall I show you what the consequences will be?" He raised his hand, palm up, in front of him. An object in his hand shimmered with flashing colors of blues and greens, the colors wrapping and swirling around his arm like a colorful snake.

"Yes, Master, I understand. You needn't show me," hissed Malpar through clenched teeth. "I will not fail you again. The girl must have taken it with her. I will find it. You need not be concerned." He casually slipped one hand behind his back, palm flat, waving it back and forth as though shooing away a pesky fly.

"Excellent! I am glad we understand each other." The Master smiled. He lowered his hand, and the shimmering lights disappeared. The glass flickered, then became a mirror reflecting their pensive faces.

Lucy laid the mirror down and stepped back. "Iam said the mirror was a portal, like a window to see into other places. Do you think the weird-looking guy was the one who trashed my room?" She righted the trunk and placed the mirror inside. "He knew I had taken the Spectrescope with me. I might be wrong, but I think he looked like the guy we just saw in the Spectrescope." She swatted the trunk lid shut with a bang.

"And I think he also looks like the ghost we saw at my house," declared Schuyler. "It must be him. But how did he get to wherever it was so fast? It was huge, like a castle with stone floors. I don't know of any buildings like that around here," mused Schuyler. She sat on the foot of the bed and tucked her legs beneath her. "The windows behind the desk were gargantuan. They reached from the floor to the ceiling."

"Let's put our heads together," suggested Lucy, plopping into a chair. "The tall man in the light-colored suit had to be a wizard or something. I saw something glowing in his hand. When he dropped his hand, the object was gone. It looked like a globe, glowing blue and green, and stripes of color swirled around his arm."

"I saw it too. The guy with the black hair was angry. His hands were clenching. He saw the glowing globe thing, and he didn't like it," said Schuyler. "I think he was afraid of it. He didn't seem quite human, though. He must be the Hayyothalan."

"Maybe—his hair didn't look like hair. It was more like feathers," replied Lucy, perplexed. "It must have been a costume or something, don't you think? He was wearing a cape and stovepipe boots, after all. Who do you know that wears a cape? He was skinny. His skin reminded me of the moldy gray yogurt I found in the back of the refrigerator last week."

"Ew," said Schuyler, wrinkling her nose. "Did you notice the taller guy? I couldn't stop looking at him, and yet I didn't think I should. I almost felt compelled to look at him. I can't explain it, but I don't think he's safe. You know what I mean?"

"Yeah, I felt the same. He had eyes like bright gold, was so incredibly handsome. I just wanted to stare at him all day," Lucy said, staring off at nothing. "I've never even met anyone like that." She shook her head. "Didn't the guy in the bird costume call him Master?"

"I think so. What else did you see? It was a big room, with massive windows, and the desk was big and fancy. There were two chairs—a leather swivel chair and a high-backed chair in front of the desk—but the room was empty of any other furniture."

"There were papers on the desk," said Lucy, getting up and wandering around the room, waving her hands like an interior decorator giving directions for furniture placement. "The room was paneled with tons of bookshelves and gobs of ancient-looking books. It made me think of my great-aunt Isabel."

"Your great-aunt Isabel?" giggled Schuyler.

"Yeah, she's ancient too. She's Grandma's sister, and she still likes to pinch my cheeks like when I was a little girl," Lucy lamented, smiling wryly. "Her house smells like an antique store. Wait, it is an antique store, with old furniture and little animal figurines all over the place. Every time we visit, she serves us tea in tiny cups. I sat my cup on the table and ended up sipping on a cat figurine instead. When she dies, we can hang a sign in the window and call it Bella's Antiques, now open for business!"

"Lucy! That isn't very nice," sniggered Schuyler. "It's hilarious, though."

"Hey! Wasn't it raining outside the castle? If it was, it means it wasn't around here because we've had sunshine all day," Lucy reasoned.

"You're right. It was rainy and gloomy. Where do you think it could be?" Schuyler leaned her head to the side, pondering the question. "Do you think it was a castle? They could be somewhere in Europe, maybe England or Ireland. They have tons of castles."

"They could have been in the States somewhere. America does have a few castles."

"Iam said we could see through the mirror to someplace else, and others could see us." Schuyler's hand flew to her cheek. "Oh, Lucy! You don't suppose they saw us, do you?"

"No, they were too involved in their conversation to notice us." Lucy was distracted by something she had seen but couldn't quite figure out what it was. She would worry about it later.

"Good, I don't think I want to meet up with the black-haired guy. He was creepy." Schuyler shivered. "Speaking of creepy, we should leave soon if we are going to check out the cemetery before it gets dark." Schuyler stood and put her hands on her hips. "I won't be caught dead going to a cemetery after dark," she stated, nose in the air. "No pun intended."

*　　*　　*　　*

The small white church on the Maple Street hill sat back away from the road, its double doors with the leaded glass windows looking forlorn in the fading light. Most of the paint had chipped off the clapboard siding, adding to the little church's neglected appearance. The name sign had been removed and sat behind the bushes next to the front steps.

Lucy and Schuyler walked around the side, past tall, shaggy arborvitae to the back of the church. The cemetery lay just beyond a short scruffy lawn, enclosed by a weathered wrought iron fence. The gates hung crookedly from the gateposts, missing the locks and hinges that had broken off long ago.

"Seriously?" moaned Lucy. "Why does it need to look like a creepy Hollywood movie setting? All we need now is fog and vampires. Grr."

Schuyler snickered quietly to herself.

Beyond, several gravestones stood like sentinels in the long grass. Dozens of the stone markers leaned in various directions. Beside one grave, a pitted and stained stone angel listed so far to one side, it was in danger of toppling over.

Lucy and Schuyler searched the headstones, looking for markers bearing the name of Stewart. A light breeze gently stirred the grasses around the gravestones. Old, weathered trees with heavy branches creaked menacingly above their heads.

"It's almost too quiet here, isn't it?" whispered Lucy. She glanced at three oddly shaped headstones with round globes perched on top of them. They cast eerie shadows along the ground.

"Why are you whispering? There's no one to hear us, and I don't think the residents will mind," snickered Schuyler.

"Fine," Lucy retorted loudly. "There are more graves here than I expected. It could take a while, so should we split up? We need to hurry. It will be dark soon."

"We could just forget the cemetery and go home," Schuyler said, grinning at Lucy, her head nodding up and down expectantly. "Yes?"

"No."

"Drat."

"We need to do this." Lucy stood very still. "Schuyler, did you see those weird stones with the round balls on top?" She pointed at five standing unusually close together.

"Yeah, why?"

"I thought there were only three when we first came in, but now there are five." Lucy squinted her eyes at the weird gravestones. "They give me the chills."

"I don't remember how many there were. They're only grave markers. I don't think they bite," Schuyler teased. She knelt by a faded stone marker and brushed dirt away from the name, but it was unreadable.

"I guess. I'll take the left side. We'll work our way toward the back. Let me know if you find them or need anything. Okay?" Lucy massaged the prickles on her arm.

Schuyler nodded. "Are you nervous?"

"Yeah, a little, I guess."

"I am too." Schuyler smiled weakly at Lucy. She rubbed at her own goose bumps.

They walked carefully through the silence of the gravestones, slowly edging toward the back of the cemetery. The sun was minutes from setting when Schuyler yelled.

Lucy jumped, her heart beating like a bass drum. "Geez, Schuyler, a little warning, please?" Lucy placed a hand on her chest and took a deep breath.

"I found them! Darwin and Helena Stewart! They had two children who died young," exclaimed Schuyler. "A son named Arlan, who was an infant, and a daughter named Dorcas. She was eight years old when she died. Oh! That is so sad. They lost their whole family."

"If he didn't have any family left, why is he still here?" Lucy shivered slightly, folding her arms together. "Is it cold, or are we just that nervous? It feels like the refrigerator door was left open."

"It's freezing out here! It shouldn't be this cold in the middle of July. The sun isn't even down yet. Brr!" Schuyler rubbed her hands over her arms where sudden chills were making her skin prickle.

"Uh, Schuyler? Are those things following us?" Lucy pointed a shaky finger at a grouping of the weird headstones. She pulled the Spectrescope from the backpack and peered through it. A purple mist outlined each of the creepy tombstones.

"Oh, Lucy!" whimpered Schuyler, grabbing Lucy's arm. "I didn't see those a few minutes ago. Where did they all come from?" Glancing behind Lucy, she gasped when she saw even more of the strange stones behind them. The bracelet began to feel warm on her wrist, but it wasn't vibrating yet.

The gravestones with the round globes on top were surrounding them. In the failing light as the sun dipped behind the tree line, they looked menacingly like stone people. Lucy and Schuyler moved closer together. More stone creatures appeared from nowhere, cutting off their chance to escape.

The sky darkened. Hundreds of dark shapes with flapping wings descended into the trees. Giant black crows filled the branches, their loud cawing intimidating in the quiet of the cemetery.

The girls clutched each other as a swirl of black smoke and ash formed in front of them. The air stank with an acrid smell of sulfur as the swirling column developed into the shape of an enormous crow, then into a human form. A creature with a face like a crow and black feathers covering his head stood in front of them. Slanted beady black eyes surrounded by ash-gray skin stared coldly at them. He wore a cape and knee-high stovepipe boots.

"Putrid little girl, hand me the Spectrescope, and I may let you live," hissed the bird-man. It was the same raspy voice she had heard in the tree that night and again in Schuyler's bedroom.

"Who are you?" asked Lucy, her voice quavering. "Why do you want the Spectrescope?"

"Just give it to me!" screeched the bird-man, swiping a hand toward Lucy to grab the Spectrescope.

The crows flew from the trees, swirling in the air and cawing loudly. Birds dipped toward Lucy and Schuyler, their beaks clicking madly. Lucy gripped the Spectrescope and swatted at the birds, knocking several to the ground.

The bracelet vibrated. Schuyler quickly raised her arm as it exploded into the shield, covering her and Lucy, protecting them from the birds.

The manlike entity startled and jumped backward, causing the crows to scatter. Lucy and Schuyler ducked. The birds swooped back and dove in circles above their heads.

The bird-man moved swiftly. Sweeping behind Lucy, he grabbed the head of the Spectrescope and jerked it.

Lucy gripped the handle as the Spectrescope split into two pieces. The creature held the magnifying head, and the handle left in Lucy's hand became warm. Molten metal flowed like mercury upward from the handle where the magnifying head used to be. It quickly developed into a brilliant, shimmering sword. Lucy raised the blade, amazed at how light it felt in her hands.

The bird-man screeched, shielding his face with his arms, and leaning away from Lucy and her sword, he dropped the Spectrescope head.

"Impossible!" he screeched. "How do you come to command the Spirit Sword of the High King, you putrid little human?" he hissed at her, slowly backing away.

Lucy held the sword before her, slowing turning it from side to side. The blade gleamed with a light of its own.

Emboldened, Lucy stepped toward the entity, brandishing the sword like a well-balanced baseball bat. Keeping her eyes on him, she reached down, fumbled in the grass for the Spectrescope head, and stuffed it in her pocket.

"Back off, bird-boy. Leave us alone, or I'll poke you with this sword." Lucy had a death grip on the handle. She was breathing quickly, and the blood was pounding in her ears.

"Oh, you are brave now, human. Your shimmery little sword won't save you," hissed the entity. "You don't know how to use it. The Master who commands me will laugh when he hears about this."

Schuyler stepped forward and held the shield in front of Lucy. The bird-man's eyes widened when he saw the emblem on the shield. It frightened him. He shuddered visibly.

"Who are you talking about?" Lucy retorted, stepping from behind the shield to circle the bird-man. "The man in the light-colored suit? Is he your Master? He said you would be punished for your failure, remember?"

"How do you know about the Master?" The bird-man clicked his beak. His beady eyes glistened as his gaze darted quickly about, his head jerking at angles.

"Who is he? Why does he want the Spectrescope?" Lucy stepped closer to the bird-man, careful to remain out of his reach.

"He is my Master. He will not be kind to you. The sword has no power over him." The bird-man glared at Lucy. "The Master has searched for millennia or more to find the Spectrescope, and he will have the magic it contains. You cannot stop him. The Master always gets what he wants in the end. A daemon is coming who will not be scared of your pretty sword." With a swirl of his cloak, the bird-man morphed into smoke and ash and disappeared on the wind.

The black crows circling overhead disbanded and flew away as the stone creatures slowly moved toward Lucy and Schuyler. Holding her shield high, Schuyler stood with her back to Lucy as Lucy brandished the Spirit Sword.

"How do we get past these things?" Schuyler whispered, peering over the top of the shield at the stone people. "Oh, I wish I had a weapon," she wailed.

Schuyler's shield began to glow, and a sheath appeared on the backside near the handgrip. Sparkling with purple gems, the hilt of a small sword appeared inside the sheath. Schuyler's jaw dropped. She pulled it carefully from the sheath. It was wide and thick, and it was shorter than Lucy's Spirit Sword at about two feet in length.

"Whoa! Who are you?" whispered Schuyler. "You're beautiful."

Glowing red letters appeared as if written by an unseen hand. They swirled and formed themselves into the words: *I am Zazriel, the strength of the King.* Schuyler's eyes widened in surprise. She grinned and yelled, "Wowza!"

Lucy jumped. "Holy moly! Where did that come from?" Lucy gasped as she gazed at the beautiful sword.

"Ask, and you shall receive!"

"Okay. Let's see if the swords scare them." Lucy lunged toward two of the stone creatures. *"Hi-yah!"* she yelled, swiping the sword in an arch toward the gravestones.

The stone creatures stopped advancing, but a way around them still wasn't clear. Lucy lunged again, yelling and swinging the sword. She struck one of the tombstones, and it crumbled into dust. Several of the gravestones retreated, but others advanced from the shadows.

"Well, one down, more to go," quipped Lucy, faking a jump at a marker. It stopped moving.

"I don't think the stones can hurt us. They're only trying to scare us. Move toward the gates as you swing at them. If we can get out of the cemetery, I don't think they can follow us." Schuyler stabbed two more of the creatures, causing them to crumble.

"How do you know?" Lucy swung her sword toward two more of the creatures. *"Hi-yah!"* she yelled, striking another gravestone. It disintegrated.

"I just do somehow. Let's find a way out. It's almost dark. I do not want to be in a cemetery after dark!"

Lucy struck two more stone people, and they crumbled into dust. A gap in the circle appeared. Lucy and Schuyler ran through it and out the cemetery gates.

7 A Nighttime Visitor

Lucy and Schuyler didn't stop running until they arrived at the park at the end of Maple Street. They sat down hard on a bench near the pond to catch their breaths. Lucy leaned forward, gripping the edge of the bench as she sucked air into her lungs. Perspiration trickled down the sides of her neck.

"I don't . . . know if I . . . like this ghost hunting . . . business after all," Schuyler gasped, wiping the sweat from her face with the hem of her shirt. Her chest hurt, and her throat was dry.

"Yeah . . . it's a lot . . . different . . . from what I thought . . . it was going to be. Though, I'm not sure what I expected," agreed Lucy, with halting breaths. She laid the sword across her lap. Sweat dripped from her face, splashing on the gleaming metal.

Meanwhile, a man with dark-brown hair and a heavyset woman sat on a bench in the shadows on the pond's far side. They watched intently as the two girls dropped down on the bench, carrying swords and a shield. Their identities were indistinguishable in the dusk.

"Oops!" Lucy exclaimed, glancing around. "We'd better hide these artifacts before someone sees them." She pulled the Spectrescope head from her pocket, and the sword melted back into the handle. She clicked the head-piece into place and dropped the completed Spectrescope in the backpack.

Schuyler slipped Zazriel into its sheath and pressed the button on the inside of the shield. It morphed back into the bracelet.

The man leaned toward his wife and whispered. She nodded her head, still watching.

"How did that bird-man get here so fast?" Lucy gasped, still trying to catch her breath. "We just saw him minutes before through the mirror." She pulled two bottled waters from her pack and gave one to Schuyler. They gulped the water down. "I think you're right. He was the thing in your bedroom earlier."

"He's more than a ghost to be able to change shape like that," Schuyler said between deep breaths. She leaned back, resting against the bench.

"He wasn't a ghost. He's the creature who was outside my bedroom window the other night crawling around, scratching on the roof. I recognized his raspy voice tonight."

"Wow. Creepy," Schuyler said. The girls remained quiet for a few minutes, resting and thinking. Then Schuyler said, "If the guy in the suit wants the Spectrescope so badly, why doesn't he come after us instead of sending the bird-man?"

"Dunno. Wait, didn't the guy in the suit call the bird-man by name? I'm sure it was the same creature we saw in the mirror. Do you remember his name?"

"Something that started with an *M*, I think. Something like Map, Marp, Marple," replied Schuyler, her voicing trailing off as she thought.

"Not Marple, it's Malpar! His name is Malpar!" cried Lucy.

"The Spectrescope must contain a lot of powerful magic. It seems to be invaluable for some reason to the guy in the suit. He wants to get it, and Iam says you must never let it out of your sight."

"I know, right? It just feels like terrible things would happen if the Master, as Malpar calls him, would happen to get hold of the scope."

"I wonder if the Master will consider this attempt to get the Spectrescope as another failure. He threatened to punish Malpar if he failed again. Maybe we won't be seeing Malpar the bird-man anytime soon," said Schuyler hopefully, pressing her hands together like a prayer.

"I wouldn't count on it. Malpar is determined to get the Spectrescope. He said a daemon would be coming who wouldn't be afraid of the sword. If I thought Malpar was creepy, I bet the next thing will be creepier still," replied Lucy with a shudder.

The man and woman watched a few more minutes. They faded further into the shadows and were gone.

"Hey, Schuyler? Back at the cemetery, how did you know the gravestones wouldn't follow us or try to hurt us?" Lucy asked.

"It seems everything that has happened to us so far has only meant to scare us. I don't think anyone wants to hurt us, at least not yet," Schuyler reasoned.

"You're pretty smart, you know?" said Lucy, smiling wryly at her friend.

"Yeah, I know. C'mon, we better get home. I'll walk with you to your house. Maybe your mom can give me a ride home. I know it isn't far, but I'd rather not walk home in the dark."

"Why not stay the night at my house? Mom won't mind. She can take you home in the morning on her way to work. Do you think your mom and dad will let you stay?"

"Yeah, it shouldn't be a problem. You can come home with me in the morning to make sure Malpar isn't in my bedroom," said Schuyler, her lips pressed in a thin line. "I'd rather be sure he's not haunting my bedroom, or I'll never sleep in there again."

The streetlights were popping on, casting pools of shadows across neatly groomed lawns. Lucy's neighbors, Bill and Vivian, were sitting on their front porch enjoying the evening and sipping lemonade.

"Evening, Miss Lucy!" Bill called out. He waved at the girls. "And how are you, Miss Schuyler?"

"Hi, Mr. Bill, and hello, Mrs. McGoo. How are you?" Lucy asked, climbing the steps to their porch as Schuyler followed and greeted the McGoos. "You've been baking again, haven't you, Mrs. McGoo? Your house is the best-smelling house in the whole neighborhood!" She breathed deeply of the aroma wafting through the screen door.

"You know me, I love to bake," said Mrs. McGoo, smiling. She stood, patting her ample hips. "I love to sample my cooking too!"

"Come sit with us and have a lemonade," Mr. Bill said. "Vivian just made it. You girls look warm. Your faces are flushed. A nice, cool lemonade is just what you need."

"I'll go get two more glasses, and then you girls can tell us what exciting adventures you've been up to today," said Vivian. She disappeared into the house to get the glasses.

When she returned, Lucy told Mr. Bill and Vivian how she and Schuyler had been wandering through the cemetery behind the church on Maple Street hill when a strange fellow named Malpar chased them from the graveyard.

"Oh, dear! You must have been so frightened," exclaimed Mrs. McGoo. "Whatever did you do?"

"I swung my magnifying glass at him like a baseball bat!" declared Lucy.

"He didn't like it when Lucy called him 'bird-boy' either," Schuyler interjected.

"He wasn't very nice, and he had a face like a crow with a beak for a nose and beady black eyes," said Lucy. She finished her lemonade.

"Now, Lucy! Bird-boy? That doesn't seem very kind, does it?" asked Vivian.

"Well, no, but he wasn't very friendly to us either," said Lucy. "A girl has to stand her ground sometimes." Mr. Bill winked at Lucy and nodded in agreement.

"It's getting late. Thank you for the lemonade, Mrs. McGoo. It was so good, and we were thirsty. Goodnight!" said Lucy, making her way to the edge of the porch and waving goodbye. The girls skipped down the porch steps, crossed the lawn to Lucy's house, and disappeared through the back door.

The McGoos watched the girls until they disappeared inside Lucy's house. They saw the back light turn off and knew the girls were safe. Bill leaned over and whispered to Vivian. She nodded.

"Malpar, the bird-boy," he said with a snicker. Then he laughed out loud and slapped his knee. "Bird-boy!"

Lucy and Schuyler found Mrs. Hornberger in the kitchen, taking the dishwasher's clean dishes and putting them away. She placed two bowls on the counter and then scooped ice cream into each for a snack for the girls to eat while she phoned Schuyler's parents, telling them that Schuyler could stay the night.

Neither Lucy nor Schuyler said anything about their adventure in front of Lucy's mom. When they finished their ice cream, they cleared their dishes from the kitchen table, putting them in the sink for washing. Lucy blew her mom a kiss before heading for the stairs.

A giant, furry spider dropped from the balcony and swung menacingly in front of her face. Lucy rolled her eyes and then winked at Schuyler.

"Argh!" cried Lucy, sprinting for the stairs. The spider jerked out of sight and disappeared with Dale into his bedroom.

"Lucy, your brother, is strange," said Schuyler, following Lucy up the stairs.

"Normally, I would agree with you. But after some of the things we've seen today, Dale seems almost normal!"

Lucy dropped the backpack on the floor next to the trunk and plopped on her bed. Schuyler pulled out the trundle and snuggled into the pillows, putting her feet up on the edge of Lucy's mattress.

"I bet Iam knows something about Malpar," Schuyler commented. "He seems to know some rather strange stuff."

"I wonder if he knows the Spectrescope can be separated or that it turns into a sword when you need it. I wish he were here so we could ask him."

"I want to know about the daemon the bird-man said is coming. That sounds scarier than Malpar," said Schuyler, wrapping her arms behind her head, "as if he isn't scary enough."

"I'll get the Spectrescope and sweep the room to be sure we're alone. I hope no one is hanging around in the corners." Lucy pulled it from the backpack and held it to her face. Slowly she swept her gaze around the room. Satisfied the room was clear, she laid it on the nightstand.

"We're good. I guess we should get ready for bed." She went to the dresser and took a clean pair of pajamas and a small overnight kit from a drawer. She handed them to Schuyler. Lucy and Schuyler kept an overnight kit at each other's house since they slept over often. They even had a spare set of clothes. The worn set would get laundered, so it was always ready for the next sleepover.

After they finished their nightly routines, the girls played computer games till Mrs. Hornberger called up the stairs, "Lights out, girls. Time for bed!"

They crawled into their beds, and Lucy turned off the light.

"*Hi-yah*? Really?" Schuyler snickered in the dark. "You sounded like a teenage ninja!"

"I thought it might scare them," Lucy grumbled, then she chuckled. "It did sound goofy, didn't it?" She snuggled under the covers and snickered. "You didn't do so bad with your sword either, you know."

"Pretty cool, huh? I'm a ninja! I'm a teenage ninja too!"

They lay in their beds, giggling. Scents from the warm summer night wafted in through the open window. They were asleep within minutes.

*   *   *   *

"Lucy," a voice whispered.

"Mmmm?" Lucy murmured.

"Lucy," the voice whispered again.

"Mmmm, what?"

"I am waiting for you. Come outside."

Slowly waking, Lucy pushed herself up on one elbow and yawned. She pulled back the curtain and peeked out the window. A tall, thin man in a brown suit and with longish white hair stood just inside the pool of light shining from the streetlamp in front of her house. He was looking up at her window, smiling.

He raised his hand and waved.

Iam!

She shrugged into her robe and slid her feet into her slippers. Creeping down the back stairs, she carefully avoided the squeaky step near the bottom. She went through the kitchen and out the back door. Her slippered feet padded softly on the cool cement path along the driveway leading to the front of the house. *This feels like two spies sneaking around for a clandestine meeting*, Lucy thought. She snickered quietly.

Iam waited for her under the streetlamp. His white hair glowed softly in the light while his blue eyes twinkled, and his mustache wiggled. Lucy smiled at him.

"Hello, Lucy," he said softly. He gazed at her bright, upturned face with admiration. He raised a hand and wiped a tear from his eye.

"Iam! I have so much to tell you! Schuyler and I have been ghost hunting!"

"Have you now? How exciting! You must tell me all about it." He leaned slightly forward, his hands clasped in front of him.

Lucy excitedly recounted her adventures with Schuyler. She told Iam all about the ghost in the corner of Schuyler's bedroom and the strange warning to Lucy, the trip to Hall House Museum, her messed-up bedroom, the Spectrescope and the mirror, and the scary episode with the crows and gravestones. Finally, she told him about the bird-man, Malpar, and how she thought he was the spirit that appeared to them as a ghost at Schuyler's house.

Iam listened intently, his head nodding periodically at something Lucy said, and occasionally he murmured "Oh my" or "Indeed." His eyebrows floated up and down on his forehead like flotsam on the ocean.

Lucy finished her story.

"Iam, what is Malpar?" asked Lucy. "I've never heard of anything like him before. He had said the Master was sending his favorite Hayyothalan. I think he was talking about himself."

Iam stared at the stars winking out as dawn approached. "It's so long a time since I have seen one of his kind," he said sadly. "Malpar is a Hayyothalan from an ancient race of creatures. Their magnificent plumage of brilliant colors was a delight. The ancient peoples of earth used to call them Birds of Paradise. They served in the courts of the High King of Ascalon." He sighed softly. "They were a gentle, high-spirited, and loving race. They were pranksters who loved to make people laugh. They could shape-shift too."

"You speak of them in the past tense. What happened to the Hayyothalans?" asked Lucy. She watched his face closely. His eyes were moist.

"The High King loved them dearly. The Dark Prince was a handsome and beguiling creature who bewitched them with his trickery and lies, and many turned against the King. It broke the King's heart, but he banished them and many other creatures from Ascalon in the True East for their rebellion. The Dark Prince was exiled for his lies and deceit and for the rebellion he caused. The remaining Hayyothalans retreated to the farthest parts of the kingdom, hiding in shame for what the others had done."

"Oh, how terrible," uttered Lucy. "Will they never get to see their home again? Won't the High King ever forgive them if they're sorry for what they did?" Lucy grieved for the beautiful creatures.

"There is a way, dear Lucy," whispered Iam softly. "In time, many will find it. They need only to ask."

They stood in the predawn silence listening to birds' waking chirps and the occasional bark of a dog. "I don't understand," said Lucy as she swatted at a mosquito trying to land on her cheek. *Some things never sleep*, she thought. "Why are Malpar's beautiful feathers so black?"

"I suspect he has much anger and bitterness hidden deep within his heart. He is a changeling, remember. Perhaps the black form of a crow was appealing, a way to hide in the shadows from his memories," Iam said softly. "When a person allows such strong feelings to rob them of joy and happiness, their spirit slowly withers away. All that is good becomes lost, and only the poison of guilt remains. It seeps through the very skin, affecting every thought, action, and choice," replied Iam, sorrow filling his voice.

"Iam? Is Malpar dangerous? Would he try to hurt us?" She stifled a yawn.

"No, dear Lucy, Malpar is not capable of hurting anyone. He will scare you and try to make you think he is a great and formidable creature. Fear is a great motivator," said Iam. "Although he was deceived and followed evil instead of good, there is still good in him. He will use many tactics to get what he wants, but in the end, he will only scare you." Iam looked earnestly at Lucy. "Were you scared, Lucy?"

"No, maybe, yeah," Lucy finally admitted. "When he grabbed the head of the Spectrescope, and it broke, I didn't think we would ever getaway. Then the sword grew out of the handle. If I hadn't had the sword, I don't know what would have happened."

"It was your honesty and strength of character that drew the sword forth, dear Lucy. Never doubt that," replied Iam, smiling now. "The sword has not been seen for many, many generations. Indeed, this is good news, very good news."

"Iam, we saw Malpar talking with a tall, dark-haired man. Malpar referred to him as Master," Lucy said. "Do you know the man he called Master?"

"Yes, I know him. His name is Darnathian. You must guard the Spectrescope, Lucy. It holds many secrets. If it falls into Darnathian's hands, the effects would be devastating." Iam looked deeply concerned.

"Why does Darnathian want it?" Lucy asked.

"The Spectrescope contains ancient magic," Iam began. "The old magic is immensely potent. Darnathian wants to use the power against the High King to defeat him and take his throne. The Spectrescope is also one of two keys. The High King separated these keys to protect their secrets. They must not be allowed to come together. The secret they hold is too precious ever to be revealed before it is time."

"Keys? Like for locked doors?"

"Something like that," he whispered. Iam casually glanced around to be sure they were alone and then leaned toward Lucy. "It's a gate, and it protects a priceless piece of antiquity that is supremely magical. There is nothing like it in the known universe or beyond. If Darnathian uses the power of the artifact with the ancient magic of the Spectrescope, the effects would be catastrophic."

Lucy grimaced. "Okay, that is a little scary. Will the Spectrescope tell me the secrets?"

"Perhaps it will someday. When the time is right, the secrets will be known, but not before."

"I think I understand. If I learn well enough, it may tell me, is that right?"

"Trust what you have learned, Lucy. Trust what the Spectrescope will teach you. The answers are there. The Spectrescope is revealing aspects of itself to you, aspects not known for millennia." He gazed intently into her eyes. "Remember, the tools in the trunk will also help you. Trust, and learn well," Iam replied firmly.

Lucy sensed Iam wouldn't tell her any more about the Spectrescope. Looking at him, she realized he made her feel safe, loved, and accepted. He was like a grandpa, and her heart wanted to remain with him a little longer. "Iam, where is Ascalon? I have never heard of it. Is it in Europe?" asked Lucy.

"The sun rises each morning in Ascalon where it draws its warmth and light. When you look toward the True East when the sun is rising, it is there you will find it. You must pass through the Evermore Gate behind the sunrise to enter Ascalon. Speaking of the sunrise, Lucy dear, you should get back to bed." Iam pointed toward the east, where the skyline was turning pink. "I'll wait here a bit longer till you are safely back in bed. Now, run along!" He motioned her along.

"Will I see you again soon?"

"If you should need me."

"Goodbye, Iam," Lucy said as she padded back around the house and into the kitchen, locking the door behind her. She tiptoed up to her room, where Schuyler still slept peacefully and crawled into bed. Pulling the curtain aside, she looked out the window. Iam was still standing under the streetlamp with his hands stuffed casually into his pockets. Lucy smiled.

Iam raised his hand and waved.

"Sweet dreams, dear Lucy," he mouthed.

He faded out until he completely disappeared.

Man! I wish I could do that!

* * * *

Malpar stood in the shadows behind the Williamses' house, waiting for the daemon to arrive. The Hayyothalan had seen many bizarre things, but still, he was apprehensive. The low-level daemon he was expecting could be very unpredictable. He didn't need any help to distract the girl and accomplish his task of retrieving the Spectrescope, but the Master had sent for it anyway. It was never wise to question the Master.

He would do whatever it took to get the Spectrescope. He didn't want to be punished again by the Master. Or be sent to Shinar. No one ever returned from Shinar. He had heard stories about the pit where the eternal blackness wraps about you, squeezing the breath from your lungs. The more you struggle, the tighter its grip becomes, but you hardly notice because of the agonized screams of souls in the dark.

Malpar squeezed his eyes shut as memories haunted him. He tried to push them away. *Oh, why did I listen? How could I believe such a lie?* Brokenhearted, he slowly released a ragged sigh.

The air around him became crisp and cold and stinking with a foulness the Hayyothalan could barely tolerate. Malpar shivered and pulled his cloak tightly around him. A mist appeared, swirling like fog in the wake from a passing vehicle until a form materialized directly in front of him. Malpar took a deep breath to steady his nerves.

The daemon had arrived.

It stood before Malpar with a hateful glare. The eyes were so dark they appeared like hollowed-out empty sockets above pale, sunken cheeks. A black suit emphasized the creature's willowy form, and it carried a bowler-style hat. The Hayyothalan could only stare back at the spectacle.

"What are you supposed to be, or rather, who are you supposed to be?"

"I am the ghost of Darwin Stewart," it replied. "I thought it was very creative of me to take this form. Darwin Stewart was a formidable man. He should have no problem scaring the girl into relinquishing the artifact," said the daemon.

"I guess it is better than your usual hideous form," mumbled Malpar.

"Shall we get started?" the daemon said, placing the bowler hat on his head.

 8 Ghostly Recordings

"Lucy! Lucy!" Schuyler whispered excitedly into the phone. "Mom took me to the library today. I got a book on ghost hunting. It's *so* interesting. I've already read most of it, and I've got my dad's digital recorder. He doesn't use it anymore, so he said I could have it!" Schuyler leaned sideways and peeked into the kitchen, where her mom pulled pans from the cupboard and plopped them on the counter.

Lucy sat cross-legged on her bed, filing her nails. "A ghost-hunting book? Digital recorder? What's all that about?" The nail file paused in midair.

"We need to know more about what we're supposed to be doing," replied Schuyler. "I'd never even seen a ghost or spirit before Malpar. I don't have the first clue how we're supposed to hunt them. I figured we'd better start learning before Malpar and his daemon show up," Schuyler explained before pausing to take a breath. "Okay, so this is what we need to do to draw out the ghosts."

"Schuyler, somehow I think the ghosts will find us," Lucy interjected with a giggle. "What did your mom say about your choice of books to read? Didn't she think it was a little weird?" she asked, leaning back on her bed and propping her feet up on the headboard. She switched the phone to speaker mode and continued filing her nails.

"Well, yeah, she did. So I told her it was for you."

Lucy groaned. "Gee, thanks, Schuyler. Your mom probably won't let us do any more sleepovers if she thinks I'm into ghosts."

"Oh, she's okay with it. She's always thought you were a little weird anyway. She says that's what's so fun about you. You're unpredictable."

Lucy laughed. "I love your mom! She's so sweet. She never says or thinks bad of anyone. So, what does the ghost-hunting book say we're supposed to do with a digital recorder?"

"Well," said Schuyler, launching into her literary persona, "with a digital recorder, you can capture a ghost talking. It's something called an EVP. That is short for electronic voice phenomenon. According to the author, ghosts are residual electrical energy left behind when a person dies. The energy imprints itself onto the digital recorder allowing the ghost to leave you a message. Sometimes this energy will imprint itself onto an object or even the walls of a room."

"We can already see and hear Malpar, or whatever he is. How does the book explain that?"

"That is the fascinating part! He's called a 'full-bodied apparition,' and he's very unusual. It's rare to see an FBA!" Schuyler's voice fairly crackled with excitement. "Even the author admitted he hadn't seen an FBA, and he's a professional!"

"If they're that rare, how did people know they exist? I mean, really? We've never even seen ghosts before we had the Spectrescope. I've heard ghost stories all my life, but I always thought they were just that, stories people told to scare one another."

"Like the stories you tell your younger cousin to scare him?" Schuyler asked, stifling a giggle.

"Well, yeah!"

"You really shouldn't scare him, Lucy," admonished Schuyler. "He's younger than you and still pretty gullible, you know."

"But that's why it's so much fun!"

"So, the book says the most obvious time to look for an EVP is just after you've asked a question. But you can also just leave the recorder on in an empty room, and then you can check it later for sounds or speech. Oh, Luce! Isn't this exciting?"

"Could be. I think I have an old recorder around here somewhere. It's the cassette-tape kind. Do you think that might work?" Lucy rummaged through the desk drawers for the recorder.

"It should. The book mentioned digital recorders specifically, but it did say they used the old-fashioned cassette or reel-to-reel recorders before digital recorders," Schuyler said. "Even Houdini, the famous magician, was interested in ghosts and spirits. It's in the book."

"What else did the book say?" Lucy asked, grabbing the phone and crawling into the closet, pulling out shoes and boxes.

"Gobs of things! Did you know you can also use a camera to take pictures of ghosts?"

"What? Take a picture of a ghost? How's that even possible?" exclaimed Lucy, sitting back on her heels.

Schuyler shielded the mouthpiece with her hand and whispered. "The camera shutter is so quick it can capture images the eye isn't fast enough to see. Isn't that wowza? You should see some of the photos in this book. They're cool. Creepy, but cool."

"What library did you get this book from?" Lucy asked. "The small library near the school doesn't have that kind of stuff." She bumped a box off the top shelf. It hit the floor, spilling beads and costume jewelry all over the carpet. Lucy groaned.

"Mom had to go downtown this afternoon, so she dropped me at the main library for a couple of hours. I think the librarian probably thought

I was strange, asking for books on ghosts and ghost hunting." Schuyler laughed. "She kept following me around."

"Wait till we write a book someday about our ghost adventures. The librarian will be like, 'Well, piffle! She was a ghost hunter after all!' " snickered Lucy. She scooped up the beads and stuffed them back in the box.

"My grandparents gave me a camera for my birthday. The picture resolution on my old cell phone isn't the greatest, and Gramps is hoping I'll want to be a photographer like him someday. He's so cute." Schuyler giggled. "I'm going to walk through the house and take some pictures. Maybe I can get Malpar's picture if he's hiding in a corner somewhere," she said, though she didn't believe it was possible.

"That would be cool. I don't have a camera, but I can set up the tape recorder to see if it can record any ghost voices while I'm out." Lucy sighed. "I have to go grocery shopping with my mom again. She's always running out of something. I swear she grocery shops every other day!"

"The book says that after you set the recorder, you should announce out loud that you are leaving the room," Schuyler instructed. "If anything happens after that point, you'll know it wasn't you. Call me later and let me know if you catch anything, okay?"

"Okay, good tip. Let me know if any anomalies show up in your pictures," said Lucy. "And Schuyler? You won't say anything about this ghost hunting to anyone, will you? I think we should keep it a secret, at least for now."

"Will do! Bye!"

Lucy put her cell phone on the dresser and rummaged through the dresser's drawers till she found the cassette tape recorder and a new cassette tape. Unwrapping the cassette, she put it in the machine only to discover the battery compartment was empty. She ran down to the kitchen and searched through the junk drawer for a supply of new batteries when a stern voice interrupted her progress.

"C'mon! Lucy, we need to get going. I have to get a few things from the grocery store for dinner tonight," Mom said, coming into the kitchen. "Don't forget, you promised you would help with dinner by making the salad."

"I'll be right back. I just need to take these up to my room. Where's Dale?" She grabbed the batteries and pushed hard on the old drawer to close it. It shut with a bang.

"Dale went to a friend's house for the afternoon. He should be back in time for supper."

"Okay, cool!" Lucy sprinted up the stairs. She placed the batteries in the recorder and tested the tape. It worked. She wondered where to put it.

She decided to set it on top of the old wardrobe in the corner of the upstairs foyer. No one used it anymore, so it sat empty. *I don't think anyone will know it is up there. It's a perfect place to hide it*, she thought, grinning. *It could get exciting! Schuyler will be so jealous if I record a talking ghost!*

Lucy climbed on a chair, placed the recorder on top, and slid it to the back of the wardrobe. She pressed the Record button and jumped down.

"Okay, I'm leaving now! Goodbye!" she roared.

"To whom are you talking? I already told you Dale isn't home," said Mom from the bottom of the stairway.

"Uh, I was just saying goodbye to my teddy bear!" Lucy grimaced. She leaned over the railing and grinned maniacally down at her mom.

"For heaven's sake, just get down here so we can go!"

"Fine!" Lucy picked up her backpack and stomped down the stairs.

She quickly thumbed through the newspaper on the kitchen counter, grabbed the sales flyer for the grocery store, and followed Mom out to the SUV. She scanned the pages, jotting down a few items on her notepad.

They split up when they reached the grocery store. Mom grabbed a cart and disappeared down an aisle. Lucy headed for the produce section to secure the lettuce, grapes, dried cherries, and apples she needed for the fruit salad. Her items were quickly found and added to her basket. A bag of apples completed the list. The task finished, she turned abruptly, bumping into someone.

"I'm sorry!" Lucy groaned inwardly, then said, "Hi, Paul."

Paul was, without a doubt, the cutest boy in school and very athletic, playing basketball and football. All the cool girls liked him. Girls in Lucy's class constantly talked of his tall, lean frame, blonde hair, and the slight dimple in his chin, but it was his eyes Lucy noticed. Their particular shade of dark blue reminded Lucy of a deep lake under a stormy sky. Though mind you, he had one major flaw.

He was painfully shy around Lucy.

Lucy had spent most of the last semester of school avoiding him. After she had tutored him in history, he always seemed to be lurking around somewhere. She hoped she wouldn't have to dodge him around the supermarket too.

"What are you doing here?" Lucy asked, in what she clearly thought was a jaunty greeting. She forced a smile.

"My mother is the store manager," he replied, smiling sheepishly at Lucy. He pushed his produce cart stacked with vegetables to the side aisle. "How is your summer going?"

"Oh, fine," said Lucy, swinging the basket in front of her. "How is your summer?"

"Okay, I guess," he replied with a shrug. "I work here most days." Paul felt conspicuously tall next to Lucy. His ears went pink, which made his eyes seem even bluer. "Mother pays me to do chores around the store. It's not so bad." He plopped a bag of potatoes onto an endcap display. "It gives me some pocket money to spend."

"Wow, this is a big store." Lucy made a pretense of looking around the store. "It must keep you busy."

"Yeah, we could use some extra help in the evenings. Sweeping the floors, that kind of stuff."

"I should let you go. You wouldn't want the boss to catch you loafing, even if she is your mother. See you later. Bye!" Lucy wiggled her fingers and darted down the aisle toward the checkouts.

"Bye," said Paul at her retreating form. He was always a little bewildered around Lucy and unsure how to get to know her better. He shrugged, pulled another bag of potatoes off the cart, and plopped it on the display.

"Are you done dillydallying?" snapped Mom as Lucy came into sight. She was waiting near the checkout lane, drumming her fingers on the cart handle.

"I ran into Paul from school," Lucy offered.

"The boy you tutored in history? Did you ask him about tutoring him again this summer? I'll check around to see what hourly rate you should charge."

"Mom, no, I didn't ask him. I'm not interested in tutoring anyone this summer."

"Guess you're gonna be doing a lot of babysitting instead," Mom complained. "Got your ingredients for the salad?"

"Yes," said Lucy holding up the basket of fruits and lettuce. She pursed her lips to keep from snapping back a retort.

"Good, let's get checked out."

Soon, Lucy was pushing the cart of bagged groceries through the parking lot. A loud squawk caught her attention. Perched on the arm of the lamppost was a large black crow, its beady black eyes staring at her. The crow cocked its head and winked at her. She gasped. Malpar?

She reached behind her, touched the backpack, and securely zipped it. She hoped Malpar wouldn't cause a scene in the parking lot. How would she explain it to her mom?

"Let's hurry home and have an early dinner," Lucy exclaimed. She charged ahead to the car, the groceries bumping about in the cart.

"Why the sudden rush?" asked Mom. "Hey, slow down with that cart! I've got eggs in there!"

"I want to call Schuyler after supper, that's all," Lucy replied, puffing for air. She opened the hatch of the SUV and shoved the bags haphazardly into the back. She glanced back at the giant crow. More crows were gathering, sitting on lampposts all around the parking lot.

"We might as well eat early. You need to finish the laundry, and I have a busy day at the office tomorrow. I need to get there early, so I'd like to get to bed on time. If Dale isn't home in time to eat with us, he can always heat his dinner in the microwave."

"Great! I can't wait to call Schuyler and find out—" Lucy stopped mid-sentence, biting her lip. She had almost blurted out their secret. She wasn't used to keeping secrets from anyone.

"Find out what?"

"Oh, just to find out if she did anything interesting today," Lucy replied nonchalantly.

"That's nice, dear," Mom responded as she put the bags of groceries into a neat order. Lucy dumped the last grocery bag in and squirreled the cart over to the cart corral while keeping an eye on Malpar.

Lucy fidgeted on the ride home and watched for any sign of being followed. In the side-view mirror, she spotted a flock of crows flying just above the treetops behind the car. In the lead was an enormous blackbird. It must be Malpar. Iam did say the Hayyothalans could shape-shift.

When they arrived home, Lucy took the groceries from the SUV's hatch as she scanned the yard and the neighborhood, certain Malpar would show up any minute. Her arms full, she charged into the house, dropped the groceries on the counter, and went back out to get the last bag. It was eerily quiet outside, but she didn't see a bird anywhere.

Dale wasn't home yet when dinner was ready, so it was just Mom and Lucy at the dinner table. They were both too preoccupied with their thoughts to notice the other wasn't speaking much.

Mom broke the silence. "Your salad is delicious. Did you get the recipe from a book?" she asked. She pushed the food around on her plate and sighed.

"I got the recipe from Mrs. Williams. She's such a good cook. Everything she makes is just delicious," Lucy said before swallowing a spoonful of the fruit salad.

"Mrs. Gleason called today. She needs you to babysit Friday evening," Mom said, poking a fork at the meat on her plate as if she expected it to bite back. "She and Mr. Gleason are going out for dinner. They should be home around midnight so that it won't be too late. Mr. Gleason can drive you home afterward. I told them you would be happy to babysit."

"Aw, Mom!"

"Lucy," Mom interrupted, "we need the money for your school supplies. It is a good opportunity to put some cash aside."

"I know, but Schuyler—"

"End of discussion."

"Yes, ma'am, I'll be happy to babysit Friday," Lucy murmured. She plopped another spoonful of salad onto her plate.

"You and Schuyler can just find another time to do whatever it is that you do. Helping out is more important."

"Okay, okay," she grumbled, picking at her dinner.

A few minutes later, Lucy cleared the dishes from the table, loaded the dishwasher, and did a load of clothes in the dryer before going upstairs. She crawled onto the wide window ledge in the foyer and pulled her knees to her chest.

Outside, the insects buzzed, and neighborhood children laughed as they played. It seemed ages since she had been carefree, not realizing the concerns within her own family. Granddad had passed several years before, leaving Grandma to live with Great-Aunt Isabel who had a heart problem, and Mom was on a reduced salary, having to timeshare her job. Lucy suddenly understood the meaning of the "weight of the world." She breathed out a long sigh.

At least Schuyler was going to research the Stewarts' family history. Any information she could find about them would be helpful. Maybe they could devise a way to get rid of the ghost or spirit, or whatever Malpar was. *How do you get rid of a ghost or spirit?* Lucy wondered. She'd ask Schuyler if the book covered that particular topic. *Ghosts, you just can't live with them.*

The tape recorder! Lucy hopped off the windowsill and ran to the old wardrobe. She pushed the chair into place, climbed on it, and reached to the back of the cabinet. The recorder had turned off, and the tape wound entirely to the other side. She pushed Rewind and took it to her room.

She climbed onto the bed with it and pressed Play. She heard herself yelling, "Okay. I'm leaving now! Goodbye!" followed by Mom's voice. Lucy fast-forwarded the tape a few seconds.

"Fine!" Lucy's voice said, followed by stomping as she went down the stairs. The next thirty minutes of tape contained only white noise occasionally interrupted by bird chirps and city noises from the open windows.

Lucy stared at the recorder. It hadn't recorded anything. Either it was impossible to record a ghost talking, or there just wasn't anything there to register.

Phooey, she thought. Suddenly, the sounds changed from the hissing white noise to something growling. She gaped at the recorder. The skin on her neck prickled.

"Lucy," an ominous deep voice growled.

Lucy gulped.

"Are you listening, Loooo-seeee?" It pronounced her name as though it were two separate words. Her skin prickled, and her body tingled.

"Give us what we want, and we'll go away, Loooo-seeee," the voice growled through the recorder.

We'll go away? Lucy thought. *How many of them are there? Does the voice belong to Malpar, trying to scare me, or something else?*

"GIVE US THE SPECTRESCOPE!" the voice screamed, sending a shiver of fear trickling down her spine despite the warm breeze wafting through her window.

The backpack was on the foot of her bed. Lucy pulled out the Spectrescope and scanned for any glimmer, mist, or shadow of a ghost, but there was nothing. She explored the upstairs, checking the bathroom, the closets, and even Dale's room. She didn't find any ghosts.

She was alone.

The tape recorder was still running. White noise spilled from the speaker.

"Didn't find us, did you?" snarled the voice.

Lucy froze. *How could it know I would search through all the rooms? It couldn't have known, could it? Is it watching me even now?*

"Don't worry," the voice growled. "We'll be back. Right now, we're visiting a friend of yours." A sinister laugh spilled from the speaker, echoing through the stillness of the room. "We're at Schuyler's house."

Schuyler! The tape recorder crashed to the floor as she climbed over it, grabbing her cell phone from the desk. She was shaking so hard she could barely punch Schuyler's number.

The phone rang several times before someone answered. Lucy heard scuffling sounds and what sounded like someone fumbling the phone. *Was that a whimper?*

"Schuyler, is that you?" Lucy yelled. It seemed forever before a voice responded.

"Oh, Lucy!" whimpered Schuyler. Her voice frightened Lucy, causing the tiny hairs on Lucy's arms to stand on end.

"There's a terrifying ghost in my house! Please, help me! I'm home alone!"

9 Night Games

"I'm coming! Keep your bracelet on!" Lucy was shaking so hard she dropped the cell phone. She snatched up the cell, and, grabbing the backpack, stuffed the Spectrescope in it. Turning quickly, she flipped open the trunk, grabbing for the hat. It tangled with the silver vest. She tried to shake it loose but shaking it made the tangle worse, so she stuffed them into the backpack as she rushed out of the bedroom.

"Just where do you think you are going in such a hurry, young lady?" Mom demanded as she came up the back stairs and stepped into the foyer.

"I have to go to Schuyler's! Can you drive me, please?" Lucy begged. "I need to see her tonight! Please, Mom?"

"Oh, for goodness' sake," groused Mom. "Why on earth do you have to go to Schuyler's? Can't it wait till tomorrow?"

"No! Tomorrow may be too late. We have to go now. Please, Mom?" Lucy steepled her hands in front of her.

"Too late for what? Are you two playing some ridiculous game again?" snapped Mom. "I suppose you're planning to stay overnight too?" She stomped back down the stairs.

"Definitely!" Lucy replied, rushing down the stairs after her.

Schuyler's house was only a couple of blocks away, but the drive to it seemed to take forever. Mom was mad. Lucy was glad because she didn't ask what was going on. How do you explain you are going ghost hunting?

The SUV had barely come to a stop when Lucy pushed opened the door, jumped out, and charged toward the house, the backpack bouncing on her shoulder.

"Thanks, Mom! I'll call you in the morning," yelled Lucy. "I love you!" She ran up the steps past the colorful terra-cotta pots of flowers. Their cheeriness did nothing to dispel the queasy feeling in her stomach. She heard mom's SUV squeal away from the curb.

The front door opened, and Schuyler stood there, shaking and still clutching her cell phone. She wrapped her arms around Lucy, nearly knocking her off her feet.

"Thank goodness you came!" squeaked Schuyler. "Mom and Dad went to a dinner conference, and they won't be home for hours." Her eyes were large orbs in her pale face. "What are we going to do?" she whimpered.

"What's been happening? Did your bracelet turn into the shield?" Lucy asked, lightly holding Schuyler's hand, hoping to instill confidence she found waning in herself.

"No, nothing," said Schuyler, who held out her arm with the bracelet. "It didn't vibrate either. Do you think that means no immediate danger?"

"Maybe, did you see who it is? Is it Malpar?"

"No, it's the ghost of a man. I don't know who it is, but he's tall with dark hair, and his eyes are so black they appear empty and hollow. He's frightening!" Schuyler shivered. They stepped into the entryway, and she closed the front door. "I don't think I'd be so scared if it were Malpar, not after what Iam told you about him."

"Malpar might be the least of our worries. Where did you see the ghost? Did he say anything?"

"I only saw him in the photos I took this afternoon. Oh, that would be frightening if I saw him in person and he said something. I'm so glad you came!" She managed a weak smile. "I feel a little better now. I don't usually mind being alone while Mom and Dad are out, but this is different. I don't feel so brave now."

"We'll be fine," said Lucy. She hoped she sounded braver than she felt. "I've got the Spectrescope with the sword, and you have your shield and sword. I also grabbed a couple more items from the trunk, just in case they're magical. We should scope the house to find this ghost. Have you seen Malpar?"

"No, I haven't, not since the other night. Why?"

"I wonder if Malpar knows this ghost since he's a spirit too. Where are the photos?" Lucy asked. She dropped the backpack on the floor.

"They are still in my camera," said Schuyler, taking it from the foyer table behind her. She held it so they could both view the screen as she scrolled through the photos.

"Look! He's in almost every picture, glaring at the camera. He looks as though he hates me for being here. He's so evil looking!" Schuyler pressed a hand against her chest as though she were going to faint.

Lucy gawked at the camera. Nearly every photo contained a pearly, semi-transparent image of a man with dark hair slicked back from his forehead, sunken cheeks forming a dour expression, and wearing an old-fashioned suit with a high collar. His eyes were the scariest things Lucy had ever seen. They appeared so black and hollow it was as though he had no eyes at all.

The ghost was reflected in the hall mirror, sitting casually in a living room chair. In one photo, the spirit wore a round brimmed hat. Another, featuring him grinning sadistically from behind the glass of the dresser mirror, was the creepiest of them all.

"Yikes! He is creepy. You didn't see him when you were taking the pictures?" asked Lucy, scrolling through the photos again. "So far, he only appears in the mirrors."

"No! I swear I would have run from the house if I had seen him in person!" She shuddered. "My bracelet felt a little tight a couple of times. It didn't morph into the shield, so I didn't think anything of it. Do you think he was close to me then?"

"Maybe your bracelet didn't change because he was in the mirror," said Lucy. "Do you think the ghost could be the landowner, Darwin Stewart, we found out about at the museum?" Lucy handed the camera back to Schuyler.

"Yeah, it's a possibility. Remember, the journal indicated Stewart died sometime in 1864 while serving in the Michigan Infantry." Schuyler was shivering. She folded her arms across her chest for warmth.

"If we could find some old pictures of the Stewarts, then we would know. Only, why would he show up now?" Lucy paused. "Wait, you don't think he could be the daemon that Malpar was referring to, do you?" Lucy rubbed her hands over her arms. Blowing her breath out, she watched it steam in front of her face. "Why is it so cold in here?"

"Ooh," Schuyler whimpered as she tugged Lucy's sleeve. "I think someone is here! Remember how cold it got at the cemetery? Get your Spectrescope! Hurry!"

Lucy grabbed the Spectrescope from the pack and, holding it to her face, scanned the foyer and the living room. Those rooms were clear. Next, she checked the stairs up to the second-floor landing and stopped. "Uh-oh," she said. The Spectrescope revealed the ghost of a man standing at the top of the stairs. It was the ghost in the photos.

"Schuyler, our ghost is at the top of the stairs looking at us. And he's hideously creepy," Lucy whispered slowly. She took several deep breaths. "Keep your bracelet ready."

Schuyler gasped and nodded and raised her shaking arm.

"Good evening, Lucy," said the ghost. "I'd have thought you would respond a little more quickly to a friend in distress." He stared at the girls from the landing. Lucy recognized the voice from the tape recorder and gulped.

The ghost was nearly transparent and unearthly pale. Slowly descending the stairs, its feet made a muffled sound on the stair tread that brought with it an overwhelming sense of dread.

"Where is he?" Schuyler whispered to Lucy. The bracelet vibrated the closer the ghost came, and she held her arm stiffly in front of both of them. It erupted into the shield. She withdrew Zazriel from its sheath, careful to keep it hidden behind the shield.

"Right here next to you," the ghost said vehemently. With a flourish of spinning smoke and ash and the acrid smell of sulfur, the spirit suddenly appeared in solid form right next to Schuyler.

Schuyler squealed, stepping backward away from the full-bodied apparition. She held the shield high, separating Lucy and herself from the ghost, and then she pointed Zazriel at him.

The ghost was even more frightening in solid form. The dark circles around its eyes made them appear blacker, more lifeless than they had looked in the photos. The dark-brown hair capping its head was combed straight back from the forehead and had streaks of gray at the temples. His dark suit and vest were narrow at the waist with long tails at the back. A stiff white shirt with a tall collar completed the costume.

"Give us the Spectrescope! Now!" the ghost roared, lunging at Lucy and swiping a pale hand toward the Spectrescope. In a flash, his face twisted hideously into that of a bull and then back into a man again.

The girls squealed and ran, retreating into the living room. Lucy pulled the head of the Spectrescope from the handle, releasing the sword. Schuyler held out the shield and pointed Zazriel toward the ghost as he approached.

Lucy kept an eye on the ghost as she placed the head of the scope in her pocket. Leaning forward with both hands wrapped securely around the hilt, she brandished the sword like a bat. The blade gleamed in the dim light of the living room lamps.

"No! You're not getting the Spectrescope. Who are you? Why do you want it?" Lucy demanded.

"You don't know what you're playing at, you stupid girl. Give us the Spectrescope. You can go back to your silly little life, and we will leave you alone. It is too powerful to be controlled by a mortal, much less a girl," the ghost spat vehemently.

"It chose me to guard it, so I guess I will. Iam said someone would try to take it." Lucy glared at the ghost. At least, she hoped she was glaring. She was breathing hard by this time and shaking.

"Iam? That old fox? Is he still telling stories about the High King that never was?" the ghost retorted. He flickered in and out of focus. "If you listen to that old fool, you won't be around for very long. You may have the Spectrescope now, but it will soon be in our possession. The Master has waited thousands of years to retrieve it. I guess a few more days won't matter." The ghost suddenly evaporated into smoke and ash and swirled threateningly around the girls. "Make no mistake. We will have it soon." The wind of his sudden movement whipped their hair and slashed at their clothes before he disappeared altogether.

Lowering the sword, Lucy breathed deeply. The ghost was gone for now. She dropped onto the sofa. She looked at Schuyler, who was still holding the shield and sword protectively in front of her. "Are you okay?"

Schuyler nodded. Her face was pale, and a strand of hair stuck to her nose. She was rooted to the spot where she stood, shaking.

"C'mon, we should scope the rest of the house. If we find Malpar, maybe we can trick him into telling us who the ghost is."

"Okay," Schuyler squeaked. She slowly lowered the shield. Her hand shook as Zazriel slid back into the sheath.

Lucy and Schuyler slowly worked their way through the living room. The old furniture had been whitewashed and updated with trendy colors and new fabrics, and a pale yellow brightened the newly painted walls. The overall effect was stylishly casual country chic, fresh, and very cheerful. It was one of Lucy's favorite rooms, but not tonight.

Tonight it felt like unfamiliar territory. Shadows lurked in the corners, and the breeze from the windows ruffled the hem of the couch, making it look as though the sofa were moving. The atmosphere was electric, and the room felt mysterious and unfriendly. Lucy's skin prickled.

They searched through the dining room and then cautiously entered the kitchen. Mrs. Williams had left dozens of jars of homemade strawberry jam sitting on the counter, waiting to go to the basement for storage. A corner table under the window held a toaster and napkins in a holder. The window was open, and a slight breeze ruffled the clean white curtains.

Nothing appeared out of place in the kitchen. They went through the back hallway and up the stairs to the second-floor foyer. They searched each room along the hallway as it made a square around the stairs at the house's center.

Back in the foyer, two chairs and a small round table sat near a potbellied stove. A door in the corner creaked open. It was the weird connecting door to the back of Schuyler's bedroom closet. The door creaked open a little further.

Lucy saw a purple glow in the Spectrescope. She poked Schuyler in the shoulder and pointed. Soon, Malpar appeared to them in his solid bird-man form. Schuyler was almost relieved to see this spirit instead of the creepy ghost now haunting her house, though she still kept a hand on the Zazriel sword.

"It was you!" exclaimed Lucy, gripping the artifact. "You ransacked my bedroom and nearly gave me heart failure in the cemetery. Why are you doing this, Malpar?" Lucy asked. "Do you know the other ghost who is now haunting Schuyler's house?" She held the relic close to keep it out of his reach. Despite what Iam had told her, she felt tremors shaking her legs because she still didn't trust the Hayyothalan.

"I must retrieve the Spectrescope!" retorted Malpar. "You shouldn't have the artifact. It is dangerous for you. You do not know how to command it." He held out a hand toward the ancient relic. "Give it to us, and we'll go away," he said, stepping closer.

"I can't let you have it, Malpar."

"Take your friend and leave this place. The spirit who has come can harm you," said the Hayyothalan. He shook his head. "The struggle has raged for thousands of your earth years. So many lives were changed and damaged. Why should you want to be involved, human?"

"I don't know. I only know I must," said Lucy, a kernel of understanding beginning to grow in her brain and her heart.

"Who is the ghost haunting my house?" asked Schuyler, peeking over the top of the shield at the bird-man. "Why are we just seeing him now? Has he always been here?"

"He is not just a ghost, he is a daemon, and he is very dangerous. He does the Master's bidding, terrible things."

Schuyler's eyes popped open, her eyebrows nearly disappearing over the top of her head. She stood motionless, watching the bird-man. Her face was as pale as a fake Halloween ghost.

"All the more reason I must stay and get rid of it if I can," Lucy gulped. She didn't like this ghost hunting very much.

"Go, Lucy. Iam wouldn't want you or Schuyler to get hurt," reasoned Malpar. "He will understand if you give us the Spectrescope."

"You know Iam?" Lucy asked incredulously.

"Yes," came the soft, hissing reply as Malpar dipped his head slightly, and then he puffed up his chest and stood tall. He stepped forward in his stovepipe boots, his cape swaying with the movement.

"Stay right there, Malpar, or I'll poke you with my sword," said Lucy, trying to sound brave but feeling more than a little intimidated by his tall, menacing form. "Is he a wizard? He can do some bizarre stuff, like disappear and all." Like Schuyler, she kept her hand on the hilt of the artifact.

"He is more, so much more, and powerful. He is many things to many peoples. He is the High King who is greatly loved," Malpar said, "and greatly feared."

"The High King? Like in the story of Ascalon?" Lucy asked. Iam was right. There was a whole other world beyond what she could see, and it existed within her world, right under her very nose. *Iam is the High King? That doesn't make sense.* Lucy was so confused.

Malpar flickered like a light bulb shorting out. He held his hands outstretched, waiting for Lucy to make her decision. "Give us the artifact, Lucy, before you get hurt. We will leave you alone once we have the Spectrescope."

"I'm sorry, Malpar. I can't," Lucy replied. "I have to see this through and protect the Spectrescope and my friends. The Spectrescope cannot fall into the wrong hands. If Iam is the High King, then he is counting on Schuyler and me."

The Hayyothalan hissed angrily and disappeared. The closet was empty except for Schuyler's clothes.

"Well, that was cheery," Lucy said, heaving a sigh. "At least we know a little more about the ghost or daemon, whatever that is." She plopped hard into a chair by the potbellied stove and stretched her legs in front of her.

"What now? Mom and Dad will be home soon. I can't say, 'Hey, Mom, Dad, we have a nasty ghost haunting our house.' "

"Let's not say anything yet. My guess is the ghost and Malpar are gone for now, but we know they will be back."

"Oh, no! I just remembered something," said Schuyler, jumping to her feet. "We didn't check the secret passages or the attic. We should check those, too, don't you think?" She pointed down the hall.

"The secret what?" Lucy exclaimed, her mouth dropping open as she stared wide-eyed at Schuyler. Then she remembered the spooky narrow hallways they used to play in when they were children. "Holy moly! I like, totally forgot about those! It's been forever since we played there."

"Yeah, the secret passages were our favorite hiding places. The house is nearly two hundred years old, after all. Dad thinks they provided some sort of insulation against heat and cold for the interior rooms. According to Dad, it's not uncommon for older houses to have them tucked under the roof's eaves. I used to play hide-and-seek with my dad there too."

"Where are they?" Lucy asked. "I don't remember where they are at, and I didn't see any doors when we were searching the rooms."

"There's a door in the spare bedroom. Here, I'll show you," Schuyler replied, taking the lead and heading toward the room across from the stairs.

She opened the bedroom door, motioning for Lucy to follow. The spare bedroom held just a few furnishings, but soft pastel colors and an old-fashioned bedspread made it cozy and inviting. The white beadboard detail gave the room a country appeal that Lucy liked. Schuyler grabbed her arm, pulled her into the room, and closed the door.

Schuyler leaned forward and pressed a panel of the beadboard, and it popped open, revealing a small entryway into a very narrow passage.

"Whoa. It is awesome." Lucy exclaimed, peering inside. "I love your house. It's so weird! How did you ever know there was a hidden door here?"

"Dad grew up in this house and later inherited it from my grandparents. He played in the passages when he was a little boy."

"I wonder what they used it for?" mused Lucy. She leaned further into the passage to run her hand over the tiny slats that formed the wall. Globs of plaster that had at one time oozed between the slats were hardened into weird and dusty shapes.

"Who knows? You'll need a flashlight. There aren't any lights in there," Schuyler said, opening the nightstand drawer and handing Lucy a big flashlight. "You can go first since you have the Spectrescope."

"Gee, thanks," said Lucy, grabbing the flashlight. A bright beam of LED light illuminated the narrow passage. The tall ceiling height emphasized the narrow path, which was just wide enough for a person to walk through.

"Where does this passage go?" Lucy asked, stepping inside.

"It follows the outline of the interior rooms. There is another access door just to your left. It goes into my dad's office. It used to be a bedroom," said Schuyler. She squeezed into the narrow passage behind her friend.

"Cool." Lucy panned the light up and down the small hallway. "Where does the door at the other end lead?"

"What door? There's only the access panel to my dad's office, just like this one. There aren't any other doors to this passage."

"Then what do you call that?" Lucy focused the beam on a door at the end of the passage. It was an aged, dark-wood door with a black, round knob and no discernible lock. Large, black hinges scrolled across the wood panels like garden snakes.

Schuyler's mouth dropped open.

"I swear! I have never seen that door before. We've played in this passage hundreds of times and that door was never there," exclaimed Schuyler. She squeezed past Lucy to get a closer look.

"Well, it's here now. Do you think we should open it? I mean, where could it go? We're at the back of your house, right? Maybe it's a closet."

"Don't open it," Schuyler warned and whirled to face Lucy. Fear flickered across her features. "What if there's something bad on the other side? Suppose it's the door the ghost came through?"

"Don't be silly. A ghost doesn't need a door to enter. Ghosts can walk through walls," Lucy said. "You're the bookworm. Didn't the ghost-hunting book say anything about that? I'll open it just far enough to get a peek of the other side," she said, trying to sound brave. She traded places with Schuyler, who held her arm in front of her waiting for the bracelet to morph.

Slowly turning the knob, Lucy pulled the door open a crack and peered inside. Shining the flashlight through the gap, she saw what looked like shelves stacked on one another. Confused, she opened the door further, panning the beam up and down. "It's a staircase! It's steep, but just a staircase."

"What? It doesn't make sense. The attic is above us, and there is a door in the front hall to the attic stairway," said Schuyler. "Where can it go?"

"We've come this far. We might as well find out." Lucy shined the light up the stairs. "It looks like it goes to the attic. Are you sure you never saw this before? It looks old like it has always been here."

"I don't remember ever seeing it before, but I was little, so maybe I just don't remember it."

Lucy held the Spectrescope up. It was clear, and the symbols weren't glowing.

"Let's go check it out. I don't see any ghosts in the Spectrescope," she said, flashing the light around the steep staircase.

"Uh, okay," Schuyler said. She cautiously stepped toward the staircase, then turned and disappeared back through the access door. "Wait a minute. I'll be right back!"

Lucy tried to keep her balance as she climbed the steep, narrow steps with the Spectrescope and the flashlight in opposite hands. Another beam of light appeared below Lucy's beam.

"Good idea. It's dark and creepy in here," Lucy said, glancing down where the second beam of light shone. "Oh, no."

"What does 'oh, no' mean?" Schuyler asked, her voice rising in pitch. The flashlight jiggled in her shaking hand.

Lucy lowered her voice. "The stairs have lots of dust, and there are footsteps in the dust that aren't mine!" she whispered. "The tracks go up and down the steps as if someone went up and came back down."

"Or came down and went back up," Schuyler squeaked. "Do you still think we should follow the stairs?"

Lucy paused and looked at the footsteps. The dust made her nose tickle. "What's in the attic? It's not full of clutter, is it? Please say no." Lucy shuddered. Tight, dark, cluttered places were high on her list of phobias, and she avoided them whenever possible. She was already feeling claustrophobic in the cramped, dusty space.

"It is empty. Mom says it's too much work to drag anything up there for storage. No one has been up there in ages."

"That is good. If this goes to the attic and someone is up there, we should see them first. At least, I hope so," said Lucy. Her beam bounced off the attic roof at the top of the stairs, where dust particles floated through the light. She crept up the stairs.

"What's that noise? That bumpety-bump?"

Lucy paused and listened. "I don't hear anything."

"Ooh, I think it's me," whimpered Schuyler, placing a shaky hand over her heart. She closed her eyes and took a deep breath. A moment later, she opened her eyes. "Okay."

A nervous smile lifted the corners of Lucy's mouth. It was somewhat comforting to know that Schuyler was not feeling too brave either.

"Do you have your cell phone?" asked Lucy.

"Yeah, why?"

"Punch in 911 but don't press Send. Just have it ready in case we need it," Lucy said quietly. She gripped the Spectrescope hard to keep her hand from shaking.

"Okay." Schuyler pulled a bright-pink cell phone from her pocket and punched in the numbers. "Got it—let's go," she said shakily, following Lucy up the old wooden stairs. "Before I lose my nerve," she mumbled.

Lucy tucked the Spectrescope under her arm. Holding the flashlight, she turned the lens, widening the beam and bathing the stairs in more light. Grabbing the scope again, she slowly moved up the steps. Schuyler followed close behind.

The stairs led to a large room with short walls on either side and slanted ceilings meeting in the center at the roof's ridgepole. The room was not completely dark. Each of the two walls contained windows, the ambient light from outside splaying across the floor.

In the center of the room was the stairway leading down to the second floor. A short railing ran around the opening on three sides. Just above the stairs, a light bulb dangled from the ridgepole in the center of the room.

Lucy stepped into the attic and flashed the beam around the room. The shaft made the shadows in the corners seem darker. She found the light switch on the corner post of the railing and flipped it on.

The attic was empty.

10 The Vanishing Staircase

"Would your dad have had reason to go up to the attic? It could explain the footsteps in the dust." Lucy sat cross-legged on the foot of Schuyler's bed, squeezing a pillow.

"He would have used the front stairs, not the secret passage." Schuyler curled up with the other pillow and leaned against the headboard.

"Yeah, but if he were working in his office, it would have been closer to use the access door to get to the attic."

"He wouldn't have any reason to go up there, and it is empty."

"What if he heard a noise in the attic and went to check it out?" Lucy countered. "Maybe he thought a squirrel got in somehow. They like attics."

"We've never had any animals get into the attic that I know of, and I haven't heard him mention anything about strange noises."

"Excuse me? Do you always listen to your parents?" Lucy said, rolling her eyes. "Now, that is strange!"

"Don't be silly. I could ask Dad when they get home." Schuyler checked the time on her watch. "They should be home any time, now."

"How are you going to explain why we were in the passage? Won't they think it a little weird, even for us?"

"I'll just tell them we were ghost hunting, like the guys in the book I got from the library," Schuyler said with a sly smile. "After all, the book was for you."

Lucy squinted her eyes and stuck out her tongue.

"I'm hungry. Let's go get a snack." Schuyler retrieved the ghost-hunting book from the desk and led the way down to the kitchen. She tossed it on the corner table where the toaster sat and went to the refrigerator.

"What d'you want to eat? I'm kind of hungry for a toasted bologna sandwich." Schuyler's voice was muffled behind the refrigerator door as she rummaged for the bologna in the deli drawer. "How about you?"

"Ooh, that sounds good. I'll get the bread and the clothespins," Lucy offered, grabbing a loaf from the pantry and opening a drawer from which she withdrew two wooden clothespins. Sitting down at the table in the corner, she pulled the toaster in front of her and carefully laid out four slices of bread.

Schuyler put bologna, butter, and mustard on the table along with plates and a knife. She spread butter on one side of each bread slice then placed a round of bologna on each of two pieces. The combination was then carefully pinched together with the clothespins and placed into the front of the double-slotted toaster. Putting the other bread slices in the back slot, she pushed the button down. The clothespins stuck out the top.

The kitchen soon smelled like warm bologna and toast. When the toaster popped up, the clothespins held toasted bread with hot bologna, singed and curling around the edges.

"Perfect!" Schuyler dropped a hot sandwich onto her plate. Lucy grabbed the other sandwich and squirted mustard over it before slapping it all back together and taking a bite.

Unnoticed, an ink-black shadow slowly crawled up the far wall and across the kitchen ceiling before coming to rest in a dark corner, making the corner nearly pitch black.

"This is such a weird way to make a sandwich, but it tastes so good!" Lucy mumbled. She licked her lips and took another bite. "How did you ever think this up?"

"When Dad was a kid working on his grandpa's farm in the summer, he made sandwiches for his lunch. He likes hot sandwiches, and they didn't have a microwave, so he improvised. Not bad, huh?"

"It's brilliant! Want another?" asked Lucy, pulling more bread from the package. They each munched down another sandwich and drank tall glasses of milk.

Schuyler opened the ghost-hunting book and began flipping through the pages. The black shadow slowly slithered along the ceiling edge to the nearest corner. Her bracelet steadily grew warmer as the shadow came closer. Schuyler noticed the heat on her arm but assumed it was the natural temperature in the kitchen. Her mom had made jam that afternoon, and the kitchen was still a little steamy.

"This book is interesting," she said. "It gives a brief history of ghost hunting. For instance, did you know, President Abraham Lincoln and his family saw ghosts and talked with mediums? Supposedly, he dreamed about his own death shortly before he was assassinated. Then, he came back as a ghost and appeared to Winston Churchill!"

"Whoa! I wonder what Winston Churchill thought. Maybe I should offer to inspect the White House for other presidential ghosts!" Lucy laughed. "What else does the book say?"

"It defines different types of ghosts, where to find them, how to talk to them, and what kind of equipment to use to hunt them. Unfortunately, it doesn't say anything about how to get rid of a ghost. You're the ghost hunter. Got any ideas?"

"Uh, well, not exactly. I need to talk to Iam."

"Lucy! You mean, we've got two ghosts in our house, and there's no way to get rid of them? What're we going to do?" Schuyler looked at Lucy with disbelief. "I've always wanted a pet, but this isn't quite what I had in mind. Why haven't you asked Iam? I'm sure he could tell you."

"Up till now, I'd never really thought about it. It seemed more like a game or a grand adventure," said Lucy. "There's got to be a way to get rid of him and Malpar. Don't worry. We'll figure it out." She helped clear the table and put the dirty dishes in the dishwasher and then followed Schuyler back upstairs to her room. The shadow silently dissolved into the ceiling and disappeared altogether.

As Lucy plopped in the chair at the desk, Schuyler suddenly turned and ran from the room. Lucy stared after her, shouting, "Where are you going?"

Schuyler went down the hall into the office, which her dad shared with her mother. After rummaging through a stack of papers next to her mom's desktop computer, she grabbed a crumpled piece of paper and ran back to the bedroom.

Pushing Lucy aside, Schuyler squiggled into the chair, opened the laptop, and connected to the internet.

"Mom signed up for YourOldAncestors.com to research her side of the family. She's working on a scrapbook project to put together a family album, and I've been helping her." She typed in the web address. "I thought maybe we could use the website to find information about Darwin and Helena Stewart, and we might even find some old pictures."

"Brilliant!" said Lucy. "This should be fun. Do you know how to navigate through it?"

"It's not hard. I've already found a few family things. We need to know who this other ghost is, and then maybe knowing who he is might help us get rid of him." Her fingers tapped rapidly at the keys.

"So, if we know his story, it might help us figure out a way to get rid of him. At the very least, we'll know who he was," Lucy reasoned.

"Exactly. Malpar did say he wasn't just a ghost; he also called him a daemon. We need to find out exactly what that is. I know it's a long shot, but it might help."

"That's brainy, you know?"

"Yeah, I know," Schuyler said with a smirk.

Lucy snorted and punched her friend lightly on the arm. "What if he is a daemon? Isn't that still an evil spirit or something?"

Schuyler googled the word *daemon*, then leaned back in her chair, her eyes widening. "Oops, this isn't good," she said, pointing at the screen. "Look."

The daemon definition was "a divinity or supernatural being of a nature between gods and humans; archaic spelling of demon." Lucy swallowed hard. Schuyler looked as though she was going to be ill.

The sound of a car in the driveway, followed by slamming doors, told the girls that Mr. and Mrs. Williams were home. Coming in the door, Mrs. Williams laid her evening purse on the foyer table and pulled her shawl from her shoulders. The girls noisily tromped down the stairs to greet them.

"How was dinner?" Schuyler asked, giving her mom a quick, tight hug. "Did you have a good time?"

"It was lovely. The lecture wasn't as stimulating as the conversation around the dinner table, but it was still a pleasant evening," replied Mrs. Williams.

"Hello, Mr. and Mrs. Williams," said Lucy.

"Oh, hello Lucy," said Mrs. Williams. She gave Lucy a quick squeeze. "Did you come to stay the night with Schuyler?"

"Yes, if that's okay with you?" asked Lucy. She smiled expectantly at Mrs. Williams.

"Wonderful!" exclaimed Mrs. Williams.

"Lucy, you are always welcome," Mr. Williams added. "We enjoy having you, and you are Schuyler's BFF," he said, smiling. "That is almost like family!" He stepped into the foyer, closing the front door behind him.

"Thanks!" said Lucy. She bounced on the balls of her feet and swung her arms. The grin on her face widened. "I love coming here."

"Hey, Dad! Did you go up to the attic recently?" Schuyler glanced sideways at Lucy. "We found footsteps in the dust on the old stairs at the back of the secret passage."

"The old stairs? Why are you talking about the passage? There aren't any stairs there," said Mr. Williams, looking confused. Then he grinned. "Are you girls spoofing us again? That's a good one! Footprints in the dust on a stairway that doesn't exist! It is original. I'll give you that." He laughed heartily.

"Dad! There truly are stairs in the passage! They go up to the attic. We were just up there!" Schuyler insisted, her face registering disbelief at his remark.

"Now, honey, you've played in that passage hundreds of times. You know there aren't any stairs. Wait, I get it! This is one of those games you two play," said Mr. Williams, grinning. "Okay, let's go check out those footprints in the dust."

Mr. Williams led the way up the stairs and through the foyer to the spare bedroom. He snatched the flashlight from the nightstand.

"Do you want to go first, or shall I?" he asked, winking at Lucy.

"You can go first, and we'll be right behind you," said Schuyler, pulling Lucy into the room.

"The secret panel is opening to reveal a hidden passage," whispered Mr. Williams spookily. He tucked his tall, thin frame through the panel and into the passage. The beam of his flashlight revealed a blank wall at the end where the door had been.

"Oh, dear, I guess the door is only visible to those with the secret password. Do you girls know the password?" Mr. Williams waggled his eyebrows and pinched his lips into a silly grin.

"No, I guess we don't. We need to work on that, don't we, Schuyler?" Lucy quickly interjected. She tugged on Schuyler's shirt hem.

Schuyler nodded.

"Yeah, we're still working on that part," said Schuyler. Since her dad thought they were playing a game, it was best to let him continue to believe that for now.

"You girls sure have active imaginations. I'm glad you're using your heads instead of playing all those video games that kids your age are doing. It's a better way to exercise those little gray cells, right?" He tapped his head. "Okay, then. Let's solve the mystery of the missing door another time. It's late, and we should all be in bed." He closed the panel and turned off the flashlight.

"You are fun, Mr. Williams. You join right in the game. Most adults just ignore us," said Lucy, following Schuyler back to her room. "Goodnight!"

"Goodnight girls, sleep well," said Mr. Williams. He dropped a kiss on Schuyler's cheek and then stuffed his hands into his pockets and whistled his way down the hall.

"Your dad is cool. I've never met my dad. If he's still living, I don't know where. Who knows? Maybe someday," said Lucy as she plopped on the foot of the bed.

"Seriously? Have you never met your dad? Don't you get birthday or Christmas cards or anything from him?" asked Schuyler.

"Nope, zilch, nada, nothing! It's okay, though. I don't understand it, but I don't know the whole story either." She pulled her legs up under her. "Maybe someday I will. I don't think about it much."

Schuyler pulled the trundle from under the bed and started fluffing the blankets. Lucy retrieved her overnight case from the top shelf of the closet.

"I wondered why you never mention him. I figured you'd tell me when you were ready. You know, Mom says things happen for a reason. Maybe you wouldn't be you if you had a dad. Everything would be different. You wouldn't have gone to the flea market with your mother because money is tight, and you wouldn't have found the Spectrescope," said Schuyler. "That's possible, you know."

"Yeah, but, if this is supposed to be my destiny, wouldn't the Spectrescope have found me anyway?" asked Lucy, flipping clean pajamas onto the bed trundle.

"Maybe, maybe not, but it's comforting to know you're where you need to be right now, like here with me," said Schuyler. She hugged Lucy.

"Thanks, Schuyler."

"Oh, the laptop! I left it on when we went downstairs. I'd better turn it off, or we can play our favorite game," said Schuyler, giving Lucy an expectant look.

"Shopping! Let's hunt something other than ghosts for a while," declared Lucy.

Shopping Cart was their favorite pastime. They could sit for hours surfing from one website to another, selecting their favorite clothes, shoes, and accessories. Adding the items into the cart, they could watch the total go up without checking out. It wasn't an actual game, but it was fun to see who could spend the most.

Sitting crossed-legged on the bed, Schuyler placed the laptop between them. Pulling up the screen, she tapped the trackpad to bring the computer from hibernation. It had disconnected from the internet, and the screen was blank. Suddenly a message began typing itself across the screen. "Don't go to sleep tonight. Some things go bump in the night."

"Lucy!" exclaimed Schuyler, pointing at the screen.

"Oh, no," whispered Lucy. "I hope they won't do something while your parents are in the house."

"Luce, what are we going to do? Mom and Dad won't believe us. They'll just think it's a game. Dad already thinks we made up the hidden staircase."

"I don't want any harm to happen to you or your parents, but I don't know what to do. After your parents go to bed, maybe we can find the ghost before he can do anything," Lucy suggested. "Maybe we can trick him somehow into telling us how to get rid of him."

"What? Like how's that going to work?" Schuyler wrung her hands. "Ooh. Mom and Dad won't be asleep for a while yet. Did you bring anything magical with you from the trunk?"

"The hat I like to wear, and a silver metallic vest. It got tangled with the hat, so I just stuffed both in the backpack." Lucy unzipped the large pocket and pulled out the hat and vest.

A small silver object tumbled out of the hat, rolled and bumped across the floor, spun like a top, and then fell over. It sparkled with blue and white gems.

"What's this?" Schuyler picked it up and admired the simple design. "It's a belt-shaped ring! I can imagine a courtly little marmoset wearing it to hold up his trousers," she said with a laugh, her tension easing a little.

"How did that get in there?" Lucy wondered. "I found it in the corner of the trunk one day. It had tarnished, but it polished up beautifully. It's kept in my dresser drawer when I'm not wearing it, so I don't know how it would have gotten tangled in with the hat."

"What are the blue stones? They're a beautiful tropical blue, like the blue oceans you see in travel posters," said Schuyler. She tried the ring on her finger, but it didn't fit, so she gave it back to Lucy.

"I dunno. It's unique. Blue's my favorite color, so of course, I like it!" Lucy laughed and stuffed the ring into the backpack.

"Are the hat and vest magical too? I hope they are because this ghost is creepy," whimpered Schuyler. "We are going to need help, especially if the ghost is a daemon."

The Ghost of Darwin Stewart

"The guess the only way to find out is to put them on," said Lucy. She slipped the thin silver vest over her head. The intricate weave of the vest shimmered slightly in the lamplight but didn't do anything magical. Lucy twisted and turned in front of the dresser mirror, trying to get a better look.

She turned to face Schuyler with her arms outstretched. "Voila! How do I look? Is this the new fashion trend, or what?" The carefree inflection in her voice didn't match the cold gnarly feeling she had in her stomach. The worried look on Schuyler's face made her stomach do flip-flops.

"Well, it could be if you are brave enough to wear it to school in the fall." Schuyler laughed halfheartedly. "You could start the metallic trend in girls' fashion."

"Here, you try the hat on, Miss Fashionista," said Lucy, plopping the hat on Schuyler's head.

Mr. Williams rapped on the bedroom door. "Time for lights out, girls." He turned the doorknob, and the door began to creak open.

"Hold on, Dad!" Schuyler waved her hands frantically at the beds. They scrambled under the blankets to hide their jeans and T-shirts.

"Goodnight, Dad! Love you! See you at breakfast!" Schuyler called out, whipping the hat from her head and stuffing it under the blankets.

"Goodnight, Mr. Williams! Thanks for letting me stay the night!" Lucy yelled.

Poking his head just inside the door, Mr. Williams smiled at them. "You're welcome here anytime, Lucy. As I said, you're practically one of the family! Goodnight, sweetheart, sleep well," Mr. Williams said, looking at Schuyler. "Oops, you forgot to turn off your computer. I'll get it for you."

"Dad!" Schuyler exclaimed, pulling the covers up tight to her face. "Really!"

"Oh, uh, right, sorry. My bad! Well, lights out. See you girls in the morning!" he said. His head quickly disappeared behind the door. It shut with a click.

"Good save, Schuyler! If your dad had come in the room, he would have seen I'm wearing my shoes in bed!" Lucy pointed at her sneakers sticking out of the bedcovers.

"I was worried he'd see the message on the computer. We don't need him asking questions." She closed the computer and put it on the desk. "Well," she said, reaching to turn out the light, "I guess now we wait."

*   *   *   *

Lucy sat cross-legged on the trundle, dozing as she leaned against Schuyler's bed. Her head lolled slowly from side to side. Schuyler lay curled up under the blankets with the flashlight gripped tightly in her hand.

Sliding slowly down the side of Schuyler's bed, Lucy's head finally came to rest on the pillow. The motion startled her awake. She sat up and blinked. With one hand, she took the Spectrescope from under the pillow, and with the other, she rubbed her eyes. Looking through the scope, she swept her gaze around the room. Still sleepy, she tried to focus on the closet door where something odd was happening.

The doorknob slowly turned. The door squeaked open, coming to rest softly against the stopper on the wall. The clothes gently swung on their hangers as though an unseen hand had searched through them, and the peculiar door in the back of the closet was open.

Her sleepy mind didn't immediately take her into boogeyman land or even into hungry-hungry-zombie-want-to-eat-you-now land. It was as blank as a chalkboard at the beginning of the school year. After all, it was an old house, and old houses do strange things like swing doors open, and the breeze from the window had probably moved the clothes about on their hangers.

It wasn't until she saw purple that her mind began to register danger!

Then several things happened at once.

Lucy's silver vest morphed into a medieval-style breastplate, covering her upper body.

Schuyler's bracelet exploded into the shield, nearly expelling her from the bed. She squirmed to throw back the bedcovers so she could rush to help Lucy.

Purple spots appeared on the carpet leading from the closet directly to the foot of their beds. Through the Spectrescope, Lucy could see the purple figure of a man standing next to the trundle. He stood gazing down at her for what seemed like minutes. The angry look on his face sent chills down Lucy's spine. *The ghost!*

The ghost morphed into a cloud of smoke and ash, swirling around Lucy. He shoved her forcefully into the blankets on the trundle. She struggled under the weight of the vest as she battled with the ghost, who was somehow solid yet not. The Spectrescope dropped from her hand and slipped from view under the edge of Schuyler's bed.

Schuyler saw the swirling cloud pushing Lucy down, engulfing her. Jumping from the bed, she grabbed Lucy by the arm and gave a jerk, pulling Lucy to her feet. Hands in the cloud pushed hard against both girls, propelling them backward, before swooping from the room through the closed bedroom door. Schuyler grabbed the hat from under her bedcovers and slapped it on Lucy's head.

"Thanks," said Lucy, breathless. "You okay?"

"Yeah, I think," said Schuyler. "What happened?"

"I fell asleep. When I woke, the ghost was standing by the bed, watching me. C'mon, we've got to find him before he wakes and scares your parents, or worse." Schuyler eased open the bedroom door as Lucy retrieved the Spectrescope, stepped past her, and began sweeping her way down the hallway.

"I can see his footsteps, they're glowing purple," whispered Lucy. "They disappear down the hallway toward the guest room."

"Glowing footsteps? It could be a temperature difference. They mentioned something in the book about temperature variations. Maybe that's what you're seeing."

"Whatever it is, it's creepy."

"Where did he go? Do you think he went through the secret hallway? Maybe that's why the door appears and disappears, he uses it as a portal," said Schuyler, her voice barely audible.

"Let's go find out. We'll have to be careful. I don't want to alarm your parents."

"I'm scared, Lucy. They could get hurt, but they won't believe we have a ghost in the house even if we try to warn them."

Following the footsteps, they cautiously made their way down the hallway to the guest room. The door was open and the secret panel ajar. Lucy held the Spectrescope tightly in one hand as she pulled the panel fully open. Schuyler handed her the flashlight. Shining the beam of light into the cramped space, Lucy looked inside. The purple glowing footsteps, which were beginning to fade, stopped at the foot of the staircase.

"See anything?" asked Schuyler. She retrieved the spare flashlight from the nightstand.

"The door is back, and it is open. Do you have your camera?" whispered Lucy.

"Great idea! It's in my room. Don't go in there until I get back!" Schuyler answered, her voice low. She pressed the stone, and the shield morphed into the bracelet as she disappeared down the dark hallway and returned with the camera, the flashlight stuffed in her pocket.

"I'm shaking so hard I'm afraid I'll drop it," said Schuyler, wrapping the camera strap around her wrist.

"Schuyler, the ghost is standing on the bottom step. I can see him in the Spectrescope. I'll shine the light on the stairs. You snap a photo."

Bending down next to Lucy, she snapped a digital photo of the stairs at the end of the secret passage. The camera's flash revealed the ghost standing on the stairs, his arm covering his face and eyes.

"There he goes!" cried Lucy. "Quick!"

The ghost turned and ran up the dark, narrow staircase toward the attic. Lucy and Schuyler followed quickly behind, their hearts pounding. They followed up the stairs and stepped into the attic room. The ghost was standing in solid form near the south window, watching them. Schuyler's shield reappeared, and she held it in front of her.

Suddenly, the ghost morphed into a swirling cloud, flowing across the room to reappear directly in front of them. The girls stepped sideways away from the spirit. Lucy held tight to the Spectrescope, and Schuyler snapped several more photos of the ghost. Anger twisted his pale features.

"Give us the Spectrescope!" the ghost roared. He swiped a pale hand toward the Spectrescope, but Lucy flinched backward. The spirit twisted again into smoke and ash, the acrid smell of sulfur filling the room. Swirling furiously, he flowed down the main staircase in the middle of the room. "Catch me if you can!" he taunted as he squeezed under the closed door at the bottom.

"Oh, my gosh! I hope he's not heading toward Mom and Dad's room!" cried Schuyler. They hurried down the stairs to the door, but the ghost had locked it. She turned the knob, but it wouldn't budge.

"This door is never locked," she said, twisting and pulling on the doorknob. "I don't even know if we have a key. What are we going to do?"

"Quick! The secret passage! We can get out that way," Lucy directed.

They ran down the vanishing staircase, squeezed through the passage, and slipped into the guest bedroom. Lucy paused in the hallway, listened, and swept the hall and foyer with the scope.

"I don't see or hear anything. We should check the hallway near the attic door," said Lucy softly, leading the way. "There! I can see his footsteps.

They go down the hall toward the other bedrooms and then just disappear." Lucy's hand flew to her mouth. "Oh, my gosh! I think I can hear him walking around somewhere. Do you hear that?"

Thump, thump. Something was moving around downstairs in the kitchen. The girls quietly went down the stairs and crept through the house, making their way toward the kitchen.

Crash!

"No!" whimpered Schuyler. "I think some of Mom's jam jars just got broken. I was supposed to take them downstairs to the cellar."

"You're worried about jam? We've got a ghost in the house! Shh! I think he's in the cellar now," said Lucy.

"Drat! I hate the cellar. It's creepy on a normal day," groaned Schuyler.

"I don't know what we can do about it except try to corner him. Keep the camera ready," said Lucy.

"Okay, here goes," said Schuyler, opening the cellar door. Holding the Spectrescope tightly, Lucy stepped in front of her and went down the steps into the cellar.

Schuyler flashed the beam of the flashlight around the narrow room at the bottom of the stairs. Lines of shelving filled with jars of homemade jams and jellies stood in ominous welcome. The shelves cast strange shadows crawling along the walls as Schuyler moved the beam. The uneven floor was roughly hewn bedrock. The girls' sneakered feet quietly gripped the rock without making a sound.

Schuyler stopped suddenly, tugging on Lucy's sleeve. "Lucy, the hat turned into a helmet! When did it do that? I didn't even see it change!"

"Dunno, it's lightweight, so I never noticed it. Guess there's a reason for it. One good thing at least if I trip on these floors, I won't bang my head," she said with a weak lopsided smile.

"I don't see anything," whispered Schuyler, staying close. "Do you see him?"

"I can see where he's been. His footsteps are glowing. Use your camera. Maybe we can flush him out with the flash. At least we can show your mom and dad there really is a ghost in the house," Lucy replied, pointing. "Over there!"

Schuyler flashed off several pictures, the blinding light from the camera making green spots appear in front of their eyes. The last two flashes revealed the ghost standing in the far corner. The spirit, solid in form, leaned on the shelving corner, sneering at them.

Lucy summoned all of her courage. "Who are you?" she demanded. "What's your name?"

"You may call me Darwin Stewart," the ghost replied, his black eyes lifeless in the beam of Lucy's flashlight.

"Why does the Master want the Spectrescope?"

"Didn't Malpar explain it to you?" he sneered. "I should think the Hayyothalan would have divulged all he knew about it to you. He is a weak, pathetic excuse for his race. Let me enlighten you," he said with a leering smile.

"Well, go ahead, tell us," said Lucy, holding the Spectrescope in front of her like a weapon. "Why do you want the Spectrescope?"

"It holds the key the Prince requires to complete his quest," the ghost answered. His voice was hollow sounding, menacing, and icy.

"Prince? Who is he?" Lucy asked, slowly making her way a little closer to the ghost. Schuyler followed, holding the shield in front of her body. Her other hand was on the hilt of Zazriel.

"Darnathian, of course, he's the prince of Ascalon, and he wants the Spectrescope back," sneered the ghost of Darwin Stewart. He ran a finger through the dust on the lid of a jam jar. "Ooh, yum, red raspberry," he said. "That was my favorite in my earlier life."

"I don't believe you. Iam said there—"

"You believe that old fox?" interrupted the ghost calling himself Darwin Stewart. "He's a deceiver, that one, and clever too. Let's see if he helps you out of this." He pushed the shelving unit over.

"No!" Schuyler screamed. She watched in horror as her mother's jars cascaded off the shelves toward the floor. The jars hit the stone with an ear-splitting crash amid the jeering laughter from the ghost.

The shelving unit crashed into the next unit, causing it to topple, sending more jars of jams and jellies crashing to the floor to shatter and splatter the walls with their sticky contents.

"Stop!" screamed Lucy. Dropping the flashlight, she raised her hand toward the disastrous scene. Everything stopped in midair as if frozen in time. The shelves defied gravity, leaning at weird angles, and while some jam jars hung suspended, others were frozen in place while shattering and exploding their contents into the air.

Lucy stood transfixed, Schuyler's mouth hung open, and the ghost was horrified.

Lucy lowered her hand, and everything was in motion again. Quickly, she raised her hand, and the process stopped once more.

"No! That's not possible!" cried Darwin Stewart. "No one can command the power of the Spectrescope except a—" He left the sentence unfinished as he vanished into smoke and swirling ash. Milliseconds later, the shield, vest, and helmet morphed back into their original forms.

Lucy and Schuyler stood looking at one another, puzzled expressions on their faces as they surveyed each other and discovered their armor was gone.

"WHAT IS THE MEANING OF THIS?" Mr. Williams roared from the foot of the cellar stairs.

Nearly startled out of their skin, Lucy and Schuyler turned to see Mr. Williams standing on the bottom step of the stairs and staring in disbelief at the toppled shelves and broken jam jars.

Crash! Bang! Splat!

Lucy had lowered her hand when she turned away, letting the scene continue. She cringed. Shattered jam jars oozed their stickiness everywhere. Strawberry chunks slowly dribbled down the walls to the floor.

"Look what you girls have done! EXPLAIN YOURSELVES!" Mr. Williams's face was crimson with anger. His body shook as he placed his hands on his hips and struggled to control himself.

"Dad! It wasn't us! It was a ghost!" Schuyler sobbed. "We would never have—"

"ENOUGH! Don't even try to blame this on some lame ghost story. You girls were still playing your ghost hunting game and now look what you have done! Your irresponsibility has destroyed months of your mother's hard work. All her effort smashed to smithereens. She was going to sell that jam to raise the money for Christmas. And *now* look at it. Gone!"

"But, Dad—"

"Don't 'but Dad' me, young lady! I am very angry with you right now."

"Dad, please, you don't understand. We have a ghost in the house!" sobbed Schuyler. "Please, look at the photos. I snapped his picture." She thrust the camera into her dad's hand.

"These are nothing but flashbacks from the light reflecting off the windows," retorted Mr. Williams, a muscle twitching in his cheek. He dropped the camera into the pocket of his robe.

"And you, Lucy Hornberger! This is all your fault! If you hadn't started all this stupid ghost-hunting nonsense, this wouldn't have happened," he shouted.

Lucy's stomach turned stone cold and queasy. *I should have done something*, she thought, tears running down her face, her body shaking. "I am so, so sorry, Mr. Williams."

"Well, I'm sorry, too, Lucy. I never expected such behavior from you. You and Schuyler can no longer be friends. You are not welcome in this house."

"But, Dad! It wasn't our fault!"

"I'll deal with you in the morning, Schuyler! Right now, I want you both to go back to bed. When I explain this to your mother, it's going to break her heart," Mr. Williams barked.

"I can call my mom to bring me home," whimpered Lucy between sniffles.

"Oh, no, you don't. You're not getting off that easy. I'll take you home tomorrow after you help Schuyler clean up this mess," he fumed, pointing a shaking finger at the jam oozing all over the floor like a bad scene from an old science-fiction movie. "I will be calling your mother in the morning. You can be sure of that."

11 Banishment

"Lucy Hornberger! I am so ashamed of you! How could you be so careless? Knocking over all of Mrs. Williams's jam jars! I WOULDN'T BLAME THE WILLIAMSES IF THEY NEVER SPOKE TO US AGAIN!"

Lucy trudged slowly up the back stairs to her room, dragging the backpack and carrying the overnight kit and spare clothes she had kept at Schuyler's house. She could hear her mother's tirade continuing in the kitchen. Even the cat followed her upstairs, taking refuge under the bed.

She dropped everything on the trunk lid, plopped on the bed, and rolled face-first into her pillow. The afternoon sunshine streaming through her window did little to warm her soul. She kicked off her jam-smeared sneakers with her face still mashed into the pillow.

Her clothes were dirty from scraping jams and jellies from the cellar floor. Mr. Williams had disposed of the broken glass. Worst of all, even more than her mother's tirade, was Mrs. Williams's face. It had looked like all her life energy had been sucked out of her as she surveyed the destruction.

I wish Iam were here. He would listen to me. Maybe he could tell me what to do, Lucy thought. She sobbed into her pillow for several minutes.

"Lucy," a voice whispered. "Wake up."

"Hmm?" Lucy mumbled, pushing herself up from the pillow. Dried tears made her cheeks feel stiff and gunky. "Iam?" She peeked out the front window but didn't see anyone on the street below. The afternoon sun had slid a little closer toward the horizon. She must have dozed off for a while.

"Come outside," the voice said again.

"Where?" She glanced about for the owner of the voice.

"To the porch, dear one," it whispered.

Lucy went down the back stairs to the kitchen, where she found a note from her mother who had gone grocery shopping and would return later. She had scrawled the words, "YOU ARE NOT TO GO OUT OR LEAVE THE HOUSE AT ALL! I'LL BE BACK SOON!" across the bottom of the paper.

"Oh, great," Lucy muttered, rubbing her gritty eyes. She wadded the paper and tossed the note in the waste bin. Padding softly down the hall to the front door, she opened it and stepped onto the front porch. Iam sat rocking gently in the white porch swing, waiting. Bill and Vivian McGoo, who were taking their daily walk, glanced up curiously as they passed the house, seeing the white porch swing rock forlornly back and forth.

Lucy burst through the door and ran to greet him. She sat on the seat next to him and grabbed his hand in both of hers.

"Oh, Iam! It's awful! Schuyler has a terrible ghost in her house. We were hunting it last night, and it caused so much damage," sobbed Lucy. Tears carved sticky trails down her dirty face. "And now Mr. and Mrs. Williams won't let me see Schuyler anymore because they think it was all my fault!" she lamented. Her upturned face wet with tears, contorted as another wave of teardrops threatened to spill from her eyes. "We tried to explain, but they wouldn't believe us. Some ghost hunter I turned out to be. I couldn't even help my best friend! Iam, what should I do?"

"The forces of evil are strong, Lucy. You have the Spectrescope, and you are learning what it needs you to do. Trust what you have learned. It can help you."

"Iam, you don't understand!" She threw up her hands. "They don't believe me! How can I help them if they won't let me? I love Schuyler, and we can't see each other forever!" cried Lucy. Her eyes burned as more hot tears spilled down her cheeks.

"Forever is a very long time. I can hardly believe they meant forever," Iam said softly, "but it may be a while before they fully understand. Just give them a little time, okay?"

"It's not fair! We tried to tell them the truth, but they wouldn't believe us."

"Let it go, Lucy. Time will help the Williamses understand. It is time now for us to think." He lightly tapped his temple. "What have you learned from your adventures so far? There are clues there that can help you," he said. "Perhaps together we shall discover what the clues are. Would that be all right?"

"How can there be any clues? I don't know anything about the ghost."

"You know more than you realize, dear Lucy. For instance, what did the ghost say to you? What did the ghost do? More importantly, what didn't he do? Think carefully. It may help you in your quest to defeat him." He patted her shoulder. "Now, tell me what happened."

She told Iam everything she could remember about the eerie voice on the recorder, meeting the ghost and hunting it through the house, and the broken jars of jams and jellies.

"Hmm, very interesting," said Iam, nodding. "Anything else you can think of?" He tilted his head, his eyes wide and questioning.

"Um, he said, 'Give us the Spectrescope,' and that it couldn't be controlled by a human girl."

"Really?" Iam stroked his mustache.

"Yeah, he did say something odd like, 'No one can command the power of the Spectrescope except a—' but he didn't finish the sentence. He just disappeared. And, that's when Mr. Williams showed up," said Lucy, sighing loudly and throwing up her hands. "I am sorry, but I don't see how any of this helps get rid of the ghost." Her head drooped.

"If we carefully consider the details, we will learn something useful. Tell me again what happened in the basement." Iam tapped on her arm when she didn't look up or say anything.

"What happened when you held your hand up?" he coaxed. "Didn't something rather spectacular occur then?"

"The jars hung suspended in midair. How did that happen?" She sniffled.

"Remember, dear Lucy, the Spectrescope contains ancient magic, and it chose to help you by sharing its power to work through you. You need to ask for help, then trust what you have learned." He leaned forward to study her face, but Lucy kept her head down.

"You mean like I'm a failure as a ghost hunter and a friend?" Lucy sniffled as another round of tears threatened to fall. "Yeah, I've learned that one well enough."

Iam patted Lucy's hand. "What is that paper in your pocket?" A gentle breeze ruffled his hair. It picked up a lock of Lucy's hair, sweeping it across her face, tickling her cheeks.

"What paper?" asked Lucy, looking down at her jeans pockets, the sullen expression deepening as her brow furrowed. Sticking out of her right pocket was a pink slip of paper. *How did that get there?* Lucy wondered, pulling it out and unfolding it. A tear escaped as she blinked, plopping on the form.

"What does it say? Perhaps it is another clue."

"It's from Schuyler! It's the password to her mom's account at the Your Old Ancestors website. We were going to search for Darwin and Helena Stewart!"

"An excellent idea! You know," Iam continued, leaning closer to whisper conspiratorially, "I heard somewhere that if you learn a spirit's true name, it gives you power over him. It's worth keeping in mind, don't you think?"

"Malpar appeared and warned us the ghost could harm us, and he did call the ghost a daemon," she said, finally looking at him. "Schuyler did a word search and found out the word *daemon* is the archaic spelling of *demon*. That is kind of scary."

"Malpar told you that, did he? Oh, that is interesting," Iam said, quirking an eyebrow. A smile tugged the corners of his mouth. "What else did Schuyler write?" He pointed to the paper and leaned in to take a peek.

"It is the names of their children. We saw the names on the gravestones when we went to the cemetery. She's written two other Stewart names too. I don't know who they are. They must be relatives or something."

"Names are important, don't you think?" Iam commented. "Schuyler is quite thorough in her research, isn't she? It should prove very helpful."

"She's so smart, but sometimes it's annoying," said Lucy with a wry smile.

"Ah, the wonderful mystery of having a friend and being one too," Iam said with a twinkle in his eyes. "You must accept the good qualities along with the annoying," he added heartily. He glanced over Lucy's head, nodded slightly, and smiled.

Lucy heard a car door open and looked to see who it was. Mr. and Mrs. McGoo were just climbing into their car. They waved when they saw Lucy.

"They're such cute people. Mrs. McGoo makes the best chocolate chip cookies ever!" Lucy said, waving at the McGoos. "You should meet them," she continued, turning to face him, but he had vanished.

"How does he do that?" she said, throwing her hands up.

Entering the house, she stuffed the paper in her pocket and headed upstairs. She took clean clothes from the closet and disappeared down the hall into the bathroom for a shower. The warm water soothed her aching muscles but did nothing for the ache in her heart. How would she ever make it up to the Williamses for all the damage the ghost had done? He had wrecked more than just jars of jams and jellies.

She stepped from the shower and slipped into her bathrobe. A familiar creaking noise was coming from her bedroom. *The trunk!*

Lucy darted into the bedroom, hoping to catch whomever or whatever had made the noise, but the room was empty. The trunk lid stood open, and someone had dumped the overnight kit on the floor. They had also partially unzipped the backpack.

She quickly felt inside for the Spectrescope. It was still there.

Phew! That was close, Lucy thought as she zipped it closed. *Just in case, I'll keep the note with me.* Schuyler had written a web address on the message along with the password. Retrieving the paper from her dirty jeans pocket, she quickly memorized the details and then stuffed the note inside the backpack. She dropped the pack into the large desk drawer, inserted the key, and locked it.

While the computer was booting up, she dressed in fresh clothes and her favorite sandals and put the key in her shorts pocket.

For the next couple of hours, she tediously searched through long pages of names and records for information about Darwin and Helena Stewart.

Finally, a smiley face appeared next to an entry. Lucy clicked on it. A faded sepia-toned photograph of a man and a woman in period clothing appeared on the screen. The woman sat in a chair as the man stood next to her, his hand resting on her shoulder.

Lucy squealed. *Yes! It's Darwin and Helena Stewart! I found them. I have to send this to Schuyler,* she thought. She copied the photo to the desktop screen and then opened her email. Typing a quick message to Schuyler, she attached the photograph and hit Send.

She flipped through several more of the ancestry pop-up windows for more photos of the Stewarts. After searching through the census records and birth and marriage records, she opened the window to the YourOldAncestors.com message board. After entering the required information, several member postings popped up, including a Jerome Stewart posting in reply to another member.

Attached to the message was a similar photo of Darwin and Helena. The poses were slightly different, but they wore the same clothing. The notice stated that Jerome was a great-great-grandson of Hamilton Stewart, the only brother of Darwin Stewart, the entrepreneur. The posting date was only a few days old.

Bingo! Let's talk! Lucy typed a message to Jerome Stewart. *I hope he writes me back. We need answers— and soon.* She finished her note and was about to hit Send when an idea popped into her brain.

She typed "Jerome Stewart" into a search engine. Several social media listings popped up. She clicked on one of the listings and read the information provided. *No, it can't be this easy*, she thought as she looked at the address.

Jerome Stewart lived nearby.

She wrote down the address and phone number on a piece of paper and tucked it in her pocket. Noise from the kitchen alerted Lucy that Mom had returned from the grocery store. She quietly crept down the back stairs and cautiously entered the kitchen.

"Hi, Mom, can I help you with anything?" asked Lucy, noticing her mom was still distraught as the canned goods banged on the countertop.

"You can help me by doing your chores without my telling you and by staying out of my line of sight," bellowed Mom. "Well, don't just stand there, do something!" The canned vegetables banged onto cupboard shelves as she packed them away.

Lucy took out plates and glasses and began setting the table for dinner. She placed the cutlery next to each plate and carefully folded the napkins. Next came the salad with shredded lettuce added into a bowl, a little salt and pepper, tomatoes, chopped egg, fresh peas, croutons, and cheese. She put a plastic cover over it and squeezed it onto a shelf in the refrigerator to keep cool till dinner was ready.

Mom was tenderizing the chicken breasts and mumbling under her breath. The decorative plates of colorful roosters hanging on the wall above the counter bounced and rattled as she pounded the chicken with the meat hammer.

"Can I do anything else for you?" asked Lucy softly.

"No."

"Can I watch TV?"

"No."

"Can I go outside?"

"No!"

"*Fine!*" Lucy retorted, stomping up the back stairs to her room. She slammed the bedroom door behind her. Sitting down hard at the computer, she sighed, then surfed some of her favorite websites and checked her email.

The instant messenger blinked, indicating there was a new chat message. It was from Schuyler. Lucy clicked the message icon.

Are you okay?

Sort of, Lucy typed.

Lots of yelling?

Yes. And pounding and stomping. How long are you grounded?

Until further notice. You?

Until I'm twenty-three. Did you get the photo?

Yeah, I couldn't believe you found them so quickly. Although I'm not sure how I feel now that we know who they are, Schuyler typed.

Why?

After several moments, Schuyler still had not responded. Lucy typed, *Are you still there?*

Yeah, just trying to figure this out. Do you think your mom will let you go to the library?

Maybe, when?

Tomorrow. One?

I'll try. I'll tell Mom I want to read that new vampire book. I'll text you in the morning. A loud voice abruptly interrupted the quiet clicking in the room.

"Lucy Hornberger! DINNER!"

Have to go, she typed and quickly logged off and went down to the kitchen. Dinner was on the table, and Mom and Dale were glaring at her as she entered the kitchen.

Dinner dragged on for what seemed like hours to Lucy, who spent most of the time pushing the food around her plate. Her stomach was queasy, and a feeling of dread engulfed her like a black cloud.

Finally, dinner was over and the table cleared. Lucy washed the bowls and pans, put dishes in the dishwasher, and covered the leftovers to store in the refrigerator.

Lucy finished her chores, quietly snitched a couple of cookies from the cookie jar, and went out to the porch swing. The evening was cool now that the sun had gone down below the horizon, turning the sky a purply pink. She curled her legs under her, snuggled into the oversized pillows, and absentmindedly nibbled a cookie. She wasn't hungry, but it was something to do. She rocked the swing back and forth.

A large black bird landed in the tree near the porch. It sat and watched her for several minutes before it swooped down and landed on the porch railing. Clicking its beak at her, it spoke in a raspy voice, saying, "Good evening, Lucy."

Lucy was startled at the sudden movement, and her mouth formed a thin tight line when she realized it wasn't an ordinary blackbird.

It was Malpar.

"What are you doing here?" Lucy asked through clenched teeth, a cookie suspended in midair on its way to her mouth.

"What do you think I am doing here? Stupid girl, you must give us the Spectrescope," Malpar replied. His crow eyes were black like small, round, glittering beads. He cocked his head to one side. "Haven't you had enough trouble yet?"

"I won't give you the Spectrescope, and you can tell your ghost friend to go away. He won't get it either," Lucy said, lowering the hand that held the cookie. She glanced past Malpar. The McGoos were walking by the house again. They were gaping at Lucy and the large black crow perched on the railing as they quickly walked across the street, disappearing around the corner and out of view. A moment later, two white doves fluttered into sight and landed on the telephone wire across the street.

"That's too bad," hissed Malpar, twisting his head and blinking at Lucy. "My Master doesn't give up easily. You may not like what my ghost friend does next. Are you sure you won't reconsider, stupid girl?"

"I'm a little tired of the name 'stupid girl.' For a Hayyothalan, you aren't funny anymore," Lucy said bravely, closely watching the bird.

A look of anguish flitted across the bird's features. "How do you know about the Hayyothalans? Our race is nearly extinct." Malpar was confused. "They're an ancient race, not part of your world. How do you know this?" He hopped closer along the porch rail, earnestly looking at Lucy, searching her face.

"Iam told me about them," Lucy said softly, noticing the change in Malpar. "You were beautiful and clever and funny once, don't you remember?"

"It does not matter anymore. That was long ago," the bird whispered, turning his head away. "My Master now is clever and powerful. He will get the Spectrescope, and you will not survive." He looked back at Lucy. "Please, just give us the object, and we'll go away. What does it matter to you?"

"I think you know more about that than I do, don't you, Malpar?" Lucy said as she leaned forward toward the bird, the cookie still in her hand. "Why do you serve this Master? You don't seem very happy or willing. Talk to Iam. He can help you. I know he would."

Malpar stared earnestly at Lucy, then dropped his head.

"Lucy Hornberger! Don't you dare feed those birds! I don't want those dirty things messing up my clean porch!" roared Mom from behind the screen door, her form appearing a moment later in the frame.

Malpar screeched and flew away.

"Who were you talking to, anyway?" Mom demanded her hands on her hips. "Don't you dare tell me you were making up more fairy tales, or you'll go upstairs and straight to bed!"

"Okay, bed it is," said Lucy, heading for the door. The doves gracefully flew from the wire and disappeared around the side of the house.

*   *   *   *

The dungeon-like hallway's stone walls echoed Grehssil's shuffling footsteps as he made his way toward the Master's chambers. He dreaded giving the news he had received from the Hayyothalan, but as Malpar had not come himself, Grehssil would have to deliver the bad news. Pausing before the heavy door, he took several deep breaths, knocked twice, and then turned the handle before stepping into the room with his head sufficiently bowed.

"Master, the Hayyothalan has sent news. He and the daemon have discovered a startling fact about the girl," offered Grehssil, tightly clasping his hands in front of himself to keep them from shaking.

The Master growled a low throaty sound that raised the scant hairs on Grehssil's arms. "This had better be great news to warrant this interruption, you worthless creature." Darnathian looked up from the ancient tome he had been searching through, his eyes glowing bright amber as he stared at the servant. "Well, I'm not getting any younger here, Grehssil."

The servant took a hesitant breath and then nervously blurted out, "She commands the power of the Spectrescope."

"*What?*" bellowed Darnathian, erupting from his chair and knocking the book to the floor. "No! The Hayyothalan is wrong! Only a Sho-are can command the power of the scope! She is a mere human girl, how can she— unless she is from the ancient lineage of Issachar!" he screamed. Flailing his arms, he sent an energy bolt of blue-green at the servant. Grehssil, dropping to the floor, narrowly missed being blasted to smithereens. The bolt hit the chamber door, charring the old wood. Grehssil scrambled across the floor to hide in front of the Master's desk, out of view. The blackened timber smoldered, wafting a pungent odor into the air.

Shaking with rage, Darnathian paced the room. The fire in the grate burned furiously, leaping into the room and raising the temperature by several dozen degrees. "That crafty old fox thinks he can still outwit me," he muttered, his hands clenching and unclenching rapidly. "The girl is going to be more difficult to eliminate than originally planned, but I will eliminate her, just like all the others before her. They had their special tools, too, but never the Spectrescope. That has remained hidden for millennia or more. If she has the scope and its power, she is indeed special," groused Darnathian as he stopped his pacing to stand behind the desk again.

"Grehssil, I need you to—where are you, you spineless jellyfish?" roared Darnathian, glancing about the room.

A shaking hand floated up from in front of the desk as a tiny voice squeaked, "Here, Master."

"Get up, you fool. I need you to retrieve something for me," said Darnathian with an evil smile. "Then, once you have my special tool, give it to the Hayyothalan."

*   *   *   *

Lucy was up early the following day. She straightened her bed, tidied her room, showered, dressed, and went downstairs to the kitchen. Mom wasn't up yet. She had the kitchen to herself, so she quickly went about making breakfast.

She rinsed the coffee carafe and put several heaping scoops of flavored ground coffee in the maker. After adding the right amount of cold water, she closed the top, put the carafe into the maker, and turned it on.

She took out several eggs along with a carton of cream from the refrigerator and placed them on the counter. She pulled the frying pan from under the cooktop, put it on a burner, and turned it on to simmer. Dropping a glop of butter in the pan, she swirled it around, watching it melt.

Retrieving two bowls from the cupboard, she carefully cracked the eggs, dripping their contents into one bowl and placing the empty shells in the other. After adding a short pour of cream, a little salt, and pepper, followed by frantic whisking, Lucy had the egg mixture ready for the frying pan.

The comforting aroma of coffee, scrambled eggs, and toast filled the kitchen. Lucy poured orange juice into glasses and set them on the counter. Lucy removed the eggs from the burner as her mom padded sleepily into the kitchen, wearing a cotton robe and matching slippers.

"What's all this?" She yawned, took a mug from the wooden cup holder on the counter, and filled it with coffee.

"Well, I've been in so much trouble recently, I thought maybe a little thoughtfulness might be nice," said Lucy tentatively.

"Well, it is a pleasant change not having to make breakfast for once. Thanks, honey."

"You're welcome. Thanks for not grounding me for life. I truly am sorry for what happened at Schuyler's house. I don't know how I can make it right, and I miss her so. Maybe I can get a job somewhere."

"You place too much time and energy in your fantasy world. You can't live in a fantasy and the real world at the same time. Life doesn't work that way. The sooner you learn that, the better."

"I know," Lucy replied, watching her settle into a chair at the table. "Mom, do you believe there is an invisible world? I mean, invisible beings existing right alongside us in our world? Just because we can't see something, it doesn't mean it doesn't exist, does it?" Lucy gently asked.

"Luce, if you can't see it, it just ain't real. Learn that already, okay?" griped Mom.

"Yes, Mom," Lucy softly replied. "Ready for scrambled eggs and toast? I warmed up the honey." She scooped up eggs onto a plate, then added toast with butter and a drizzle of honey. After giving the plate to her mom, she filled one for herself and joined her at the table.

"I'm sorry, Luce," her mom continued after Lucy had taken a bite of toast, and with a sigh, she set down her coffee cup. "I guess I am a little hard on you sometimes. It's just that you're so much like your father, believing in ghosts and spirits and whatever fantasy that comes along. I don't want you to grow up believing a lie." She took another sip of her coffee.

"But, what if I do believe it?" asked Lucy, sitting up straighter. Wow, this was a first, her mom opening up a little bit. "What if I really am a ghost hunter, and spirits are real, and, like a different dimension exists right next to ours, and they are connected somehow."

"Then I would say I'm locking you in your room and calling a counselor to talk sense into you!" Mom snapped back, slamming down the coffee cup and splashing its contents onto the table.

Lucy pinched her lips. "Okay then, good talk," she whispered, looking down at her plate to avoid the stern look on her mom's face. They ate the rest of their breakfast in silence.

"May I go to the library this afternoon? I would like to read that new vampire book. Would that be okay?" asked Lucy.

"If you get your chores done, yeah, I guess that's okay. I will be working late at the office. I'm organizing the upcoming company sales meeting, so I may not be home when you get back. Dale will be home tonight. Just don't go bothering the Williams family. I think it best if we give them a little time to calm down, if possible," said Mom. She walked over to the cooktop for a second scoop of scrambled eggs. "I didn't know you knew how to cook eggs. They taste good."

"Thanks," said Lucy with a wry smile.

Together, they cleared the table, putting dishes in the dishwasher. Lucy made a plate of scrambled eggs and toast for Dale and left it on the counter. Mom grabbed another mug of coffee and muttering, "Just like her father," she headed down the hall and disappeared into the office to pay bills.

Lucy finished her chores quickly. After dusting and vacuuming, she packed away the vacuum sweeper, put the furniture polish back in the cupboard, and checked the newly washed windows for any streaks. Satisfied, she turned toward the stairs. A fluttering noise outside the open window at the foot of the stairs made her stop. A flock of blackbirds was sitting on the power lines across the street. Lucy gaped at the large grouping and then sprinted up the stairs.

Pulling her bedroom curtains back, she peeked out the window. More birds gathered on the wires and in nearby trees, watching the front of the house.

In the center of the grouping was a large black bird, much bigger than the others, looking toward the house. Malpar!

12 Discoveries

Anxiously, Lucy grabbed her backpack from the bottom desk drawer. She peeked out the window again, shut the bedroom door, and crossed the hallway to the back stairs.

"Hey, what's up, Squirt?" Dale asked, coming up the back stairs eating a cookie.

"I'm going to the library. You?" Lucy asked, hoping to keep her voice steady. She passed Dale and skipped quickly down the steps.

"Rock climbing."

Lucy stopped and turned abruptly, holding tight to the railing to keep from stumbling back down the stairs. "Rock climbing?" she asked. "Seriously? When did you take up rock climbing?"

"When they hired a cute new girl at that big sporting goods store out near the mall," Dale replied with a smirk. His eyebrows danced on his forehead.

"Go figure. Well, don't break anything when you fall off the wall," Lucy retorted.

"Yeah, right, you're in more danger of all those rickety old book racks falling on you!" Dale shot back.

"I'm not worried about the books. I'm worried about the birds," said Lucy as she ran down the stairs.

"Huh?" Dale said, frowning. *Girls. Whatever.* He disappeared into his room and shut the door.

Lucy stuck her head in the office doorway. "Going to the library now! Love you, Mom!"

"Don't be gone long. You're still grounded until you're twenty-three!" Mom yelled back at her. Lucy sighed and rolled her eyes.

She quietly opened the kitchen door and slipped outside. Crouching low, Lucy made her way behind the bushes at the back of the house, frequently peeking through the branches at the birds sitting on the power lines in front of the house as she cautiously made her way through the backyard. Staying close to the neighbor's garage to keep out of sight, she crawled into the bushes along the yard's back. The bank dropped sharply down, creating a hill that was nearly impossible to climb.

From here, Lucy could look down on the next street. The houses sat about twenty feet lower because the road cut into the side of a large hill. Lucy's house was on top of the mound, while the neighbors behind were at the bottom.

Following the embankment and pushing through the bushes, the branches picked at her clothing and scratched her skin. Despite the discomfort, she crept behind a neighbor's garage to a well-worn path on top of the ridge. It led to another path between the houses where the street leveled out.

Keeping low and using the scrubby bushes as cover, Lucy hurried along the following path. She glanced around to see if anyone had followed and then ran furiously up the street, the backpack bouncing wildly on her shoulder. When she reached Maple Street hill, she turned and headed toward the library.

Schuyler was waiting, sitting on a bench in front of the library. She stood and waved when she saw Lucy.

"Get inside, now!" Lucy panted as she ran toward Schuyler. "Being watched!"

"Huh?" said Schuyler.

Lucy grabbed a hand and jerked Schuyler off the bench, running toward the buildings double doors and dragging her friend behind. Pulling hard on the heavy door, it opened slowly, and they ducked inside. Lucy stood panting in front of the checkout desk. The clerk frowned and stared at them.

"Malpar is back," Lucy panted. "He was watching the house just now." Pulling a small bottle of water from the backpack, she took a sip before continuing.

"What?" Schuyler's mouth fell open.

"No food or drink allowed in the library!" barked the desk clerk. Lucy took another swallow before capping and putting the water bottle back in the pack, scowling at the clerk as she zipped it.

"How did you get away? Do you think he saw you?" Schuyler whispered.

"I snuck out of the house and took the old path between the houses on the ridge. He was sitting on the power lines in front of the house when I left. He had a bunch of feathered friends with him."

"That is kind of scary. The last meeting we had wasn't so pleasant. We'll have to be careful when we leave here."

"Shh!" hissed the clerk sternly, scowling at the girls. Schuyler pursed her lips as she glared back at the desk clerk and, grabbing Lucy's hand, led her to their usual corner in the history section. It was the best place to sit and talk. They plopped down and sat cross-legged on the floor.

"Malpar came to see me last night. He tried to reason with me why I should give up the Spectrescope," explained Lucy. "He was speechless when I called him a Hayyothalan. It was as though he had forgotten. He was shocked I even knew about the Hayyothalans. And his attitude changed like he was sorry he was doing this to us. He said his Master would eventually get the Spectrescope and we would be dead."

"What? Ew! I don't like the sound of that at all!" exclaimed Schuyler, eyes huge. "If he was sorry, why is he still doing it?"

"I think he has to do it, or his Master will do something terrible to him."

"Then why stay with this Master? Why not run away?"

"I don't think he has a choice. I believe he has to stay and do what his Master wants," Lucy said. "The Master must have some kind of power over him."

"Who is this Master, I wonder?" Schuyler mused, fidgeting with the bracelet.

"It's the guy we saw in the mirror," Lucy offered. She pulled two pieces of hard candy from the backpack, handed one to Schuyler, and then popped the other into her mouth. The butter caramel was her favorite.

"The tall guy in the white suit? After seeing what he was able to do, no wonder Malpar is scared of him. He must be an evil wizard or something," Schuyler reasoned.

"Yeah, evil wizard," Lucy replied, thinking. "I asked Iam if he knew who he was, and then he explained the guy in the suit is the Dark Prince named Darnathian. Remember? Iam warned us about him. He wants the Spectrescope because of its ancient magic. Iam also said it is one of two keys that open a gate somewhere, and in the wrong hands, it will have devastating effects. What the heck does that even mean? Yeah, Iam knows more than he's letting on."

"Why wouldn't he just tell you?" Schuyler asked. "You're the ghost hunter the Spectrescope selected. If anyone needs to know what the devastating effects would be, it's you."

"I don't know. Iam told me a story about Malpar, the Hayyothalans, and a Prince. The Prince wanted to be King and tried to turn the Hayyothalans against the real King. The King was heartbroken and eventually banished the Prince and his followers from the kingdom. Malpar is a Hayyothalan. The guy in the mirror is the Prince. So who is the High King, and where is he? That's what I'd like to know."

"Malpar did say something about Iam as a High King. But that doesn't make sense, does it? He's the vendor from the flea market," whispered Schuyler, slowly flipping through a history book she'd pulled off a lower shelf. If the desk clerk checked on them, it would look as though they were discussing history. "But, Prince or High King, I think they are both wizards of some kind since they can manipulate things and disappear as they do."

"I agree. Mom thinks I was going to the library to get a book, so we don't have much time," Lucy said, searching through the backpack and handing Schuyler several pages. "Here is the information I downloaded from the ancestry website. I think we need to see Jerome Stewart. He was on the Stewart family tree, and he still lives nearby. Maybe he can tell us the story of Darwin and Helena Stewart."

"Do you think he can help us?" asked Schuyler. "It's a bit of a long shot, isn't it? I mean, my mom and dad don't know that much about our ancestors. They never really thought much about them till Mom came across an old photograph in a family Bible. No one knew who the people were." Schuyler paused to put the book back on the shelf.

"Well, it's worth a try. It may be a long shot, but anything Jerome can tell us has got to help," Lucy said. She shrugged into the backpack and headed toward the door.

"Uh, Luce?" asked Schuyler. "Aren't you forgetting something?"

"What?"

"You're supposed to get a book from the library, remember?" Schuyler snickered, pursing her lips.

"Oh, yeah! I forgot," Lucy sheepishly replied as she headed toward the help desk.

"Excuse me! Do you have that vampire book everyone is talking about?" she asked the still-scowling desk clerk.

"Yes, we do. I just put a copy back on the shelf. I'll get it for you. One moment, please," the librarian curtly replied and went to retrieve the book.

"Vampires? Really?" asked Schuyler, a quizzical look on her face.

"What? Did you think I was going to read a ghost story?" Lucy said, grinning.

*   *   *   *

The old house was a two-story Victorian built around the turn of the century. The porch was large and deep with decorative moldings and corbels typical of that style of home. The paint was peeling in places, giving it a shabby-chic allure. Summer flowers bloomed around the yard in abundance, their colors brilliant against a neatly groomed green lawn.

Lucy and Schuyler walked up the narrow brick walk toward the front steps. Lucy stopped suddenly. Schuyler bumped into her.

"What if he won't talk to us?" asked Lucy. "I mean, how do you ask someone about their relatives? I can't say, 'Oh, by the way, I think Darwin is haunting my friend and me.'"

"We'll think of something. Go on, ring the bell," Schuyler prodded. She pushed Lucy up the porch steps toward the front door.

"Yeah, okay." Lucy saw the front door was open, allowing a warm, yeasty aroma to drift through the screen door and past her nose.

"Oh, that's a good sign," piped Schuyler. "There's nothing more welcoming than the fragrance of freshly baked bread!" She leaned closer to the door and breathed in the delicious fragrance.

Lucy rolled her eyes. "You and your stomach," said Lucy, shaking her head. "Well, here goes." She pressed the doorbell.

A spritely old gentleman appeared at the door, wearing a white shirt and gray trousers. He smiled when he saw the girls. "Hello," he greeted them kindly. "How can I help you girls today?" He opened the screened door. His gray hair stuck up all over his head.

"Um, hello, are you Mr. Jerome Stewart?" asked Lucy. The gentleman smiled, nodding his head. "My name is Lucy, and this is my friend, Schuyler," she began, smiling shyly. "I found your name on the ancestry website message board, and we were wondering if we could talk to you about Darwin and Helena Stewart. They were ancestors of yours, weren't they?"

The old gentlemen appeared slightly confused. "You want to know about Darwin and Helena? How do you come to know their names? I thought you were selling magazines or cookies," he said. "Are you doing a research project or something?"

"Well, no. We both live in Stewart Heights. We've noticed many of the street names refer to the Stewart family. When we were in Maple Hill Cemetery recently, we saw the headstones of Darwin and Helena Stewart," explained Lucy, a tremor of apprehension flitting across her face. "We were wondering if they are relatives of yours if you could tell us more about them."

"Really now? A couple of history buffs, huh? It's refreshing to see young people take an interest in the history around them. Why don't you girls take a seat there on the veranda? I'll ask Mrs. Stewart to bring us out some refreshments. How does that sound to you young ladies?" Mr. Stewart asked, a big friendly smile on his wrinkled face.

"Oh, we don't want to impose on you, sir," said Lucy.

"Nonsense! We're glad to have the company," he insisted. He disappeared into the house. "Marian," he called out, "we have visitors."

There were two large wrought iron sofas, side chairs, and a coffee table. Lucy and Schuyler sat on one of the couches. Mr. and Mrs. Stewart appeared shortly, carrying trays of lemonade and lemon tart bar cookies. Lucy suddenly realized it had been hours since she had eaten.

After the introductions had been made and the drinks and cookies passed around, Lucy hesitantly spoke.

"Mr. Stewart, we saw their names on the gravestones, so I looked for Darwin and Helena Stewart on the ancestry website. That's where I saw your posting and wondered if you could tell us about them. We thought it so sad that both their children died. Did they ever have other children? Are the streets named after them?"

"It is such a pleasant surprise to know history is still interesting to the young." He pushed his glasses back up on his nose. "Darwin was my great-great-uncle on my father's side of the family. He was quite a prosperous landowner. They say Darwin helped many families settle in the area and become landowners themselves. He had nearly a thousand acres of land on which he farmed wheat and corn, but the property's mainstay was the sawmill. There were numerous furniture factories in Grand River Valley back then," Jerome expounded. "He also operated a carriage house for travelers, which was like a motel in those days."

"He was married later in life to a beautiful young woman named Helena," he continued. "Together, they had two children, a son, Arlan, who died before his first birthday, and a daughter, Dorcas, who died around the age of seven or eight, I think. She took ill with a fever. Records show it was a hard winter that year. Many of the neighboring families lost loved ones due to illness. Darwin and Helena never had any more children." Jerome paused long enough to take a swig of lemonade.

"You have to remember, dearie, they didn't have medicines back then like they do today. When someone took an illness, it was a solemn thing," Marian Stewart chimed in.

Lucy grinned. Mrs. Stewart seemed very genuine and kind, though her voice was high pitched and nasally. It made Lucy want to giggle. She was glad Mrs. Stewart didn't talk often.

"Darwin died in 1864 of something called consumption," Schuyler interjected.

"Tuberculosis," said Mr. Stewart. He shifted his portly frame in the chair. "Darwin enlisted in the Michigan regiment of the Union army, where he was assigned to the medical unit to help attend to the wounded. He became sick with tuberculosis shortly after enlisting. He died during the winter of 1864."

"The community," interjected Mrs. Stewart, "named several streets after him and his family. Darwin and Stewart are two such streets. They named Hamilton Street after his brother, my husband's great-great-grand-father. They were both very successful businessmen."

Mr. Stewart nodded. "Darwin's wife, Helena, tried to keep the carriage house open and run the farm herself, but she died suddenly," he continued. "Some folks thought Helena was heartbroken over her husband's death, and others believed her to be grief-stricken over her children. My father believed she died in childbirth. There's no way to know for sure because of poorly kept birth records. Most likely, it was influenza of some sort."

"What kind of man was Darwin? Do you think he was a kind person?" Lucy asked.

"He seems to have been esteemed by the community to have had the honor of streets named after him," said Mr. Stewart. "Let me ponder a moment." He tapped a finger against his temple. "I think he served on the city council and the board of directors for the bank, isn't that right, Mrs. Stewart?"

"I believe so, dearie," chirped Mrs. Stewart.

"He was also instrumental in bringing the railroad into town," continued Jerome. "If the railroad hadn't come to the area, industry and the growth would have been affected. So, yes, I think he must have been an honorable individual."

"Could Helena have had another child without anyone knowing? Someone must have known about it. What do you think happened to it?" Schuyler asked.

"I really don't know. I doubt those stories were true. If Helena did have a child, it might have died with her in childbirth. If the child lived, Hamilton Stewart would have been the baby's legal guardian as Darwin's next of kin. Helena didn't have any other family that we know of. I don't think there ever was a child," said Mr. Stewart, shaking his head. "You've never found anything about a child on that website, have you dear?" Mr. Stewart said, addressing his wife.

"No, never, not one mention of any orphaned baby in the family histories, dearie," replied Mrs. Stewart.

"You don't think he would haunt someone, do you?" asked Lucy, hesitantly.

Mr. Stewart suddenly looked bewildered. "Haunt someone? You mean like a ghost?" He looked from Lucy to Schuyler. "Do you think my Uncle Darwin is haunting someone? Is that what you came here to find out?" he asked, his voice rising rather heatedly. "You're looking to hear ghost stories?"

"Honestly, Mr. Stewart," Lucy said quickly, "we didn't know what to expect when we came here. Schuyler's house sits on land we think belonged to Darwin Stewart, and there's a ghost in her house who looks like the man in the photo of Darwin and Helena." Lucy shrugged. "We're just trying to figure this all out."

"We don't know what to expect or what we should do," said Schuyler earnestly. "We were hoping for any information that might help us make the ghost go away."

"You've got yourselves quite a problem. I'd say you both have overactive imaginations. That's what I think," Jerome said with a laugh. "We've had quite an entertaining afternoon, haven't we, Marian? Just imagine! Darwin is a ghost! Maybe you girls shouldn't go exploring through cemeteries again anytime soon."

"I think our young guests are quite serious, Jerome. I don't think I would want anyone's ghost living in my house either," said Mrs. Stewart, her brown eyes twinkling in a slightly wrinkled face. "Why don't you take the trays into the kitchen, dearie?"

Mr. Stewart grunted, picked up the food trays, and carried them into the house. He chuckled to himself as he disappeared into the kitchen.

"I wouldn't pay him any mind," Mrs. Stewart whispered to the girls. "We never knew much about his ancestors until I signed up for that website. I never told him what else I found out about his great-great-uncle, the honorable Darwin Stewart," she said, clucking her tongue. "He was a spiritualist. You might want to do a little research on that next time you go to the library."

Lucy gaped at Mrs. Stewart. "How did you know we were just at the library?"

Mrs. Stewart smiled and pointed to the library card peeking out of Lucy's pocket.

"Oh, yeah," Lucy laughed, impressed that Mrs. Stewart was so observant. "What is a spiritualist, anyway? Is it someone who believes in ghosts?"

"They not only believe in ghosts and spirits, but they also believe they can talk to them," replied Mrs. Stewart. "Darwin Stewart used to hold séances in hopes of contacting his first wife, Daphne. Helena was his second wife." She winked at Schuyler.

"His second wife? We didn't find any other gravestones with the name of Stewart. Where would Daphne be buried?" Lucy asked.

"No one knows. There were no photos or records of Daphne. I only found a brief reference of her. Otherwise, we also wouldn't have known about her," replied Mrs. Stewart. "Darwin Stewart was childless and much older than Helena. Men often married younger women so they could have children. Most likely, he wanted an heir to his estate."

"So, with no living children, who would have inherited his estate? Hamilton Stewart?"

"Hamilton Stewart most likely, or perhaps it was simply dispersed if there wasn't a will," said Mrs. Stewart. She leaned toward Lucy and put a hand on Schuyler's shoulder, pulling her close.

"I happen to believe in ghosts too. And I want to warn you. If Darwin Stewart held séances trying to contact his dead wife, he could have opened a portal to the other side. It could be very dangerous for you. Maybe you should just leave the ghost alone; it might go away and never bother you again."

"Somehow, I think it's here to stay for a while. I am glad you told us about the Stewarts. Maybe what you told us can help."

"I hope so. You're both such sweet girls. I hate to think you have a ghost haunting either of you. Do be careful, okay?" Mrs. Stewart hugged each of them.

"Thank you, Mrs. Stewart. I'm delighted to have met you. Thanks for the treats! They were delicious!" Lucy walked over to the screened door. "Goodbye, Mr. Stewart! Thank you for talking to us," she yelled through the screen.

"Goodbye, girls. If you see my great-great-uncle Darwin, tell him I said, 'Hello!' Darwin and Helena, ghosts! Heh, heh, heh," came the muffled retort.

They could hear Mr. Stewart laughing loudly in the kitchen. Lucy looked sheepishly at Schuyler as they left the porch and waved goodbye to Mrs. Stewart. In a nearby tree, a large black crow eyed them warily.

*   *   *   *

"So, what now? Do another computer search for Daphne?" Schuyler asked. They were on their way back to the library. The sky was getting dark, and storm clouds were rolling in and hiding the sun, making the horizon a weird shade of purple tinged with green.

"I'm not sure. What if Helena had a child, but it also died in childbirth? Maybe that's why the ghost is still here. He's looking for Helena's child," Lucy replied.

"Okay, I suppose it could explain the creepy guy."

"Have you seen him since the other night?"

"No, thank goodness. I haven't slept much either," squeaked Schuyler, glancing at the darkening sky. "We'd better hurry. I think it's going to storm." She started to run just as large pellets of rain began hitting the ground.

"Let's go to my house. It is closer. You can hang out there till the rain lets up. Mom is at work, and Dale is at the mall rock climbing," Lucy yelled through the increasing rain. She ran as fast as she could toward home. The rain came down harder and drummed loudly on the pavement.

"Rock climbing?" said Schuyler.

"Don't ask," came the caustic reply.

The girls burst through the back door and stood dripping water on the kitchen floor. The backpack landed on a chair at the counter. They kicked off their soggy sneakers before Lucy ran upstairs to grab a dry shirt for herself and an extra one for Schuyler.

Lucy took clean towels from the dryer in the laundry room, handing one to Schuyler so they could dry their hair. After they dried themselves off, Lucy put the dripping sneakers into the dryer to thump and thud as they tumbled. The wet tops landed in the laundry basket of dirty clothes.

No one was home. Metrocom, usually a relaxed cat, was crouching under a chair in the dining room with his back arched.

"Metrocom! Hey buddy, what are you doing under the chair?" said Lucy. She knelt on the floor to coax him out of his hiding place.

"Rrreow!" the cat hissed. It streaked into the living room, taking refuge behind the couch.

"What's up with the cat?" Schuyler watched as Metrocom's tail disappeared behind the couch.

"I don't know. I've never seen him act this way before." Lucy followed the cat into the living room. "Metrocom! Come on, sweetie, it's just Schuyler and me. Why are you so scared?" Lucy climbed on the couch and peered over the back cushions. The cat's tail slithered like a snake along the floor, disappearing under the sofa. A muffled "rrreow" followed.

"So weird. I wonder what got his fur up?" said Lucy. She jumped off the couch, turned towards Schuyler, and shrugged her shoulders. "Let's grab something to eat. We can do a computer search later. I'm hungry."

"What's on the menu?" Schuyler asked, climbing into a chair at the kitchen counter.

"Hmm, not sure," said Lucy as she opened the refrigerator door. "Um, let's see. We have leftover cold chicken from last night's dinner and some fruit salad. The salad is delicious. I made it!" she said, taking the plate of cold chicken and a container of salad from the refrigerator.

"Oh, bravo! Cheerio and all. Just pat yourself on the back, girlfriend!" Schuyler laughed. She squiggled the chair to the counter and leaned on her elbows, clasping her hands in front of her.

"Well, it is good!" Lucy whined. The plates chinked as she took them from the cupboard.

Behind her, the knob on the basement door turned slowly.

"Whose recipe did you use?"

"My own. I kind of make things up as I go. It's really delicious. I used orange gelatin and orange juice instead of cold water, shredded carrot, some fresh pineapple, and freshly grated ginger for a little spice." Grabbing a large serving spoon from the utensil drawer, she liberally heaped the orange carrot salad on the plates. "Then, when it thickens, I mix in a little salad dressing and whipped cream and let it chill for a couple of hours, and voila! A yummy dessert salad!" Lucy said with a flourish, dropping a cherry on top of each salad.

The basement doorknob clicked open.

"Good job, Lucy! My mom would be proud of you," Schuyler said. She admired the plate Lucy placed in front of her. "I'm challenged in the cooking department. I'd probably put too much of something in the gelatin, and it would never set up. It would be gelatin soup!" She laughed at herself as she leaned forward in the chair. She scratched at the itchy skin under the bracelet.

A small squeak echoed through the kitchen.

"Your mom is such a good cook. All you need to do is watch her. You'll pick it up eventually," Lucy said with a grin. They giggled.

The basement door slowly inched open. Lucy plunked down in the counter chair next to Schuyler, pulling the plate of honey-baked chicken across the counter, and began filling up her plate. "Pass the honey and bread, please." Busy devouring their lunch, they did not notice the basement door creeping open.

"It's getting quite dark outside," said Schuyler, glancing outside the kitchen window. She helped herself to a second serving of chicken. As they ate, the wind outside whipped up and slashed the bushes against the house. Soon rain pelted at the glass and blew in through the open window, dousing the counter in water.

The Ghost of Darwin Stewart

"Oh no!" Lucy cried, pushing back from the counter and running to close the window. "Help me? Mom usually leaves a few windows open to air out the house. You check the living room, and I'll go shut the windows upstairs."

"Done!" said Schuyler, hurrying through the kitchen and dining room, checking windows as she went. The living room windows were all shut. "Any other rooms you want me to check?" she yelled up the front stairs.

"No, she never leaves the windows open at the back of the house unless it's an upstairs window," Lucy answered, coming down the front stairs. "She's too afraid someone will crawl through the back windows to rob the house. Those windows don't even open. They're nailed shut."

"Seriously? How would you get out in a fire? Break a window?"

"Probably. Let's finish lunch," Lucy said, heading back to the kitchen.

"Hey, Luce? Was that door open before?" Schuyler asked, pointing at the open basement door.

"I don't know. It's normal, though. It creeps open when the wind blows hard. Drafty old house," she said, slapping the basement door and slamming it shut. "Want some lemonade?" She opened the refrigerator door, removed a large pitcher of fresh lemonade with sliced lemons floating on top, and set it on the counter.

"Uh, Luce, my bracelet is getting tight," whimpered Schuyler, pulling at the bracelet. "Ouch!"

Lucy opened the glass front door of the cupboard and froze. She saw the creepy ghost from Schuyler's house reflected in the glass. He stood in front of the basement door, his face twisted in a leering grin as he stared back at her. Then the ghost became a dark, swirling mist.

"Schuyler! Run!" Lucy grabbed the backpack, her shaking hand struggling with the zipper.

The shield erupted from the bracelet. The chair toppled to the floor as Schuyler jumped. The mist swirled angrily through the kitchen as the girls took refuge behind the shield. The ghost shot up the back stairs.

"Quick! Lucy! The Spectrescope!" Schuyler shouted. Lucy pulled it from its pocket and followed the ghost. The backpack landed on the stair with a thud.

The second floor was much colder than the living room. When the girls got to the top of the stairs, they saw no sign of the ghost or its mist.

"I don't see anything!" Lucy cried.

"You don't see anything? It's got to be here!" Schuyler said.

"I don't see anything in the scope! Maybe it's not working."

"Maybe you're using it wrong."

"What do you mean I'm using it wrong? You look into it, and it shows what you need to see!"

"Keep trying! I only meant maybe you should look for anything weird. It has to be here somewhere," said Schuyler, looking cautiously around the landing for the dark mist or any other manifestation.

"Got it! There's a weird purply glow in the scope. It went down the hall toward my room. It's almost like an afterglow, but it's not the mist itself, whatever it is," Lucy said, pointing down the hallway. The bedroom doors were all slightly ajar.

They quietly made their way toward Lucy's room. The door was open, but the space was empty. The mist was gone.

"What was that thing? Is your house haunted now too?" asked Schuyler. She lowered the arm with the shield.

"It was the ghost of Darwin Stewart. I saw his reflection in the glass cupboard door just before he morphed. He must already have been here and spooked the cat. Where did he go? The glow I saw in the scope faded away." Lucy swept the room with the Spectrescope. "This room is freezing. Could he still be here somewhere?"

The closet door suddenly burst open. A blast of sulfuric air whipped past Lucy's face, flipping tendrils of hair across her cheek. A faint whisper followed the stinky blast swirling around her, pushing at her and trying to knock her down.

"What the!" Lucy cried. She swatted wildly at the air around her. "Do you see anything?"

"I don't see it, but I can hear something. It sounds like whispering. Can you hear it?"

"Lucy, you must give us the Spectrescope!" came the breathy whisper a second time. A foul-smelling air swirled around her face, touching her skin like a feather. She shivered.

"It wants the scope," Lucy said. "No! Go away and stay away! I won't give it to you *ever*!" she yelled at the ghost.

Crack! Lightning flashed through the windows, blinding their eyes. The thunder rumbled loudly, shaking the whole house.

Another flash of lightning flickered on the ghost standing in solid form across the room, glaring at them. "Give us the Spectrescope, and we'll leave you alone. What good will it be to you after we scare you to death," the ghost growled, holding his hand out for the Spectrescope.

Lucy stepped in front of Schuyler. She pulled the magnifying head from the handle and slipped it into her pocket. The sword flowed molten from the handle, growing upward until it stood gleaming in its entire length. Lucy held it firmly in both hands, brandishing it, ready to swing at the ghost.

"Oh, so brave now that you have your pretty little sword. You do not scare me," the ghost sneered. "I'm not afraid of a little girl." He morphed again, this time into a dark purple mist. Swirling violently around the girls, he flowed from the room into the hallway and along the floor.

Lucy ran after him, holding the sword in front of her. She found him at the end of the hallway near the back staircase. Schuyler huffed up behind her with the shield held high, her hand on Zazriel.

"Ha, ha, ha," the ghost laughed, sounding like an old car coughing and sputtering. He morphed into the solid form of Darwin Stewart. "Can't catch me, you can't catch me," he taunted.

A sound made Lucy turn. Malpar stood behind them, hissing and trapping them between the two spirits.

"Now what to do, I wonder," said the ghost. "Things aren't working out for you, are they, stupid girl."

The lightning continued to flash outside, and heavy rain pinged incessantly against the windowpanes. Lucy swung the sword at the ghost, catching his lapel with its tip. The spirit disappeared entirely. She carefully stepped backward, looking from side to side for the ghost, but couldn't find him.

Schuyler was holding Malpar back with the shield. Each time he tried to advance toward them, she blocked his view and his way past. He did not attempt to hurt her, only to get past her to Lucy and the Spectrescope.

He made one more attempt to pass her when Schuyler lunged at him.

"Aaargh!" Schuyler shrieked. With her fingers tightly gripping the shield's hand strap and the other hand on the outer edge, she ran toward Malpar.

"Squawk!" yelled Malpar, surprised by Schuyler's bold move. He morphed into his bird form and flew into one of the bedrooms. Lucy and Schuyler charged after him, but the room was empty.

Back in the hallway, the girls were alone, the atmosphere vibrating as the thunder continued booming around them. Slowly, they lowered their weapons and waited, listening. They didn't say anything for several moments.

"That was interesting," Lucy finally said. "Darwin Stewart isn't bound to the house. I thought ghosts only haunted a place that held meaning for them." The sword liquefied back into the handle, and she put the head back on it. "I guess maybe our house could be on the old Stewart property too. We never checked the records for this house."

"Yeah, I was thinking of that. The Stewarts did own a lot of property, so it's possible. Do you think maybe he's bound to the property and not just to our house?" Schuyler asked, still holding the shield for the moment.

"I don't know. I'll ask Iam when I see him. He should know," Lucy said. She turned to go downstairs. "We should check the rest of the house to make sure they're gone. Then we can finish lunch."

"Do you think they've gone back to my house?" Schuyler asked hesitantly, still standing in the hallway. "I'd hate to think Mom and Dad are home alone with two creepy spirits in the house."

"There's no way of telling. We know they'll keep trying to get the Spectrescope, but who knows what they'll do next."

A chilling rush of acrid air swept around the girls suddenly, followed by a vast cloud of smoke and ash pushing at them. "Oh! Here we go again," cried Schuyler, holding up the shield.

Covering her eyes against the smelly cloud, Lucy stepped backward and landed on Schuyler's foot. Twisting her ankle, she fell awkwardly into Schuyler, and they crashed to the floor. Lucy banged her head hard on the floor as the Spectrescope flew from her hand and skidded across the hallway floor. The girls lay tangled together as the cloud separated into two separate forms.

"Oh, this wasn't nearly any fun at all," the ghost lamented. He stood between them and the Spectrescope. "There you go, Malpar, pick up the Spectrescope and deliver it to your Master. I'll stay here and have a little more fun with the ghost hunters!" laughed Darwin Stewart heartily.

Malpar looked at the scope lying on the floor. Slowly, he walked over to where it lay and bent to pick it up.

"No! Malpar, please don't do it!" cried Lucy. She struggled to her feet, reached a hand to help Schuyler, and looked anxiously at the bird-man. "Darnathian mustn't get the scope. It would be horrible! Remember the High King, Malpar? What would he want you to do?"

Malpar's hand faltered.

Lucy saw a faint tremor of his hand before he reached out and grasped the handle of the Spectrescope. He stood holding it, a look of reverence on his face as he studied the symbols on the handle.

His hand began trembling uncontrollably. "What is happening?" Malpar cried, dropping the scope to the floor. The Spectrescope glowed molten red before returning to a golden glow.

"My hand is burned! It burned my hand!" he screamed, holding his blistered hand by the wrist to control the trembling. "The pain! Make it stop!" A foul odor like singed leather filled the hallway.

"Shut up, you fool!" the ghost yelled at Malpar. "So, the legend is true! Enchantments protect it, and the protector must freely give it to cancel the spells. Before this is over, you will give us the Spectrescope, you wretched little girl. Of your own free will, you shall give it to us!" The ghost stepped forward, grabbed Malpar by the arm, morphed them both into smoke, and disappeared through the wall.

"Oh, Lucy! What're we going to do?" said Schuyler, shaking. The encounter with the two spirits had left her more than a little rattled.

"I can't believe I dropped the Spectrescope! Stupid, stupid! What would we have done if they had gotten it?" Lucy chided herself, bending to pick it up. "That would have been bad, very bad."

"They didn't get it, and that's all that counts," said Schuyler, pressing the stone. The shield morphed back into the bracelet. "You can't blame your-self. It was an accident you tripped and fell."

"It shouldn't have happened at all! Iam warned me I have to protect the Spectrescope. I've got be ready next time."

"Why did the scope burn Malpar now?" Schuyler asked. "He grabbed it when we were in the cemetery, but it didn't burn him then. Today, his burns were deep."

"I was still holding it, remember? Then it broke into two pieces. Maybe that's why it didn't burn him. It must be enchanted or something. The ghost and Malpar couldn't take it. I must give it. But I would never give it to them. They must know that."

"Of course they know it, Luce. It also means they will have to persuade you somehow to give them the scope."

"I'll never give them the scope, no matter what!" declared Lucy.

"You shouldn't say that," Schuyler scolded. "You don't know what they will do or what they are capable of doing. You may not have a choice."

"I know." Lucy sighed, sagging against the wall. "But Iam is counting on me to keep it safe. It is part of a key, and there's always a choice," she said quietly. "You gotta go home. Go check on your mom and dad." She turned and tromped down the stairs.

"Wait! What if they come back? You heard what the ghost said. They expect to have the Spectrescope soon. You need me here to help you," Schuyler retorted, following Lucy down the stairs.

"What I need is time to figure this thing out," Lucy said, walking into the kitchen. "We still don't even know how to get rid of them." She threw her hands up in the air. "Does *any* of the stuff the Stewarts told us help? Maybe it has nothing to do with it at all. I just don't know!"

Lucy sat down at the counter and rubbed her temples. "I don't know what to do. It's not like the Spectrescope came with an instruction booklet. I need to talk to Iam, but he keeps disappearing before I can ask him anything," she said, giving Schuyler a worried look. "You need to check on your mom and dad. Whatever you do, don't tell them you've seen me. They're mad enough already."

"Yeah, I guess you're right. You will call me, won't you, when you know something?" asked Schuyler as she opened the back door. The storm had passed, leaving only a light rain falling.

"I will. I promise," Lucy replied.

13 Babysitting Gone Awry

The rest of the week was uneventful. Lucy and Schuyler online messaged each other every day, but the ghost had not returned. Even Malpar was a no-show. Life slowly returned to normal, and they forgot about the spirits for a while.

Lucy hurriedly gathered her dirty dinner dishes and placed them in the sink to wash later when she got home. Running up the back stairs to her room, she grabbed the backpack and the Spectrescope from off the trunk and turned to leave when she caught her reflection in the dresser mirror.

Oh, you've got to be kidding! Lucy grimaced as she looked at the big purple stain on the front of her shirt. "Mom! I'll be down in a minute after I change. I spilled grape pop all over my shirt." The offending shirt was removed and flung to the floor.

"Lucy! Hurry up. I've got to get back to the seminar," Mom yelled up the staircase. "I'll drop you at the Gleasons on the way. C'mon! Let's go!"

"Piffle! I can't find my pink Paris T-shirt! Mom, did you see it?" Lucy shouted from the closet.

"It's in the wash. It doesn't matter what you wear. Just get a move on!" Mom hurried up the stairs and poked her head around the door. "They're little boys. They don't care how you look. I can't be late again," she huffed, going to Lucy's dresser and pulling out a sleeveless knit shirt. She tossed it to Lucy and stomped down the back stairs. "I'm in the car!" she hollered on her way out of the house. The kitchen door slammed behind her.

"Fine!" Lucy grumbled, pulling the shirt over her head. She stuffed the Spectrescope with the library book into the backpack, zipped it up, and ran down the back stairs. Searching the pantry yielded two trail-mix bars and a can of diet cola. She would need them for a snack after she put the boys to bed.

Mom was waiting in the SUV with the motor running. Lucy tossed her backpack on the floor and pulled the seat belt across her chest. Mom had the car in reverse before she clicked it into place.

"Geez, Mom," Lucy mumbled.

"I told you I was in a hurry. I have to get back to the seminar. The speaker is covering the registration desk for me," Mom fretted. "Do you have your cell phone? Is it charged?"

"Yes, Mom, it's in my pack and fully charged," said Lucy, holding tight to the grab handle above the door as the vehicle careened around a corner.

"Good, if you need anything after the Gleasons leave, you can call the McGoos. I already asked them if they were available in case you have an emergency," said Mom.

"If I have an emergency, I'm dialing 911," said Lucy.

"You know what I mean," said Mom, exasperated. "Scraped knees, bumps, cuts, bruises, and that sort of thing. You won't be able to reach me. After the seminar is over, I'll have to take a few things back to the office. I should be home before you, though."

The SUV screeched to a halt at the Gleasons' house. Mrs. Gleason was waiting on the big front porch. Lucy hopped out with her backpack, and the SUV squealed away from the curb and disappeared down the street.

"Oh," said Mrs. Gleason, a frown creasing her features. "Does she always drive like that?"

"No, only when she's upset with me, which lately, is most of the time," said Lucy with a snort as she climbed the steps to the porch. "Hi, Mrs. Gleason, excited about your dinner get-together tonight?" she asked.

"Oh yes! Thank you for asking. You're so sweet. It's with some of our friends we haven't seen since college, so it's been a while," she replied with a chuckle. "It should prove to be an interesting evening for sure!" A sparkling clip held her long dark-brown hair, and she wore a simple but elegant black dress.

"Wow! You look stunning!" exclaimed Lucy, admiring the clean lines of the dress. She found she was taking more interest in feminine things since becoming a teen, and at nearly fourteen years old, she was almost grown-up.

"Well, thank you, Lucy. Mr. Gleason and I should be home before midnight," said Mrs. Gleason, opening the screen door for Lucy. "He can drive you home so your mom won't have to wait up to come to get you. The boys have already had their dinner. They can have a snack and a glass of milk around seven, then off to bed at eight. After that, the evening is all yours, dear."

"Thanks, Mrs. Gleason," said Lucy, stepping into the living room.

Sounds of *rat-a-tat-tat, boom, rat-a-tat-tat* filled the room. Two boys sat in front of the television. Bradley, who was six years old, and his seven-year-old brother, Christopher, were inseparable. They did everything together and even looked so much alike with their white-blonde hair that most people thought they were twins. Close in height and build as well, the young boys were highly energetic and resourceful.

"Hi, guys! What're you playing?" asked Lucy.

Sharing a seat on the ottoman, which was way too close to the television, they were busy blowing up their opponents in a video game. They each waved a hand in response to her question but didn't turn around.

"Okay then, good talk," said Lucy, turning back to Mrs. Gleason. "May I take them to the park? I won't keep them out long. Maybe burn off some energy and get a little fresh air." *And get away from the video games*, she thought.

"Great idea! They need a little exercise. They've been playing that game most of the afternoon. I had things to get done, so I didn't insist they go outside to play. At least it made it easy for me to keep an eye on them," said Mrs. Gleason. "There's money in the cookie jar on top of the refrigerator for ice cream," she whispered with a wink. Lucy nodded.

"Ready, sweetheart?" asked Mr. Gleason as he entered the room. He was wearing a blue suit with a matching blue knit shirt underneath the jacket. He never wore a tie as he found them too confining. "Hi, Luce— thanks for watching the boys. Have fun!" He grabbed his wife's arm and ushered her out to the car. Lucy stepped to the front windows, pulled the curtains back, and watched them drive off. She sighed heavily. *It is going to be a long evening*, she thought.

"Let's go to the park for a while," said Lucy, reaching over and switching off the television. "Grab your helmets, and we'll ride the bikes around the block before we go to the park."

"Aw, c'mon! I don't want to go to the stupid park. I want to finish my game!" Christopher whined.

"Yeah, same goes for me!" agreed Bradley. He reached for the television remote, but Lucy grabbed it and held it out of reach.

Quietly taking a deep breath and lowering her voice, she said slowly, "We are going to ride bikes and go to the park. If you each behave, I will buy you an ice cream cone from Two Scoopers on the way home." She paused for effect. "If you don't behave, you will not get ice cream, and you will go to bed early. Deal?" She looked sternly at each brother.

"Okay," came the joint reply. The boys scrambled to their feet and rushed to their rooms to get their helmets.

Lucy shook her head. She remembered the first time she babysat the boys. They had broken a prized vase and overturned a planter, scattering dirt across the dining room carpet. The Gleasons returned home to find Lucy on her knees cleaning the mess and the boys standing in the corner with their noses pressed against the wall, screaming at total lung capacity. Her memory was now permanently etched with the Gleasons' shocked expressions. She thought they would never ask her to sit the boys ever again. Oddly enough, the boys asked for her each time their parents were going out. *Of course,* Lucy thought, *no one else is dumb enough to babysit them except me. Yay!*

"We're ready," the boys announced, rushing into the room and carrying their helmets and a favorite toy each. "Can we go now?" they asked.

How do they say the same thing at the same time? It's creepy! Lucy thought, looking at their upturned smiling faces. *I don't know what's more bizarre, the talking thing or the way they're smiling at me.*

"Did you both use the bathroom?" asked Lucy. "Remember my rule? Always use the bathroom before leaving the house. I don't like going into dark, unclean public restrooms."

They disappeared into the bathroom, bumping each other out of the way to get to the toilet first. "No fighting!" Lucy yelled.

She picked up the backpack and went into the kitchen. She grabbed wipes and three bottles of water and put them in the pack. Going out to the garage, she got the bikes down off the wall hooks. Mr. Gleason was a neat freak. The organized garage had the items most often used easily accessible.

She rolled the boys' bikes out onto the driveway and then went back to get Mrs. Gleason's bike. It was a turquoise twelve-speed racing bike with slimline tires. She parked it on the driveway with the others as she admired its sleek, clean lines.

What's taking them so long? Lucy thought. Entering the kitchen, she found the boys standing together, staring down the hallway. "What're you doing?" she asked.

Neither boy said a word but raised an arm each, pointing to the end of the hall. Lucy looked down the hallway. Stuffed animals and toys were piled one on top of another at the end of the hallway. The stack reached almost to the ceiling.

"Oh, honestly! That's what took you so long? We had a deal, remember?" Lucy groused, exasperated. She rolled her eyes upward.

"We didn't do it!"

"What do you mean you didn't do it? I can see your toys stacked to the ceiling!"

"We didn't do it," said Bradley.

"They were stacked there when we came out of the bathroom," said Christopher.

"All my toys were in my room," said Bradley.

"My toys were in my closet," said Christopher.

Lucy threw up her hands. "Forget it! C'mon, let's just go to the park!" She grabbed their hands and pulled them through the kitchen. "We'll discuss this later. If you behave the rest of the evening, our deal still stands. You get ice cream, but only if you behave."

"We still didn't stack our toys like that. We thought you did," said Christopher.

"I was getting your bikes down so we can ride to the park!" They walked through the garage out to the driveway. She didn't notice the bikes were facing the opposite direction from how she had left them.

It only took a few minutes to ride around the block and over to the park. Lucy put the bikes in the racks as the boys hurried to the merry-go-round.

She found a bench nearby where she could sit and watch them play as they pushed each other on the merry-go-round.

After a while, Christopher returned for a drink of water. Bradley sat on the edge of the merry-go-round, waiting for Christopher to return, his arms wrapped around the steel tubing on either side. Lucy waved at Bradley to let him know she was watching. He smiled back.

Lucy pulled bottled water from the backpack, uncapped the top, and gave it to Christopher, who took a long swig before handing it back. Dirt already streaked his cheeks, so she retrieved a wipe and washed his face. He hugged her neck and ran back toward the merry-go-round. He stopped.

"Where's Bradley?"

"Bradley!" yelled Lucy, jumping up. Her heart sank into her stomach, and she started to shake. Frantically, she looked around the park, searching for the small blonde-haired boy. "Bradley! Where are you? Answer me, honey!"

She spotted him lying sprawled over the top of a large cement barrel tunnel, his small hands grasping tightly to the edges to keep from sliding off. He must have darted across the park without her noticing. How did he get up on the barrel, though? She tossed the backpack on her shoulder, took Christopher's hand, and raced toward the cement barrels while pulling Christopher along beside her.

"How in the world did you get up there?" asked Lucy, reaching up to grab him. He rolled off the barrel and into her arms. "You are one quick little man." She laughed nervously. She hugged him close, holding him for a moment to reassure herself that he was okay. Lucy hoped he couldn't tell she was still shaking.

"I don't know how I got up there," he whimpered, burying his face in her shoulder. "I was on the merry-go-round, and then I was here. I want to go home. This place is scary."

"It's only your imagination," she said, rubbing his back and gently rocking him back and forth. The natural motion appeared to calm him a little. It helped calm Lucy some too. "You just scared yourself once you got up on the high barrel," she said. "It's okay, sweetie. Everyone gets scared sometimes. You just got to the park. Don't you want to play a little longer, maybe go on the swings?"

"No," he mumbled against her shirt. "There were shadows on the merry-go-round and shadows in the barrel tunnel too."

Shadows? Lucy furtively glanced around, instantly on high alert.

"Why don't we ride our bikes over to Two Scoopers and have some ice cream? Ice cream always makes things better," she said, bending and standing him on his feet.

"I'm still scared. Can I ride with you, Lucy?" Bradley whimpered.

"You're going to be just fine. Besides, if you ride with me, who will ride your bike home? You know what? I think you want me to tickle you," she said, grabbing Bradley and tickling until he squealed, and a big smile brightened his face. "Need more tickles? Or ice cream?"

"I want ice cream," piped Christopher, tugging on her shirt hem.

"Okay, ice cream it is." They walked back to the bench to retrieve the vampire book, water, and wipes and then rode the bikes to the ice-cream parlor. A dark shadow followed them, darting swiftly between the tree branches.

Two Scoopers was busy, and the lines were long. It took several restless minutes to get the boys their favorite ice-cream cones, orange-vanilla twist. Lucy sat between them on the picnic bench while the boys happily licked at their cones. The episode at the park had left her apprehensive and restless.

Trying to act casual, she pulled out a trail-mix bar and munched it while pretending to read the vampire book. Her food was tasteless and unsettling. Usually, she enjoyed watching families laughing together under the shade of the canopy or children chasing each other, but tonight her heart beat hard, and anxiety gripped her. Even her skin felt cold and clammy.

It was just another warm summer evening in the city with car horns honking and dogs barking in the distance. Everything appeared normal.

Except for the crows gathering in the trees.

After the visit to Two Scoopers, Lucy led the little group as they casually rode back to the house and put the bicycles in the garage. She hung the bikes on their wall hooks and followed the boys into the house. Outside, the crows were gathering again, flitting quietly among the tree branches. The boys ran ahead into the kitchen. Lucy sneaked a look at the gathering birds, then put the overhead door down and checked the side-door lock. She joined the boys in the kitchen and locked that door as well.

"Can we watch television?" they asked in unison. They pointed toward the living room.

Lucy squinted her eyes at them. *That is so creepy! Sheesh, as if I'm not already creeped out.* "It's getting late. Your mom said in bed by eight o'clock. By the time you wash up and get into your pajamas, it will be time for bed. If you hurry, I'll read you a bedtime story before lights out."

The boys hurried down the hallway toward their rooms.

"*Lucy!*" they screamed in unison. Lucy rushed into the hallway and skidded to a stop behind the boys. Her heart pounded, and her breath caught in her throat. The stuffed animals were no longer stacked in a pile but were hanging suspended in the air, floating eerily near the ceiling.

"Oh, my goodness! Too funny!" Lucy quipped, clapping her hands. "Did your dad sneak in and tie those up there? I bet he did." She nervously laughed as she gazed at the bizarre sight, rubbing the prickling skin on her arms as she did. "Your dad, what a prankster!"

"I want my toys back!" cried Bradley. "Can you get them down?"

"I'll get them down while you go clean up and put your pj's on," said Lucy, giving both boys a gentle push into the bathroom and closing the door. "Now, don't come out till you are ready for bed."

She flew to the kitchen and grabbed the backpack. The zipper stuck as she pulled hard on the slider, but it finally opened far enough to put her hand in and pull out the Spectrescope. Placing it to her face, she tip-toed through the kitchen to the living room. *Oh, no, please, don't let any ghosts be here tonight*, she thought as she scanned for weird anomalies. The Spectrescope wavered in her hand. All clear so far.

Lucy raced back to the hallway and pounded on the bathroom door. "Hey, guys! Almost ready for bed? Don't forget to brush your teeth!"

"Aw," came the muffled reply.

Putting her ear to the door, she heard the water tap turn on and giggles erupting from the boys. *They're fine and probably flooding the bathroom*, she thought, shaking her head.

The floating toys hovering near the ceiling gave her the creeps. The plastic eyes seemed to look straight at her, taunting her. Chills marched down her back. She had to get those things down somehow.

I wonder, she thought. Holding the Spectrescope in one hand, she raised the other hand toward the ceiling and whispered, "Down." A giant farting walrus bounced off her head with a burp and joined the two dozen other stuffed animals and toys on the floor.

Glancing at the bathroom door, Lucy thought the command, *Separate*. The toys zoomed into the air again and returned to their bedroom shelves. It was as though the incident had never happened. *Now, if only I can convince them it was a dream*, she thought.

* * * *

Grehssil stood with his scrawny arms folded across his chest and wrapping around his body in an attempt to keep from shivering or quaking in fear.

He didn't know which. The tapping sound of his foot echoed against the walls as he waited near the stone staircase.

The Hayyothalan was late. Malpar had better have a good excuse, or the Master would have his feathers plucked, but that was for the bird-man to worry about. Grehssil had worries of his own.

He had found the special tool the Master had demanded. His pocket felt heavy with the weight of its importance. Grehssil shuddered as he recalled the delight on the Master's face when he had presented it to him. The Master had taken it greedily from his hand and, turning it over, had inspected the small object. It had levitated from his hand to float in the air before the Master, and as it gently turned about, it had sparkled in the firelight. Grehssil could see the fine detailing etched in its surface. The tiny innocuous object was shaped like an ax-head and was quite lovely.

"Yes," the Master had declared, his amber eyes glowing brightly. "This will do nicely. Give it to the Hayyothalan. He will know how to use it. When the time is right, little Miss Hornberger will find herself suffering from a severe lack of confidence. She will begin to realize how inept she is, and then she will feel discouraged and isolated from her dear friends. She will realize it was all just a pack of lies, and she will no longer trust her precious Iam, the old goat. Poor girl," the Master had sniggered. "You did well, Grehssil. It is called the Wedge of Discouragement. Of all the tools in my toolbox, this is my favorite." Then the Master had laughed wickedly. Grehssil shuddered again at the memory.

A swoosh sounded in the stone hallway, causing the servant to jump. Malpar appeared amid a cloud of ash, walking toward him. Grehssil would never entirely trust the Hayyothalan, but then who among the Irredaemon ever really trusted one another? The bird-man's stark beady eyes unsettled Grehssil for some reason. It was as though the Hayyothalan could look straight into his soul.

Grehssil mentally shook himself and, gathering his wits, stepped forward to greet the Hayyothalan. "You're late, Malpar. The Master is expecting you to complete your mission soon. He has a tool for you to use, he does," he said. "It is the Wedge of Discouragement. You are to give it to the girl." He stretched out his arm and opened his hand. The tiny silver object lay sparkling in his palm.

Malpar stared intently at the object, then raised his piercing gaze to Grehssil's face. He watched a droplet of perspiration slide down the side of the servant's nose. Tilting his head sideways with a quick jerk, his hand darted out to snap up the wedge. Turning abruptly, he strode back down the hallway to disappear with a swoosh into a cloud of ash.

Grehssil breathed a sigh of relief and slumped against the wall. *What a day*, he thought, *with a millennium to go.*

*   *   *   *

"Read it again, Lucy!" begged Christopher, kicking his feet under the covers and sending stuffed animals bouncing to the floor for the umpteenth time.

"Yeah! Read it again!" Bradley chimed in while jumping on the matching twin bed on the other side of the bedroom.

"I've read it three times already tonight! If I have to read about green eggs and ham even one more time, I'm going to be sick!" said Lucy. "It's time for lights out. Your mom said to be in bed by eight o'clock, and technically you are in bed, but it's way past time for lights out. So, settle down and go to sleep." Lucy pulled the summer blankets up around Christopher, tucking him in. "You both need to settle down if you're going to sleep in the same room tonight. If you don't, I will send Bradley back to sleep in his room. Got it?"

A thump announced the other brother had just ricocheted off the wall. *Grrr.* "Bradley! Stop jumping on the bed! You know what happened to the five little monkeys. Your mom will be mad at me if you fall off and bump your head!" Lucy grabbed Bradley mid-jump and tipped him down to land amid the pillows and stuffed animals. She tickled him under his chin, causing an eruption of giggles and squeals.

"Tickle me, Lucy! C'mon! Tickle me!" bellowed Christopher, thrashing about and messing up the covers.

"What was in those ice cream cones? Pure sugar?" Lucy grabbed Bradley as he popped up again. "Okay! Time out! Stand in opposite corners and do jumping jacks for the next five minutes. Do you want to jump? Well, start jumping, boys," she said, pointing them to opposite corners. They squealed with delight as they rushed to comply.

"I can jump longer than you can!" taunted Bradley.

"No, you can't! You're just a little kid," retorted Christopher.

"Keep jumping until I say stop!" Lucy commanded, miffed.

Three minutes into their punishment, the boys were slowing down and whining that they were tired. "Oh, that's too bad," said Lucy, sitting cross-legged on one of the twin beds and picking at her chipped nail polish. "You still have two minutes to go. Keep jumping. You're doing a great job. You both know how to do a fine jumping jack."

"Aw, c'mon Lucy, we're tired," chimed both boys.

"Oh, well, if you're that tired, you can finish your two minutes of jumping another time," Lucy sighed, rolling her lips into a thin line to keep from smirking. "Hop in bed, and I'll tuck you in again."

Each boy shuffled to his bed and climbed in. Lucy straightened the covers and placed their favorite stuffed animals around them, then kissed them goodnight. She turned off the light and walked to the door. They had nearly disappeared under the array of critters on each of their beds. The nightlight on the dresser emitted a soft glow with just enough light for Lucy to see. The boys were already falling asleep. *Phew!* Lucy thought, quietly closing the door.

Lucy padded down the hallway, pulling the Spectrescope from her jeans' back waistband where she had quickly stuffed it when the boys rocketed from the bathroom earlier. She quickly scoped the house again before plopping down on the living room couch. The lens was clear.

But the symbols were glowing.

She pointed the Spectrescope at the light-colored carpet as the symbols glowed, rotated, and morphed into new shapes. They spun faster until the glow projected the images across the floor as the movie played out.

Images she quickly recognized confirmed her fears. The shadows in the park Bradley had spoken of were Malpar lurking in the shadows, watching the little group. The movie showed Malpar springing from the shadows at the park's edge to grab Bradley off the merry-go-round and deposit him on the largest tunnel. Lucy gulped. What if it had been the daemon and not Malpar? She squeezed her eyes shut and took a long, slow breath.

The Spectrescope vibrated in her hand as the symbols morphed again. New shapes revealed a crow, an upside-down triangle, a girl, and the tall figure of a man circled by a fanged serpent. Lucy shuddered. She assumed the girl's symbol was probably her, and the serpent's image was super scary, but she couldn't figure out the meaning of the triangle. Of all the characters, it glowed the longest before fading out, and that had her worried. Really worried.

Lucy curled her legs under as she snuggled back into the couch. She reached for the afghan Mrs. Gleason always keeps on the back of the sofa and wrapped it about her shoulders. A sudden chill froze her to the core and had little to do with the room's temperature. Frightening thoughts ran through her head. How could she fight against these spirits and keep those around her safe? And what did the triangle mean?

Reaching for her cellphone, Lucy decided to text message Schuyler, hoping her friend could respond without getting in trouble with her parents.

R U there? Lucy typed, then waited. She pulled the afghan tighter. The blackness of night just outside the big window threatened to swallow her. Shadows lurked around every lamppost, then flitted away in the headlights of passing cars, only to come slinking back once again. Her eyes felt as though they were straining to pop from their sockets as she stared into the darkness.

Lucy flinched violently, sending the cellphone skittering across the couch when the *beep-beep* indicated Schuyler had responded. She scrambled to retrieve the phone.

Here. What's going on? The message read.

At Gleasons.' Malpar is stalking us. New symbols. Scared, she typed.

I wish I were there.

Me2.

Remember Iam said Malpar's only scary. As long as it's him, you should be fine, Schuyler typed. *I know he's still creepy, but it's something.*

Lucy smiled wryly and typed. *Thanks. It helps—new symbol.* ∇

Meaning?

Don't know.

Headlights flashed through the living room, followed by the slamming of car doors. Lucy peeked out the window to see Mr. Gleason helping his wife from the car. *Have to go. Gleasons home,* she typed, then added a smiley emoji and two hugs.

14 Daphne Makes an Appearance

After the active and somewhat unsettling evening with the Gleason boys on Friday, Lucy spent a quiet weekend reading the vampire book and writing in her journal. She even put fresh polish on her nails in an attempt to forget about the spirits for a while.

Following breakfast on Monday morning, Lucy jogged up the back stairs to her bedroom, opened the window beside the bed, and turned on the computer. Mrs. Stewart had said her husband's great-great-uncle Darwin had been a spiritualist. She pulled up Wikipedia and searched for the word *spiritualist*.

"One who believes in the existence of spirits and talking with the dead. The spiritualist believes it is possible to recall a spirit temporarily by conducting a séance to communicate with the dead," stated the website.

Wikipedia doesn't say anything about horribly annoying ghosts or how to get rid of them. I bet whoever wrote this article never saw a ghost, Lucy thought, pursing her lips.

She searched again when another website caught her attention. It warned against séances. The writer said séances could open doors or portals to another dimension or reality that are very difficult to close. *Mrs. Stewart was right. She had warned us about that too*, Lucy thought. Her head dropped to her arms on the desk while the cursor blinked on the screen. She closed her eyes. Thoughts rambled through her head as she tried to make sense of everything that had happened since she found the Spectrescope.

Her cell phone beeped, indicating she had a new text message. It was from Schuyler. *If you can get away*, the message read, *meet me at the old carriage house on the corner.*

Why? When? Lucy typed.

Now. Got info. I got the key to the house. I will explain later.

Sorry? What house?

Really? Mrs. Walters's house. R U coming?

Wow. Okay. On my way. Lucy frowned and rolled her eyes. Schuyler could be so dramatic sometimes.

Lucy left a note on the kitchen counter to let Mom and Dale know she had gone for a bicycle ride. Mom was at work, and Dale was at a friend's house. She grabbed her backpack and checked that the Spectrescope was inside before securing her bike from the garage. Pumping as fast as her legs would allow, she flew down the street on her bicycle, the backpack securely strapped to her shoulders. It took a few minutes until she turned the corner and saw Schuyler on the front porch of the old carriage house, her bicycle lying in the bushes.

Lucy coasted to a stop in front of the brick two-and-a-half-story house. It was bigger than she remembered, with tall windows. A round turret on the corner of the house rose menacingly into the air, ending with a pointed shingled roof. It seemed to have a sad mood about it somehow, as though it missed its glory days. A small plaque, embedded into the brick, sat in the wall's center above the door. In the shade of the porch roof, it was nearly invisible.

Schuyler was peeking in the front windows along the wraparound porch. "What's up? Why are we meeting here?" Lucy asked, dropping her bike in the bushes next to Schuyler's.

"Remember? Mom used to clean house for Mrs. Walters," Schuyler began. "Well, Mrs. Walters has gone to live with her daughter and her family in their big house. They will sell the house, but Mrs. Walters asked Mom to check on the house periodically until then. And I have the key!" Schuyler grinned, holding up the brass key.

"I am still confused," Lucy said, swiping the old key from Schuyler. "Why do we want to poke around in Mrs. Walters's house?" She inspected the key, then handed it back.

"Because all the antiques are still in the house," Schuyler said, gaping stupefied at Lucy.

"Mrs. Walters's antiques?" Lucy asked, giving Schuyler a sideways glance with raised eyebrows.

"The Stewarts!" Schuyler gasped. "Their antiques have been passed down to each new owner since they were alive."

"Holy moly! That's awesome! But should we be poking around in the house without anyone knowing it? It's kind of like trespassing, isn't it?" Lucy wanted to check the house for clues but hesitated because she didn't know Mrs. Walters, and it wouldn't be right without asking her permission first.

"It's okay. Mom hasn't checked the house in a few days, so she asked me to run over here to check it out. That's how I got the key. Mom knows I am here, so it's not like breaking and entering," Schuyler said, grabbing Lucy's hand and dragging her toward the door. "C'mon! Let's see if we can find something that can help us."

The peeling paint on the wood columns, the ornate balustrades, and railings of the wrap-around porch hinted of a past of glory. The cream-colored brick, still firm and solid, stood rigid like a soldier-at-arms. One shutter hung at a slight angle next to the living room window. Lucy could see through the sheer curtains. Most of the furniture was gone, the room empty. The remaining pieces emitted a lonely emptiness that gave her a sudden case of chills.

"Wait. How did you find out the house belonged to the Stewarts?" Lucy asked.

"The county government has a website. I searched through the parcels using the address. The owner's information was minimal, but an attached document declared the antiques were never to be sold and had to remain with the house. Then I went to the Your Old Ancestors website searching through photographs." Schuyler reached in her pocket, pulling out a folded paper. She held it out to Lucy. "I found an old photo of the Stewarts standing in front of the house, confirming the original owners were Darwin and Helena Stewart. I printed a copy. Look at the date and name of the house in the photo. Now, look up."

"Wow," Lucy muttered, gazing at the photo of two people and the one face she knew as the ghost. "Wait, what?" She glanced at Schuyler, who was pointing at a brick embedded above the door. Lucy tilted her head up and gasped. "Holy moly! It's still there! It is the same house."

"Told you."

Schuyler fumbled the key into the old-fashioned door lock and, twisting the doorknob, pushed her shoulder into the door with a shove. The door was stuck. "Lucy, get your shoulder in here and help me push," Schuyler commanded.

"Yes, boss,'" Lucy whined and then snickered. She stuffed the photo in her jeans pocket.

"Oh, do it. I can't wait to poke around inside!" Schuyler pulled Lucy toward her, and together they pushed hard against the door. It opened suddenly with a loud pop, a groan, and a creak. Their combined momentum sent them tumbling to the floor of the foyer, where they lay giggling.

Lucy rolled over, looked up at the foyer light hanging from the high ceiling above them, and then screamed at full lung capacity. Schuyler squealed, scrambled to her feet, and fled down the hallway. Lucy rushed past her, grabbing Schuyler's shirt on the way and propelling them both through a doorway. Lucy slammed the door and leaned against it as Schuyler stumbled forward into the room, which happened to be the kitchen.

"Lucy! What happened? What are we screaming at?" Schuyler puffed, pulling her shaking hands through her curls, tucking stray strands behind her ears. "You scared me right into tomorrow!"

"Shh!" Lucy hissed. Lucy's trembling hands fumbled with the zipper on the backpack, finally pulling it open to reach in for the Spectrescope. Lucy opened the door slowly to peek down the hall toward the front door and to the chandelier suspended from the ceiling. The Spectrescope was clear.

Lucy stepped into the hall, methodically scoping the rooms on either side until she stood again in the foyer beneath the huge ugly light. Looking closely at the monstrosity, she thought she saw a very faint purple residue around the chandelier's ball finial. It vanished so completely while she stared at it, she couldn't be sure she had seen it. Schuyler followed behind, tiptoeing to keep from making any noise.

"Phew! All clear," sighed Lucy, lowering the scope. "I'm sorry, but that monstrosity freaked me out," she said, pointing a shaky hand at the chandelier. "I thought it was a giant monster of some kind. I swear I saw eyes looking back at me, and there was a slight purple hue to the ball, but I think whatever might have been there is gone."

A feeble light filtering through the door's sidelights and transom cast shadows about the dim foyer, making it difficult to see. The gigantic bronze Victorian light suspended from the ceiling hung by a thick chain. Lucy scrunched her face, thinking how it resembled a human being hanging upside down. The multiple arms of the light supported dingy yellow globes, and the ball finial at the bottom had embedded crystals.

The front door, which had swung closed again, slowly creaked open. Lucy and Schuyler grabbed each other and squealed together in unison. A man's head with an unruly shock of brown hair appeared around the edge of the door.

"Is everything okay in here? Vivian and I were walking by when we heard screaming coming from inside," said Bill McGoo, leaning further into the doorway. Vivian McGoo hovered behind her husband, her hands clamped over his shoulders.

"Mr. Bill and Mrs. McGoo!" Lucy exclaimed, clearly relieved. She quickly slipped the hand holding the Spectrescope behind her back, tucking it into the waistband of her jeans. "Oh, my gosh, it is good to see you! We're sorry we scared you. Well, we scared ourselves," she said, pointing up at the chandelier. "It's kind of creepy, don't you think?" Lucy said, grimacing and shrugging her shoulders as the McGoos looked up at the light.

"Well, I can certainly see why that thing would scare the daylights out of just about anyone. What on earth? Whoever thought a thing like that would be nice to see? It looks like a bat tried to eat an octopus, for goodness' sake," said Mrs. McGoo as she smiled commiseratively at the girls.

"Beats me, Viv," said Bill. "Hey, what're you girls doing in old Mrs. Walters's house?" Bill tried to scowl at Lucy and Schuyler, but the twinkle in his eyes gave him away.

"We have permission," Schuyler offered. "Mrs. Walters is living with her family. Until the house sells, she asked my mom to check on the house for her. Mom is busy today making an order of her specialty cakes for a fundraiser, and since it's been a few days since she was here last, she sent me," she said. "Oh, and of course, Lucy." She smiled a little too eagerly at the McGoos.

"I thought you two weren't supposed to see each other anymore," said Bill, pinching his lips together to keep from smiling.

"Oh, you heard about that, huh?" said Lucy, sighing as her gaze dropped to the floor. "I'll never live this one down. Probably everyone in Grand River Valley knows by now."

"Bill! Don't pick on the girls like that," scolded Vivian, her hands on her ample hips now. "You certainly weren't an innocent angel at their age, remember?" Vivian snorted.

"I can't remember that far back, Viv. I'm older than dirt," he quipped. "You, too, I might add. Heh, heh, heh," snickered Bill. He looked at Lucy, winked, and said, "I've always been an angel."

"Oh, shush," said Vivian, poking Bill in the arm. "It's not so bad, sweetie. I think your mom only mentioned it when we were chatting the other day because she knows we're close," she said, patting Lucy on the shoulder. "If it will cheer you up, I'll go home right now and make you a batch of my famous chocolate chip cookies."

"Thanks, Mrs. McGoo. I'd like that," said Lucy, leaning in to hug the lady. "You're the best, and your chocolate chip cookies will cheer me up!"

"I'll send along some cookies for Schuyler, too, so you can give them to her the next time you're not together," said Vivian, turning to wink at Schuyler, who was grinning and nodding vigorously.

"And not to worry, Lucy. Viv and I never saw you two together today, did we, Viv?" asked Mr. Bill.

"Saw whom, dear?"

Bill snickered. "Come on, let's go, Viv. The girls are okay, and you've got some baking to do. Besides, they need to get exploring through the old house."

Once the door closed and the girls were alone again, they broke into giggles. Lucy retraced her steps to the kitchen to retrieve the backpack, pulled out two water bottles, and handed one to Schuyler. "They are the cutest darn couple I've ever met," giggled Lucy. "I'm glad they showed up. It made me feel better somehow."

"I feel better too," said Schuyler, "except now I'm hungry thinking about those chocolate chip cookies Mrs. McGoo is going to make."

"You're always hungry. I don't know how your mom keeps up with you. Here, have a granola bar," Lucy said, rummaging in the backpack and handing one to Schuyler.

"Ooh! My favorite LUNA bar. Thanks, Luce," Schuyler said, pulling the wrapper open and taking a big bite.

Lucy shook her head. "So, where do we start? Any ideas? Please tell me we don't have to go to the basement or the attic. Those places are always so creepy. I mean, really? I think our basement would scare even a ghost. Bleh!" Lucy gave an exaggerated shudder.

"You are such a dork," Schuyler snickered. "Anyway, the antiques are in the living quarters of the house, so the brave ghost hunter doesn't need to go to the attic."

"Yeah, yeah, yeah," retorted Lucy. "Lead the way O Great and Wise One," she said, bowing and swirling her hand in salute.

Smirking as she munched, Schuyler led the way through the main floor of the house. They found a solitary antique sideboard cabinet in the breakfast room at the back of the house just off the kitchen. The empty formal dining room was next through the archway. Wandering through the parlor, they found it held only a pair of identical carved wood and upholstered chairs placed on either side of the large fireplace. The engravings replicated a coiling serpent with fangs bared in the fireplace mantel.

"As if the bat-eating-octopus light in the foyer wasn't creepy enough," said Schuyler, pointing a cautious finger at the carvings, "this will give me nightmares tonight. Yikes!"

"You're not kidding. Who thinks these things up, anyway? Didn't they have design schools back then?" Lucy tugged the sleeve on Schuyler's shirt. "C'mon, let's keep looking. There has to be something here that can help us," she said, hefting the backpack higher on her shoulder. "The parlor is through here." She led the way through the curved archway.

"I wish we knew what we're looking to find. It must be a personal item, something of significance to the Stewarts," said Schuyler, rubbing her hand over the carved wood trim around the archway, this time featuring flowers and vines. "Maybe a wedding ring or a baby rattle. We need to figure out who these people were and if there's something we need to know."

Lucy advanced farther into the parlor, her sneakers squeaking on the wood floor. The nearly empty parlor, just off the foyer at the front of the house, contained a circular room that was part of the old Victorian-style house's turret design. Near the round-room windows sat an old side table topped with a lamp and a crocheted doily. The table legs curved outward, ending with brass caps shaped like toes. The lamp was entirely another matter.

"Seriously?" Lucy exclaimed. "I would be in an eternal state of freaked out if I lived in a house with stuff like this. Look at the lamp!"

The lamp was tall and narrow, with a round potbelly squatting on three legs, each shaped like a lion's powerful rear leg, complete with toes and claws. Adding to the creep factor were the two scrolled humanlike arms reaching upward with hands that curled inward. The velvet and silk shade was patterned with a design that Lucy thought looked suspiciously like eyes, open and staring.

"Ew! Maybe we've seen enough, and there isn't anything here to help us. I think we should go now, yes?" Schuyler grabbed a handful of Lucy's shirt, pulling her into the foyer and toward the door.

"Schuyler, this was your idea in the first place," Lucy said, arching her eyebrows. "I think we need to keep looking. Who knows if we find that special something or even an old document. We need to find out all we can." She smiled wryly at Schuyler. "Who's the brave ghost hunter now?"

"Okay," squeaked Schuyler. She rubbed nervously at the bracelet. "I guess we go upstairs next, huh?" She leaned around the big ornate railing, looking up toward the gloomy second-floor landing. The railing wrapped around the length of the hallway, which was open to the foyer below. There appeared to be light coming from the room at the top of the stairs.

Lucy followed Schuyler slowly up the stairs to the room with the strange light emanating from within. Inside, a large stained glass window depicting dryads and fauns dancing around a tree with a flame at its core loomed over the small sitting room. A single bench sat in the middle of the room.

"Ooh, Luce! It looks like something out of The Chronicles of Narnia. Although I don't recall a tree with a flame, do you?"

"No, but it's intriguing, though, isn't it? I feel like I want to step into their world and join them in the dance. I know it is silly, and yet," she sighed, "I feel like there's something more going on there." Lucy shook herself from her musing.

"Yeah, I think I could sit here for hours, watching, waiting for them to move and come to life. It's so beautiful. Maybe this is what we're looking for?"

"No clue," Lucy said. She pulled out her cell phone, snapped a couple of photos of the glass mural, and then recorded a short video. "Okay, let's keep looking." The phone got stuffed back into her pocket. She peeked into the adjoining room near the top of the stairs, discovering the bathroom. Continuing down the dim hallway, she held the Spectrescope to her face as she scanned. Lucy startled violently as the hallway lights flashed on.

"Oops," Schuyler grimaced, her hand on the light switch. "Sorry!"

"Uh, no problem," Lucy gasped, nearly hyperventilating. "I think we're even now. Guess we're both a little jumpy." She gently turned a knob, opening the door to the first bedroom. It was empty except for the curtains and another of the three-legged lamps sitting on the floor in one corner. The room had a bay window matching the one in the formal dining room just below it.

"Are you going to check the closet? I hate weird closets," whispered Schuyler. "They give me the creeps." She walked farther into the room, pointing at the door in the corner, presumably the closet.

"What do you mean?" Lucy laughed, rolling her eyes. "Some people have a walk-in closet. You have a weird house with a walk-through closet." She snorted. "Okay, open the closet door, and I'll scan it for ghosts."

Schuyler took a deep breath, threw the door open, and then hurried behind Lucy. Peeking around Lucy's shoulder, she saw the closet was empty. "Okay, that wasn't so bad," she admitted confidently.

"Wow, bravery in action. How about you open the other door? Or don't you think we should check behind the skinny little door at the back of the closet?" Lucy asked wryly.

"What? There's another door?"

"It's probably another interior space like at your house," Lucy said, peeking into the closet. The door was barely discernible in the beadboard paneling under a thick coat of old paint.

"Oh, you want me to open it?"

"Yes."

"Drat," said Schuyler. She pinched her lips and stepped into the closet. A string hung from a light fixture above the door. She pulled the string, and the light bulb popped on, basking the empty closet in dim yellowish light. A shelf above the clothes rod was covered in thick dust, making her sneeze. Bending down under the rod, Schuyler ran her hands around the edge of the door, looking for a way to open it. "I don't think it does open. There isn't a knob, and pushing on it doesn't do anything. It probably hasn't been opened in a long time."

"Let me try," said Lucy, exchanging places with Schuyler. She stuffed the Spectrescope under her arm and felt around the door's edge like Schuyler had but couldn't find any clue as to how to open it. "Okay, let's leave it for now. Maybe we can figure out how to open it later."

They checked the next door. It was another empty bedroom and closet, this time without a secret panel.

The last door was different from the others. The wood was dark with age and had a serpent roughly etched in the center. Given all the strange oddities of the old house, Lucy and Schuyler hesitated in front of the door.

"I'm not sure about this," Lucy whispered. "The Spectrescope is getting warm, which probably means there is something nasty behind this door. Can you activate the bracelet before it detects an entity?"

Schuyler nodded and pressed the purple center stone, which caused the bracelet to melt into flowing metal, forming the shield. Schuyler reached into the sheath and withdrew Zazriel. "Okay," she whispered, "I'm ready."

Lucy started to turn the handle, then stopped. Schuyler frowned and tipped her head at the door, silently questioning. Lucy nodded, took a deep breath, and opened the door. A heavy, nauseating odor assaulted their noses, causing both girls to scrunch their faces.

"Ew," Schuyler squeaked. "What is that stench?"

Lucy held the Spectrescope tightly as she scanned the large bedroom containing all the ornate antique furnishings. She felt she had stepped backward in time by one hundred and fifty years. Gold and burgundy tapestries covered the large ornate bed, and floral hand-painted oil lamps sat on the heavy dresser and side chests. The curtains, fashioned from the same rich tapestries as the bed, looked nearly new. A small chair sat before a dressing table featuring a large oval mirror. An incense burner on the tall chest was the source of the disgusting odor.

Schuyler edged into the room, her gaze taking in all the details. It was immaculate, given the dusty condition of the other rooms. She lowered the shield slightly but kept a firm grip on the sword. The circle of the turret, like the parlor, held another table and three-legged lamp. Schuyler shuddered as she stared at it, tickles crawling up her spine and down her arms. She could have sworn one of the eyes on the lampshade had blinked at her.

Lucy gently nudged her shoulder, then pointed at the mirror. It was filling with a golden swirling mist. In her hands, the Spectrescope glowed a warm yellow, and the symbols spun around the handle, coming to rest in a new configuration. There were a dove and a shining sun. Lucy showed it to Schuyler, who nodded, and together they approached the dressing table.

"Who are you?" Lucy asked as the mist settled into a human shape. "What are you doing here?" She watched the fog clear, and the face of a young woman appeared. The delicate features and almond-shaped eyes held no malice in them, only curiosity. The woman's long brown hair, which fell in folds to her shoulders, was soft and shiny. Something was alluring and comforting about the young woman who appeared as solid as they were. It drew both Lucy and Schuyler closer to the mirror.

"I am Daphne," she said softly. "I mean you no harm. You want to know about Darwin. I can help you, Lucy." Her voice was soft and breathy. "Hello, Schuyler," she said, smiling at Schuyler.

Schuyler stood gaping, her focus temporarily distracted as she dropped her arm with the shield. "Oh, my goodness! How can you know all that?"

Daphne smiled wider. "An angel told me."

"Oh," whispered Schuyler.

"Are you real, Daphne?" Lucy asked. "I mean, you look so solid, not anything at all like the other ghosts we've encountered." Lucy slapped a hand to her cheek. "I'm sorry, that was rude."

"It is all right. It's only natural that you would be curious. And, yes, I'm quite real and alive," replied the young woman. She laughed softly.

"Daphne, is this mirror a portal?" asked Lucy, tapping on the glass. "Can you come through it? Where are you?" She flattened her hand against the glass.

"No, it is only for this special moment that it is functional," Daphne explained. "Not all mirrors are portals. They only reflect what you need to know. I am in Ascalon, and I cannot cross back over to come to you, Lucy."

Daphne placed her hand on her side of the glass next to Lucy's and sighed. "You are very dear to all of us, and if I am to help you, we must hurry."

Lucy dropped her hand, smiling wistfully at Daphne. "Is the ghost haunting us your husband?" she asked, watching as a myriad of emotions flitted across the face of the young woman. "If you can't or don't want to answer, it's okay. It must be confusing for you to understand why your husband would haunt anyone. Can you tell us anything that might help us?"

"I haven't much time, so I'll answer the best that I can. The High King allowed me to contact you because he knew I wanted to help," Daphne said.

"Who is the King? Malpar referred to Iam as the King, but that doesn't make any sense," Lucy said, perplexed. "He's the vendor we met at the flea market. He can do some crazy wizard-like stuff, but Iam, the High King? He's more like someone's sweet, old grandpa than a King."

"Lucy," Daphne said, her eyes wide in bewilderment. "He is our Forevermore. He is gracious, good and merciful, and all-powerful. Surely, you must know that by now."

"I'm sorry. I don't understand," Lucy said, smiling wryly. "If Iam is the High King of Ascalon, why wouldn't he just tell me?"

"He is known throughout the universe by many names. You must learn for yourself, Lucy, who he is in your world. When you know in your heart who he is, you will begin to see clearly and understand. For now, I can only help you with the ghost."

Lucy sighed, her shoulders drooping. "I thought Malpar was scary, but this ghost entity is way worse. And I'm worried."

Daphne's image flickered in the mirror as she turned aside to acknowledge someone who was out of the view of the mirror. Lucy noticed a blur of activity and heard muffled voices in the room behind the young woman. She leaned closer to the mirror to eavesdrop but jolted upright when Daphne popped back into view.

"Darwin was a good man. Misguided, but a good man," Daphne continued. "We were very much in love, but I died in childbirth with our first child, and the child also died."

"Wait!" Lucy interrupted. "I'm confused. You said you 'died,' but you are alive in Ascalon? I don't understand. How is that even possible?" Lucy glanced at Schuyler, who was staring, transfixed at the young woman.

"I haven't time to explain, dear Lucy. For now, I must tell you certain things you need to know. Darwin was devastated. He held séances in the house, believing he could contact me. It opened a portal to the Dark Prince's realm. It is still in this house, and it must be closed for all your sakes." She hesitated, sadness marring her lovely features. "The entity haunting you is not my husband. It is a low-level Irredaemon who took the form of my husband. Ghosts are not the souls of departed loved ones. They are Irredaemons and unredeemable. You must resist this daemon, and he will flee from you. Do not believe anything the daemon tells you. It is all lies. Trust what you know is true. Truth is stronger than lies."

"How can I resist him? How do I get rid of him?" Lucy pleaded. "I don't understand. Everyone talks in riddles! Please, just tell me what to do!" She threw her hands up and nearly bounced with agitation.

"You must trick the daemon into telling you his real name. Then, in the name of the High King, he can be sent to Shinar, and the portal closed," Daphne said, leaning closer to the mirror. "The Belt of Truth has the power to do this. Learn to use the truth, and it will strengthen you. Each of your tools is divinely powerful. You must learn to use them. You have been chosen and endowed with the ability to finish your task. And remember, Lucy, help is all around you. You only need to ask and then trust what you have learned."

The mirror flickered. Daphne looked at each of them in turn, waving her hand as she began to fade away. "Goodbye, and be sure you wear your armor!" She was gone.

"I am asking! Wait, don't go. I still have questions," Lucy yelled at the empty mirror. "Argh!" She stomped so hard around the room, the lampshade with eyes began to bounce.

This time, Schuyler saw several of the eyes blink. She whipped Zazriel through the air, pointing it at the lamp. All the eyes snapped shut. "Ooh, you better not be watching us!" she snarled.

The eyes remained shut.

15 Oh, What to Do

"Argh!" Lucy yelled again, throwing her hands up. "This is so frustrating! 'Trust what you have learned. Help is all around you. The truth will strengthen you,' " she mimicked. "What does all that even mean?" Lucy stopped pacing and stared into the mirror that now reflected her worried image. "Daphne! Come back!" she said, rapping her knuckles on the glass. "Please?"

"We have to get going, Luce," Schuyler said, still pointing Zazriel at the lampshade. "We can do a quick search of the attic. Daphne said the portal opened is still here, and it needs to be closed. I am not sure what that means, but I do know it's probably not something either one of us is going to like." The lampshade eyes remained shut as she sheathed the sword. She tugged on Lucy's sleeve and nodded her head toward the door. "C'mon," she said.

"I guess the attic is a logical place to look, but I want to go back to the room with the glass mural. There's something about the room I can't explain," Lucy said, making her way down the hallway to the little sitting room.

Schuyler followed Lucy into the hall, closed the old door, and then popped it open again and stuck her head into the room. Nothing moved or blinked. With a sly smile, she slammed the door shut with a bang. "Made you jump, I betcha," she whispered.

Lucy sat on the bench and stared at the window. The dryads and the fauns were still frozen in place around the tree with the flame. "What is it I am missing here?" Lucy whispered. She memorized every detail in the glass mural. There were the dryads with flowing blonde hair in regal gowns, the fauns who were dancing on their hooves, and a bright flame inside the tree with the vivid red fruit. Each of the participants held something in their hands, but Lucy couldn't discern what it was. The longer she stared, the more she became mesmerized by the scene. A few stars in the royal blue sky appeared to twinkle as she stared.

"What do you see, Luce? Is there something here that we're missing?" Schuyler entered the little room and sat next to Lucy.

"I don't know. I feel like it's right there in front of me," Lucy said, reaching out to grasp a handful of air, "but I can't catch it, no matter how hard I try."

"It's so beautiful," Schuyler crooned. "I just yearn for them to be dancing and moving, but that's dumb because it's just a glass mural," she said, shrugging her shoulders. "I don't know what it is, but I feel anxious as I look at it."

"I feel that way too! I even have goose bumps," Lucy said, rubbing her arms. "Well, let's search this room really quick. Your mom probably expected you home long before now. You don't need to get into any more trouble. I've caused you enough as it is."

Lucy took another look at the mural, shook her head, and then stood to scope the small room. She pointed to the corner of the room near the doorway. A narrow door with a purple glow appeared in the Spectrescope.

Schuyler pinched her lips together, nodded, and moved to stand next to Lucy. She pressed the purple stone, turning the bracelet into the shield. The gems on Zazriel's hilt sparkled in the multihued light from the window.

Lucy reached out a shaky hand and pressed the wall. The door became visible and slowly swung on squeaky hinges until it rested against the wall. "Schuyler, get the flashlight from the pocket of my backpack."

Schuyler grabbed the flashlight and shined the beam into the dark space. There stood another door with black scroll hinges. Her mouth fell open. It was identical to the door with the vanishing staircase at her house.

"Oh, boy," Lucy whispered. "I think we found the portal Daphne told us about." Taking a deep breath, she stepped into the closet. The Spectrescope prickled with heat and vibrated so violently, Lucy nearly dropped it. She gripped it tight and froze as chills marched up and down her spine. In the lens of the Spectrescope was one word: *No*.

Lucy heard growling coming from behind the ancient door.

Slowly, she retraced her steps backward into the room and firmly closed the wall panel. She pulled the head from the Spectrescope and deposited it in her pocket. The Spirit Sword glistened with an ominous blue glow in her hand.

"Why did you stop?" Schuyler asked. She sucked in a deep breath and her brow furrowed when she saw the Spirit Sword. She hurriedly stuffed the flashlight into her pocket and yanked Zazriel from its sheath. "What's wrong?"

"I think we need to go," Lucy whispered. She pushed her friend toward the door while keeping the sword pointed toward the panel she had just closed. "Go!"

"Got it. Running!"

They bolted down the staircase, exploding into the foyer and out the front door, with Lucy slamming it behind them. Schuyler sheathed her sword, grabbed the key from her pocket, and fumbled as she tried to lock the door. Lucy took the key and locked it.

"What happened back there?" Schuyler asked shakily.

"The Spectrescope warned me not to open that door," Lucy said, replacing the head on the Spectrescope as the sword slipped into the handle. "Look, the message is still there," she said, showing Schuyler the lens. "I heard something growling. Whatever it was, I don't think the Spectrescope wanted us to open that door until we know we can close it permanently." She blew out a shaky breath and kneaded the tingles on her arm.

"Are these artifacts returnable?" Schuyler muttered, rubbing at her growing tribe of goose bumps. "I think this is a little more dangerous than we originally believed, and I, for one, don't want to be scared to death before my fourteenth birthday!" She shakily rubbed her wrist where the bracelet had returned.

"You'd better get home. We can text later," Lucy said as she placed the Spectrescope in the backpack. "If we figure out what it is everyone thinks we know, maybe we can find a way to get rid of these daemons."

"Okay. I'll text you after everyone goes to bed. Bedtime nowadays is early," Schuyler moaned. "Dad still isn't speaking to me, and Mom doesn't seem to have any energy. She's been sleeping a lot lately, and I am worried. I don't know what to do."

"If only I could make it up to your parents," Lucy said sadly, slinging the backpack over a shoulder. "I miss them."

"I guess we'll figure it out. At least, I hope we do."

They retrieved their bicycles from the bushes and then rode in opposite directions. Lucy took the long way around toward home. As they peddled away, two white doves landed on the porch railing of the old carriage house. The skinny dove bobbed its head up and down like a bobblehead. The chubby dove clucked its tongue as though complaining.

"Lucy!" Mom hollered up the back staircase. "I hear clicking. You'd better not be texting with Schuyler. I don't want you bothering Schuyler or her parents. It was 'lights out' ten minutes ago. Switch off and go to sleep. You need to be at the Gleasons' early in the morning."

Lucy quickly texted good night to Schuyler, then set the phone's alarm for the morning. They had brainstormed through several texts but were still unsure what to do about the ghost. Daphne had said to trick the spirit into revealing his name and then banish him to Shinar. What did that mean? Lucy didn't know. Schuyler had finished reading the ghost-hunting book from the library, and Lucy had searched several websites, each with no luck.

"Yes, Mom! Goodnight!" Lucy bellowed. She rolled her eyes. *Why did I have to get the bedroom nearest the stairs? Mom can hear a mouse fart in the attic next door. Grrr*, Lucy thought. She rolled over, turned off the table lamp, and pulled the covers up around her with a huff.

Lucy lay in the dark, listening to the usual night sounds drifting through the window, a dog barking down the street, crickets chirping, and a police siren wailing in the distance. She thought of the bizarre events that had occurred to her and Schuyler since she had brought the Spectrescope home and the trunk with its weird collection of tarnished oddities. She had called out for Iam though he still hadn't shown up. *Am I on my own now, with all these ghosts wreaking havoc on my friends and me? Have you left me, Iam?* Lucy thought, and soon she snuffled and snorted as she drifted off to sleep.

"I am still here, sweet girl. I will never leave you," a familiar voice whispered in her ear.

"Mmm, okay," Lucy muttered sleepily. Rolling over, she snuggled deeper into the covers. The night sounds drifting in through the open window gradually quieted down as the night wore on. Only the occasional squealing of a siren could be heard way off in the distance.

Lucy's nose began to twitch and scrunch as a burnt and sulfuric odor assaulted her sinuses. Sneezing, she sat up and rubbed the sleep from her eyes. Sniffling, she rolled over the edge of the bed and felt for the bottom drawer of the nightstand from which she retrieved a tissue and blew her nose. She sniffed the air several times. The odor was still there.

"Heh, heh, heh," a low, raspy voice laughed. "Not used to the stink yet?"

Lucy jolted upright, forcing her eyelids wide open to see in the dark. There in the corner and sitting in her desk chair was Malpar in his human form. His beady eyes glowed red in the shadows. Her hand darted under the pillow to grab the Spectrescope.

"What are you doing here?" Lucy hissed quietly. "I'm not giving you the Spectrescope."

"I must keep you from feeling too comfortable. Are you uneasy, human girl?" sniggered Malpar. "I need you to know I can get to you anywhere, anytime, and in any way. Maybe I will influence your dreams, or should I say your nightmares? Didn't your precious Spectrescope warn you I was here?" His head jerked sideways, the light from the streetlamps reflecting off the shiny feathers on his head.

Lucy glanced down at the Spectrescope in her lap. Bewildered, she gazed at the odd image of a man with slumped shoulders followed by a broken-heart symbol, then turned her gaze back to the bird-man.

"What do you mean 'influence my dreams'? You can't possibly know what I dream in my head."

"Are you sure about that?" Malpar sneered. "Why don't you drift off back to sleep then? Maybe you will see if I can influence your dreams," he rasped.

"What about you, Malpar? What do you dream about?" Lucy asked. "Do you dream about serving in the courts of the High King of Ascalon? Can you remember the beauty of Ascalon or the love you felt for the High King?" She leaned forward to observe the bird-man. The low light from the streetlamps was just enough to reveal the emotions flitting across his face.

"I have no dreams, not anymore. What good will it serve, longing for something you can never have again?" Malpar lamented. His head dipped so low Lucy thought he would fall from the chair. "We define ourselves by our choices, Lucy. I chose poorly."

"You made a mistake, Malpar. I make mistakes all the time. Ha! Ask my mom. She can tell you," Lucy said, rolling her eyes. "I guess, though, it's how we learn so we don't make the same mistake again. Talk to Iam. He can help you. I know he would."

"My Master would send me to the Abyss for even thinking about the High King."

"Malpar, when you were in the Master's chambers, how did you know Schuyler and I were watching you through the mirror?" Lucy asked, studying the bird-man. "I remember you waved your hand behind your back. You were trying to warn us to back off, weren't you? Why would you do that?" The weird head jerking still creeped her out, but there was a noticeable change in his demeanor. For a brief moment, Malpar seemed amused.

"The Master did not know the Crystalline mirror was open," Malpar replied with a smirk. "He is always so bloated with his importance and his greed for power. It is easy at times to fool even him." He closed his eyes and breathed deeply. "There was the most heavenly freshness to the air. It held the fragrance of young, untouched souls, filled with curiosity and life."

Malpar went to stand by Lucy's bedside, gazing down at her. His beady eyes searched her upturned face, her clear gray eyes looking back at his. He detected an uneasiness his nearness brought to her, and he took a step back. His focus fell on the Spectrescope in her lap. He clicked his beak, lifted his head, and stood tall.

"Give me the Spectrescope, Lucy, or I'll influence more than just your dreams," Malpar hissed. "I must have it." He held his hand out for the scope.

Clenching her jaw and licking her lips, Lucy breathed deeply and drew herself up straight too. "No," she said firmly.

"Lucy Hornberger! What are you talking about?" Mom complained as she opened the bedroom door and stepped into the room. "I can hear you all the way downstairs—oh my!" she said, gagging and waving a hand in front of her nose. "What is that stench?"

As Mrs. Hornberger stepped into the room, Malpar morphed into a black mist and slithered like spilled ink through the shadows across the floor. Unnoticed, he flowed into the backpack and hid the Wedge of Discouragement before flowing out a corner of the open window. *See how you like* that, *stupid girl!*

"Stench?" Lucy asked innocently. "Oh! Do you mean that stench? I'm sorry. I tooted." She frantically waved the covers toward the window.

"Tooted? For goodness' sake! What have you been eating?" Mom grumbled. "Forget I said anything. Why are you talking to yourself at this hour of the night?"

"I sneezed and woke myself up! Can't a girl sneeze without getting into trouble?" Lucy griped. "How come you always assume it's me being the problem and never Dale? Huh?" She blew loudly into the tissue.

"Go back to sleep," said Mom, "quietly this time." The door closed with a thud.

You know, I'm not sure who the bigger problem is right now, Mom or Malpar, Lucy thought, falling back on the pillow and yanking the covers over her face.

* * * *

"Lucy! Time to get up!" Mom yelled up the back stairs. "You're babysitting the Gleason boys today, remember? C'mon! Get a move on."

"How can it be morning already?" Lucy grumbled, rolling over and tucking the pillow around her head. "It's too early to get up."

"Lucy! Now!"

"Okay, I'm moving." Lucy reached out a hand, felt around for the small top drawer of the nightstand, and then opened and closed it with a bang. "Getting dressed now," she mumbled, rolling onto her back and drifting off to sleep again.

Honk! Honk!

Lucy bolted from the bed, heart pounding and ears ringing. Mom was standing in the doorway, holding an air horn.

"What's the big idea?" Lucy yelled. "You nearly gave me a heart attack!"

"I found your Granddad's old air horn in the hall closet the other day," Mom said with a smirk. "Huh, I guess it still works."

"So *not* funny, Mom," Lucy grumbled, folding her arms across her chest. "My ears are ringing. I won't be able to hear for days. At least your ears are ringing too."

Mom reached up and pulled bright-pink foam plugs from her ears. "What did you say, dear?"

Glaring at her mom, Lucy grabbed some clothes and then stomped down the hallway to the bathroom and slammed the door.

Mom sniggered quietly. "You're not the only person who can play shenanigans around here," she said, polishing the bell of the horn with the sleeve of her cotton robe. Turning, she stepped lightly down the back stairs, giggling.

Lucy stomped her way through her morning routine. The air horn incident had put her in a gloomy and grumpy mood. Drawers banged and doors slammed as she went about her tasks with a scowl. The breakfast dishes would have been cracked, chipped, or broken from her rough handling if her mom hadn't intervened.

"You'd better straighten out your face and your attitude, young lady," said Mom, who was stacking the dishes in the dishwasher. "The Gleasons aren't going to trust you to babysit the boys if you show up at their house looking the way you do."

"It's your fault I'm grumpy. Nice way to wake up your daughter with an air horn, no less!"

"Consider it payback for the empty eggshells in the carton yesterday," said Mom, putting her hands on her hips. "I didn't realize they were empty until they started floating on top of the water! How do you expect me to make hardboiled eggs with no eggs? You've pulled that trick one too many times, missy."

"Fine!" Lucy snapped back. "I won't pull that trick again."

"You'd better not be pulling any tricks. Now, out," commanded Mom, pointing to the back staircase. "Go get your things ready to go to the Gleasons. Maybe a full day of babysitting crafty little boys will change your attitude."

"Doubt it!" Lucy snapped as she stomped upstairs.

Swimming at the community pool was always a favorite activity for the boys and a respite for Lucy. Since it was a weekday, Lucy didn't expect very many people to be using the pool. Grabbing the backpack, she began stuffing it full.

By the time Lucy was ready to leave, there were a first-aid kit, snacks, bottled water, her swimsuit and towels, cell phone, and the vampire book in the bag. The Spectrescope was zipped securely into one of the outside pockets, and on a whim, she wadded up the hat and vest together, stuffing them into the other. *Maybe the sunshine can sweeten my mood.* She paused, thinking. *Nope, it's not going to happen.*

"Geez, this thing weighs more than it usually does," Lucy grumbled to herself as she dragged it, bumping and thumping down the stairs. "Maybe I need to do pushups or something."

"What's up, Squirt?" Dale asked. Packages of bread, cheese, and cold cuts lined the counter where he was making a sandwich, slathering mayo over several slices of bread. "You look tired. Couldn't sleep?"

"Dude, we just had breakfast. How can you even be hungry?" Lucy asked, gaping at the sandwich piling up on Dale's plate. Her mouth snapped shut as she shook her head. "And no, I didn't sleep well. Who can sleep with an air horn blasting?" she snarled, exiting the kitchen and slamming the back door behind her.

"Huh? What was that about?" Dale said as he watched out the window at her retreating back. "Teenage girls, glad I'm not one of 'em."

Mom was checking her phone messages while waiting in the SUV with the motor running. Lucy climbed in, wedged the backpack between her feet, and buckled her seat belt. Slinking down into the seat, she folded her arms and stared straight ahead at the windshield. Neither acknowledged the other on the very silent five-minute ride over to the Gleasons' house, located in a newer development.

Lucy exited the SUV at the curb with a quick look at Mom, who seemed somewhat bewildered for some reason. A small smile flittered briefly across Mom's lips before disappearing into a straight, tight line. Slinging the backpack over a shoulder, Lucy lumbered up the driveway to the porch steps. She glanced back and frowned upon seeing Mom pull demurely away from the curb. *What's up with her driving? She usually drives like she's racing in a NASCAR event*, Lucy thought. Shrugging, she plodded up the steps.

Ringing the Gleasons' doorbell caused a chain of events. The boys could be heard through the screen door whooping and hollering at each other in the kitchen, the cat screeched somewhere in the house, and Mr. Gleason yelled from the upstairs bathroom that he needed a bandage for the cut he just got from shaving. Mrs. Gleason, who came streaking through the house clutching a box of bandages, quickly unlocked the screen door.

"Molly! I need those bandages!"

"Morning, Lucy! Be right back!" yelled Mrs. Gleason over her shoulder as she rushed up the stairs. "Coming, dear!" Her hair, formerly in a ponytail, was now half-undone, with wild strands flying behind her as she ran.

"That is mine, Bradley! Give it back! You had the last one!" Christopher bellowed from the kitchen.

"It's my toaster tart. I put it in the toaster. Get your own!"

Why me? My head hurts already, Lucy thought, shuffling into the kitchen, which could have been a scene from a disaster movie. The backpack dropped to the floor as she surveyed the scene. The boys had each grabbed the toaster tart, mashing it and leaving them with the sticky, crumby jam fingers now being used to pull each other's hair. A toppled milk glass dripped its contents over the edge of the table, and a soggy cat was licking milk from its fur. Dishes were upturned, and cutlery lay scattered on the floor as the boys squabbled. Lucy nearly whimpered. *What will I do with them for an entire day?*

"What're you guys doing?" Lucy scolded, rushing to grab their clenched fists and separating the boys. "Stop hitting each other! Your mom is going to be mad when she sees this mess."

"It was my toaster tart!" yelled Bradley.

"Was not! It was mine!" screamed Christopher.

"And I don't care!" bellowed Lucy, marching them to the sink to wash their hands. Pumping folds of creamy soap into her hand, she stood between them and slathered their sticky fingers. "Now, rinse." She adjusted the water temperature. Glowering at each other, they reluctantly stuck their hands under the faucet.

"Molly! What're you doing? Ouch!" Lucy heard Mr. Gleason yelling in the upstairs bathroom. "I don't want the styptic stick! That thing burns like crazy. Just put a bandage on it. Ouch!"

"Oh, hold still!" Mrs. Gleason responded. "Don't be such a baby!"

"Wow. I guess everyone is having a bad morning," muttered Lucy, handing towels to each boy to dry their hands. Using a wet dishrag, she washed sticky jam from their faces and pulled crumbs from their hair.

Retrieving the dirty cutlery from the floor, Lucy added them to the plates and glasses already in the sink. "If you both have finished with breakfast, you can go to your rooms and quietly play until we go to the pool."

"I'm still hungry," Christopher wailed, plopping down in a chair at the table. "I didn't get to eat anything yet," he grumbled. "Will you make me some pancakes?"

"Yeah! Pancakes!" Bradley mimicked. "Pancakes! Pancakes! I want pancakes!"

"All right, already! Sheesh," said Lucy. "Give it a rest, little dude. I will make pancakes if you both sit quietly and don't fight with each other—otherwise, no pancakes. Cold cereal, maybe, but no pancakes. Got it?" Lucy glared at each of them.

"Got it," they said in unison.

How do they do *that? It creeps me out,* Lucy thought with a shudder. Turning the faucet on again, she ran water in the sink to wash the dishes and added a squirt of dish soap. While the sink was filling, she put a frying pan on the stove to heat, began mixing ingredients for the cakes, and dropped a dollop of butter in the hot fry pan.

"Lucy," the boys said.

"Nope, I can't hear you. You're sitting quietly, remember?" Lucy said, preparing to spoon batter into the pan, her back to the sink.

"Lucy!" they yelled, then erupted into giggles.

Lucy turned, glowering, to see them giggling and pointing to the sink where the dish soap had frothed into a mountain of bubbles and water cascaded over the counter and down the front of the cabinets.

"*No!*" Lucy bellowed, dropping the spatula into the batter bowl. The bowl teetered on the edge of the counter as she grabbed hand towels from a drawer. Swabbing up the water from the counter and cabinet fronts, she flicked the faucet off with an elbow. The towels dropped to the floor, where she used her foot to swipe at the growing puddle. She was flailing at the mountain of bubbles, trying to push them back into the sink, when the odor of something burning wafted past her nose. "Oh, no!" she whimpered, turning to the stove. The butter was smoking, charring the pan, and spitting hot greasiness all over the stovetop and the surrounding counter.

"Lucy! You're burning something!" Molly Gleason screamed, running through the kitchen doorway to the stove. She snatched a nearby hot pad, grabbed up the smoking pan, and turned the burner off. "What on earth are you doing? You are so easily distracted. You've got to learn to be more focused. The butter could have started a fire!" Her frazzled ponytail was hanging even lower over her shoulder. "Assuming that used to be butter." She dropped the pan into the dishwater, causing it to sizzle and hiss.

Lucy felt a wave of discouragement wash over her. It seemed everything she did only made things worse the harder she tried.

"I know! I'm so sorry! I was trying to clean the boys up and make pancakes for their breakfast," Lucy explained. "It won't happen again, Mrs. Gleason. I'll wash these dishes, then concentrate on the pancakes. One thing at a time," she said, pushing up her sleeves and plunging her hands into the dishwater. She scrubbed hard at the charred pan.

"I will make the pancakes," Mrs. Gleason said firmly. "You can finish those dishes, if you would please, then you can get the boys' things together for the trip to the pool this afternoon."

"Yes, ma'am," Lucy said as she quietly washed and stacked the clean dishes in the drainer. When Bradley and Christopher finished their breakfast, they disappeared into the living room to play video games.

Mrs. Gleason and Lucy finished the dishes and cleaned up the rest of the kitchen mess, then Mrs. Gleason hurried upstairs to shower and change. Lucy plodded down the hall toward the boys' rooms. A dark, intangible cloud seemed to surround Lucy. Her feet felt as though they weighed twenty pounds each at the end of thick wooden legs. *What is wrong with me today? I can't do anything right*, she thought. *Mom was cranky at me. Even Mrs. Gleason thinks I'm a mess-up.*

Lucy filled the boys' small backpacks with extra T-shirts and shorts, towels, and water toys before lumbering back to the kitchen for snacks and juice boxes. Entering the kitchen, she quickly pinched her lips together and hoped she didn't start laughing.

Mr. Gleason was wearing a large Elmo bandage over the cut on his chin.

He had just snapped the lid on one of two totes filled with brochures and catalogs for the company's booth at the trade fair downtown. Stacking one tote on top of the other, he carried them through the kitchen's side door and out to the car.

Mrs. Gleason, wearing a pantsuit and her wet hair neatly combed, was quickly filling a picnic basket with sandwiches, fruit, and drinks. She flipped the top shut with a bang. Clutching the picnic basket in one hand and her purse and phone in the other, she rushed past Lucy and followed her husband out the door.

"Okay, goodbye," Lucy said, frowning as she watched them through the kitchen window as they frantically packed the car. Mrs. Gleason headed back to the house.

"Sorry, Luce," said Mrs. Gleason, leaning in through the doorway. "We're both feeling muddled today. It's so unlike either of us. The event starts at one o'clock. The salesman helping Patrick backed out at the last minute, and I had to cancel my outing today with my sister so I can help Patrick at the trade-fair booth," she rambled. "We won't even be able to get away for lunch, so I had to pack a lunch to bring with us. And we still need to stop by his office to get the supplies the other guy was supposed to bring," she lamented. "It's just all so discombobulated."

"Once you get to the show and can relax a little," Lucy offered, "I'm sure everything will be okay."

"I hope so. Thanks for watching the boys," Mrs. Gleason said. "There's money in the cookie jar and take-out menus on the top of the refrigerator."

"I can make something for the boys. I don't mind cooking," Lucy said.

"Don't even think about cooking after that little mishap this morning!" growled Mrs. Gleason, causing Lucy's head to snap back, wide-eyed and lips pinched. "The boys will be much safer if you order take-out food. Not to mention, less risk of you burning down the house!" The side door banged shut behind her. A heated exchange of words followed the sound of a car door slamming.

Lucy stared at the space Mrs. Gleason had just occupied. "Okay," she whispered, her chin trembling. Lucy crawled into a chair at the snack counter and dropped her head on her arms. Feeling utterly discouraged and dejected, she listened to the squealing tires and raised voices drifting away in the distance. Tears squeezed between her closed eyelids and fell softly to the counter. After a few minutes, she sniffled, slid from the chair, dried her eyes, and swiped a towel across the wet counter.

Picking up her backpack, she shuffled toward the living room and plopped on the couch. She absentmindedly watched the boys as they played several of their video games. Despite the happy but raucous giggles, Lucy couldn't manage even a tiny smile at their antics. She retrieved the vampire book to read a few pages, but it eventually fell to her lap unopened. The chiming of the mantel clock disrupted her brooding.

"Hey, guys!" said Lucy, trying to get Bradley's and Christopher's attention. They ignored her and leaned toward the television, their eyes laser focused on the video. "Guys!" she bellowed, reaching over and turning off the television.

"We're still playing," they said in unison. "Turn it back on!"

"No, it's almost time for the community pool to open. You want to go swimming, don't you?" Lucy cajoled. "Let's get you both into your swim trunks, and then we can head over to the pool. Maybe, if we get there before noon, Mr. Arthur will let us in early. Afterward, we can get ice cream at Two Scoopers."

"Fine," grumbled Bradley, tossing down the game remote.

"I guess," grumbled Christopher as he joined his brother, and together they trudged to their rooms to change.

"Alrighty then," Lucy muttered, and gathering all the backpacks, she plodded out to the garage where the bikes were hanging on ceiling hooks. She got them down and pushed them out to the driveway. Lining them up, she placed each boy's backpack on his seat. Mrs. Gleason's turquoise racer was leaning against a back wall. Lucy retrieved it and put it next to the others. Tightening the straps on her backpack, she slipped it on.

"Boys! C'mon!" Lucy yelled as she entered the kitchen. "Are you ready yet?" She heard the video game playing again. *Grrr!* Lucy thought. *It's going to be a long day.* She went back into the living room where the boys were sitting together on the ottoman playing the game. They still hadn't changed. Standing in front of the television, she turned it off.

"We're still playing," they said in unison. "Turn it back on!"

"I just asked you both to go get ready and put your swim trunks on! We're going to the pool." Lucy stormed.

"You did not," they said in unison.

"I'm not going to argue with you," Lucy said, squinting her eyes at them. "Go get your suits on!" She pointed to the hallway. "Now!"

"Fine," grumbled Bradley, tossing down the game remote.

"I guess," grumbled Christopher as he joined his brother, and together they trudged to their rooms to change.

Lucy blinked several times as she watched them. *Talk about déjà vu, huh.* She turned toward the kitchen and tripped over their backpacks.

What? I thought I put these with the bikes. Shaking her head, she picked up the bags, went out to the garage, and froze in her tracks.

The bicycles were hanging from the hooks in the ceiling, and Mrs. Gleason's turquoise racer was leaning against the back wall. *Huh? Wow. I really am losing it. I could have sworn I got those bikes out already. Brain fart!* Sighing, she went through the routine again and placed all the bicycles on the driveway.

What is keeping them already? They'd better not be playing that video game, thought Lucy as she walked into the kitchen. "Boys! Let's go!" she yelled. Loud squeals and giggles emanated from the living room where the video game was playing.

Taking a deep breath, Lucy walked calmly into the living room, turned off the television, and placed the gaming console on top of the nearby bookcase.

"We're still playing," they said in unison. "Turn it back on!"

"I have asked you both twice now to go get ready and put your swim trunks on. We're going to the pool to swim and have fun," Lucy hissed through clenched teeth.

"You did not," they said in unison.

"I did too! I'm not going to argue with you," Lucy said, glaring at them. "Go get your suits on!" She pointed to the hallway. "Now!"

"Fine," grumbled Bradley, tossing down the game remote.

"I guess," grumbled Christopher, and joining his brother, they trudged toward the hallway.

Lucy turned and tripped over the boys' backpacks. She stared wide-eyed at the packs on the floor. *What is this? I feel like I'm in a bad movie that keeps replaying. Well, it stops here,* she complained to herself.

Without saying a word, she grabbed each boy's hand and stomped down the hallway, pulling the complaining boys behind her. She entered the first bedroom door. "Christopher, please go get your swim trunks on, and no fooling around. I'm going to wait right here with Bradley until you finish dressing, and then we're going to do the same thing for Bradley," Lucy ordered. "Now, go."

Confused and frustrated, Christopher quickly scrounged through his dresser drawer until he found his trunks. Retreating into his closet, he changed into them, then stepped into the hallway where Lucy nodded approvingly. She straightened his T-shirt.

Turning the other boy around, she gently pushed him toward his bedroom. "Bradley, it's your turn. Go get your swim trunks on, honey," Lucy said quietly. He hurried into his room and returned a few minutes later, wearing his swim trunks and a T-shirt like his brother.

"Good job, guys," Lucy offered. She was feeling anything but confident, but she would worry about that later. "Okay, let's head for the pool. Sound like a plan?" Raising her eyebrows, she smiled weakly.

"Okay," Christopher muttered as he followed Lucy and Bradley to the garage. "Lucy? Are you mad at us?" he asked, scrubbing his shoe at the ground.

"No, honey, I'm not mad at you," Lucy said while getting the bikes down again. "I am just having a bad day. You know, when things don't go quite the way you expect them to. It's like getting vanilla ice cream when you wanted chocolate, you know?" He was struggling with his backpack, so she helped him slip it on.

"I think so," Christopher said, getting on his bicycle. "I hope Two Scoopers will have a lot of chocolate ice cream today. You need some bad."

Lucy dropped her head and pinched her lips together to suppress a grin. A dimple appeared in both of her cheeks, which made Bradley giggle. She snorted. *Who knew? The wisdom of little boys*, Lucy thought.

"Are we getting ice cream? I want ice cream," Bradley chimed in. "I want a scoop of chocolate and a scoop of peanut butter and a great big scoop of cookie dough right on top!"

"Well, okay then, little man," Lucy smiled wryly. "You'll be bouncing off the walls with a sugar high by the time your parents get home." Climbing onto the racer and feeling exhausted already, she peddled slowly and led the way to the neighborhood pool and park.

 16 More Troubles

Arthur, the park attendant, saw them approaching on their bicycles and waved. "Ah already unlocked the gate for ya, Lucy," he said as they hopped off the bikes. "It's good to see ya. Ah kinda hoped you might be a-comin' round sometime this week," he said, swinging the gate open and waiting while Lucy helped the boys place the bikes in the rack and then relieved them of their backpacks. He scratched lightly at his thinning gray hair, then stuffed his hands into the pockets of his baggy bib overalls. "Seems it's a been a month o' Sundays since ah seen ya last."

"You're a kind man, Arthur," Lucy said, "and thank you for unlocking it early. I need this downtime." Lucy liked Arthur. He reminded her of Happy, one of the Seven Dwarfs, because his cheeks disappeared into deep craters when he smiled, and his missing teeth gave him a comical appearance.

"You sound sorta discouraged, Lucy." Worry etched his face, puckering the wrinkles around his brown eyes even more. "You tired or sumthin?" asked Arthur in his easy southern drawl. Closing the gate, he walked with her to the pool as she pulled life jackets from the backpacks for each boy. The boys ran ahead of her and jumped into the shallow end of the pool.

"You could say I'm having a bad day," Lucy said and then groaned as she watched the boys roughhousing and splashing water everywhere. "Christopher! Bradley! Come get your floaters on! Remember Lucy's Rules!" she shouted. The boys splashed each other, then climbed out to get their life jackets.

"Aw! We don't need those dumb things," Christopher complained. "Our mom doesn't make us wear them."

"Well, I'm not your mom, and when you're with me, you wear them. Lucy's Rules," Lucy said firmly as she snugged Bradley into his and tightened the straps.

Kneeling in front of Christopher, who was struggling with the snap buckles, Arthur chuckled as Christopher muttered under his breath about "stupid rules." He took the jacket from Christopher, pinched the clips open, and handed it back. "Rules are good things ta have, son. They're ta keep ya safe. If ya disobey the rules, ya could get hurt, and then your mama would be frightfully mad at Lucy. Ya wouldn't want Lucy ta get in trouble now, would ya?"

Christopher looked at the older man. "Nah, Lucy's okay," he said, glancing sideways at Lucy, who was still fidgeting with Bradley's jacket straps. "We really like her," he whispered.

"Don't tell her that, okay?"

Arthur chuckled. "Nah, that's jus' fine," he whispered. "Your secret is safe with old Arthur." Grinning, Arthur stood and patted the boy on his head. "You have fun today, son. And remember what ah said."

Lucy realized she had forgotten to put sunscreen on the boys before leaving the house, so she slathered nearly the entire tube onto their bodies, making them look like miniature ghosts. Christopher took off running toward the pool and cannonballed into the water with a big splash.

"I kinda think you're gonna have a mite of trouble with those boys, Lucy," Arthur said as he watched the younger boy try to cannonball into the water like his brother. But Bradley didn't quite manage to roll tight enough. The effect looked more like a turtle splashing flat on his back. Arthur let go with a laugh and slapped his thigh as Bradley came up sputtering with a massive grin on his face.

"Arthur, it's going to be a very long day," said Lucy, plunking down on a chaise under the shade of the pavilion, her shoulders slumping. She pulled out a big beach towel, covered the chaise with it, and settled in with the vampire book from the library. Keeping the kids in sight over the top of the book, she sighed. "How's your day going, Arthur?"

"Oh, ah keeps busy. There's sure enough ta do around here, what with the summa' in full swing now. There's the pool and all the trimin' to do and grass ta cut. Well, that's 'nuff about me. How's come you're havina bad day?"

"I can't seem to do anything right today. Mom was cranky with me. I burned the butter and flooded the floor at the Gleasons' house," Lucy said, a breathy sigh escaping her. "If the Gleasons would have had time to get someone else to babysit the boys, I wouldn't be here. Everyone is mad at me, except maybe you, and the day isn't over yet." She clutched the book to her chest as she wrapped her arms around herself, a sudden chill washing over her.

"Well, if you need anythin', jus' remember help's always available ta them that ask," Arthur drawled. "Bye now, Lucy," he said, waving. He slowly sauntered through the gate, closed it, and moseyed off to trim bushes on the other side of the fence surrounding the pool.

Lucy absentmindedly watched him for a few minutes as he went about snipping and shaping the bushes, his movements precise and efficient. *Wait. What did he say?* Lucy thought. *"Help's always available to them that ask"? Huh, that is rather weird.*

"Cannonball!" Christopher squealed, launching himself into the pool. A giant wave spouted upward, sending a wall of water cascading over Lucy as she sat holding the library book.

Thoroughly drenched, her mouth open and eyes scrunched shut, Lucy gasped and bounded from the chaise. The soaked book fell to the ground unnoticed as she stomped through puddles to the edge of the pool. Water snaked its way down her face, arms, and legs in rivulets as she stood glaring, tight-lipped, at Christopher, who was floating in the middle of the pool.

"Uh-oh," Bradley said, pointing at Lucy. "I think you're in trouble." He paddled to the opposite side of the pool, crawled out, and sat on the edge. "I didn't do anything, just so you know."

"Out! Now!" fumed Lucy, pointing toward the steps. "That was bad. Very. Very. Bad. You know the rules. Sit in the corner, and don't you dare say even one word. Not one word. Got it?" She quaked all over as she followed Christopher to the corner of the enclosure and knelt to remove his life jacket. Lucy could barely undo the snap buckles with her trembling fingers.

"I'm sorry! I really am!" Christopher whimpered. "I didn't think you would get all wet." He stood still as Lucy tugged at the exasperating buckles. "I'm sorry, Lucy." He sucked in halting breaths.

Lucy looked at Christopher without saying a word. His eyes, brimming with tears, were as huge as saucers as he looked back at her. His bottom lip quivered as he bravely stood there, waiting for her to erupt at him.

Lucy sniffled, blinked, then suddenly leaned forward and planted a kiss on his cheek. "You are just acting like a little boy. A bad little boy, but a boy just the same," she said, slipping his jacket off. "However, rules apply to everyone. You are not supposed to splash people who are not in the pool. You have to learn to follow the rules." She hugged him back as he wrapped his arms around her neck and squeezed. "Your time-out is twenty minutes. Sit."

"Okay," he said contritely, and, dropping to the ground, he sat with his back against the fence and drew his knees to his chest.

"What about me?" a little voice asked.

"What about you?" Lucy asked, turning to look at Bradley sitting on the pool's edge. He kicked his feet in the water while surveying the scene. "Did you break the rules?"

"No."

"Then you're not in trouble."

"Okay. Can I have my water toys?" Bradley asked.

"They are in your backpack. You may come to get your toys," Lucy said, retrieving his backpack and holding it out to him. He padded over to take his toys out, then threw them in the pool. "Are we still getting ice cream?"

Lucy snorted. *One-track mind.* "Yes, we can still get ice cream later if there are no more infractions."

"What's a frack-shun?" Bradley pinched his brows together.

"Infraction, it means 'no more rule breaking.' Got it?" Lucy shook her head. *I'm waiting till I'm ninety to have kids*, she thought, rolling her eyes.

"I didn't break any rules. I should get ice cream," Bradley stated, then confidently walked down the steps into the pool and swam out to where his toys floated in the middle.

Yup. Waiting till I'm ninety, Lucy thought, walking back to the pavilion and picking up the wet book. Holding it by a corner of its cover, it dripped water down her arm. *Just great*, she thought. *No way they're not going to notice this.* Dropping it on the chaise, she grabbed another towel from her backpack and toweled off. She put the book on the used towel, laying it open in the sun and hoping the heat would dry it out. Most of the pages were wet, so she wasn't too hopeful.

She sat in the shade of the pavilion, but the slight breeze was making her chilly, so she dragged the chaise into the sun. The warmth felt good on her skin, and hopefully, it would dry her damp clothes. She had brought extra clothes but didn't feel like making an effort to change out of her wet things. Who knew? The way her day was going, she'd probably fall into the pool.

Curling up and snuggling into the towel, she watched as Bradley played with his toys. Glancing around, she frowned, wondering why they were the only ones in the pool on such a hot summer day. The sun shone white hot in a cloudless sky above them. So, where were the other children? Not that she minded; it was blissfully quiet with only the gentle splashing from Bradley.

A fluttering sound came from behind her. She sat up and swung around in the chaise. A huge black crow hopped along the fence rail toward her. His head jerked as she stared at it, squinting. Then the crow winked at her. Malpar!

"Lucy?" Christopher asked. "Is my time up yet? My butt is getting tired from sitting on it."

Lucy quickly glanced at her watch. "Yup, your time is up, little man," she said, looking back at the pool. Bradley was still splashing his toys around. "You can go swim now, but put your life jacket back on," she said. "Need help?"

"Nope, thanks, Lucy!" said Christopher, slipping his jacket on and snapping it shut as he padded toward the pool.

Lucy swung around again, looking for the bird-man, but he was no longer sitting on the fence rail. Reaching down, she felt around for her backpack while watching for the bird-man to reappear somewhere. The boys splashed in the pool, oblivious to their surroundings. Lucy checked the Spectrescope for messages and then scoped the pool enclosure for any spirits. It was clear. They had the pool to themselves.

*   *   *   *

Eventually, a few other children arrived at the pool with their parents. The boys spent the afternoon playing in and around the pool with friends amid squeals and giggles. Lucy alternated Bradley and Christopher's pool time with quiet time spent in the shade of the pavilion. She had brought books and their gaming tablet to entertain them while they dried off, drank water, or ate snacks. Though the remainder of the day went without incident, Lucy was still discouraged and apprehensive. By late afternoon when they got to Two Scoopers for ice cream, everyone was tired and fussy.

Two Scoopers had already run out of Christopher's favorite soft-serve ice cream, orange-vanilla twist, so he had to settle for two scoops of orange sherbet with a scoop of vanilla ice cream sandwiched in between. "It's not the same! I don't like it!" he wailed.

"Honey, it's the same, only different! It's orange and vanilla, just like your twist cone, only it's hard ice cream," Lucy explained. He wailed while he ate it.

Bradley decided he wanted something different. But Two Scoopers had run out of cookie dough ice cream too. So Bradley whined.

"How about if we put chocolate and peanut butter ice cream with something else? Vanilla, maybe?" Lucy pleaded.

"No!" Bradley cried.

In the end, Bradley chose a scoop each of chocolate and peanut butter ice cream, topped with a scoop of superman ice cream. Lucy thought she would gag, but at least it kept him quiet for a while. When the boys finished their treats, they all peddled sluggishly toward the Gleasons' home.

She helped the boys get cleaned up, changed into fresh clothes, and then ordered pizza for an early dinner. The boys had ravenous appetites and gobbled up their share of pizza as Lucy picked at the slice on her plate.

After dinner, they rode their bikes to the playground. The boys chased each other around, played on the swings, and rode the merry-go-round. Lucy was exhausted just watching them.

The sun was still hours from setting when they rode home and stored the bikes in the garage. As they entered the kitchen, Bradley threw up, splashing puke all over the floor and cabinets. It wasn't a pretty sight. Lucy threw a hand over her nose and mouth to keep from gagging and barfing herself. She threw paper towels over the mess on the floor to cover it while she quickly washed the slime from Bradley's face. Then Christopher threw up just as she finished cleaning the floor.

Being careful not to breathe too deeply, she started over.

Lucy was still kneeling over the second mess when she heard the Gleasons' car pull into the driveway. Lucy could hear them bickering outside while they unloaded the car. Quickly wiping the wet cloth across the floor, she was rolling up to stand when Mrs. Gleason screamed.

"My babies! Whatever did you do to them?" Mrs. Gleason wailed.

"Good heavens!" said Mr. Gleason, stepping into the kitchen behind his wife.

Lucy slipped, and landing on her butt on the wet floor, looked up wild-eyed at Mrs. Gleason, who was staring at the boys.

The boys looked decidedly sick. Bradley had begun to whimper, a sheen of sweat beading on his pink forehead, and Christopher was moaning and clutching his stomach. "I don't feel so good," he lamented.

"What did you feed them, for goodness' sake? They were fine this morning when we left, and after a few hours in your care, they are sick as can be!" Molly Gleason groaned and placed her hand on Bradley's forehead. "He's got a fever! Patrick, get the car ready! We're taking them to the urgent care clinic."

"I was cautious with them, Mrs. Gleason. I swear!" Lucy said, scrambling to her feet. "They spent equal time in the pool and the shade. I made them drink plenty of water, and we brought fruit and nuts and granola for snacks. No junk food, except ice cream when we went to Two Scoopers. Honest, I don't understand."

"What did they eat for dinner? You didn't cook anything, did you?" Mrs. Gleason snapped. "I expressly told you, 'No cooking!' "

"I ordered a pepperoni pizza!" Lucy huffed, throwing her hands up. "It's their favorite thing to order when I babysit. After dinner, we rode the bikes to the playground for a while and then came home." Lucy frantically looked from Mr. Gleason, who was holding Christopher, back to Mrs. Gleason. "It was just a typical day."

"Well, I've had enough of your excuses, girl," Mrs. Gleason snapped. "Get your things. We'll drop you home on our way to the clinic." She picked up Bradley and hurried out the door.

"Yes, ma'am," Lucy snapped. Picking up her backpack, she stomped after Mrs. Gleason out to the car. Mr. Gleason tagged behind, carrying Christopher, who was still whimpering.

Molly Gleason sat between the boys in the back seat, leaving Lucy to crawl into the front seat where she sat clutching her backpack. Instinctively, she felt around in the side pocket for the Spectrescope to make sure it was still there. Mr. Gleason backed the car slowly down the driveway. Lucy glanced at her watch. Still time. "Would you please drop me at the library instead? I can walk home from there," Lucy asked, now feeling measly and her voice nearly nonexistent.

"Fine," said Mr. Gleason, and turning the car onto the road, he drove toward the library.

"Thank you, Mr. Gleason."

"You can be sure," Mr. Gleason began, his posture stiff and unyielding, "we will be calling your mother to let her know how disappointed we are with you. Don't expect to babysit for our children ever again."

"No, sir," said Lucy as she slunk lower into the car seat.

Mr. Gleason parked at the curb in front of the library a few minutes later. Lucy got out and carefully closed the door. Just as she stepped back from the curb, the Gleasons' car roared down the road and disappeared around a corner. Sighing, she turned, trudged into the library, and groaned.

The grumpy librarian was on duty.

The Ghost of Darwin Stewart

Her hair was in its usual bun, and her glasses perched on the end of her nose. She was busy counting the books that piled up on the counter next to her. Ignoring Lucy, she swung her chair around and tapped furiously at the computer keyboard, leaning forward to squint at the screen.

"Um, excuse me," Lucy said. "I need to return a book possibly."

"One moment, please," the librarian said curtly and continued to bang at the keys.

Lucy shifted from one foot to the other as she waited. Pulling the soggy book from her backpack, she held it below the counter's edge and out of the librarian's sight. Licking her lips and swallowing, she looked at the woman who was still harassing the keys.

"Excuse me, how much longer, please? I'd like to get home before it gets dark."

"That's the problem with you kids," the woman said. "You're always so impatient. What do you need?"

"I need to return a book, if possible."

"What do you mean 'if possible'?" The woman grunted and leaned forward to stare at Lucy over the top of her glasses. "Do you need to return a book or not?"

Lucy held up the soggy vampire book.

"Well, how careless!" she scolded. "That's going to cost you, young lady. You can't damage books and then expect to return them. You will have to pay for a new book instead." The bun bounced about as she flipped through the pages of a directory, her finger finally following the print lines across the page and down a column. She reached for the pencil tucked behind her ear, wrote something on a piece of stationery, and handed it to Lucy.

"That much?" Lucy exclaimed, reading the paper. "It'd be cheaper if I just bought it from the bookstore at the mall and returned the new one!"

"Well, too bad you didn't think of that," the librarian replied, returning the pencil to its spot behind her ear. "Next time, use those little gray cells you're carrying around inside your head. If you had asked for help, I would have suggested you do just that. The library is now closed. Goodbye," she said, walking around the counter and over to the doors. Jangling the keys in hand, she tapped her foot as she waited for Lucy.

Feeling discouraged, Lucy stuffed the soggy vampire book into the backpack and trudged through the doors. A resounding click echoed as the bolt slid home, locking the doors behind her.

Lucy dropped her backpack on the bench in front of the library. She lowered herself onto the seat, wishing she could melt into the wood. Her mouth fell open as she laid her head against the back and stared at the dark threatening clouds gathering overhead. A large blackbird landed on the seat next to her with a flutter of mighty wings. She didn't need to look. She knew it was Malpar.

Snapping her mouth shut, she sat up and glared at the bird. "What're you doing here? Come to laugh at the pathetic ghost hunter?"

"Lucy, you must give me the Spectrescope," said Malpar. "Why should you involve yourself in a battle that has raged for millennia?" He tilted his head, looking very much like an oversized pigeon, and blinked at her. "Just hand over the Spectrescope, then you can forget about all of this and go back to your life." Malpar clicked his beak and stretched out a wing as if expecting Lucy to hand over the Spectrescope.

"No," Lucy said, her pouty voice barely a whisper. Her bottom lip slipped further out as her head drooped.

"Lucy, if you do not do as the Master wants, he might harm you and your friend." Malpar hopped along the bench till he was right next to Lucy. He stretched his neck toward her and stared. Lucy felt as though she were a specimen in a science project, and he was waiting for her to turn into mucus or something.

"Go away. I don't want to talk about this anymore. I just want to go home." Lucy snatched her backpack from the bench and trudged down the walk. She didn't need to turn and look. She knew Malpar was still watching. After a moment, a flutter of wings told her he had flown off.

A big droplet of moisture splattered on her cheek. *Great, just great*, she thought, glancing up. *This day just keeps getting better.* She plodded toward home, the backpack feeling like a tremendous weight on her shoulders as the rain pelted down.

17 Schuyler Disappears

"Thanks for taking me to the bookstore, Mr. and Mrs. McGoo," said Lucy as she climbed from their car, a new copy of the vampire book clutched in her hand. "I guess it won't matter if I finish reading the ending before I return it to the library. It's already late, so what's another day or two of late fees?" she muttered.

"Do you think a plate of my chocolate chip cookies might help?" asked Mrs. McGoo, wrapping a pudgy arm around Lucy's shoulders as they stood on the driveway. "Maybe they could put a smile back on your face? How about it? Want some gooey chocolate chip cookies?" she queried, a sympathetic smile dimpling her weathered puffy cheeks.

"Thanks for the offer, Mrs. McGoo, but I don't think even your cookies could help right now," said Lucy. "It is best if I just go curl up in a corner with a book and stay out of everyone's way. That way, I can't get into any more trouble," she lamented. "At least, I don't think I can."

"Aw, it can't be as bad as all that, Miss Lucy," said Mr. Bill. "You've had a long face for several days. Won't you tell old Bill why you're so down?" he said as he swiped a hanky across his brow, mopping at a bead of sweat.

"Whew, it's a warm one today. How about a glass of Viv's sweet lemonade and some cookies while we sit on the porch and chat? What do you say?"

"Well, maybe later, Mr. Bill," said Lucy, plodding slowly toward the side gate with her head drooping. She waved before she rounded the corner of her house and entered the kitchen.

"Aw, our poor girl," said Vivian. "She's so disheartened. I could throttle that Malpar. I'd like to—"

"Just wait, Viv. It'll turn out all right," said Bill. "You'll see."

Lucy watched the McGoos from the kitchen window as they took their purchases into the house, the screen door banging shut behind Mr. Bill's slim form. *They're so sweet. I'm glad they're our neighbors*, she thought.

Lucy found a note from Mom on the kitchen counter saying she would be home late from the office, Dale was at the mall, and he wouldn't be home early either. *Wonderful, no one home to tell about my troubles. Not that anyone would care anyway*, Lucy thought. She stomped on the trash compactor's lever, crumpled up the paper, and tossed it into the bin, then slammed the bin shut.

"Hey, Metrocom!" she yelled. "Where you at, little dude? Metrocom!" Lucy listened for an answering "meow" but only heard the soft hum of the refrigerator. She peeked into the living room but didn't see the cat any-where. *Not even the dumb cat cares enough to come to greet me*, she thought, trudging up the back stairs to her room.

The backpack and the book landed with a thud on top of the trunk. Lucy kicked her sneakers off as she crawled onto the bed and rolled into a fetal position. Hot tears leaked from her eyes, wetting the bedspread and making Lucy sniffle. Even the afternoon skies had clouded over again, pelting the roof and the shingled ledge outside her window with huge rain-drops. She wrapped her arms around her legs and curled up tighter. She stayed like that for a while and cried softly. It seemed everything was going wrong.

The Williams were mad because of the destroyed jam and jellies, and they still had a creepy ghost in their house. Mom was furious and mortified because of the incidents with the Williams and the Gleasons, not to mention the ruined book, and the Gleasons were mad because the boys had gotten sick. Malpar was haunting Lucy trying to get the Spectrescope, and she still needed to return the replacement book to the library.

Where is Iam in all of this? What gives? Lucy thought, pushing down into the pillows.

The house was silent. A door creaked open somewhere. Lucy bolted upright, her ears straining to hear any sound. A soft *thud, thud, thud* came from the direction of the kitchen near the back stairs. Chills crawled along her skin as she reached for the backpack, unzipped the main compartment, and put her hand on the Spectrescope inside.

"Is anyone home?" Dale bellowed.

Phew! Lucy thought and quickly swiped her hands over her face to wipe away the remaining tears.

"Iam," she whispered, "I need to talk to you. Where are you?"

"Who were you talking to, Squirt?" asked Dale, poking his head around her doorway.

"No one, I guess," Lucy said, wrinkling her nose at him. "Ew! You stink. Where've you been? You're all hot and sweaty."

"Rock climbing at the mall."

"Again? Did you ever meet the new girl?"

"Yeah, when Harry introduced her as his new girlfriend," he said with a grimace. "Can you believe it? A dork like Harry and a babe like that, go figure." Harry had been Dale's best friend until last Christmas when Harry set off a stink bomb in the boys' bathroom at school. Dale got blamed for it and received a three-day suspension from school. Harry never owned up to it, and they had barely spoken since.

"Harry? Really? She isn't as bright as you thought." Lucy smirked. "Don't worry. You'll probably meet gobs of cool girls when school starts up. I mean, really? Who could resist a big strapping guy who thinks he's a ninja?"

"Gee, thanks, Squirt. I think I'll just go to my room and mope now," said Dale. "You know, I like rock climbing. It's challenging." He disappeared down the hallway. "Hey, what's for dinner?" he bellowed from his bedroom.

"Probably pizza," Lucy yelled back, "and just as soon as you order it. Mom's working late again tonight, so we're on our own."

"Oh, yeah, I forgot," he yelled. "Want some? I'll order one for you too."

"No, thanks anyway. I'm not hungry. I'll just make a sandwich or something later."

Lucy plopped on her stomach on the bed and stretched out, looking out the window for Iam, but he wasn't there. She closed her eyes and soon drifted off to sleep for a while.

"Lucy," a voice whispered.

Lucy stirred and rolled over.

"Trust," the voice whispered again. "Trust what you have learned. You are never alone."

Yawning, she pushed herself up on one elbow, leaned over, and looked out the window. The lowering sun had finally reappeared following the late afternoon rain, and the rays were bathing the broken clouds in a peachy tint. She glanced up and down the street, hoping to see Iam, but the road was empty except for a few children playing. Sighing, she rolled over, threw her pillow on the floor, and got up. Her reflection gazed back at her in the dresser mirror, the large gray eyes confused and bewildered. *Where is he? He said he would come if I called. Doesn't he hear me anymore?*

Straightening her shirt, she ran her hands over her jean shorts to smooth the wrinkles out and went down to the kitchen, where she found a note from Dale taped to the counter. He was meeting some friends for pizza and a movie instead and would be back late. *Perfect,* she thought. *Home alone with a ghost on the loose whose sidekick is a smelly bird-man.*

Dirty dishes were piled on the counter, forgotten. Laying the cell phone on the counter, Lucy grabbed the plates and dumped the soggy food into the garbage disposal. Flipping the faucet on, she rinsed the plates and glasses before putting them in the dishwasher.

Her stomach rumbled. Deciding on a sandwich, she took the bread from the cupboard and grabbed the peanut butter from the pantry shelf. Her cell phone rang. Swiping the screen, she tapped Speaker and unscrewed the peanut butter jar.

"Hello?" she asked as she swirled a knife through the peanut butter and plopped it on a piece of bread.

"Lucy!" screamed Mrs. Williams. "The ghosts took Schuyler!"

"*What?*" cried Lucy, dropping the peanut butter jar and knife onto the sticky bread. Anxiety gripped her chest.

"The ghosts! The ghosts took Schuyler!" Mrs. Williams sobbed.

"*Ghosts!* How many are there?" Lucy exclaimed, her mouth falling open.

"Oh, please forgive us, Lucy! We had no idea it was all true. You've got to help us," cried Mrs. Williams. "You can help us, can't you? Schuyler told us you have some sort of connection with the ghosts. We don't know what else to do!" wailed Mrs. Williams.

"Where is Schuyler?" Lucy's hands trembled, and she gripped the counter hard. She squeezed her eyes shut, swallowed, and breathed deeply. "Tell me what happened. Please, I need to know."

"We were all going out for dinner and a movie when Schuyler ran back into the house. She said she had forgotten something. When she didn't come out after a few minutes, Stephen went to get her and couldn't get in the house. Schuyler was pounding on the door, and it wouldn't budge,"

Mrs. Williams whimpered. "She's still locked in the house. Stephen said he looked through the window and could see a horrible-looking ghost standing behind her, laughing!"

"Mrs. Williams, listen to me. You've got to get away from the house. I don't know what I can do, but I am leaving now. Don't go near the house!" Lucy ended the call, stuffed the phone in her pocket, and ran up the back stairs to her room.

With the Spectrescope safely tucked inside the backpack, she removed the silver metallic vest and slipped it on, then stuffed the hat into her waistband. Moving quickly, Lucy grabbed the buckle ring from the dresser and slid it on her finger. Turning to leave, she noticed the trunk lid was open. Briefly staring at it, she knelt and rummaged through the trunk for the antique mirror.

Hands shaking wildly, Lucy looked at her bouncing image in the mirror. *I'm about as ready as I'm going to be*, she thought and stuffed the mirror into the backpack as well.

She clomped down the stairs two at a time, the backpack bouncing wildly on her shoulder. She rushed through the kitchen door, the screen banging shut behind her, and cut through the side-yard gate.

Mrs. McGoo was sitting on her back porch stoop. "My goodness! Where are you going in such a hurry?" The welcoming aroma of chocolate chip cookies wafted on the warm evening air.

"Later!" yelled Lucy, waving a hand and rushing past Mrs. McGoo down the driveway. She cut around the front of the McGoos house, across the lawn, and disappeared down the street.

"Bill, it looks like something is finally afoot. She's in a mighty big hurry."

"Yup, it sure looks that way, Vivian," said Bill, stepping through the kitchen door. "I don't think even your famous cookies can help her right now. If you are ready, shall we go?"

* * * *

Lucy ran past Mr. and Mrs. Williams and up the steps to the house.

Mr. Williams had his arm around his wife's shoulders, hugging her tightly as they stood on the sidewalk. She whimpered between sobs that shook her entire body. Mr. Williams looked positively green.

Gasping hard, Lucy stared at the house, taking in details of the blank windows, the door shut tight, and the absence of any light. The sun cast hideous orange hues across the face of the old house. She pulled the Spectrescope from the backpack and dropped the bag on the porch floor. Taking a deep breath and gripping the scope firmly, she walked to the front door. Something shiny on the ground caught her eye. She picked it up, and her heart skipped a beat.

It was Schuyler's bracelet.

Shaking, she put the bracelet in her pocket. Struggling to fill her lungs with air, she faced the door just as it crashed open, hitting the inside wall. The screen door ripped itself from its hinges. Lucy ducked, but not before it clipped her in the face and cut her cheek as it sailed into the yard.

Mrs. Williams screamed, then fainted.

Mr. Williams gasped and gripped his wife's arms. He half carried, half dragged her away from the house, and laid her in the grass.

In the dark doorway floated a pale gray face. The ghost of Darwin Stewart leered at Lucy. The lifeless black eyes narrowed.

Smoke and ash swirled violently, and an acrid smell filled the air as the ghost morphed into solid form and stood in the open doorway. He grabbed Lucy by the arm and jerked her inside as the heavy oak door slammed shut behind them.

Standing in the small foyer, Lucy glared at the ghost. A sickly smile slowly drifted across his cold features as he watched her through blank, lifeless eyes. The spirit seemed to be in a type of flux. He was fading in and out of focus. Lucy swallowed, squared her shoulders, and stepped toward the ghost.

"Are you getting brave now?" he sneered. "Just what do you think you can do to save your little friend? Before this night is over, you will give me the Spectrescope if you expect to see your friend again."

"I'll do whatever it takes to fight you and get her back. She's my friend!"

"It is useless for you to fight. There's nothing you can do to me," the ghost taunted, "I'm a spirit." He floated in a circle around her.

"There has to be a way to defeat you, and I'll find it. I won't give up until I've got my friend back and you're gone!" yelled Lucy, twisting to follow him as he circled her.

"Let's make a deal, Lucy Hornberger," he said as he came into focus. "If you can find and rescue your friend, I will let you both live. I get the Spectrescope, and you get your friend back." He stepped closer to Lucy, bending lower to put his face next to hers. He twisted his head, stretching his neck. "You won't defeat me." He dematerialized.

Lucy breathed a little easier once he disappeared.

"Schuyler! Where are you?" Lucy opened the foyer closet door, looking inside. "Schuyler! Make a noise if you can hear me!"

She ran through the living room, searching behind the chairs and the couch. She searched the hallway and the bathroom. The dining room and kitchen were empty, as was the porch room. Standing in the middle of the kitchen, she slowly turned and faced the basement door.

"Please, not the basement. I hate this basement," Lucy groaned. She opened the door and switched on the light, navigating through the clutter on the narrow stairs. Two small bulbs hanging from the rafters dimly lit the root-cellar basement's cut stone walls and uneven stone floor. The metal racks that once held Mrs. Williams's jars of homemade jam were empty, except for a few surviving jars. Lucy winced at the memory.

"Schuyler? Are you down here?" Raising the Spectrescope to her face, Lucy carefully swept her gaze around the cellar. There was no trace of the ghost or Schuyler.

The cellar contained two halves, one side used as the jam storage area and the other used for the laundry, furnace, and utilities. Lucy edged closer to the laundry room and peeked around the doorway for the light switch. A lone light bulb illuminated the dark, windowless room.

"Hello?" Holding her breath and listening, she tiptoed into the musty room, and the scope held tight in her shaking hand. A purple glow appeared in the Spectrescope.

Almost immediately, an acrid sulfuric odor filled the space, and a mist swirled around her. Hands within the smoke pushed at her and pulled her hair. Lucy grappled with the hands, but she lost her balance and fell against the wall. The mist dispersed. She raised the scope and saw a purple glow flowing along the floor and up the cellar stairs. Panting, she chased after it.

The glow passed through the kitchen and dining rooms and up the stairs to the second floor. *Of course! The attic!* Lucy thought. She followed it up the stairs and down the hallway to the guest bedroom.

The door was stuck. She rattled the knob and pushed hard against it, forcing it open. Lucy exploded into the room and fell to the floor, bumping her head on the nightstand. Scrambling to her feet, she gingerly touched her head where an egg-sized knot was already forming.

Glancing at the Spectrescope, the purple glow disappeared under the wall panel leading to the secret passageway. Lucy took the flashlight from the drawer, opened the hidden panel, and shined the beam down the passage. The door to the vanishing staircase was there.

She stepped into the passage, and the secret panel closed behind her with a thud. *No!* Lucy thought and pushed it with her shoulder, but it wouldn't budge. Shining the beam ahead, she made her way to the old wooden door. Tucking the flashlight under her arm, Lucy turned the knob and opened the door. She placed her foot on the bottom step and paused. The Spectrescope didn't reveal any new ghost tracks.

"Schuyler? Are you up here?" she called, her voice cracking. Her sneakered feet made no sound as she crept up the stairs toward the shadows in the attic.

"Hmm, hmm!" came a muffled reply. *Thump, thump.* "Hmm, hmm!"

"I'm coming!" Lucy hurried up the stairs. Schuyler was bound and gagged on the attic floor, leaning against a wall. Rushing to her, Lucy dropped the flashlight and the Spectrescope in Schuyler's lap and knelt to untie the ropes binding her hands and feet.

"Hmm, hmm," Schuyler mumbled, bumping her head against Lucy's forehead.

"Ouch! Oh, sorry," said Lucy, removing the gag tied around Schuyler's head. "Are you okay? He didn't hurt you, did he?"

"Thanks," said Schuyler, licking her mouth. "I'm okay, only shaken up a bit. What about my mom and dad?" She gaped at the blood trickling down Lucy's cheek. "You are hurt! Your cheek is bleeding!"

"Your mom and dad are fine. They are locked out of the house, but they are safe," said Lucy, reaching a hand up to her face. The blood on her fingers was unsettling her. "It's just a scratch. My head hurts worse. I fell on my way through the spare bedroom and hit my head on the nightstand," she said, trying to loosen the bonds on Schuyler's hands. "Your mom called me, did you know?"

"I'm so glad. What about Iam? Did you talk to him?"

"No, I called out to him, but he didn't answer. I guess we're on our own," Lucy said, tugging on the rope. "I can't get the knot untied. I'll have to cut it."

A black mist slowly crawled up the stairs, flowing along the floor behind Lucy. It morphed into the form of Malpar. Schuyler squealed. Lucy stood and turned to face him.

"What do you want?" said Lucy, noticing as she watched the bird-man that something about his demeanor was different.

"Lucy," Malpar said, "give me the Spectrescope, and I will help you get out of here. The daemon you know as Darwin Stewart won't let you go, you know that." Malpar watched Lucy standing in front of her friend with her arms outstretched and blocking access to Schuyler.

"I can't give it to you, Malpar. I promised Iam I would protect it. He's counting on me to keep it safe. Please, help us if you can," Lucy pleaded, "but I can't give you the scope."

"I cannot help you. You are on your own." He slowly dissolved into a black mist. "Use the divine power of the Spectrescope, Lucy. I have seen it," his voice echoed as he disappeared.

"What was that about?" Schuyler asked, struggling to untie her feet with her hands still bound.

"I'm not sure. He's right, though. We're on our own," Lucy said. "C'mon, we gotta get out of here." She took the Spectrescope from Schuyler's lap and scanned for any sign of the ghost. The attic was clear. Reaching to untie Schuyler's hands, a sudden swooshing sound made them look up.

"Oh, great, not again," Lucy groaned. The staircase vanished. Slowly, an outline of a door appeared on the wall, and then a solid door formed, identical to the one at the bottom of the vanishing staircase.

"I don't think I want to know where that goes," Schuyler mumbled as they both stared at the new door.

Lucy had a bad feeling. She hurriedly grabbed the bracelet from her pocket and stuffed it into Schuyler's hand since the rope still bound her wrists. Lucy turned toward the sound of the door creaking open, revealing a long, creepy corridor with chandeliers down its entire length.

A blast of foul air swirled around them as something invisible grabbed Schuyler and pulled her, kicking and flailing, across the floor toward the corridor.

Schuyler screamed. "Lucy! Help me!"

Lucy flung herself to the floor, grabbing for Schuyler's legs. She missed. Pushing herself up, she lunged again as Schuyler disappeared into the corridor. The Spectrescope slipped from her grasp and slid across the slippery floor. The door slammed shut inches from Lucy's outstretched hands.

"Schuyler!" Lucy cried. "No, no!" Tears stung her eyes as she crawled to her feet, grasping the doorknob and tugging on the locked door. Tears coursed down her cheeks. With her back against the door, she slid to the floor and wept. *I am such a failure!* Lucy thought. *I wish I'd never gone to that stupid flea market! How useless can I be?* She pulled her knees to her chest and sobbed.

Sniffling, she swiped the back of her hand across both cheeks and crawled across the attic space to the Spectrescope, took hold of it, and stood up. *Oh, Iam, where are you? I can't do this alone. I don't know what to do. Please, help me.*

The Spectrescope vibrated in her hand.

Of course! The Spectrescope! Daphne said the tools were divinely powerful. Malpar said it too. Looking at the scope in her hand, Lucy wondered what she was so supposed to do next. "Can you help me?" she asked the Spectrescope.

The rings under the scope began spinning and projected moving images through the lens and onto the wall. As the scene played, Lucy saw Malpar sitting in the chair in her room's corner, watching her sleep. As her mom entered the room, Malpar morphed into a black mist and slithered across the floor toward the backpack. Lucy watched his inky, mist-like form flow through the bag and then out the window as the movie faded.

Did Malpar place something in the backpack? Lucy thought as her skin began to crawl with a cold prickle of fear. *Oh, no! What am I going to do now? I left the backpack on the porch, and there isn't time to go back for it.* A crushing wave of discouragement washed over her, nearly dropping her to the floor. A tear slipped down her cheek and splashed on the lens of the Spectrescope.

The Spectrescope vibrated again as the symbols started glowing. They changed to reveal two new shapes. The first shape looked like the vest she was wearing, and the second shape was the triangle symbol she had seen before.

"Wait, my vest was in the backpack. Could something have slipped into a pocket?" Lucy asked, and, searching the metallic vest's front pockets, she found the triangle hiding deep in a corner. The minuscule object, shaped like a wedge, was also etched with symbols. Whatever the thing was, Lucy could tell it was evil.

"Can you get rid of it?" she asked the Spectrescope.

The Spectrescope glowed brightly, and an amazing warmth flooded through her hand and body. Images began to appear again in the lens, and Lucy understood. She tilted her hand and dropped the wedge to the floor, holding her hand above it. The wedge started to glow like the embers of a fire until it turned white hot and erupted into little flames. Lucy almost gagged at the heat and the stench it emitted as it dissolved into dust. With a wave of her hand, the dust blew away and was gone. Lucy blew out a puff of air, took a slow, deep breath, and then blew it out too. She felt renewed, as though a tremendous weight had lifted from her shoulders. *Thank you, Spectrescope.*

Squaring her shoulders, Lucy walked to the door and turned the knob.

18 The Hallway of Doors

Lucy stepped into the long narrow hallway to search for Schuyler. Crystal chandeliers hung at intervals, illuminating the space in harsh refracted light. The crystals swayed gently and tinkled, sending sickly colored rainbows across the walls and chills down Lucy's back. Doors lined the hallway, five on each side. Every door was unique with ornately carved wood, plain and austere fronts, or garish paint colors. The whole effect was of some strange, ill-fitting puzzle.

Whoa, where is this place? Is this still Schuyler's house? Lucy wondered, stepping farther into the hallway. The door in the attic wall slammed shut and disappeared behind her.

Trapped, she was in a strange hallway with no exit.

Lucy raised the Spectrescope and peered through the lens. The weird purple glow she had seen earlier was bubbling along the floor midway down the corridor. Her hand shook as she stared at the image in the scope.

The purple glow slowly morphed into a shape. The familiar smoke and ash merged at the end of the hall, and the stench was undeniable. She lowered the Spectrescope and watched as the ghost of Darwin Stewart materialized.

"I have your little friend," the ghost drawled as he twisted his head slowly from side to side. "She isn't happy with our accommodations, though I can't understand why. This is such a lovely resort, don't you think?" His face held a leering smirk, but his eyes were a lifeless void, like a gaping black hole in space, the light sucked out of existence.

Lucy felt as though she could get sucked through those eyes into the void and lost forever. She averted her gaze to focus on the leering smile instead. She shivered as the hand clutching the Spectrescope tightened its grip.

"Let's play a game, shall we? If you want your friend back, you must find her. She is behind one of these doors. If you can rescue her, the game is over. She is unharmed, but there is no guarantee *you* won't be. That is unless you are ready to give me what I want—give me the Spectrescope." His image wavered as he stood glaring at her.

He vanished and reappeared directly in front of her. He was standing so close Lucy could smell his foul breath. "There are ten doors. Three will let you pass, bringing you closer to your goal. Seven are the wrong choice. For each wrong choice you make, I will add another door. For each correct choice you make, a wrong door will disappear." He leaned forward and lowered his face near hers. "Choose wisely," he said. He threw his head back and hysterically laughed as he morphed into smoke and ash and disappeared through the crack under a door.

Lucy trembled and stared at the unending hallway of doors, unsure of what to do next. "How can I choose? I don't know how," she whimpered. "This could take an eternity."

"Choose what?" Schuyler asked, standing beside her, a bewildered look on her face.

"Schuyler! I thought I'd lost you!" Lucy cried as she hugged her friend. Slivers of ice pricked her skin, scratching and chilling her while the stench of something rotten wafted up to her nose and nearly gagged her. Aghast, she sprung back as the ghost morphed again.

"How pathetic you humans are, so easy to manipulate," said the ghost of Darwin Stewart, his face contorted with disgust. "Choose!" he yelled, swirling into smoke and ash before slithering down the corridor and blending into the shadows.

Shaking, Lucy gripped the Spectrescope tightly in her hand. "Oh, Iam!" she whispered. "How can I?"

"Trust," whispered a voice inside her head. "Trust what you have learned."

The Spectrescope became warm in her hand. She gazed down at it and turned it around. The symbols were glowing. They moved in fluid animation, like droplets of mercury sliding around the ring, blending into one another to form new characters as they became still. The new symbols were incomprehensible. Lucy turned the scope over several times. No matter how she tried, she couldn't decipher their meaning.

Frustrated, she looked forlornly down the hallway. A smile spread across her face. The carved characters on the nearest door matched those on the Spectrescope. She walked up to the ornately carved door and turned the handle.

"Trust," the voice whispered again. "Trust."

I fell asleep this afternoon, and I heard a voice—only, it wasn't a dream. It was Iam telling me to trust, she thought, her hand still on the handle. *That's what the voice is telling me now*, Lucy thought. *Trust.*

Holding the scope tightly in hand, she opened the door and stepped through the doorway. The door slammed with a resounding echo. She was in the hallway again.

"What?" Lucy whispered.

It was the same hallway, only different. Now there were eight doors instead of ten. One wrong door had disappeared as the ghost had said, along with the door she had just entered. She moved along the hallway, looking at each door in turn, trying to decide which door she should open next. Glancing at the Spectrescope in her hand, she thought, *Please, help me choose.*

The Spectrescope glowed, and the symbols moved again. Lucy walked the hallway, studying the characters in the wood. She stopped at the door on her left. The symbols on the Spectrescope were the same as on the door. Placing her hand on the knob, she opened the door and walked through.

Again, she was back in the hallway, and two doors had disappeared. Six doors remained. *Great! Only one more door*, she thought. She walked up to the last remaining door bearing carved symbols. *The first two doors had characters, so this must be the right door.* The harsh light from chandeliers gave a creep factor to the symbols carved in the wood. They looked strangely alive in the three-dimensional relief. She grasped the door handle, gave it a turn, and walked in.

She found herself standing in her own bedroom at home, holding the library book. Her hand was still on the knob of the open door, and she saw the hallway of crystal chandeliers behind. Puzzled, she stepped farther into the room as the handle pulled from her grasp and the door shut with a bang. Lucy was standing in her room at home, and she heard her mom yelling downstairs.

"Lucy Hornberger! You get down here this instant!" her mom yelled up the back stairs. "The library just called. Your book is a week overdue! I reminded you to return it the other day. Now you'll have to pay a late fee. You might just as well have bought it for the good it did to borrow it from the library!"

"How did I get here? I don't understand," she said. She looked around the familiar room with the old-style dresser and faded wallpaper. It was as she had left it earlier in the evening. She looked down at her clothes; they were the same shirt and jean shorts she had put on that morning, with a shimmery silver vest over the shirt. *What's this?* Lucy thought.

"What are you talking about?" Mom demanded as she stormed into Lucy's bedroom.

"I have to go see Schuyler! Can you take me to the Williamses house? I need to know what happened to Schuyler!" Lucy cried, throwing the book on the bed.

"Schuyler? Who the heck is Schuyler?" asked Mom, her face puckered in familiar irritation.

"What do you mean 'who's Schuyler?' She's my friend since forever! You know, the curly-haired girl I've known since grade school." Lucy said heatedly. "She was in trouble, and I was trying to help find her. I was just at her house. I opened this stupid door in a crazy hallway, and poof! I'm in my bedroom!" She went to the bookshelf in the corner and grabbed a framed photo from the shelf. She thrust it at her mother. "See? The curly-haired blonde girl named Schuyler!"

"What girl? You're holding a dog for crying out loud! Are you talking about a dog?" asked Mom, her exasperation with Lucy reaching its limit.

"It's not a dog! That's my friend Schuyler Williams! And she's lost, and I've got to find her!" Lucy yelled.

"Look at it! That was the dog we found lost at the beach one day. You wouldn't let go of it until the owners came to get it," she huffed, thrusting the photo back at Lucy. "You needed to know it was happy with its family." Mom crossed her arms with a huff and a glare.

"I don't understand," Lucy sniffled, studying the photo. "It was my friend Schuyler, really it was."

"Well, that's it. You've finally gone completely nuts!" Mom sneered. "You tell so many stories, you're starting to believe them yourself. You have to stop living in a fantasy world. I've warned you before, Lucy, if you can't see it, it just ain't real. Stop this nonsense already. Got it?" Mom huffed and stomped from the room, slamming the door on her way out.

Lucy looked down at the photo. The Lucy in the picture was smiling at the camera and hugging a large blonde and curly-haired dog. The girl and dog were at the beach, and they looked happy.

"No! Mom! Come back! None of this right." she yelled. "I remember this picture. Mr. and Mrs. Williams took Schuyler and me to the beach for a picnic. They took this photo of us," cried Lucy. "It was Schuyler." Her legs gave out from under her, and she plopped on the floor, crying.

She sat there for several minutes. Confusion gripped her mind. Why was she crying? She couldn't remember. Finally, she squeezed the tears from her eyes, sniffled, and got up from the floor. She put the photo back on the bookshelf.

It was hot in the room, so she went to the window, pushed back the curtains, and opened it. It was completely dark outside. No streetlamps, no crickets chirping, just empty darkness. Not a breeze or even a breath of air floated through the opening. Lucy frowned and swiped at the tears still clinging to her cheeks.

Not bothering to change her clothes, she pulled the covers back and crawled into bed. The overdue library book fell to the floor with a thump. Leaning out of bed, she reached down and picked it up. Only it wasn't the vampire book anymore. On the front of the dust cover was an old-fashioned magnifying glass. It seemed strangely familiar, but she couldn't remember why. She fanned the pages of the book. They were all blank.

Lucy slipped out of bed to retrieve the backpack from the desk drawer. The bag was gone. Still, something bothered her, so she removed the book's dust cover, tossing the book on the bed. Studying the magnifying glass image on the cover, she tore the paper away until she held only the magnifying glass.

"Spectrescope!" Lucy screamed, gripping the paper image and holding it out in front of her. The room swirled into a vortex, sucking her down until she crashed in a heap on the tiled floor of the strange hallway. The crystal chandeliers swung menacingly above her. The door she had wrongly chosen slammed shut with such force it shattered some of the crystals.

Lucy sat on the floor, gasping, clutching the real Spectrescope once again. Breathing heavily, she rocked back and forth, the motion calming her somewhat. Slowly Lucy got to her feet and straightened her clothes. Swallowing hard, she gripped the Spectrescope tightly in one hand, and with the other, she tugged at the metallic vest to make sure it was real.

"Lucy," a voice whispered in her head. "You forgot to trust. You are never alone, dear child."

More tears spilled down her cheeks, and her face flushed as she listened to the voice. It was altogether both chastising and comforting. "You are never alone, dear one," the voice whispered. "Trust."

"I'm sorry. I will trust. But could you please help me to trust more?" Lucy asked, looking at the Spectrescope in her hand. A tear slipped from her cheek and fell into the mesh of the metallic vest. Where the tear disappeared, the material coalesced into solid metal. It grew until the entire vest became a breastplate of armor. Lucy ran her hand over the new breastplate and found it was warm to the touch. It appeared rigid but was as malleable as the original vest had been, making it light and comfortable to wear.

"Please help me, and show me the door I need," said Lucy, holding up the Spectrescope. The scope grew warm again as the symbols became fluid, circling the ring until they became one inert symbol.

It was the serpent.

* * * *

Lucy looked down the corridor at a myriad of mismatched doors. The ghost had lied in telling her only one wrong door would be her consequence. It took her several minutes of walking along the hallway to find the door with the matching symbol. Standing in front of the door decorated with a giant serpent, Lucy hesitated. The ornately carved symbol on the door raised its head to look at her. The eyes glowed like living amber, brilliant in color.

The serpent raised its head and slithered around the door, entwining itself around the door handle. Wary and watching it closely, Lucy slowly moved her hand toward the handle to open the door. The snake hissed and struck out at her hand, but she jerked it back before it could sink its teeth into her skin.

The serpent continued to slither around the door, coming to rest again around the handle. Remembering the incident with the stuffed toys, Lucy firmly grasped the Spectrescope in one hand, raised the other, and yelled. "Immobilize!" The snake solidified except for the eyes, which glowed like glass stones reflecting a raging fire.

"Oh, Iam, I wish you were here," Lucy whispered. "I'm so scared."

"Remember, you are not alone, dear one," the voice in her head whispered, "but you must wear all of your armor."

"I trust. I really do," Lucy said haltingly, tugging the hat from her waistband and plopping it on her head. Finally, she twisted the belt-shaped ring from her finger. It increased in size until it was large enough to wrap around her waist.

"Could I have a shield, too, please?" she asked the Spectrescope. It glowed brightly in her hand. When the light subsided, she was wearing a bracelet similar to Schuyler's, though it was larger and etched with a tree instead of holding a purple gemstone.

"That's so cool! Thank you!" Lucy exclaimed, peering at the bracelet. The Spectrescope vibrated once again. Lucy looked at it, swallowed hard, and nodded. Feeling more encouraged, Lucy turned the handle, opened the door, and stepped through. Then everything changed.

19 Spirit Warfare

Lucy sensed a vibration on her wrist. As she held her arm out to examine the cause, a large shield emerged seamlessly from the bracelet. Larger than Schuyler's shield, it was decorated with a flag, held by a brilliant white fox, and displaying an elegant golden crown on a field of purple. The shield was extremely lightweight considering its size, and in a sheath next to the handgrip was another sword.

The hat Lucy wore morphed into a helmet, covering even her ears. It was so lightweight, she barely knew it had changed from a hat to a helmet.

The belt around her waist now gleamed of polished silver metal and was encrusted with blue and white gemstones that scintillated in the dancing firelight from the great stone hearth across the room. The jewels had grown to the size of small rocks.

The door Lucy had opened led into a vast dining room with a high-beamed ceiling. Cut and polished stone tiles formed the elegant walls that matched the stone floor, and in the center of the room was a dining table so large it could seat nearly a hundred people. Roaring fires blazed in massive fieldstone fireplaces at both ends of the room. Windows along one side spanned from floor to ceiling, the panes reflecting the blazing fires. The entire room appeared to be burning. The thick darkness outside the windows thoroughly obscured the location of the place. Lucy couldn't tell whether it existed in her world or some other.

Iron candelabras, looking suspiciously like twisted bones, sat unlit on the mantels. The bizarre patterns frozen in the wax from previous burnings dribbled down the sides of the candles.

The high-backed chairs surrounding the table, reminiscent of those Lucy had seen in pictures of historic castles, were covered in tapestries. Each chair told a different story of strange yet beautiful mythical creatures, many of whom she had never seen before, being hunted by hideous forms that were scarier than any nightmare she had ever had.

The door disappeared behind Lucy as she stepped farther into the fire-lit room. The Spectrescope gave no sign of the ghost, but movement at the end of the table caught her eye. Schuyler was strapped and gagged in a chair near the fireplace. Her head drooped forward, and her chin rested on her chest. She seemed unhurt and unaware that Lucy was in the room. She still gripped the shield bracelet Lucy had pushed into her hand before being dragged into the hallway.

"Schuyler!" Lucy cried, running toward her.

Schuyler looked up suddenly, terror swelling in her eyes as she violently shook her head back and forth. Straps bound her wrists to the chair's arms, but she was able to wave her hands, urging Lucy to stay back.

Lucy nodded, pulled the headpiece from the Spectrescope, and stuffed it in her pocket. The sword flowed from the handle, gleaming in the firelight. She grabbed the back of Schuyler's chair and swung her around, swiping the blade across the straps binding Schuyler's arms and feet. Schuyler flexed her wrists, then tugged and pulled at the gag in her mouth. It was tied tight, cutting into her cheeks. Lucy shoved the bracelet onto Schuyler's wrist.

"Hang on, I'll cut it," said Lucy, carefully running the blade across the knot. It split, and Schuyler yanked it from her mouth as a lock of her hair fell to the table.

"Thank you for joining us, Miss Hornberger," said the ghost of Darwin Stewart as he stepped out of the fire.

They scrambled away from the ghost. Lucy used her foot to shove a chair in front of them, positioning it between the spirit and themselves. "You okay?" she whispered as she watched the ghost. Schuyler nodded.

"Spectrescope," Lucy whispered. "Schuyler needs armor." Lucy raised the Spirit Sword as she gripped the shield tightly.

A helmet and a breastplate appeared on Schuyler. The shield had already erupted from the bracelet, and Schuyler withdrew her sword. "Thanks," she whispered, glancing down at the breastplate she was wearing. Firelight reflected off the gleaming metal.

Darwin Stewart casually picked up the lock of Schuyler's hair, twirling it between his pale fingers. "Our friend here has been telling me how much she enjoys your company. I'm so glad you came. Our games will be so much more exciting with your participation." The skin surrounding his black, lifeless eyes crinkled as his mouth twisted in a humorless grin.

"The game is over, Darwin Stewart," said Lucy heatedly, "I played your game of 'find the right door,' and I found my friend. It's over, now let us go."

"You're mistaken. The game is just beginning!" the spirit laughed, and morphing into smoke and ash, he swirled violently through the room. The candles detached themselves from the candelabras and flew at the girls. Schuyler raised her arm, and the candles crashed into the shield, leaving wax smudges on the metal before falling to the floor.

Next, the candelabras flung themselves at them. Lucy swiped her hand sideways. The iron candelabras crashed against the stone wall and broke into pieces.

Darwin Stewart flew along the floor, gathering up the broken pieces. He whipped the shrapnel at the girls. Lucy swiped her hand again and tossed the iron pieces into the flames.

The ghost growled and swirled into the fire, stirring up sparks and sending them raining into the room. The fires raged in their grates. Fiery arrows shot from the flames and hit the raised shields, then dissolved.

More arrows flew from the shadows as Lucy turned. They hit her breastplate, disintegrated into sparks, and went out.

Fireballs shot from the opposite fireplace. Lucy raised her sword and swung, knocking several to the floor where they extinguished as others smashed into her shield. Schuyler followed Lucy's tactic and swung her sword at the fireballs. Several more rounds of fireballs launched at the girls simultaneously from both fireplaces. Lucy yelled. "Freeze!" The luminaries immediately turned into solid ice spheres, dropped, and shattered as they hit the floor.

Schuyler dodged an arrow but squealed as she tripped over a chair and fell, narrowly avoiding another round of the flaming missiles. Lucy saw the ghost in the flames, hurling them toward Schuyler.

"Immobilize!" she screamed, her hand raised toward the flames. The flames froze in midair, giving Schuyler time to scramble to her feet. Lucy lowered her hand, allowing the fire to engulf the chair. It burned ferociously into ash. The ghost growled in anger and flew into the room.

"Enough!" roared Darwin Stewart. "Give us the Spectrescope, or these humans will perish!" He flung his arm wide, and two chairs sitting in the shadows at the far end of the room shot backward from the table. Mr. and Mrs. Williams each had an apple wedged in their mouth and struggled against the bonds holding them to the chairs.

"No!" screamed Schuyler, rushing toward her parents. The ghost flung out his hand. Another chair shot forward, blocking her path. "Mom! Dad!" she cried. "I thought you said they were safe!" she accused Lucy.

Lucy gulped. Her insides quivered like gelatin. "Let them go!" Lucy yelled, trying to glare at the ghost. "It's me you want, and the Spectrescope."

"I think not, you stupid girl," he retorted. "Pay the price. Hand over the Spectrescope willingly, or your friends will perish." He pointed at the Williamses, and dozens of fiery arrows from both fireplaces flew in their direction. Schuyler screamed, struggling with the chair. It kept moving to block her path.

"Arrows!" Lucy yelled as she raised her hand, clenched it, and the captured arrows hung suspended in midair. Twisting, she flung the arrows at the ghost of Darwin Stewart. "Return!"

The arrows shot toward the ghost and sliced right through him. He morphed into the black mist and reappeared next to the Williamses at the other end of the room. In each hand, he held a dagger, and with a flick of his wrist, they floated from his hands and pointed themselves at the Williamses throats. Rebecca and Stephen Williams sat petrified as the daggers hovered dangerously close to their necks.

"Lucy!" screamed Schuyler. "Do something!" She gripped the back of the chair and tried to fling it aside, but it wouldn't budge. She beat on it with the shield to no avail and then started whacking at it with her sword.

"Release the Williams family, and I'll give you the Spectrescope," said Lucy through gritted teeth. "Prove to me they are safely away from here, then I will freely give you the scope."

"No, Lucy! Don't!" Schuyler warned, sheathing her sword. She pressed the stone, which caused the bracelet to reappear on her wrist. She gripped the back of the chair for support. "Isn't there something else you can do? You know it will be disastrous if the Master gets the Spectrescope."

"It's okay. It's not like I asked to do this," Lucy said, her voice barely a whisper. She laid the shield down. "I'm sure Iam will understand. At least, I hope he does." Shaking, she took the headpiece from her pocket and replaced it as the sword disappeared into the handle. She held it out to the ghost. "Get them all out of here. Please," Lucy whispered, her voice cracking.

"So polite, of course, I would be happy to oblige," said the ghost with a laugh. Waving his hand, the cords holding the Williamses untied themselves. The apples disappeared from their mouths. They stood, rubbing at their wrists where the bonds had chafed the skin. They watched silently with terrified eyes but didn't move.

"Malpar!" The ghost yelled.

Malpar stepped slowly into the dining room through a door next to the fireplace. He was in his human form, and his feathered head gleamed in the firelight. He glanced briefly at Lucy before dropping his gaze to the Spectrescope, which she held in her shaking outstretched hands. As he reached out and took it, he looked deeply into her clear gray eyes. Then his beady, birdlike eyes blinked swiftly and darted sideways at the ghost. "Fear," he whispered before taking the Spectrescope and disappearing.

Then the Williamses disappeared.

Schuyler gasped. "It was all a lie! They weren't even real! You tricked us." Schuyler glared at the ghost, anger creeping up her neck and turning her face pink.

"You can leave now. Go through that door back to your pathetic world. You will find nothing has changed," said Darwin Stewart, pointing at the door through which Malpar had entered. "Go before I change my mind."

"Schuyler! Go!" Lucy squeaked, but Schuyler ran and stood by Lucy.

"Not likely, girlfriend," she snapped and pressed the stone. The shield erupted again from the bracelet. "You need me." She raised the shield and withdrew Zazriel. The short sword gleamed in the firelight as she pointed it menacingly toward the ghost.

"How precious," sneered the ghost. "Now you're both here with me for all eternity. You'll learn to fear the dark like you never did in your world." He morphed into the black mist, his acrid smell polluting the air. The spirit slithered across the floor toward them and rose in front of them, morphing into the ghost. He turned and walked toward the fire.

The belt around Lucy's waist was growing warm. She looked down. The stones were glowing. One stone began to wiggle and then jumped into her hand. She wrapped her fingers around it and clutched it tight. "Wait!" Lucy yelled.

"What do you want, stupid human girl?" The ghost sneered and turned around. "Want to play more games? We have all of eternity to do that!" The ghost laughed. The sound echoed off the stone walls of the great dining room, sending chills down each girl's spine. Morphing, he swirled around them, twisting strands of their hair as he passed.

"Schuyler, stand behind me," Lucy whispered. She grabbed Schuyler's hand and gave it a quick squeeze. "I think I know what to do." She turned back toward the ghost, who had changed back into his human form and was leering at them.

"What kind of stupid name is 'Darwin Stewart'?" Lucy asked, trying to project a bravado she certainly didn't feel. She was quaking inside and hoped she didn't throw up anytime soon. She gulped air and swallowed hard. "I bet that isn't even your real name."

The ghost reared up in front of her, the empty black eyes inches from her face. Lucy balled her hands into fists, willing herself to breathe calmly. The foul odor was overwhelming and thoroughly terrifying. When the ghost opened its mouth and breathed on her, her stomach retched from the stink of decaying flesh emanating from it.

She barfed on him.

The ghost growled long and loud.

"Putrid girl! You shall suffer for this, and you will fear me!" he screamed as he swirled away from her into the flames. He reappeared moments later in front of the fireplace. The vomited discharge was gone.

"Darwin Stewart is a stupid name," Lucy chanted over and over, still clutching the blue gemstone. She jabbed Schuyler in the ribs and nodded her head toward the ghost. Schuyler quickly joined in the chant.

"Stop it, you horrible human girls!" the ghost ranted at them. "Stop it, I say!" He morphed into his acrid smoke and ash, swirling violently around them and ripping at their hair and clothes. The girls clung to each other as they continued the chant.

"So tell us horrible humans what your real name is, or are you scared?" Lucy taunted, her hair whipping violently and stinging her face.

"A great daemon like me? Afraid of you?" the ghost sniggered, morphing into his human form. "I am Fear itself!" he said, puffing up his chest. "You shall have all of eternity to learn to fear me!"

"Lucy, the stone," a voice in her head whispered. "Read the words aloud, then shatter it against the ground."

"I don't think so!" Lucy yelled at the daemon. She held it up and shouted the words that were glowing within the stone. "*You shall fear the King, your High King, for he is great and powerful. He has done great and mighty things!*"

Lucy threw the blue stone down as hard as she could. It smashed against the stone floor and exploded into a mass of blue smoke, encompassing the daemon completely. When it cleared, a rope of flames had wrapped around the daemon, binding his arms and legs.

"No!" The daemon screamed, struggling against the flaming cords. "Master Darnathian! Help me!"

Another stone popped up from the belt. Lucy caught it and repeated the sequence. "*The High King preserves his chosen ones; his enemies shall he destroy,*" she yelled, and she shattered the second stone. More blue smoke roiled around the daemon. As the smoke cleared, both girls took a step backward, distancing themselves from the daemon. The burning rope still bound him.

And he was covered in worms.

The daemon screamed and writhed in agony as he thrashed about, worms crawling over his eyes and covering his head. Schuyler turned away, squeezed her eyes shut, and covered her ears, trembling from head to foot.

Lucy gulped hard, and clenching her fists, leaned forward and screamed as loud as she could. "*FEAR! In the name of the High King of Ascalon, I banish you back to Shinar!*"

The screaming daemon was gone.

The great room filled with a freakish silence, disturbed only by the twin fires' pop and crackle as the girls stood alone in the empty room. Their skin prickled in the sudden emptiness.

Schuyler, who was still quaking and nearly exhausted, slumped into the nearest chair. "Oh! My! Goodness! I'll never be able to watch a spooky movie again." She slapped a hand over her eyes. "I think that image has permanently burned my eyes."

"You're not kidding about that," Lucy whispered, still staring at the spot where the daemon had disappeared. The glowing gemstones in Lucy's belt slowly faded out till they reflected only the flickering firelight.

"How did you know what to do?" Schuyler asked, pressing the stone with a shaky finger. The shield changed back into the bracelet.

"I had help," Lucy said, pulling a chair out and finally sitting down. She rubbed her arms to keep her hands from shaking. "The belt got warm like the Spectrescope does when it's trying to tell us something. When the stones popped into my hand, a voice in my head told me what to do. I know it was Iam's voice, but I didn't know the stones would react like they did, though I'm so glad it worked."

"I don't understand. How did you know the daemon's real name?" Schuyler nervously twirled a lock of hair around her finger.

Lucy pulled her legs up under her as she sat in the chair. The heat from the fireplaces had settled down once the daemon was gone. The warmth felt so good on her skin, she slumped into the seat, a sigh escaping her throat. "I didn't. Malpar told me." She glanced about slowly at the enormity of the stone room. "I remembered what Daphne said about tricking him into telling us his name. She said, 'in the name of the High King,' we could send him to 'Shinar.' When the daemon said he was Fear itself, I knew that was his name, just as Malpar had said when he took the Spectrescope from me. Although, I didn't realize then that Malpar was telling me the daemon's real name."

"I don't get it. The daemon and Malpar were working together to get the Spectrescope for the Dark Prince. Why would he tell you the daemon's real name? Do you think Malpar is on our side now?"

"I don't know. I saw so much sadness on his face when he took the Spectrescope from me. Maybe he is changing. I hope he is." Lucy wrapped her arms around her legs and rested her chin on her knees. Letting out another shaky sigh, she closed her eyes for a few moments.

"What about the Spectrescope? Iam said it would be very, very bad if the Dark Prince got hold of it."

"They may have the Spectrescope, but it won't do them any good," Lucy said, pinching her lips into a cheeky smile. "I know something the Dark Prince doesn't."

Schuyler squinted her eyes at Lucy. "So, what do you know?"

Lucy just grinned and waggled her eyebrows. "C'mon, let's get out of here," she said as she got up, retrieved her shield, and headed for the door the daemon had told them to use. "We have to figure out how to get the Spectrescope back."

"Do you think we should go through that door?" Schuyler asked. "What if it's another trick?"

"Only one way to find out. Ready?"

"No, but let's do it," Schuyler said, following her across the room. They stood motionless in front of the door, looking at it. Lucy reached for the knob, but the door emitted such a foul smell, she halted.

"Well, that can't be a good sign," Lucy said, wrinkling her nose. She glanced at Schuyler, who was pinching her nose tightly. She looked positively green.

The belt suddenly grew warm as a white stone wiggled and popped out. Lucy caught it and smiled.

"Good news?"

"Definitely," Lucy said. She held up the stone and read the glowing words out loud. "*Go in peace. Your journey has the High King's approval.*" She threw the gemstone, smashing it on the floor in front of the door. White smoke billowed up. As it cleared, it revealed the front door to Schuyler's house, and through the little window in the door, they could see Mr. and Mrs. Williams clinging together on the sidewalk. This portal would take them back to their reality.

"Together?" Lucy asked as she opened the door. Schuyler nodded. Together, they walked through the door.

* * * *

Each piece of armor had reverted to its original shape as the girls went through the portal. Lucy was holding a bracelet in her hand and was wearing a belt-shaped ring. They stepped out onto the front porch of Schuyler's house. Mrs. Williams was awake and clung to her husband as they stood on the sidewalk, speaking in hushed tones with Mr. and Mrs. McGoo.

"Schuyler! Thank goodness you're safe!" Mrs. Williams clapped her hands and rushed to throw her arms around Schuyler, hugging her tight. "How did you get her out so quickly, Lucy? It's only been a few minutes since you stepped through the door. Thank goodness the McGoos stopped by."

"What? We've been gone all night!" exclaimed Lucy. She stuffed the bracelet quickly into her pocket as she spotted the backpack on the porch floor right where she had dropped it. Kneeling, she unzipped the main compartment and rummaged through the bag.

"No, you haven't. It's only been a short time," Mrs. Williams said. "It's still dusk."

"It doesn't matter how long, you've saved Schuyler from the ghost," Mr. Williams said, joining his wife and daughter. He glanced around hesitantly. "Where is the ghost? It is gone, isn't it?"

"He's gone, Dad! Lucy defeated him!" announced Schuyler, nearly vibrating with excitement.

Mrs. Williams held Schuyler, rocking her back and forth. "You have no idea how scared your dad and I were. We're so happy you are back safe and sound." Pushing Schuyler to arm's length, Mrs. Williams's smile faded, and her brows puckered as she looked at her daughter. "That is odd. I don't remember you wearing a hat and a vest earlier."

"Oh! Um, that's what I went back in the house to get," Schuyler explained, "and my bracelet. I'd taken it off when I did the dishes."

"That's it!" Lucy exclaimed, pulling out the mirror. "If the Dark Prince has a mirror, I know where I can find him!"

"No, Lucy! You can't!" Schuyler blurted, jerking away from her mom. "You might not be able to get back. Give me the mirror!" Schuyler grabbed hold of the mirror and tugged. Lucy held tight. Instead of breaking, the frame stretched, enlarging the mirror. The startled girls each fell backward when they let go of the mirror.

The mirror dropped with a clatter to the porch floor. Its surface shimmered with fluid concentric ripples, like gentle waves against the shore.

Lucy jumped up and stood looking at the mirror. Without another thought, she dove into the mirror as if she were diving into a pool for a swim.

Schuyler watched with horror as Lucy's feet disappeared through the surface. She scrambled to her feet, preparing to do the same, but halted.

The mirror was just a mirror.

And both her parents had fainted.

*   *   *   *

Lucy fell hard onto the paneled library floor, landing with a resounding thud in front of the ornate wooden desk. She felt bruised all over. Sitting up and moaning, she gingerly touched the knot that was forming on her forehead where her face had hit the floor when she fell through the mirror. *Ow! Now I've got two goose eggs.*

A quick movement caught her eye, a hand swiping through the air. The Dark Prince had closed the mirror, sealing her on this side of the portal, wherever that might be.

She looked up as the Dark Prince Darnathian arose and smiled broadly at her from behind the desk. Malpar stood to the side, holding the Spectrescope. His expression was unreadable, but his slouching shoulders spoke loud and very clear.

"Malpar, please," Lucy pleaded. "Give me back the Spectrescope. The Dark Prince mustn't get hold of its power. That would be bad, really bad." She stood to her feet and brushed her hands over her shorts, stalling for time to figure out what to do next. *I need to ask for help, but what should I ask?* Lucy thought.

"See how she pleads, Malpar?" sneered Darnathian. "These humans are so weak and pathetic. And to think the High King would choose them over us." He slipped a casual hand into his pocket while studying the pointy manicured nails of his other hand. "Oh, what to do? How shall I dispose of this annoying human girl?" He looked directly at the bird-man. "Any thoughts, Malpar?"

"No."

"No?" Darnathian countered.

"No, you shall not destroy her. She is a Bachar," Malpar replied quietly. His small black eyes held a hardness that surprised even Lucy as he stared at the Dark Prince. "I was a fool to deny the High King to follow a vile thing such as you. I would destroy you if I could."

"Malpar! Don't. Call out to the High King!" Lucy stepped toward him. "Please, give me the Spectrescope," she said, her hand outstretched.

"Thou art a fool, bird-boy," sneered Darnathian at the Hayyothalan, ignoring his threat. He swiped his hand and sent Lucy flying backward against the bookshelves. She smashed into the shelves, dislodging several books as she slid to the floor among the tumbling ancient tomes. Malpar grimaced and turned away.

"A Bachar, indeed," Darnathian laughed. He leaned his hands on the desk and watched Lucy pick herself up from the floor. Stumbling among the fallen books, she advanced toward the Dark Prince, determination, although tinged with fear, etched in her face.

"Oh, this should be fun, Malpar. Look at the little minion," the Dark Prince snickered. "Still, she persists in the game." He swiped his hand again, sending her sprawling across the floor toward the giant fireplace. Darnathian threw his head back and laughed, his amber eyes glowing like molten embers.

"Lucy," the voice whispered in her head, "remember."

Again Lucy picked herself up, only this time she flung her arm toward Darnathian. A white-hot energy bolt flew from her fingers, striking the Dark Prince squarely in the chest. He was thrown over the desk and smashed against the huge wooden door. He lay prone on the floor, stunned.

Lucy took the bracelet from her pocket and slipped it on. The shield erupted as a round of flaming arrows flew from the shadows at the end of the room. They hit the front and disintegrated. Placing a hand on her chest, she whispered, "Armor," and the vest and hat morphed into their gleaming metal forms. She unsheathed the spare sword. It was a short, edgeless, thrusting sword, with the name *Ratha-nael* etched below the hilt.

Darnathian pulled himself up from the floor to his full height to tower over Lucy. His face contorted with anger as his fists clenched and unclenched several times. His white suit was rumpled and dusty.

"That wretched old man! I will have his throne and his power!" Darnathian roared. "Malpar, the Spectrescope is powerless! How did you not know this, you fool? I needed its power, and now the girl has the power!" Darnathian whipped his hand up and hurled a dozen hissing snakes at Lucy. "And I shall have it!"

Lucy swung the short sword, decapitating several snakes. The writhing bodies sizzled into ash as they fell to the floor. Fireballs blasted out of the hearth. She tilted the blade, deflecting the luminaries at the remaining snakes, setting them on fire.

Darnathian advanced toward Lucy, lobbing a continual barrage of blue-green energy balls at her. She quickly maneuvered the agile little sword to block and parry his attack. Any artillery hitting her armor ricocheted away or was extinguished soon.

Lucy was quickly growing tired, but the Dark Prince was so relentless in his advance, she couldn't drop the sword long enough to put on the Belt of Truth.

"Enough of this game. I'm tired of playing with you, minion girl," Darnathian growled. He stood tall and raked his hands over his suit, brushing the dust away and straightening the wrinkles. "It is time for you to die. Your death will bring me the power of the Spectrescope. Once I reunite the power with the relic, it will divulge all its secrets. I will know the location of the Life Tree."

Lucy, holding tight to the sword and shield, widened her stance and breathed deeply. Whatever the Dark Prince was preparing to do, she had to be ready because it was going to be really bad. *Oh, Iam! I need help! Please send help somehow. I can't do this alone*, she thought.

"You are not alone, dear one," the voice whispered in her head. Lucy gave a slight nod.

Darnathian threw up his hands, sending out a beam of blue-green energy that hit the shield hard. It shook on her arm but deflected the beam, bending it out and away from Lucy. The Dark Prince advanced, his eyes glowing like flames. Lucy knew if help didn't come soon, she was about to get incinerated.

Malpar screeched, the sound loud and piercing. "You will not harm her! Destroy me instead!" he cried, lunging toward the Dark Prince. "By the name of the High King of Ascalon, you will not harm her!" He spread his wings to hide Lucy from the Dark Prince as he tossed the Spectrescope to her. "Forgive me, my High King!" he yelled.

Malpar gripped Darnathian by the wrists, pinning his arms to his side. The Dark Prince cursed in a strange language as blue-green strips of light swirled like sparklers around him and the bird-man.

Lucy sheathed the sword and barely caught the Spectrescope as she ran to the sister mirror on the wall. The lights were growing brighter and swirling furiously around the room. She reached up to the mirror and pulled down on the frame. It stretched far enough for her to jump through, but it remained dark.

The Dark Prince and Malpar struggled, crashing into the bookshelves and upending the Master's chair. Lucy glanced back at Malpar. He grappled and kicked against the Dark Prince as energy cords coiled around him. They were binding his arms and wrapping around his neck, but Malpar still gripped the Dark Prince. Darnathian lifted Malpar into the air, his feet dangling while his head lolled backward, but he still clung to the Dark Prince.

"Go, child," Malpar whispered hoarsely, "remember me to the High King."

"Mirror, please help me," Lucy cried, tears cascading down her cheeks. The mirror sparkled to life. "Thank you, Malpar," she whispered and jumped through the portal.

"No!" The Dark Prince screamed and threw Malpar's body aside. He ran to the mirror as Malpar tumbled over the desk and crumpled lifelessly to the floor.

The mirror was sealed.

20 The Portal

Lucy rolled over and groaned. Her limbs refused to move without complaining, and the purple-and-green bruises resembled hideously large polka dots. The armor had morphed when she jumped through the mirror, so the hat now drooped over her face, and the metallic vest was askew. Lucy felt ridiculous. She pushed the floppy hat out of her eyes and sat up.

"Lucy!" Schuyler exclaimed, rushing to Lucy and pulling her up to her feet. "Oh, my gosh! When you disappeared into the mirror, I thought for sure I would never see you again!" She slapped Lucy lightly on the arm. "Don't ever do that again! Jumping into the enemy's lair, what were you thinking? Geez!" she scolded, then hugged Lucy.

"Ow! Not so tight!" Lucy managed a brief smile as Schuyler let go. Lucy rubbed her shoulder. "Now I know what those ninja warrior wannabes must feel like after a competition. I hurt all over. Iam could have given us a heads-up or something." She rolled her shoulders to release the stiffness that was setting in. "How long was I gone this time?"

"Not long," Schuyler said.

"Lucy!" exclaimed Mrs. Williams as she sat on the grass. The McGoos helped her up, and she hurried to the porch and climbed the steps. "Sweetheart, are you all right? Where did you disappear?" Mrs. Williams asked, examining Lucy's bumps and bruises. "My goodness!" She lightly touched the goose egg and minor scratches on Lucy's face. Cupping her hand around Lucy's hot cheek, she smiled adoringly at her. "I'll go get some salve for those wounds. I'll be right back," she said and stepped into the house.

"We've still got to close the portal at Mrs. Walters's house," Lucy whispered to Schuyler. "Think you can distract your mom and get the key?" She ignored her complaining muscles and was already tucking the Spectrescope into the backpack.

"No need, she's upstairs getting the first aid kit," Schuyler muttered, and disappearing into the foyer, she opened the table drawer and extracted the key. With a glance up the stairs, she rejoined Lucy on the porch. "Let's slip around the side while Dad is still talking with the McGoos." She sat on the porch railing, swung her legs over, and dropped discreetly to the ground.

Lucy followed and, landing softly, hunched down to follow Schuyler around the side of the house. They kept low and in the shadows as they edged along the backyard fence. Once they were safely out of view, Schuyler cautiously bumped a fence board with the toe of her sneaker. The board creaked. She touched it again, and this time it swung free, rotating on a cross board.

"C'mon, we can cut through the neighbors' backyards to the side street," Schuyler said, holding the board up so Lucy could crawl through the opening. "It's a shortcut to Mrs. Walters's house. It's almost dark, and I've been creeped out enough today."

"How'd you know that board was loose?" Lucy asked, tagging behind as Schuyler followed a well-used path between the neighboring yards.

"Oh, it's been loose for years. I found it one day when I was running away. I never told Dad about it, and he's never found it. I thought it could be handy someday."

Lucy snorted. "You? Running away?"

"Yup, I was seven and mad at my mom. I used her new scissors to pry open the bathroom window so I could sneak out. They broke, and that meant more trouble, so I was like, out of there. It was somewhat fun until it got dark. Then I got scared."

"How far did you run?" asked Lucy, hurrying alongside Schuyler as they snaked their way along the dirt path. Pushing back an overgrown bush, Schuyler stepped out onto the sidewalk, followed closely by Lucy. They were standing across the quiet street from Mrs. Walters's house.

"Just to the other side of the fence. Hey, I didn't want to get lost, you know?"

"You're something else," Lucy remarked, shaking her head. "I think I'm starting to see a mischievous side I didn't know you had."

"Yup, that is me," said Schuyler with a smirk, "something else."

"Well, let's get this over with," said Lucy, looking up at the house. The rounded roof of the turret pointed ominously skyward like a giant witch's hat in the dusk. The old house sat in shadows as night slowly fell. Lucy rolled her shoulders to hide a sudden shiver that crawled down her back. "If you keep watch at the front door, I'll go in and try to close the portal."

"Oh, no way," Schuyler admonished. "We go together." Schuyler stepped from the curb and began marching toward the old house as Lucy dragged herself behind. "C'mon, let's do this. We know more about daemon hunting than we did before when we were here."

"And we both have armor too."

They slowly approached the house, each ignoring the dark, blank windows staring back at them like empty eye sockets. Streetlamps began popping on and shedding light in pools along the ground, seemingly making the shadows even darker. Schuyler inserted the key and pushed the creaky door open, then flipped on the foyer light. The ancient chandelier's old glass globes glowed to life and cast a harsh yellow light over the entryway.

"Ew, I really don't like that chandelier. Nasty thing," Schuyler snarled, eyeing it suspiciously before stepping into the room. "With those lights on, it does look like a giant bat eating an octopus. Thanks for the visual, Mrs. McGoo."

Lucy silently entered the room, her glance quickly slipping to the shadows on the periphery of the foyer and into the hallway leading to the kitchen. Her grip on the backpack strap involuntarily tightened as anxiety settled into her core. Various expressions flittered across Schuyler's face as her gaze skittered about, and Lucy knew her friend felt that same anxiety. Unzipping the pack, she pulled out the Spectrescope, and it vibrated in her hand.

The symbols on the ring began to rotate, forming a series of strange words that Lucy didn't know how to pronounce. The lens started glowing, and she held the artifact up as words splayed across the nearest wall.

In the name of the High King, go forth. Be strong and courageous, for the King, your High King, goes before you saying, "I will never leave you or forsake you."

"Thank you," Lucy whispered as the words slowly faded away. Breathing deeply, she slowly exhaled and looked up the stairway to the shadows at the top of the stairs near the landing. Gripping the Spectrescope in one hand and placing the other hand on her chest, she whispered, "Armor."

The hat, which was askew on her head when it morphed into the helmet, snapped into place, startling her. The vest became the breastplate as the ring on her finger began to wiggle. Taking it off, she watched it grow into the belt and wrap itself around her waist. The tiny blue gemstones had also grown and were once again like small rocks, their facets twinkling in the light. "You are next," she said, nodding at Schuyler as the shield morphed from her bracelet and the grip snuggled into her hand.

Schuyler nodded and placed a shaky hand over her heart. "Armor, please," she squeaked. Instantly the hat and vest changed into the helmet and breastplate, and the shield morphed from the bracelet.

Lucy pinched her lips. "Okay, you get brownie points for politeness," she snarked. Her attempt at levity earned her a weak smile from Schuyler. Lucy bumped her shoulder into Schuyler's. "In the name of the High King, here goes nothing."

"Or something goes, if we're successful," Schuyler whispered, Zazriel shaking in her hand.

Lucy lifted the shield and clenched the Spectrescope as she slowly advanced up the stairs. Schuyler followed close behind. The harsh light from the chandelier wove its way through the balusters of the railing, casting weird shapes that looked like skinny gnomes along the walls. As they drew near to the small sitting room, they heard growling and scratching. Lucy rolled with her back against the wall on one side of the doorway as Schuyler took the other side.

"I think it's coming from the corner where the portal is," Lucy whispered, peeking into the dim, unlit room. "I hope it doesn't decide to come through before we can seal it."

"Any idea how we do that?"

"I'm working on it," Lucy mumbled. "Please help us, Spectrescope." The ancient relic vibrated, the symbols began glowing. The word "sword" appeared in the lens. "Okay, then what do I do?" The characters morphed in their shapes until they solidified into images of two girls with swords and armor and a girl holding a sword pointed forward with something exiting from the end of it. Lucy scrunched her face at the symbols, then removed the headpiece and stuffed it in her pocket.

"That face has me worried," Schuyler whispered as she clung to the wall as though it were in danger of tumbling down if she moved. "What did the Spectrescope say?"

The Spirit Sword flowed from the handle. "We fight," Lucy said, swinging around the doorframe and into the room suddenly. A fierce growl roared from the corner as the hidden panel crashed open, and a hideous daemon with blood-red eyes and gnarly warts rushed into the room. Snarling, its lips pulled back and revealed jagged teeth. It reached toward Lucy with razor-sharp claws.

Baring the shield, she thrust the Spirit Sword at the creature, but it dodged. She swung the sword, and again the creature escaped, lightly jumping sideways. Gripping the sword tightly, Lucy lunged, stomping her foot. It startled the beast, and it blanched before hunching over to growl.

Moving cautiously, she matched the creature's movements as they dodged around the room. A barrage of flaming arrows shot toward her from the shadows and bounced off her armor. "Schuyler! A little help, please!"

"Argh!" Schuyler squealed, hurtling into the room and swinging her short sword. Zazriel whined as it cut through the air and obliterated several arrows. Schuyler quickly beat down several more arrows with her shield and stomped the flames out.

Lucy narrowly avoided the creature's razor-like claws by leaping over the little bench. The beast swiped its claws, reaching for her. Turning the sword as she swung, the blade caught the tip of the creature's nail, shearing it off. The daemon howled in anger. It lunged toward Lucy just as she thrust forward with the Spirit Sword, plunging it through the daemon's body. The creature threw its warty head backward, mouth open and screaming, as it erupted into flames and disappeared, leaving a tendril of smoke behind.

Schuyler saw a shadow move when a round of arrows plunged hissing into the room. She deflected them with the shield. Copying Lucy's moves, she lunged forward with her sword, thrusting it into the shadow form. It screeched and burst into flames. Schuyler stood speechless, still pointing her blade where the creature had been.

"I'm gonna seal the door!" Lucy yelled and lunged forward, pointing the Spirit Sword at the portal. "In the name of the High King, be sealed forever!"

Brilliant beams of white-hot energy burst from the Spirit Sword, engulfing the portal and illuminating it in a blazing light. Lucy leaned forward as she struggled to stand, her feet sliding across the floor as the force of the beam pushed her backward. Screams and growls filled the small room as the portal glowed a molten red. "In the name of the High King, begone!"

Lucy stumbled forward when the energy from the Spirit Sword ceased abruptly. The Belt of Truth grew warm, and she glanced down to see a blue stone wiggling. It popped out. The words glowed warmly within the stone as she read out loud, "*You should fear the High King who has authority to cast you into Shinar. Your fate is sealed.*" Lucy threw the stone at the portal.

An explosion rocked the room, sending Lucy and Schuyler tumbling backward to the floor and crashing into the little bench at the center of the room. After a moment, stunned and groaning, Lucy pulled herself up to a sitting position. The Spirit Sword lay next to her, and the shield had changed to the bracelet. The room felt light and airy, like it was happy again.

"Are you okay?" Lucy asked. Schuyler was spread eagle on the floor on the other side of the bench and staring at the ceiling, blinking rapidly.

"Yeah, I think so," Schuyler mumbled, staring at the ceiling. "Just dazed a little. What happened?"

"It's done. Look," Lucy said, pointing at the corner. "It's gone. The Spirit Sword sealed the portal, and the power of the stone made it vanish completely. There's not even a hint that a door or a portal was ever there." She crawled over to the corner and felt along the wall. The old plaster was cool to the touch. "Nada," she said. Slowly, words appeared on the wall, saying, *With the blessing of the High King, this house shall be called Blessed, forever.*

"That's great!" exclaimed Schuyler, rolling over and sitting up. She pulled the helmet off, and it changed back into the hat, then she wadded it up, stuffing it into a pocket. The vest was back, too, along with her bracelet. "Since our armor has changed, does that mean the spirits that were here are finally gone?"

"Only one way to find out." Lucy stood, and, placing the headpiece on the handle, she scoped the room, the hallway, and finally the other bedrooms. Returning to the sitting room, she found Schuyler seated on the bench gazing at the glass mural. "It's all clear up here." She sat next to Schuyler on the bench. "We'll scope the rest of the house, too, but I think it's all gone."

"It's so beautiful, isn't it?" Schuyler said wistfully, her head lolling to one side. "I wish it were real. Silly, huh?"

"No, I get it," Lucy replied, gazing at the mural. "It makes me long for something. I mean, it feels peaceful, like there's no sadness there. Who knows? Maybe it is real—somewhere." She poked a finger at Schuyler's ribs. "We should be going. It is dark already, and your parents will be worried." Lucy stood and pulled Schuyler to her feet, then gently steered her toward the stairs.

A sudden movement at the edge of her periphery made her glance back at the mural. Nothing had changed, and the room was still peaceful and quiet, with the characters in the mural frozen in their glass world beneath the tree. She held the Spectrescope up and viewed the room.

Huh, nothing. Must be my eyes playing tricks on me again, she thought and then followed Schuyler down the stairs.

She didn't hear the soft, tinkling giggle coming from the sitting room.

21 Forgiven

"Luce, what are we going to tell my mom and dad?" Schuyler asked, closing and locking Mrs. Walters' front door behind them. "They're going to wonder where we went in such a hurry, and they're probably going to be mad and worried. This is getting so complicated," she lamented, trotting down the sidewalk and crossing the street between pools of light from the streetlamps.

"We tell them the truth," Lucy said. "They know about the ghost, or daemon really, so we tell them about the portal at Mrs. Walters' house. The portal is closed now, the house cleared, and it is blessed." Lucy trudged behind along the old worn path, her feet feeling like twenty-pound weights. "I could sleep for a week, and I still have to tell my mom about all this. I think I'd rather fight the daemons again."

"Oh! Don't say that! We may end up fighting more after today. Iam did say the battle has been raging for millennia," Schuyler said. "And we just slammed the door shut on one of their portals to our world. Those creepy things and the Dark Prince won't be happy about that," she added, holding back the loose fence board. She followed Lucy through the opening, and they headed across the lawn for the back kitchen door. Two white doves nestled in the bushes at the back of the yard. One clucked and chattered while the other bobbed its head rapidly.

"My goodness!" Mrs. Williams called to the girls from the back porch steps as they approached. She held the screen open as they came up the steps. "We looked everywhere for you girls until Mrs. McGoo spotted the open drawer of the foyer table. Of course, when I saw Mrs. Walters's key was missing, I knew you both had gone to check on the old house for me. And after all you've experienced today. You girls are just so thoughtful," she gushed behind them as they entered the kitchen. "Since we missed our dinner and movie night because of those nasty ghosts, I decided a celebration was in order. Why not have Sunday dinner on Saturday night? We can have leftovers tomorrow, but tonight we celebrate."

A heavenly aroma wafted past their noses, and Lucy inhaled deeply. Schuyler rushed into the dining room where the table held place settings for six people, and bowls of steaming mashed potatoes and green beans sat in the middle.

"I'm starving! Let's eat!" Schuyler exclaimed, pulling back a chair.

"We need to wait for Mr. and Mrs. McGoo," Mrs. Williams said, coming into the room behind them. "Vivian offered to bring fresh blueberry compote and buttermilk biscuits."

"Woohoo!" Schuyler squealed. "What else are we having?"

"Mrs. McGoo is also bringing her decadent chocolate revel cookie bars for dessert. They just popped home to grab those items, so they should be along shortly."

"I smell deep-fried chicken, right?" Lucy asked Mrs. Williams. "There's nothing that smells or tastes as good as your deep-fried honey chicken. It's one of my all-time favorites." She set the backpack on the floor in the corner and slipped quietly into a chair next to Schuyler.

"It's the least I could do to say thank you. You did save Schuyler from that horrible ghost," Mrs. Williams said, leaning down to give Lucy a quick squeeze. "I hope you can forgive us for not believing you before. I feel so ashamed over how we treated you," she explained, sniffling. "You and Schuyler have been best friends for years, and you have never given us cause to disbelieve you. I'm so sorry, honey."

"Mrs. Williams, don't be sorry. I hardly believe it myself, and I don't understand it all just yet," Lucy said. "Everything that has happened is so surreal, though I am learning more each day. I blame myself for all your smashed jellies and jams. If I had figured out sooner how to stop the ghost, maybe it would never have happened," she said regretfully.

"Lucy, you had no idea the ghost could do so much damage. I wasn't even really sure I believed in ghosts before. Well, I do now," said Mrs. Williams. "You shouldn't blame yourself," she said, patting Lucy on the shoulder. "You tried your best. Today you defeated him, as Schuyler put it, and I'm very grateful that you did."

"Thanks, Mrs. Williams," Lucy said as Mrs. Williams smiled and headed back to the kitchen. Beside her, Schuyler gasped and slapped a hand across her mouth. Reaching over, she poked Lucy in the ribs.

"Ow!" Lucy jumped and stared at Schuyler. "What was that for?"

"What about the vanishing staircase?" Schuyler whispered, her eyes wide and frightened.

"Holy moly! I forgot," Lucy muttered. "We better go check it." She got up, grabbed the backpack, and headed for the stairs ahead of Schuyler.

"Mom!" Schuyler yelled. "We're gonna go wash up for dinner."

"Don't be too long. The McGoos should be here any minute."

"Okay," Schuyler yelled over her shoulder, taking the steps two at a time.

Lucy was already at the top of the stairs, waiting by the potbellied stove in the weird little sitting area and scoping the room. Viewing each room and bathroom, Lucy quickly worked her way around the upstairs. The Spectrescope was clear. The guest bedroom containing the secret panel was last. Schuyler quietly opened the door, flicked on the light, and took the flashlight from the nightstand.

Lucy drew a deep breath, crossed her fingers, and tipped her head toward the wall. Nodding quickly, Schuyler opened the secret panel, handing the flashlight to Lucy as she stepped into the narrow passage. Lucy shined the beam toward the end of the passage, expecting to see the ancient door to the vanishing staircase.

The door was gone.

In its place was a message in large glowing letters: *With the blessing of the High King, this house shall be called Blessed, forever.*

"Well, is it clear?" an anxious voice asked.

Lucy heaved a sigh, stepped back into the room, and smiled. "Not to worry. Never again will you see a door or a ghost in your bedroom," she said, pulling her friend forward into the passage and pointing to the words.

"Oh, that's so awesome!" Schuyler sighed as the words slowly faded away. "Blessed forever. Wow," she said, looking at Lucy. "We really did it, didn't we?"

"Well, we did have help, but yeah. We did it," Lucy said with a smirk. She held her hand up and slapped Schuyler a high five. "Let's get cleaned up. I'm famished, and I am definitely eating more than my share of deep-fried honey chicken tonight. Race you to the bathroom!"

* * * *

They talked at length around the dinner table about their ghost-hunting adventures, though they refrained from giving too many details about banishing the daemon and sealing the portal. Lucy was distressed about the fight with the Dark Prince and held back from mentioning the event. Only Schuyler knew what had happened to Malpar.

Mr. and Mrs. Williams were still somewhat in shock over everything that had happened and said very little during dinner. However, the discussion got quite lively when Mr. and Mrs. McGoo began to speak about the dangers of the evil spirit world and the consequences of ignoring true spiritual matters. Lucy and Schuyler looked at each other, and while the adults were engrossed in conversation, they slipped quietly from the table and went upstairs to get ready for bed.

"I hurt all over," Lucy complained. "Even that hot soak in the bathtub didn't help." Pulling the covers of the trundle bed up to her chin and stretching out her limbs, she grimaced.

Schuyler sat cross-legged on the top bed, filing her nails. "I can only imagine what those bumps and bruises are going to look like tomorrow. You'll probably look like a circus exhibit."

Lucy laughed. "Your mom is awesome. I still can't believe she called my mom and apologized for the misunderstanding. Misunderstanding? Scary daemon ghosts, magical artifacts, broken jars of jams and jellies. That's not a misunderstanding, that's a train wreck." Lucy sat up, folded her legs, stretched her arms behind her, and then leaned forward to stretch her back. "I wonder if the Silly Buddha Hot Yoga place accepts walk-ins? Maybe an hour of sweaty, stinky yoga would take the kinks out."

"Yeah," Schuyler said thoughtfully, "that might work. You can tell your mom in the morning that we went to yoga and you injured yourself because you're an uncoordinated klutz." Pulling her lips into a goofy smile, she stared wild-eyed at Lucy, then busted out laughing. "You should see your face, BFF!"

Lucy squinted her eyes, glaring. Schuyler laughed harder. Lucy whacked her with the pillow.

"I'm sorry!" Schuyler giggled, pushing the pillow away. "But really! You should see your face," she said, pointing at the egg-sized knots on Lucy's forehead. "It looks painful. How's it feeling?" Her hair, still damp from her shower, was curling into ringlets.

"Painful," Lucy said dryly, rolling her eyes. "I'll have to get creative when I explain all these bumps and bruises to Mom." She held her arms out to view the damage. "She's gonna think I tried out for the girls, wrestling team and lost."

"You did say you were slammed against the bookshelves when you fought with the Dark Prince. You could say you had a close, personal encounter with a bookcase, and the books fell on you. Technically, it's true," Schuyler said, snickering. "Your mom probably won't ask too many questions if you explain it like that." Her smile quickly faded as she looked at Lucy. "Luce, what's wrong?"

Lucy sniffled and sat caressing the Spectrescope as it lay in her lap. Hot, heavy tears rolled down her cheeks, plopping on the lens. She grabbed it up, clutching it to her chest, and sobbed as she rocked back and forth. Schuyler wordlessly handed her a box of tissues, then crawled onto the trundle and sat next to her. After several minutes, Lucy snuffled and swiped the tears from her cheeks before blowing her nose. Blinking away a few straggling tears, she put her head on Schuyler's shoulder.

"I'm sorry I'm acting like a baby," she said between sniffles. "I know Malpar tried to scare us into giving up the Spectrescope, but when I really needed help, he gave up his life to help me. I didn't mean to cost him his existence," she said as more tears rolled down her cheeks.

"Oh, Luce, I'm so sorry," Schuyler said softly, putting an arm around Lucy's shoulders. "The important thing is, he was there to help you when you needed him. In the end, he was a good friend. Try to remember that, okay?"

"He cried out to the High King, did you know?" Lucy said, taking another tissue and drying her eyes. "He said, 'Forgive me, my High King.'

He fought bravely, but the Dark Prince used his power to conjure up energy cords to bind him." She snuffled again. "I felt so bad leaving him behind."

"There was nothing you could do. His fate was already sealed."

"I know, but it doesn't make it any easier."

"Luce, back in the castle, when you gave up the Spectrescope, you said you knew something they didn't. What did you mean by that?" Schuyler crawled back up on the bed and opened the nightstand drawer. Pulling out a bag of candy, she took a piece and handed the bag to Lucy.

"You're still hungry? How is that possible?" Lucy asked, waving away the candy. Schuyler plopped the bag back in the drawer.

"I've got a sweet tooth. Get over it," came the snarky reply.

Lucy snorted. "It's one of the secrets of the Spectrescope."

"Well?"

"Just before I found you in the gargantuan dining hall, the Spectrescope told me what to do," Lucy said. "If I freely gave up the Spectrescope to protect someone I loved, the power of the artifact would be separated from it and remain with the one who gave it up. Once I got the Spectrescope back, the power got transferred back to the artifact." Lucy gently caressed the scope, polishing the lens on her pajama top.

"Did the Dark Prince know this when you fell through the mirror?" Schuyler asked.

"Not at first, but he figured it out. Then Malpar died trying to save me," Lucy whispered, her head drooping forward. "I wish I could talk to Iam. I haven't seen him in days, and there are so many things to ask him." She slid down into the covers, still holding the Spectrescope.

"Let's get some sleep," Schuyler said, rolling over and worming her way under the covers. "Mom said she would make us a stellar breakfast in the morning with scrambled eggs and bacon and buttermilk biscuits with sausage gravy! I can't wait! My mouth waters just thinking about it." Reaching up and clicking off the light, she heard a loud snort. "Just give it a rest, girlfriend."

The Ghost of Darwin Stewart

* * * *

"Lucy," a voice whispered. "Wake up, beloved."

"Mmm mmm, Iam?" Lucy murmured.

"Lucy, come chat with me," the voice said.

"Mmm, where?"

"In the sitting room outside Schuyler's door."

Lucy sat up. Blinking and rubbing her eyes, she crept from the trundle and borrowed Schuyler's robe that was lying across the foot of the bed. Tiptoeing to the door, she carefully eased it open, slipped into the hallway, and inched it closed again.

Iam was casually sitting in one of the tufted chairs near the old potbellied stove. The room was bright and inviting, even though it was still dark outside. Lucy briefly wondered what provided the light.

"Oh, Iam! It's so good to see you," Lucy whispered as she hurried over to him and gave him a quick hug. "There are so many things I need to know, only I don't know what to ask first," she said, carefully sliding the other chair closer so she could sit in front of him. "We probably need to be quiet so we don't wake Schuyler or her parents. Should we go down to the kitchen to talk?"

"We're perfectly fine right here, dear Lucy. The Williams family won't be disturbed by our talk or the light," Iam said, a smile dimpling his weathered cheeks. "Tell me about your adventures in ghost hunting," he urged.

Lucy excitedly described their encounter with the daemon ghost of Darwin Stewart and the battle in the castle dining room and the appearance of the armor they wore. His head occasionally bobbed as she narrated her encounter with the Dark Prince, Darnathian, and his fight with Malpar. She watched as his eyebrows floated up on his forehead when she told him about sealing the portal in the sitting room at Mrs. Walters house.

"Iam, I feel so bad for Malpar," Lucy said, curling herself up in the chair. "He seemed very sad when he spoke about his home. I believed him when he said, 'Forgive me, my High King.' Will the High King forgive him, do you think? I hope so." She watched him expectantly, so many questions bouncing in her head like popcorn in a hot pan.

"You shouldn't worry yourself about Malpar," Iam replied softly. "I can see by your expressions as they flitter across your face that you have other questions you would like to ask," he said, leaning forward in his chair and resting his arms on his legs. He wore the brown tweed suit and the usual white shirt.

Lucy thought he looked like someone's easygoing grandpa with his longish white hair and white mustache and brows. She thought of him in that way, too, as Grandpa. Perhaps she would ask him someday if she could call him Gramps.

"Well, I do have a few questions," Lucy said hesitantly, pulling her legs up and wrapping her arms tightly about her knees. "When Schuyler and I were at Mrs. Walters's house, we met Daphne. She said the High King had allowed her to help us. She told us the High King is our 'Forevermore.' She said you are the High King of Ascalon." Lucy felt a bit uneasy, and she studied him closely as he thought about her statement. "You are the High King of Ascalon, aren't you?" she asked softly.

"I am," he said, with quiet authority, "the High King of Ascalon."

He hadn't moved or morphed into a different shape, though something about him appeared different. Lucy felt the hair on her arms raise and her skin prickled. Never before had she felt such a wash of emotions, melting and sinking into the core of her being. There was fear tinged with reverence, wonder colored with love, and a longing so deep she thought she would suffocate before she could breathe another breath.

For a second time that evening, she felt hot tears coursing down her cheeks to trickle over her chin and disappear down her neck. "Why didn't you tell me?" Lucy asked, her voice breathy and small.

"I wanted you to discover for yourself who I am, Lucy. It is not my nature to force you to act or follow. I ask only that you love me for who I truly am," Iam replied. "And really, isn't that what you want too? To be loved for who you are?"

Lucy sat in silence. Her mouth opened and closed several times without any words exiting. Finally, she just smiled and nodded. The questions that had bounced around her head earlier must have leaked out through her ears. She couldn't recall a single one.

"Today, in your world, I am Iam Reynard, a crafty old fox and full of cunning. But to those who discover me, well, you'll see." Iam smiled gently then, his bright, sky-blue eyes twinkling. "Now, go get the mirror. I have a special surprise for you. Go on, git," he said, as he waved his hand and shooed her toward the bedroom door. He smiled at her retreating form, padding to the door and easing it open. He was still smiling when he disappeared, taking the gentle light with him.

Lucy knelt, gritting her teeth as she unzipped the backpack, willing it to be quiet and not wake Schuyler. The mirror was sparkling as she pulled it from its pocket and leaned it against the bed. Pinching her lips, she glanced up at Schuyler sleeping in the top bed, and suddenly, just like that time at the flea market, the air around Lucy had a shimmering quality to it as though she were encased in a bubble looking out.

The concentric circles in the mirror cleared, and images formed in the glass. Through the portal, Lucy could see a large and elegant chamber hung with beautiful tapestries, and silk-upholstered chairs sat before a raised dais on which resided three throne chairs. A tall, thin creature occupied one of the smaller silk chairs. Something about the being struck her as familiar, and then she gasped. She was observing a Hayyothalan.

The creature held his body very erect in the chair, with hands tightly folded in his lap. The bird-man bore brilliant plumage in several shades of turquoise, emerald, green, and aqua that sparkled with iridescence. His eyes were bright and intelligent, and his skin appeared almost pearlescent.

Lucy heard a resounding click, followed by what must have been a large, heavy door creaking open for a moment and then a resounding thud. The bird-man quickly stood to his full height and dropped just as quickly to kneel. His large, sweeping wings fully extended and swept forward to cover him completely. Lucy could see a tall personage in a beautiful velvet robe enter the chamber, but his back was to the portal, and she could not see his face.

"Your Highness, my King," the bird-man said. Lucy nearly squealed as she recognized Malpar's voice. It was clear and lyrical. She bounced and waved her hands at the portal.

"Rise, Malpar. Stand before your King," said a deep voice that resonated throughout the chamber. "For your repentance and your service to one of my Bachar, you are forgiven and sealed. Turn, Redeemed One, and see the child who touched your heart," the King said, sweeping his hand toward the portal.

"Malpar!" Lucy called.

Upon hearing Lucy's voice, Malpar turned to face the mirror hanging on the chamber wall and saw Lucy's exuberant face. He rushed to the portal, tears welling in his eyes. "Lucy! Thank you, dear one. If it weren't for you, Lucy, I may never have seen my home or loved ones again. You reminded me of what I once was and could be again. Our great High King is so benevolent. He provided a way for us all to come home."

"I was so scared. I didn't know what to do, and then you crumpled to the floor," Lucy said, sadness sneaking into her voice and placing a hand on the glass.

The Ghost of Darwin Stewart

"You urged me to remember and to call out to the High King. Thank you, Lucy!" Malpar placed a hand on his side of the glass next to Lucy's. "One day, we will be together, and you will meet my family. They will love you as much as I do," Malpar said, smiling and bobbing his head. He still had the quirky movements that reminded Lucy of a pigeon.

"You love me?" asked Lucy. "But I didn't do anything. I didn't know how to help you."

"You did more than you know, dear Lucy, and I will be forever grateful," Malpar said. "Look at me! Aren't my feathers beautiful? I've been washed clean, and I smell good too!" He spread his wings and turned around several times, prancing in front of the mirror to show Lucy his incredible plumage.

"Yes, Malpar, you are quite gorgeous," said Lucy, laughing as she watched him frolic about the chamber. "I can't wait to meet your family. They must be ecstatic to have you home again!"

"Totally blown away would be one way to put it," Malpar quipped, waving his wings. He stopped dancing, and his face became serious. "I must go, Lucy. The portal is about to close. Please be careful. Darnathian is a sly one, and he is the chief of liars. He will not stop in his quest to obtain the Spectrescope. The artifact holds a deep secret that he must not learn. Guard the Spectrescope carefully, and guard your heart." Smiling wistfully, he placed his hand against the glass again, and Lucy did the same. "Goodbye, dear Lucy. I shall look forward to seeing you again one day."

"Goodbye, Malpar, I'm so happy you are home," Lucy said as Malpar faded from view. The mirror slowly dimmed and winked out. It was just a mirror again.

Lucy sat with her hand still against the glass for a moment, a contented smile dimpling her cheeks. She placed the mirror back in its pocket and zipped the backpack shut, placing it next to the trundle bed. Crawling carefully over to the window, she leaned on the windowsill and peeked out at the street below. Standing in the pool of light under the streetlamp was Iam. He raised a hand and gently waved. Lucy smiled and waved back as she watched him slowly disappear. Snuggling back under the covers of the trundle, she whispered, "Goodnight, Iam."

"Goodnight, dear Lucy," his voice whispered in her head.

Thoughts from the Author

Dear Reader,

Phew! That was quite an adventure! Thank you for joining me. I enjoyed creating this fantasy for you, and I hope you had as much fun reading it as I did writing it. This is the first installment of The Issachar Gatekeeper saga. Be sure to watch for the next book, *The Ghost Writer*, coming soon. I hope you will add Lucy Hornberger and The Issachar Gatekeeper to your list of perennial favorites and visit them often.

Lucy Hornberger was brought into being through influences from my childhood. Like Lucy, my mom was a single mother struggling to make ends meet, so we lived with my maternal grandparents. My grandmother would often ask, "Did you see the lady in the black taffeta dress last night?" Yikes!

Many a night I remember being woken by strange sounds in the sesquicentennial house by creaks and groans that didn't seem quite human or footsteps on the stairs in the middle of the night after everyone had gone to bed. It wasn't only my grandmother who saw ghosts—other family members eventually refused to stay the night in the old house, preferring instead to go to a hotel or even drive late into the night to return home. In my childish mind, the stories had to be true, didn't they? Eventually, I grew up and put childish ways and beliefs behind me. After all, an intelligent and well-educated adult wouldn't believe in such things.

Or would she?

The Ghost of Darwin Stewart

A Few Things to Consider

I know you are wondering: *Does she really believe in ghosts and spirits?* Yes, I do. There are numerous references in the Bible for spirits. Check these out:

- Colossians 1:16: "For by Him all things were created, both in the heavens and on earth, *visible and invisible* . . . all things have been created" (NASB, emphasis added).

- James 2:19: "You believe that there is one God; you do well. The demons also believe, and tremble" (MEV)

- Hebrews 13:2: "Do not forget to show hospitality to strangers, for by so doing some people have shown hospitality to [spirits] without knowing it."

- Psalm 103:20: "His angels [are] mighty in strength" (NASB)

- Isaiah 6:2: "Seraphim [angels] stood above Him, each having six wings: with two he covered his face, and with two he covered his feet, and with two he flew" (NASB).

- Ezekiel 10:14: "Each of the four cherubim [angels] had four faces: the first was the face of an ox, the second was a human face, the third was the face of a lion, and the fourth was the face of an eagle" (NLT).

Frightening, isn't it? (Cue the scary music.) Now, what do *you* believe?

One More Thing

Scriptural references used in this story:

- Deuteronomy 31:6: "Be strong and courageous. Do not be afraid or terrified because of them, for the LORD your God goes with you; he will never leave you nor forsake you."

- Judges 18:6: "Go in peace. Your journey has the LORD'S approval."

- Psalm 145:20: "The LORD watches over all who love him, but all the wicked he will destroy."

- Mark 16:17: "In my name they will drive out demons."

And finally, Ephesians 6:10–17 (emphasis added):

Be *STRONG* in the Lord and in his mighty power. Put on the full *ARMOR* of God . . . the *BELT OF TRUTH* buckled around your waist, with the *BREASTPLATE* of righteousness in place . . . the *SHIELD OF FAITH*, with which you can extinguish all the flaming arrows of the evil one. Take the *HELMET* of salvation and the *SWORD* of the Spirit, which is the word of God.

Cast of Characters

Lucy Hornberger—age thirteen; chosen to protect the magical Spectrescope and the trunk of relics.

Schuyler Williams—age thirteen; Lucy's best friend, assistant ghost hunter, and chosen to help Lucy.

Iam Reynard—vendor from the flea market; befriends Lucy. Reynard means fox.

Malpar—fallen creature known as Hayyothalan; able to morph from a bird to a man.

Darnathian—fallen archangel; known as the Master; the Dark Prince.

Darwin Stewart—evil ghost who haunts Schuyler's house.

Grehssil—fallen creature and servant to Darnathian.

Vivian McGoo—Lucy's neighbor; homemaker, loves to bake.

Bill McGoo—Lucy's neighbor; retired.

Rebecca Williams—Schuyler's mother; enjoys baking and homemaking.

Stephen Williams—Schuyler's father.

Jeannie Hornberger—Lucy's mother; single mom.

Dale Hornberger—Lucy's older brother.

High King—supreme and powerful being, ruler of Ascalon.

Daphne—deceased wife of Darwin Stewart.

Molly Gleason—mother to Bradley and Christopher.

Patrick Gleason—father to Bradley and Christopher; salesman.

Christopher and Bradley Gleason—the small boys Lucy babysits often.

Paul Matthews—friend of Lucy's from school; works at the grocery store.

G lossary of Terms

Ascalon—the heavenly realm of the High King.

Bachar—chosen/selected.

Daemon—fallen angels who became evil.

Hayyothalan—(*hay-yo-the-lan*) fallen birdlike creatures.

Irredaemon—fallen angels; cast from Ascalon for their rebellion against the High King.

Ormarrs—lowest level of the fallen angels.

Ratha-nael—magical sword; name means "thwarter of daemons."

Shinar—a place of never-ending darkness and sadness.

Sho-are—a gatekeeper.

Spectrescope—magical artifact known for its power and its secrets; allows Lucy to see ghosts.

Spirit Sword—hidden within the Spectrescope; also called Puriel, meaning "fire of the King."

Zazriel—magical sword; name means "strength of the King."

The Ghost Writer

Book Two of The Issachar Gatekeeper Series

Prologue

A man in a light-colored suit slipped quietly from the shadows into the room. Entirely at ease in the darkness of the unfamiliar room, he watched as the teenage boy sleeping in the bed flung an arm from under the covers and snored.

The man, known as Darnathian, smiled, twisting his head and stretching his neck. It was an odd quirk he had never managed to eliminate since losing his wings. He raised a hand, and several manuscript pages floated off the corner of the nearby desk, landing softly in his outstretched palm. He scanned the pages, then threw his head back and laughed.

"Grehssil was correct. You will do nicely, my boy," he said. "Indeed, you will do very well." The servant, Grehssil, who had a nose for ferreting out strong emotions, had been sent to locate someone within Lucy's circle of friends whom he could easily manipulate.

Everything was changing for the sleeping teenager. His feet were too big, and his lean, shapeless frame made him awkward and clumsy. His mom worked long hours at the grocery store, often leaving him home alone, and he rarely saw his dad since his parents had separated. He knew his mom loved him, but he wasn't so sure about his dad.

Yes, Grehssil had done very well.

The pages floated back to the desk and neatly restacked themselves. Frenetic lights appeared in the room, flickering blue and green across the ceiling and down the walls.

Darnathian cupped his hands together. When he opened them again, a glowing orb sat in his palm. A smile spread across his face as he studied the colors within the circle.

"Mene ru'ach tsavah yara," he uttered and tossed the orb at the boy. It exploded over the bed, and diamond-like dust settled on the boy. The particles sank into his pores, luminescing under his skin before disappearing completely.

"Ameyn," Darnathian said, and with an eerie rumble of laughter, he turned and walked through the wall.

"Yikes!" Arms and legs flailing, the boy scrambled from the covers and scratched his skin. Rubbing his hands over his bare arms and face, he gyrated about the room, his skin feeling as though a gazillion mosquitos had bitten him while he slept.

"What the heck?" Panic stricken, he searched the bed and the room for the source of the bites. The itching became less the more he rubbed his skin. Maybe his imagination was working overtime. After all, he had just woken from something like a nightmare. Frustrated and bewildered, he sat down at the desk and tried to recall the strange dream of a man in a light-colored suit laughing at him.

About the Author

 L. G. Nixon grew up hoping to one day become a writer, and after a long career in office management, she began writing. She also grew up in a creaky old house where relatives told of ghostly visitations. Her joy as a writer comes from being able to share the stories God lays on her heart. Her otherworldly realms are created in Michigan where she lives with her husband, a high-energy boxer dog named Cali, and a tailless cat named Pan. She enjoys motorcycling and skiing, landscape painting, and hopes someday to finish her pilot's license. (She wants to fly the Space Shuttle if they relaunch it, so she just might need that pilot's license!)

If you are enjoying The Issachar Gatekeeper series, drop her a note. She would love to hear from you!

Visit her website at: www.lgnixon.com